LYNN'S SEARCH

Book Four of the Evans Family Saga

C. J. PETIT

TABLE OF CONTENTS

PROLOGUE

August 14, 1873
Canon City, Colorado

Prison guard Lou Burchett followed the two released men at a distance with his rifle cocked as they headed for the heavy iron gate that meant freedom for some and usually death for the others. He'd learned through experience that even those about to walk out that gate harbored enough resentment to take a last bit of anger out on the guards after it had swung open.

As another guard unlocked the gate, Lou hoped they did try something. He wouldn't get into any trouble for shooting the bastards; he'd probably deserve a medal for keeping animals like them from returning to society.

But he didn't get his wish as the two ex-prisoners didn't even look back at him as they passed through the open gate and were now out of his control. He released the rifle's hammer, then waited for the gate to be locked again before turning and heading back for the cells.

John Coleridge walked beside Rusty Halloran as they put some distance behind them and the gray walls of the Denver Territorial Prison.

After they'd walked for almost a minute, John quickly looked behind them at the closed gate and said, "The bastard's gone."

Rusty looked back himself as he replied, "I figured he'd shoot us as soon as we walked outta there. I wish I had the guts to jump the son of a bitch before we left. He almost killed you back in '71 when we moved to this new place."

"Don't remind me. He goaded me into it, too. That cost me another twelve months of my life just a year before I was supposed to get out. I should've killed the bastard when I had the chance. I would've hanged for it, but it might have been worth it."

"What do we do now, John?"

"We got enough to get some decent clothes and a good meal, but then we need to get some real money."

"We ain't gonna work like regular folks, are we?"

"Hell, no! That doesn't get us any big money. We need to find Mike and Ollie first, though. Mike said they going to wait for us in Florence, but that was four months ago. After we look like regular guys and fill our bellies, we'll start heading that way. It's only five miles, and if we find them there, we can start figuring out how to fill our pockets."

Rusty nodded then said, "They'll be there, John. Ollie owes me for lettin' him know that his good pal Lefty was a snitch."

John grinned and said, "He may have sung like a canary to the guards, but he sure didn't fly like one when he left that walkway."

Rusty laughed as they headed for Canon City to begin their lives without bars.

CHAPTER 1

September 5, 1873
Denver, Colorado

Denver County Sheriff Quentin Wheeler stood waiting on the sidewalk in front of the county courthouse for a fast-moving buggy to pass before he stepped onto the street and quickly trotted across the bustling roadway. After reaching the other side of the street, he hopped onto the boardwalk and turned east.

Two blocks later, he turned into the office of the United States Marshal and entered the open door.

Deputy Marshal Thom Smythe was at the desk, saw him enter, and said, "Mornin', Sheriff. Need to see the boss?"

"Just to pass along some information. Is he in?"

"Yup. He's talking to Bryn in his office."

"That's even better," the sheriff replied as he removed his hat and headed past the desk.

Bryn and Dylan had heard him enter, so when he reached the doorway, they were both looking his way.

"What's the news, Quentin?" Dylan asked.

"I don't know if you got the word, but I just got a telegram from Al Tapper down in Pueblo County about a stagecoach holdup west of Pueblo a couple of days ago. The driver was killed, and the shotgun rider took a .44 in the leg. None of the passengers were hurt though."

"Does he need our help?"

"Nope. He was just letting me know because one of the holdup men was identified as John Coleridge."

Bryn said, "I'm surprised we haven't heard from him since he got out."

"He only left the prison last month because he had a year added to his sentence for assaulting a guard. The shotgun rider was a former guard at the prison and recognized all four of them; even with their masks. Sheriff Tapper is having some wanted posters made and will send them to me as soon as they come off the press."

"He lost them?" Dylan asked.

"By the time the wounded shotgun rider got in, it was too late to get a posse together, and the next day, the trail was impossible to track because of the heavy traffic on the road."

"What did they get?"

"Just under three thousand dollars. It was the deposit from the Canon City Bank that was supposed to go to Pueblo."

"Is this the first job that he's pulled since he got out?" Bryn asked.

"It's the only one where he and the other three have been recognized, but if they were on horseback and had Winchesters and Colts, then they had to have gotten the money from somewhere, and I doubt if they worked for it."

6

Bryn asked, "When you get those posters, can you send them over here for us to take a look?"

The sheriff replied, "I had him send me two copies of each because I figured you'd want to see them, Bryn. You'd have gotten the posters anyway, but probably not for another couple of weeks. Al's going to have them put on the first train after he gets them."

"Who else was with him?" Dylan asked.

"Rusty Halloran, Mike Greenburg and Ollie Thorsen. They were all in the prison with him, and Rusty was let out the same day."

"I don't know much about Greenburg or Thorsen, but I'm a bit surprised that Rusty Halloran would run with John. John may have been a crooked lawman, but he still wore the badge. I wouldn't think a hard type like Halloran would partner up with an ex-lawman."

"I'm not. John tended to take the easy way out when he worked for me, and after I got over my outrage when Bryn brought him in, I blamed myself for not noticing how far he'd gone bad. He always seemed to have too much loose cash, but I never paid much attention. After he was sent up, I did some investigating around town and found that John had been using his badge as a threat to line his pockets. I felt like a damned idiot for not spotting it earlier and had to do a lot of apologizing once I finally pulled my head out of my butt."

Bryn looked at Dylan and said, "I'm glad that Ryan is with Jack on the Double EE."

"Lynn, Al, and Garth are pretty proficient already too, Bryn. I don't think we have to worry about a repeat of Cornbread's plot," Dylan said before looking at the sheriff and asking, "Do you think they're headed our way?"

"I doubt it. All of us would recognize John right away. They'll stay clear of Denver."

"Okay. Send us the posters when you get them, and I'll pass the word to my boys; the ones with badges and the ones that are hoping to wear one when they're a little older."

"Are all of them planning on following your footsteps, Dylan?"

"They've been telling me that since they were knee-high, but ever since they discovered girls, I think their priorities have shifted. Garth is the only one who really still seems enthusiastic about becoming a lawman."

The sheriff grinned, then looked at Bryn and asked, "How about your boys, Bryn?"

Bryn smiled and replied, "They're all still boys and enjoy doing boy things. They play with their toy guns and there's not a week goes by that one of them doesn't ask when they can shoot a real gun. They're a great help to Erin, though."

"You both have some mighty fine youngsters. I've got to get back to the office. I should send those posters to you within the next four days."

Dylan then said, "You know, Quentin, we've been kind of insulated out here from the big money panic that's gripped the country. A lot of those factories back East have shut down after the railroads began falling like a bunch of dominoes. Everybody thought they could get rich by building a new railroad and when those two goliaths, Rockefeller and

Vanderbilt started their own personal war, they didn't care about the disaster they'd help create."

"Why bring it up, Dylan?"

"We've been lucky because we don't have a lot of factories or railroads out here, but I'm worried that a lot of those out-of-work, desperate men will start heading our way to hunt for gold rather than starve. We're already seeing the start of it, and I think we'll both be a lot busier soon."

"I suppose you're right, Dylan. I just hope the damned thing doesn't last too much longer."

"Well, thanks for the information, Quentin," Dylan said before the sheriff gave them a short salute and left the office.

After he was gone, Dylan looked at his brother and said, "Do you want to go and let Kyle know? John might focus any revenge on you for arresting him, but Kyle was with you and pointed him out at the trial."

"I'll head over to his office now. He doesn't have a case this morning, does he?"

"Nope. He had that burglary case yesterday, but I think he's in his office right now."

Bryn grinned and said, "It's hard to imagine Kyle as an assistant county prosecutor, but Walter says he's doing a great job. When Walter offered him the job, Kyle swore it was just because he shared our last name. That may have been partly true, but he sure has proven himself. He's only lost that one case, and that was probably because the defendant was too pretty to convict."

Dylan laughed and said, "It's kind of hard to get a conviction when the jury is all staring at the lady's legs; not that she was hiking up her skirt on purpose."

Bryn grinned, then rose and said, "I'll be back in about twenty minutes, boss," before he walked out the door, passed Thom, grabbed his hat and left the office.

———

Five minutes later, he was sitting across from Kyle Huw Evans, Esquire, Denver County Assistant Prosecutor; still the youngest attorney in the territory.

"You don't think he'll be a problem, do you?" Kyle asked.

"The sheriff doesn't think so, but Dylan said to let you know. He wouldn't know where you live now anyway."

"I remember that trial as if it was yesterday. That was the day I became Kyle Huw Evans and decided to follow the path that took me here. I can still see John Coleridge glaring at me as I pointed at him. You said that if he lived out his sentence, he'd come out of there a hard man, and it sounds like you were right."

"We were just surprised that he was so readily accepted by the other three. They were all life-long criminals, while John used to wear the badge. Dylan just wanted me to let you know so you could pass the word to Katie."

"We would have heard about it on Sunday at the family get gathering anyway. Does Dylan think he's coming here to get his payback?"

"Nope and neither does Quentin. We all know what he looks like, but it's good to be aware of the possibility. He could send in one of his new pals."

"Okay. I'll keep an eye out, but since I moved into this office, I always watch out for a back shooter. I know I haven't convicted any lifelong killers like Carbo yet, but even some of those bad boys that I've sent to Canon City for a year or two might hold a grudge when they get out, or one of their kin might express his dissatisfaction."

"If they try, then they'll be surprised when they meet the best shooting prosecutor in the territory, and they should have just written a nasty letter. I recall when you could barely hit the target at all. Now you're giving Dylan a run with your Model 3 and your Winchester."

"I don't think I'm that close, Bryn. I do like the Model 3, though. Everybody else seems excited about the new Colt, but we Evans boys will always wear a Smith & Wesson. Katie likes the Model 1 that I gave her and swears she'll beat Gwen and Erin one of these days."

Bryn smiled and said, "It's kind of funny to watch those three firing their pistols with their eyes glaring at the target. Erin told me that she pictures Bill Carbo's face staring at her and has to keep from emptying the pistol."

Kyle snickered before saying, "Katie said she only misses now because she's out of balance with that weight she's carrying. When I asked her if she was going to have triplets to overshadow Erin's twins, she threatened to have a misfire the next time we do our target shooting and hit the pistol that put the babies there."

"I hope not," Bryn replied as he grinned then asked, "Are you and Katie going to name the next one after me?"

Kyle laughed and answered, "She wants another girl, so Bess will have a sister. But if you'd like, we can name her Berwyn."

"No, that's all right. Stick with a name that you don't have to explain to folks."

Kyle was more serious when he said, "We already picked out a name for a girl. We both would like to honor the matriarch of the Evans family. We'll name her Meredith Anna."

Bryn nodded and replied, "Dylan couldn't use her name for Bethan or Cari because of Gwen's sister, Meredith, and we were out here when Erin chose Grace Lynn, so I'm happy that you chose mom's name. I hope you don't have a boy, though. I've heard that some men are named Meredith, but I doubt if any of them have Anna as a middle name."

"You never know."

"Does mom know?"

"Not yet. We're keeping it to ourselves until the baby is born healthy. I know how devastated Gwen was when she lost her last one and then to be told she couldn't conceive again was even worse."

"I know. It was seeing her children that revived her spirits. They still have six healthy children and that's rare in itself. We only realized how lucky we all had been after we almost lost Ethan last year when measles raced through the Double EE."

"Katie watched ours like a hawk for two months after that. It was a miracle that Ethan pulled through the pneumonia."

Bryn nodded as he recalled those horrible, terrifying days with the ranch full of sick children; wondering how many they would lose to the deadly disease. It had been nothing short of a miracle that they'd all survived, especially little Kyle Lynn who was just over a year old when the measles struck the ranch. Erin hadn't conceived either since that plague and she was convinced that the measles had been the culprit. She had been the only adult on the ranch to have contracted the disease but hadn't had a serious case. Yet when he'd seen her with the initial symptoms, Bryn had been terrified that he might lose her. The month of October 1872 was a period of strain and danger to the Evans family that had no defense. None of their pistols or rifles could have stopped nature's assault.

Bryn shook the memory from his mind, then smiled at Kyle and said, "Well, I'll get back to the office. We'll see you on Sunday and we'll beat you this time."

"You've got to learn to hit better, Bryn," Kyle said as Bryn stood and waved before leaving his office.

————

Kyle entered the front door, put his new Stetson hat on its peg, then as Katie stepped out of the hallway with eighteen-month-old John Lynn on her hip and almost-five-year-old Bess Lynn raced past her mother shouting, "Daddy!", while three-year-old Colwyn trotted behind her.

Kyle caught Bess as she leapt into his arms then kissed him on the cheek before he smiled at Katie and said, "He can walk, Mrs. Evans. You shouldn't be carrying any more weight than you already are."

Katie set John on the floor, then after he let Bess down, he kissed his wife and asked, "How was it today, sweetheart?"

"Not bad. Mom stopped by to check on me, as usual," she replied as she took Kyle's hand before they turned and headed for the kitchen.

They reserved the dining room for family get togethers when the large kitchen table only served as a children's table. Even though Dylan and Gwen's four teenagers sat with the adults, the kitchen table was still pretty full.

After Bess and Colwyn sat at the table, Kyle put John in his highchair, then suggested that Katie take a seat to rest her back while he at least served the supper that she had prepared. He'd learned his lesson early on in their marriage that she didn't react well to being ordered to do anything.

As he began filling the plates, he said, "Katie, I wish you'd let me hire a housekeeper to help you. We can certainly afford one and you'd be able to stay off your feet more."

Katie sighed and replied, "I suppose you're right, Kyle. I've been too stubborn to allow another woman do what I feel that I should be doing, but I am getting a bit tired by the end of the day."

He smiled at her and said, "I'll talk to the agency tomorrow."

"Sometimes I wish that we hadn't moved into Denver and were closer to the rest of the family. Those four miles seem like a hundred these days. Even mom is almost a mile away."

"We were lucky to find this one with the population boom. We can always sell this house and build a new one on the Double EE if you'd like, Katie."

She shook her head and replied, "No. I'd rather get you home earlier each day than wait for you to make that ride, especially in the winter. I'm just in one of my pregnancy moods, but I'll be fine. Just don't hire some young pretty housekeeper who would make me jealous."

Kyle laughed as he began setting plates on the table and a bowl of mashed corn and oatmeal for John.

"I doubt that you'd ever have cause to be jealous of any woman, Katie. If a woman like the young lady who was my only other dance partner couldn't impress me with her corset-enhanced bosom and charming smile, then none can."

Katie laughed as she began spooning the mush into little John's open mouth.

After everything had been moved to the table, Kyle sat down and said, "Bryn stopped by the office earlier to tell me that John Coleridge had been spotted with other three recently released convicts when they held up a stage outside of Pueblo. None of them believe that he'll show up in Denver County, but Dylan wanted to let us know."

Katie asked, "Are you concerned?"

"Not much. I agree with them that he's too easily recognized by too many people in the area to even come close to Denver."

"But wouldn't he look a lot different after all those years in the prison?"

"Maybe, but he couldn't be sure that it would be enough. It was just a courtesy notice by the sheriff anyway. Besides, I'd be pretty far down on his list and he wouldn't know where we live either. He also wouldn't know my new name or that I'm a county prosecutor."

"Do you think Erin is worried? Bryn was the one who arrested him."

"I'm not sure. You'd know better than I would."

As Kyle joined Bess and Colwyn who were already demolishing their food, Katie said, "When mom stopped by, she told me that Erin is worried about Ryan."

"Why? Has he done something? It's not another girl issue; is it? I thought that I'd have to prosecute him over the Molly Finnegan debacle. It was Bryn who bailed him out and soothed the family's ruffled feathers."

"No. I think he learned his lesson with her and seems to be happy to just have his short peccadilloes with the young women in Denver. We're all just waiting for some angry father to go after him with a shotgun."

"If it's not women, is it his drinking?"

"No. That's not out of hand; not for an Irishman. It's just that over the last couple of months, Erin says that he's been more aloof and distant. I haven't been around him enough to notice. Can you think of a reason why he'd be that way?"

Kyle took over feeding John so Katie could eat, then replied, "There was that one small argument he had with Dylan that might be the reason, but I can't understand why it would be."

"What was that?"

"I told you about it after Dylan mentioned it; but at the time, we didn't think it was a big deal. He'd asked Dylan if he could become a deputy marshal, and Dylan told him that he was more valuable helping Jack and the boys with the horses than he would be wearing a badge, and Ryan seemed offended by his answer."

"I do remember that, but I didn't think it was important either."

"Dylan told me and Bryn that the real reason was that Ryan simply didn't have the temperament for the job. He angered too quickly and made rash decisions. If he was at the other end of the emotional scale and wore the badge, he'd get himself killed soon after he pinned it on. But a man who behaved like Ryan would not only be a danger to himself, he'd be a danger to others. Toss in his drinking and womanizing and he'd be a disaster as a deputy marshal."

Katie set her fork down and said, "I wish I could tell you that you're wrong, Kyle, but I can't. I thought that Ryan would change when he left home, and for a while he seemed to be happy to be out with the horses. I don't know if Molly Finnegan was the trigger for the change, but he doesn't seem satisfied to be just working on the ranch anymore."

"Well, we'll talk to the family when we go out there on Sunday. Maybe I'll corral Ryan and talk to him myself. At least I should be able to get a better read on what's bothering him."

"I'm sure that Erin would appreciate anything you could do to help, Kyle, and I would be grateful, too."

"I'd do anything for you, Katie," Kyle replied as he slipped the last spoonful of mush into John's mouth.

———

Ryan was having coffee with Lynn in the kitchen of his own small house after having supper with the rest of the family in Dylan's big house. Lynn, Alwen, and Garth had been living in

Kyle's house after he and Katie had moved to Denver in the spring.

"I thought you were smart enough to figure it out before I even got here, Lynn," Ryan said as he swirled his half-empty cup in front of him.

"I noticed a while ago, but it doesn't matter even if it is true. He's my father and he always will be."

"Sure, you say that because he's your hero, but did you ever wonder why he and your mother never told you?"

"Maybe because it's not true. Did you ever think of that?" Lynn asked harshly, not wanting to believe what he had suspected for years now.

"Come on, Lynn. You don't look anything at all like Garth or even Alwen, who's just your cousin. You don't look like any of Bryn's boys, either. You know it's true, Lynn. Dylan isn't your father. Look at the timing. You were born exactly nine months after your hero father took your mother out of Fort Benton and killed the man who was probably your real father. Did you ever stop and think why he did killed him? I mean, the only story you've ever heard was from your mother and him. What if they're both covering up the real story? What if your hero murdered her real husband up in Fort Benton and stole her away? Nobody around here would know; and in those days, who would even care?"

Lynn snapped, "You're wrong, Ryan! My dad is the bravest and most honest man I know, and he'd never do anything like that!"

Ryan snickered and said, "A man would do anything to get what he wants, Lynn, especially if it's a woman who he fancies."

Lynn glared at Ryan and growled, "Like you did with Molly Finnegan?"

Ryan's eyes narrowed as he replied, "She lied to everybody because she didn't want them to think that she was a hussy. But she wanted it and if her brother hadn't come into the barn to get a screwdriver, she would have been welcoming me back with open arms. I'll bet your sainted hero did the same thing and maybe your real father caught him and your mother before your hero had a chance to diddle her and got killed when he found them."

Lynn shot to his feet, knocking his chair over backwards and exclaimed, "You've gone too far, Ryan! You're talking about my mother and father; not you and Molly!"

Ryan laughed, then said, "If you're so sure, Lynn, why don't you ask him? Better yet, ask them both and see what they say. If he's so damned honest like you claim him to be, then maybe you'll finally learn the truth. Then if they tell you what you don't want to hear, you'll know that you're not an Evans at all. You're the son of a murdering, thieving son of a bitch."

Lynn glared at Ryan as he asked, "Why are you doing this, Ryan? If you've known for so long; why are you telling me now?"

"Because I don't plan on staying here much longer. I'm going to make a name for myself because your marshal hero doesn't think I'm good enough to be one of his deputies. I plan on heading out of here in a few days and showing them all that I'm as good as any of them. I figure if you're just a bastard, like your Uncle Kyle, then you'd want to come along."

"Where are you going? What are you going to do?"

"I'm going to do what those famous relatives of yours and all those other lawmen couldn't do. I'm going to get those four outlaws."

Then he laughed as he said, "Hell, if you've got some of your real father in you then you could kill all of them without even thinking about it."

Lynn continued to stare at Ryan and wished that he had another argument ready, but instead, he just turned and marched down the short hallway and soon left the small house.

After he heard the front door slam, Ryan stood, walked to his cupboard and slipped out a small pint bottle of whiskey. He took one long drag and then replaced the cork before hiding it back behind the box of soap chips.

————

Lynn's mind was boiling with warring thoughts as he crossed the long yard to his parents' house. At least he was sure that his mother was his parent; but as soon as the thought arrived, he began to doubt even that certainty. *What if he'd been someone else's castoff? What if they'd found him on the way to Omaha?* Lynn's whole world was crashing around him and he wasn't sure if he could believe anyone anymore.

He pounded up the steps to the front porch and entered the house without knocking. As soon as he strode into the front parlor, he found his parents with Bethan, Cari, Brian and Conway in the room.

Everyone turned to look at him and as soon as he did, Dylan could see the angst on his face and asked, "What's wrong, Lynn?"

Lynn was close to bursting, but held back his explosive question as he asked, "Could I talk to you and mom alone, please?"

"Certainly," Dylan replied, before looking at the four younger Evans children and saying, "Bethan, can you take everyone into the kitchen? I'm sure that some of your mother's cookies are still left."

Bethan glanced at her older brother as she stood, replied, "Yes, Dad," then took Conway's hand and shooed the other two before her as she walked down the hallway.

As they left, Lynn pulled a chair across the parlor to be closer to his parents before sitting down.

"What's wrong, Lynn?" Gwen asked.

Lynn wasn't quite sure how to phrase his question, but finally just looked at Dylan and quickly asked, "Are you really my father?"

Dylan understood what he was asking and had been expecting it for years, so he was ready with his reply.

"Of course, I'm your father, Lynn. I've been your father since the day you were born."

"You know what I'm asking. I don't look like any of the other Evans and I know that mom had been married to that man in Fort Benton for a couple of days before you took her away. Is he my real father?"

"Does it really matter, Lynn? You're as much an Evans as any of your brothers, sisters or cousins. Have we ever treated you any differently than we treated Garth?"

21

"No, you haven't, and I am grateful for that, but I want to know the truth. Was that evil bastard you killed in Fort Benton my real father?"

Dylan glanced at Gwen who was visibly upset before he sighed, then replied, "Yes. Burke Riddell assaulted your mother before I rescued her, but I didn't kill him. I was there with your mother when Joseph Walking Bear, a Crow army scout, killed him for raping and murdering his young niece."

Lynn dropped against the chair's back cushion as he slowly said, "Then Ryan was right. I'm a bastard."

Gwen then snapped, "You are not a bastard, Lynn! You are our son and we both love you very much. The circumstances of your conception don't change that."

Lynn looked at his mother and replied, "They do change things, Mom. How can I be sure that the monster that you described as my father isn't lurking deep inside me? What if I suddenly want to start hurting people?"

"If there was even a hint of evil in you, Lynn, you would have known by now," Dylan said.

"That's only because I've always been with the family. What if I'm on my own? What happens then? What if I become an outlaw and you have to shoot me? How can I tell what's buried deep inside me that can suddenly change who I thought I was?"

Dylan looked at his troubled son and said, "None of us ever know how we'll react until it happens, Lynn. You just have to believe that you're going to be a good man and will make us both proud."

LYNN'S SEARCH

Lynn had his eyes on the floor as he nodded, but still had so much to think about. Suddenly, Ryan's offer seemed to be his opportunity to discover the truth about himself.

He raised his eyes and replied, "Okay, Dad. I'll be all right. It was just a shock, I guess."

"Are you sure that you're okay, Son?" Dylan asked.

Lynn nodded, then stood and slid the chair back to its original position before turning to his parents and saying, "I'm going back to the house now."

Gwen stood then walked to Lynn and hugged him as she whispered, "We love you, Lynn. Don't ever forget that."

Lynn smiled weakly at her before he turned, left the parlor and then the house.

After he'd gone, Dylan turned to Gwen and said, "What the hell is Ryan doing? We both knew that sooner or later, Lynn would realize what had happened, but now, he seems to suspect much worse. Maybe we should have told him when he was just a boy."

"Perhaps we should have, but it's too late now. I'll talk to Erin tomorrow and you can tell Bryn on the ride to the office and then tell Kyle and mom when you get to Denver. We'll just have to see what happens on Sunday."

Dylan nodded, but was fuming about what Ryan had done. It wasn't his place to tell Lynn anything.

———

Lynn didn't go to the house he shared with Garth and Alwen but headed to Ryan's place.

When he reached the small house, he just entered without knocking and headed for Ryan's bedroom.

Ryan heard him coming and was already on his feet when Lynn passed over the threshold.

"Well?" he asked, "Did you ask them?"

Lynn sat on the bed and replied, "Yeah. You were right. He told me that that evil bastard in Fort Benton was my real father, but he said that he didn't kill him. He said that some Indian did."

Ryan pulled up his straight-backed chair close to the bed, sat down and said, "That's what he said? How do you know that? It sounds like a way to make you not hate him for killing your real father. Why would some Indian want to kill your father in the first place?"

"He said that the Indian wanted revenge because the man had raped and murdered the Indian's niece."

"And you believed him?" Ryan asked in apparent disbelief.

"Yes. I believed him. I don't know why you seem to want to tear my father down, Ryan, but I have no reason to disbelieve him. He's never lied to me before, and neither has my mother. But now that I know that Burke Riddell is my real father, I'm worried that I might someday become a heartless man like him. I need to know if it's there and the only way I can find the answer is to leave the Double EE and find out who I really am."

"So, you're coming with me?"

Lynn nodded, then asked, "How do we do this?"

"Well, we both have horses, pistols and Winchesters. I have almost sixty dollars saved up. How much do you have?"

Lynn shrugged and then replied, "Almost a hundred dollars, I guess."

Ryan grinned before saying, "Well, we can ride out of here whenever we want to. We just pack our horses with some spare clothes and other stuff, including some spare ammunition and some food, then we ride off."

"Where will we go?"

"Well, your marshal father told us about some outlaws that nobody can find down around Pueblo. What if we were to find them and capture them or kill them? We'd be famous and would probably get a big reward. He said that they had stolen almost three thousand dollars, too."

"But we're not the law, Ryan, and there are four of them and only two of us."

"I know that, but you've already learned a lot about tracking and are pretty good with your guns, too. You're a lot better than I am. We aren't wearing any badges, so we can surprise them. Maybe we can become bounty hunters."

Lynn shrugged before replying, "It doesn't really matter where we go, I guess. Just let me know soon so I can pack. I'm going to head back to my house now."

"Okay, Lynn. I'll start thinking about when we should go. I think the best time might be Saturday night before the whole family gets together and they all start talking about you like you're a stranger."

"They wouldn't do that, Ryan, but I'll start getting my things together."

"Don't forget your money, Lynn."

"I won't," Lynn replied before he stood, then left the bedroom, walked out to the kitchen and left through the back door which was closer to his house.

As he walked, Lynn debated about telling Alwen and Garth the news, but decided that it didn't matter. They'd hear it soon enough on Sunday, and he didn't want to see their reaction. So, when he entered his house, he just behaved as normally as he could when Al asked if he wanted to play some poker.

He played horribly that night as his mind was on everything but the cards in his hand, but neither of them noticed.

———

After the children were in their beds and Gwen and Dylan were alone again, she asked, "Do you really think he'll be okay?"

"I'm not so sure, Gwen. It'll take some time to recover from the shock, but we can't go out of our way to treat him any differently. All we can do is to still be his parents."

"I guess they'll all have to go through something like this as they begin to prepare to go off on their own, but Lynn has a lot more on his plate. Should we tell the other children?"

"Not yet. Lynn may have explained it to Garth and Al when he got back to the house and it'll trickle out from there. If not, we'll wait until Sunday when the whole family is here, but we'll have to come up with a soft way to let the children know."

"I'm surprised that none of them have figured it out yet. I'm sure that the adults already have."

"They all grew up with Lynn as their oldest brother or cousin and accepted him as nothing else. Our older children may have started to wonder about it once they fully understood the whole boy-girl thing. Maybe it'll all be better when everyone knows, and we can finally tell the whole story. Would you be able to listen when I do that?"

"I'll tell them, Dylan. I believe I can do a better job reliving the horror of those few days living with that horrid creature. Maybe I should have told Lynn tonight, so he would have understood why we hadn't told him before."

"Well, we'll just have to see how he reacts when he hears the story on Sunday."

Gwen sighed and snuggled in close to Dylan as she tried to put that nightmare out of her mind. It would be difficult to bring the despicable memories from their dark hiding places, but she'd do it to help Lynn.

CHAPTER 2

After Dylan rode off with Bryn the next morning, Gwen walked the four hundred yards to Bryn and Erin's house leaving Bethan in charge of her siblings.

Alba was already taking care of Erin's brood when Gwen entered the kitchen and Erin smiled at her sister-in-law and asked, "Shouldn't you be armed, Gwen?"

"Oh. I forgot what Dylan said about those outlaws, but I wanted to talk to you about something that happened last night."

"Alright," Erin replied and then was surprised when Gwen left the kitchen, so whe walked down the hallway following her and wondering what was so private.

When they entered the parlor, Gwen turned and looked up at her taller sister-in-law and began quietly repeating the troubling conversation they'd had with Lynn.

After she'd finished, she asked, "Did you already suspect that he wasn't Dylan's natural born son?"

"We all guessed that some time ago, but it really didn't matter. Do you think it does now?"

"We're not sure. He seemed to accept it before he left and he's out in the pastures now, so I haven't seen how he was today. Why would Ryan goad him into asking us?"

Erin exhaled sharply, then replied, "He's been kind of cold to me for a while now and I don't understand. When I ask him about it, he pretends there's nothing wrong."

"Is it another woman issue?"

"No, not this time. I don't think he's going to go down that road again, and he doesn't seem to be drinking any more than he had before. It's something else."

"But that doesn't explain why he'd provoke Lynn like that. Is he out with Lynn and the other boys?"

"I don't know, Gwen. Do you want me to ride out there and talk to him?"

"No. Dylan and I want to tell everyone tomorrow in our own way. Maybe that will settle everything down."

"It might make things worse; at least as far as Ryan is concerned."

"Was he ever like this when you were young?"

"He wasn't like my older brother, Jack, who was a real troublemaker, and he wasn't sweet like Daniel, who is now Father Daniel Mitchell. He was a mischief maker and always seemed to be having fun, but I was three years younger than he was, so I thought it was normal. Even after I was told I was going to be a nun. I really didn't pay too much attention to how he behaved."

Gwen nodded, then said, "Well, all we can do is see what happens tomorrow and, as Dylan says, play the cards that we're dealt."

Erin laughed before replying, "Bryn says the same thing, and I guess it's true."

"Well, I'm going to head back to the house and get a start on that big pile of laundry that's been piling up."

"Don't remind me," Erin said before Gwen smiled, then turned and left through the front door.

———

Out in the western pasture, Ryan and Lynn had separated from the others and were walking their horses south.

"I'm all packed and ready to go, Lynn. I figure we can leave after everybody's asleep. We can be all the way to Castle Rock before anybody wakes up."

Lynn was beginning to regret his quick response to Ryan's suggestion, and almost told him that he wasn't going to go but didn't want to think that Ryan would believe him to be a coward. Besides, he really did need to discover how he'd react to the unknown that awaited them in the outside world. He didn't really believe that they'd be facing those four outlaws and had no idea how or where he'd find the answer to his troubling personal question.

"Okay. I'll come over to your place and then we can saddle the horses and leave."

Ryan grinned as he replied, "We're going to show everyone that we're as good as they are, if not better."

Lynn had to bite his tongue to keep from snapping back but held back his defense of his father and uncles as he rode alongside Ryan. He knew that Ryan would probably be throwing a lot of insulting barbs at his father and his Uncle

Bryn after they left, and he had to learn to put up with them. He still didn't understand why Ryan seemed to suddenly hate them so much. He knew that his father didn't dislike Ryan, despite that embarrassing incident with Molly Finnegan.

As they turned back to join the others, Lynn started reviewing what he needed to take with him. He also made up his mind that he'd leave a note for his parents, so they wouldn't worry as much. He was sixteen and although he was slightly shorter than Garth, he was thicker in the chest and had more muscle on his arms and legs, so he outweighed Alwen. Uncle Kyle had walked halfway across the country when he was seventeen and hadn't even been armed when he began the journey. He and Ryan each had a pistol and a Winchester and knew how to use them, so he would be much safer than Kyle had been when he entered the unknown.

———

Kyle looked at Dylan as he said, "I think I know what might have set Ryan off, Dylan. Remember that incident when he asked if he could be a deputy marshal?"

"I do, but it didn't seem that important."

"Maybe it was to him. I can't think of anything else that happened around the time he started becoming so dissatisfied."

Dylan shrugged, then said, "I guess we'll just have to find out tomorrow. I just hope that the older children don't begin to think that Lynn's different."

"I don't think it'll be a problem, Dylan. All we can do is see what happens and work with the cards we're dealt."

"I know, but I wish I had an ace or two up my sleeve."

Kyle smiled at Dylan and said, "You can always ask Bryn to let you borrow the king and queen of hearts I gave him when Huw and Grace Lynn were born."

Dylan grinned and replied, "He wouldn't let them go for a hundred dollars, Kyle. He keeps them in his wallet to remind him of that night."

"We'll see you tomorrow, Dylan."

Dylan rose, said, "See you then, Kyle," then left the office.

―――

As the sun disappeared over the Rockies, Lynn was in his room with the door closed as he put the finishing touches on his packing. He had to use his pillowcase for some of his extra things and even taken the extra pillowcase from the closet. He discovered that as soon as he thought he had enough, he'd find something else that he needed to take with him. Soon, both pillowcases were stuffed, and his heavy jacket and other winter outerwear were laid out on his bed. It was still technically summer, but the chilly nights had already arrived, and he could see snow on the mountain peaks. He had already packed his basic necessities into his saddlebags and left them in the barn with his mahogany gelding, Griffin. He'd asked the only Welsh speaker in the family, his grandmother, for a good Welsh name and she suggested Griffin, which meant prince.

Supper had been a decidedly awkward affair, at least between him and his parents, but no one else seemed to notice. He had come close to telling them that he was leaving with Ryan more than once, but knew that if he had, they'd be able to talk him out of his decision without much of an argument.

LYNN'S SEARCH

He'd written his short letter to his parents when he'd first returned and hoped that they would understand. He didn't want his father or Uncle Bryn, or anyone else, to try and find him.

He finally blew out his lamp and just stretched out on the bed to wait for Al and Garth to fall asleep. But when he found himself drifting off, he bolted upright and just sat on the bed.

_____

Ryan lived alone, so he had no such concerns. He had packed his things and once the sun went down, walked out to the barn and saddled his horse, a black gelding he'd named Boot, but not because he had stockings. He'd just thought it was funny because he could say Boot's black.

He saddled Griffin as well, then returned to his house where he packed some food for the first few days. His plan was to ride down to Pueblo, then head west for Canon City. He expected to find those four outlaws somewhere in between.

_____

John Coleridge and the other three outlaws were nowhere near either town as Ryan and Lynn prepared to leave the Double EE.

After the murderous stage robbery, they'd ridden on the roadway to hide their tracks for a few miles, then turned south and followed a creek until they shifted southeast and spent the night in the tiny town of Muddy Creek.

Now they were in the much larger town of Walsenburg, and while not exactly a thriving metropolis, did give them a place to spend some of their loot without bringing too much attention to themselves.

That would change soon.

———

Lynn finally stood, stretched, then began his transformation into a human pack animal. He strapped on his gunbelt, put on his heavy coat, and then hung the two pillowcases over one shoulder and his heavy saddlebags over the other. He grabbed his Winchester in one hand and held his boots in the other.

He walked to the floor, set his boots down and opened the door before picking them up again and stepping through the dark doorway. He glanced toward his brothers' rooms, then turned, silently closed his door before he tiptoed down the hallway toward the front room.

Once he reached the front door, he had to do the boot drop again and once outside, he closed the door, stepped to the edge of the small porch and sat down.

After donning his boots, he stood and began quickly walking in the light of the half-moon toward the barn. He kept glancing back at his parents' house with mixed feelings. He didn't resent them in the least for keeping the secret because he could understand their motive; but once he he they had confirmed Ryan's accusation, he knew that he had to leave to be certain that none of his natural father's evil lived inside him. He was unsure if he would ever return to the Double EE, and the idea that he may never see his family again hurt. Even with that painful thought, Lynn still believed that his decision was the right one. He hoped that he'd be able to return someday after he was confident that he was an Evans, and not a Riddell.

———

LYNN'S SEARCH

Ryan was waiting impatiently in the barn and began to suspect that Lynn had changed his mind. He knew that Lynn's quick reply that he'd be joining him was a response to the shock of learning his true lineage, but Ryan expected that after he had talked to Dylan and Gwen, Lynn would stay.

He was almost ready to leave the barn to find Lynn when he heard footsteps and soon spotted Lynn as he popped into view before the open barn doors.

"There you are! I thought you might have chickened out, Lynn."

Lynn ignored the insult and simply replied, "Let me get my things on Griffin and let's go."

"Now you're talking," Ryan said as he walked with Lynn back into the barn.

———

Five minutes later, the two loaded horses were walking out of the barn and turned toward the access road.

Once they reached the roadway, they turned south and set their horses to a medium trot.

"How long are we riding tonight?" Lynn asked loudly.

"Until we're too tired to keep going," Ryan replied.

Lynn didn't ask anything else as he stared ahead at the moonlit road but knew that they'd still be passing Double EE land for another hour or so.

There were two small towns, Petersburg and then Littleton just past the southern edge of the Double EE, but he didn't think that they'd be stopping in either town. He'd gotten the impression from Ryan that he intended to push on as far south as they could get.

———

It wasn't until breakfast the next morning that anyone noticed that Lynn was missing, and it was Bethan who first voiced it.

"Where's Lynn?" she asked.

Garth shrugged as Alwen replied, "We didn't see him when we got up, so we thought he was already here."

Dylan glanced at Gwen and said, "I'll be back in a few minutes."

She nodded as he stood and grabbed his old flat leather hat and headed for the door.

As soon as Bethan had asked the question, he had a twist in his stomach. After their talk, he and Gwen had been concerned that he was more upset than he'd let on but didn't think he was depressed enough to hurt himself. But teenagers just didn't think like adults and there was no telling what he might have done.

He quickly reached the small house and popped through the door before hustling to Lynn's room.

As soon as he walked through the door, he was relieved not to find Lynn's body, but knew instantly that he was gone. As he scanned the empty room, he spotted the sheet of paper on the dresser.

He walked slowly to the chest of drawers, picked up the paper, unfolded it and read:

Dear Mom and Dad,

I'm leaving with Ryan, but I want you to understand that I'm not angry or even upset by what you told me. I suspected it for some time now, but I still love you both and will never think less of you.

I need to get away from the comfort and security of my family to discover who I really am. Knowing that the evil Burke Riddell is in my blood tortures my mind and I'm not sure how, when or where I can solve this torment.

I understand why you chose not to tell me all these years, and I'm grateful and blessed for all that you've given me. Please don't try to find me. I hope to return to the Double EE, but only when I have my answer.

With My Love and Respect,

Lynn

Dylan read it a second time and understood how Lynn must have felt. The only part of the note that bothered him was the first line; that he was leaving with Ryan. He and Gwen had spent a lifetime raising Lynn and all of their children to be honest, conscientious human beings, and he hoped that Ryan didn't undue all of it in just a few weeks.

Dylan then left the house and headed for the barn where he found Griffin and Ryan's gelding both gone and assumed that they were probably a good thirty miles away by now.

As he walked back to the big house, he hoped that Gwen wouldn't ask him to find Lynn. He didn't believe that she would, but a mother's instinctual desire to protect her children may override her understanding.

When he entered the kitchen, everyone looked at him, but he didn't say anything until he took his seat.

He handed the note to Gwen, who looked at his eyes before turning hers to the paper.

She quickly read it before she softly said, "He's gone."

Bethan quickly asked, "Lynn left?"

Dylan replied, "Yes, dear. He rode off last night with Ryan. I have no idea where they went."

Garth asked, "Can't you find him, Dad? You're the marshal."

"I probably could find them in a day or two, but your brother asked me not to search for him."

"Why?" Al asked.

Dylan glanced at Gwen, then said, "Yesterday, Lynn asked me and your mom about his father."

Garth asked, "You're his father, Dad. Why would he have to ask about it?"

"Yes, I'm his father because I raised him with your mother since he was born, but I need to tell each of you what I told Lynn yesterday."

LYNN'S SEARCH

The children all looked at their father as Dylan began to explain how Lynn had been conceived and why he was so upset.

When he finished, Al asked, "Is he coming back?"

Gwen replied, "I hope so, and so does he. All we can do is wait."

"Do Uncle Bryn and Uncle Kyle know about Lynn?" Bethan asked.

"Yes. They all suspected it anyway because of how different Lynn looked from the rest of you and the timing of his birth."

Garth asked, "Are they still coming today?"

"Yes. Lynn may not be here, but we still need to keep going as we always have," Dylan replied, then looked at Alwen, Garth and Bethan in turn before saying, "It won't be long before each of you may leave to start your own lives, but hopefully, it will be under much happier circumstances."

"I won't leave in the middle of the night, Dad," Al said before Garth added his promise to only leave the ranch with his parents' approval.

Bethan knew that she had a few more years before she would leave, but the boys were already beginning to notice her, and she didn't think she'd be waiting much past her seventeenth birthday. Of course, that would only happen if she met some boy who met her standards and wasn't afraid of her.

Gwen looked at her husband and said, "Do you want to wait until the others come here in a few hours to tell them?"

"I think so. I'd prefer not to keep repeating the story."

Gwen nodded then handed the note to Alwen to read.

It then passed to Garth, Bethan and even ten-year-old Cari before she gave it back to her mother.

————

Lynn and Ryan were on the road again after catching a few hours' sleep south of Littleton. It was a Sunday, so road traffic wasn't very heavy. They hadn't spoken much after stopping for the night, and the lack of communication continued as they continued south as each of them ruminated on what they'd be doing over the next few days.

Ryan had already planned on spending some of his money when they reached Castle Rock. He'd packed his bottle of whiskey but wanted to save it until it was all that was available. He was depending on Lynn's tracking and other lawman skills that he'd learned from Dylan to lead them to the four outlaws. Then he'd have enough money and a reputation to go his own way. He wouldn't need Lynn after that and as far as Ryan was concerned, Lynn could go running back to the Double EE.

Lynn still thought hunting four killers was a bad idea. This was a job for a large posse and two inexperienced men didn't stand a chance. He thought Ryan's belief that surprise would be enough to overwhelm the four men was nothing short of ludicrous. Men like that didn't trust anyone. If he and Ryan suddenly ran across them, they'd be lucky to get within two hundred yards before the four outlaws had their rifles out and aimed at them.

He wasn't about to lead Ryan to the four men, even if he could find their trail. If trained lawmen couldn't find it, then he knew that they didn't have a prayer.

Yet he still knew that he needed something to push him into having to make those decisions that would send him down one path or the other. He strongly believed that he would behave as his father, Uncle Bryn and Uncle Kyle did, but needed the confirmation. He just didn't expect to find it in a confrontation with John Coleridge and his gang; wherever they may be.

———

In Walsenburg, Rusty Halloran sat across from John Coleridge at the diner and asked, "How long are we gonna stay here, John? I don't like it much. It's too close to Pueblo and I figure this sheriff musta got a telegram about us."

Ollie Thorsen then said, "I think so too, John. We're wearin' out our welcome here."

John looked at Rusty and replied, "I think we can stick around for another day or so. We're not making any noise that might attract attention to us."

Mike Greenburg snapped, "We already made the noise outside of Pueblo, John! We're four strangers and that kid deputy gave us a doubletake."

"Alright, if you're all so spooked, we'll leave tomorrow morning. The question is which direction? We can head south to Trinidad and then go on to Mexico where we'll be safe and our money will go farther, or we can head west."

"There ain't nothin' out west, John," Rusty said, "and I'm not all that keen on Mexico either. Trinidad still isn't big enough to hide in, so I think we take the train north and head up to Denver. That's big enough now that we can just blend in for a while before we do our next job."

"I told you, Rusty. I can't go back there. Too many of those lawmen know me."

"Hell, John, you don't look like you used to. With that beard and those six years of hard livin', you look like a real nasty feller; not that badge wearin', smooth talkin' boy you used to be."

Ollie laughed and said, "He's right, John. You look like a cross between a hard luck prospector and a teamster."

John still wasn't pleased with the idea, but at the same time, still harbored the desire for some payback. He thought that he'd just be fired for the bribery, but Cornbread had fingered him, and he'd served seventy-two months at hard labor. He used to believe that Bryn Evans was out of his reach, but now with his new partners, maybe he could come up with something. It would be difficult to say the least; what with the sheriff's office and the U.S. Marshal's office in town, but if he could find a way to hurt the bastard, it would be sweet revenge.

He wouldn't go as far as Cornbread had planned to do, but a simple ambush would work. He knew that both Evans lived on Bryn's ranch southwest of Denver and would leave the city each weekday. They would be so complacent in their routine that they'd never suspect an ambush. It would be his only opportunity to set things right.

"Alright," he said, "We'll take the train tomorrow, but we'll get off at Castle Rock where nobody knows me. Then we'll make the ride to Denver. Okay?"

"Sounds good to me," Ollie replied.

Rusty nodded, then took a sip of his coffee. John may think that he was the boss of their band, but Rusty knew better. He was able to manipulate Coleridge easily and one of these days, he'd let John know that he was now the number two man.

———

"I think they're those four outlaws who held up the stage west of Pueblo, boss," Deputy Lyle Arnold said to Sheriff Carney as he stood on the sheriff's porch.

"Lyle, you see outlaws in every dark alley and in every shop. Why do you think it's them?"

"It's the way they looked at me when I first saw them. I should say that it was the way they didn't look at me. I didn't recognize any of them and even when I passed them on the boardwalk, none of them even looked me in the eye. Strangers always either try to be really friendly or at least act like they're curious. These boys must have seen my badge and after I passed them because when I turned around to look at them again, none of them looked back, either."

"And that was enough to convince you that they're the outlaws that robbed a stage fifty miles away."

"Nobody up there knows where they went and it's only a day's ride."

Tom Carney sighed, then said, "Alright, Lyle. Do you know where your desperate killers are right now?"

"They were heading for Lilly's Diner, so they're probably still there."

The sheriff may have believed that his fresh-faced deputy was seeing bogeymen but couldn't afford to take the risk that he may be right. His more experienced deputy was out of

43

town, so there were only two of them and Lyle hadn't experienced any serious confrontations yet.

"Stay here while I tell the missus that I'll be gone for a bit."

"Okay, boss," Deputy Arnold replied as the sheriff disappeared into his house.

He was already nervous about a possible gunfight, but the idea of capturing four hardened killers was exciting too.

When Sheriff Carney returned, he closed the door before they stepped down from the porch and headed for the office.

"Are we going to confront them?" Lyle asked.

"Not if I can help it. I want to get a closer look at them, so I want you to stay in the office, but have the shotgun ready. Do you understand?"

"Yes, sir."

"I don't want any gunplay in the diner if we can avoid it. I hope that these boys are just passing through."

"Are you going to talk to 'em?"

"Maybe. They haven't seen me, so I should be able to at least get a good look at them. I'll take a seat at a table and have some coffee, so they won't get suspicious. If someone says, 'good morning, sheriff', I'll pretend that I don't see them and then after I finish my coffee, I'll come back to the office."

"Okay."

The sheriff was telling Lyle his plan so the young man would understand that the job wasn't always about shooting bad guys; it was trying to avoid pulling a trigger at all if it was possible.

After a brief stop at the office, Sheriff Carney began his slow walk toward Lilly's Diner, greeting the folks as he passed as he usually did.

When he entered the diner, he spotted the four men at the corner table and none so much as paid him any mind. He assumed that they'd watched him approach and were trying not to be so noticeable.

As he took a seat, Edith Royce approached his table, smiled and asked, "Did Fannie kick you out of the house this morning, Sheriff?"

He looked up at her, returned her smile and replied, "Nope. I had to go and talk to Fred Arthur, so I figured I'd have some of your coffee, Edith."

"Well, I'll be right back," she said before turning and heading back to the kitchen.

He'd taken the seat that faced the corner, so he could see the four men at the table who still hadn't even looked his way. He had to agree with his deputy that it was odd behavior. Normal human curiosity would have compelled them to take a glance at any new patrons, but they studiously avoided turning their eyes in his direction.

He wasn't sure if they matched the brief descriptions in Pueblo County Sheriff Tapper's telegram, but they didn't have any obvious differenced, either. One of them was even blonde, which had been mentioned in the telegram.

Edith arrived with his coffee, then set it down, smiled and left to bus a different table as the diners left.

Sheriff Carney made short work of the coffee, left a nickel on the table, even though he didn't have to, then waved to Edith and left the diner.

He didn't walk directly to the office, but headed in the opposite direction, suspecting that the four would be watching him through the window.

————

After the sheriff left, Rusty asked, "What do you think, John? Was he lookin' us over?"

"I'm not sure, but I think so. Why would he come in here on a Sunday morning and just have a cup of coffee?"

Ollie said, "I think we outta pull up stakes right now and get out of here before things get hot."

"I'm with Ollie," Mike Greenburg said as he glanced back through the window.

"Okay. Let's head back to the hotel, get our stuff, then head to the livery. We can ride out of here and pick up that train at the Huerfano station."

With the decision made, the four outlaws stood, left some silver on the table for their food, then quickly filed out of the diner.

————

As they headed for the hotel, Sheriff Carney had cut through an alley before he headed back east toward the jail. He may not be convinced that they were the outlaw killers yet but couldn't risk doing anything in the diner. If they were those men, and knowing the suspicious nature of criminals, he

46

suspected that they would leave the diner soon after he did. Whether they would be leaving Walsenburg or not was the second question. He began to suspect that they might be in his town to try to rob the bank tomorrow morning.

As he quickly strode to his jail, he wished that he had his more experienced deputy available. If they were the four that robbed the stage and killed the driver, then they weren't about to keep from starting a gunfight in the streets of Walsenburg, and Lyle Arnold would be a liability.

By the time he entered the back door and spotted Lyle with a Winchester in his hands and a boyish look of excitement on his face, he knew that only bad things would happen if he confronted the four in his town.

"Was I right, boss?" Lyle quickly asked.

"Maybe, but I'm still not sure. If it is them, then we're outgunned, and I don't want to see bullets flying in the streets of I can avoid it."

"We're not going after them?"

"We're going to watch from the office and see where they go. I don't want you to set one toe outside until I say so."

He could see the disappointment on Lyle's face, but he wasn't about to change his mind as he stepped past his bloodthirsty deputy, grabbed a shotgun from the rack and walked to the right window. The hotel was across the street and down a block to the east, so he had a good line of sight. He assumed that they had returned to the hotel by now. If they were planning on robbing the bank, then they'd stay inside and lay low. He was hoping that they were spooked by his attention and left Walsenburg today rather than hit the bank tomorrow. At least his other deputy should be back by then and they'd be ready.

Kyle was standing at the left window and asked, "How long are we going to wait, boss?"

"Not too long. If they're nervous, they'll leave. If not, then I'll have to come up with something."

"*We're going to let them leave?*" he exclaimed.

"If they ride out of here, I'll thank my lucky star and send a telegram to the other sheriffs."

Lyle snorted, but continued to watch the street.

————

The four objects of the lawmen's attention were walking across the hotel lobby trying to appear as innocent as possible, but all of their hammer loops were off as they stepped onto the boardwalk.

Each of them glanced back toward the diner, then scanned the buildings across the street, lingering on the sheriff's office before turning east and heading for Pappy's livery.

————

Lyle was chomping at the bit when he saw them exit the hotel and almost shouted, "There they go!"

"I can see that, Lyle. Now hold your horses and just watch. I want to get a good description of their animals when they leave Pappy's."

Lyle began tapping his right toe against the pine floor as he watched his chance for glory enter the livery.

"Are you sure this is the right thing to do, boss?" he asked.

"If Joe was here, I might think about setting out after them when they're outside of the town where there isn't a chance of endangering any citizens, but with only two of us, we wouldn't stand a chance. We'd get killed and leave the town wide open to whatever those bastards felt like doing. Our first job is to protect folks, Lyle. Don't ever forget that."

"No, sir," Lyle said with an obvious tone of disappointment.

After watching the four men ride east out of town, Sheriff Carney said, "I'm going to the telegraph office and let the other sheriffs know they were here."

Lyle asked, "Do you want me to track them for a while to see which direction they go?"

Sheriff Carney was about to turn him down but knowing which way they were heading would add a valuable piece of information to his warning telegram.

"Alright, Lyle, but you stay out of sight. Do you hear? I don't want them to know you're there. You follow their tracks until they make a turn then you come back. I don't want to hear any gunfire. Is that clear?"

Lyle had to restrain his excitement as he slowly nodded, then replied, "Yes, sir. I'll just track 'em."

"Alright. You go saddle your horse and I'll head to the telegraph office. I want to see you back here within an hour so I can send a second telegram with what you tell me."

"Okay, boss," Lyle replied as he stepped out of the jail and headed for Pappy's, where they kept their own horses.

Sheriff Carney watched him trot to the livery and hoped that he didn't do something rash. The only reason he didn't change his mind was that he knew that Lyle, like all new lawmen, had to learn when to restrain themselves.

He left the office and turned west to send his long telegram.

————

Ollie was riding alongside Mike behind John and Rusty and was almost constantly checking their back trail. Mike wasn't concerned because they hadn't seen either the sheriff or his deputy when they left town. They were already a mile out and riding at a medium trot, so the odds were that the sheriff hadn't recognized them after all. But Ollie was always a bit high strung and this time, it would work in their favor.

————

Lyle had quickly saddled his dark white gelding and left town at a slow trot, expecting that his boss would be watching, but once he passed the first bend in the road, he picked up the pace to a fast trot. He really had no intention of disobeying the sheriff, but this was his first real action since putting on the badge and his exhilaration overrode his simple instructions for staying well back of the potential danger that rode ahead of him.

He still couldn't see the four men but was leaving a large dust cloud behind him that rose well above his head and trailed a good thirty yards behind him.

————

It was that dust cloud that caught Ollie's eye as they rode almost two miles ahead of Lyle.

"Somebody's comin' up fast!" he shouted as he stared at the roadway behind them.

Three heads all turned west and Rusty snapped, "Damn it! I figured that sheriff wasn't interested!"

"Let's set up behind those trees over there," John yelled, "There's only two of them."

"What if they got a posse with 'em?" Mike asked loudly.

"They didn't have time to get a posse together," John answered before they picked up the pace to reach the trees.

Once they entered the small forest of pines, they quickly dismounted and pulled their Winchesters.

"Me and Ollie will target the sheriff and you and Mike can have the deputy, John," Rusty said as he cocked his repeater's hammer.

John didn't argue but cocked his own Winchester before each of them set up behind a tree.

As they leveled their rifles, Mike asked, "What do we do after we take them down? Do we head back into town and make hay?"

"Hell, no!" John answered loudly, "We drag their bodies into the trees, strip what we want and get out of here. If we tried to go back there, those armed citizens would be expecting us."

"Okay," Mike said as he stared west.

The dust cloud was getting larger and soon, their targets would appear around the curve.

Rusty then said, "Wait until they're close. We don't wanna miss."

John didn't comment again but was getting annoyed with Rusty acting as if he was the boss.

———

Lyle didn't see them ahead as he rounded the twist in the road, so he kept his eyes focused on the far end of the empty roadway. Their trail was so fresh that he hadn't even had to look down.

He never gave a single thought that the outlaws might be preparing an ambush. He was convinced that they were far out ahead of him and anxious to put as much distance between them and Walsenburg as possible.

So, when he approached the trees, he never even noticed the shift in the tracks away from the roadway. His first clue that the four men were no longer riding east was when he felt three .44s slam into his body at the same moment that his ears heard the reports of rifle fire.

He was still alive when the lead punched into his chest and gut, but the power of the three shots at less than forty yards knocked him from his saddle and sent him sprawling onto the dirt road, creating his own small dust cloud in the process.

John Coleridge was the first to race out of the trees with his smoking Winchester in his right hand.

"Where's the sheriff?" Ollie shouted as he followed John.

"I don't think he's coming," John yelled back as he watched the deputy for any signs of life.

As he and Ollie approached Lyle's body, Rusty and Mike headed for his horse, who had slowed and then stopped to rest.

Once John determined that Huerfano County Deputy Sheriff Lyle Arnold was no longer alive, he quickly stripped the body of his gunbelt and went through his pockets. He only found three dollars and twenty-two cents but shoved it into his own pocket before taking Lyle's badge and slipping it into his other pocket.

"Why are you takin' his badge?" Ollie asked.

"It might come in handy later. Let's get this body into those trees," John replied before he grabbed Lyle's ankles.

"Alright," Ollie said as he took the wrists and they lugged the body off the roadway.

Rusty led the white horse into the trees and once they were all well inside the pines, he tied the gelding off and pulled the saddlebags.

There was nothing worth keeping in the saddlebags, but he took the Winchester out of its scabbard, then detached the scabbard as well as Mike watched.

John and Ollie arrived, half-dragging and half-carrying the body before dropping it on the needle-covered ground near the horse.

"Now what?" Ollie asked as he gulped for air.

"That damned horse is too easy to spot, so we have to leave it here. If we take him and the body to the far end of this forest, it'll take a while for the sheriff to find them. Then, we have to figure that he's sent telegrams to the surrounding lawmen letting them know that we're in the area."

Rusty grinned and said, "That's right. You used to wear a badge, John, so you'd know how they work."

"It's an advantage, Rusty. Let's get them moved and start riding again as soon as we can. I don't think the sheriff will be heading our way, at least not for another two hours or so, and by then, we'll be long gone. We can talk about where we'll go as we ride."

"Okay, boss," Mike said as he untied the gelding, leaving John and Ollie to move the corpse again.

Rusty then attached the second scabbard to his saddle before sliding his second Winchester home as he waited for his partners to return. He may have wanted to be the boss, but he'd need John more than ever now. His lawman experience would be invaluable if they were to avoid running into more trouble over the next few days.

When John and the others returned, they mounted and soon were on the road heading east again at a higher pace than they had earlier.

"Where are we going, John?" Rusty asked loudly.

"We stay on the road for a while, then we head for Placita. It's a small town with no law about fifteen miles southeast of here. We should be able to lay low for a while. Nothing gets the law more upset than when you kill one of their own. That idiot deputy may have deserved those .44s for being so ignorant, but that doesn't matter. He was wearing a badge and they'll be looking for us even more than they were before. We have to let things quiet down for a week or so."

"A week? We're gonna have to stay in some jerkwater town for a whole week?" Mike yelled.

"Would you rather head back into Walsenburg and say 'hello' to the sheriff or maybe ride down to Trinidad or up to Pueblo to be greeted by a bunch of waiting lawmen? We have plenty of cash and we can just take it easy."

"Alright, alright. I guess I can put up with it for a week," Mike snapped back.

John didn't say anything more as they continued east and after another three miles, took the southeast road toward Placita.

———

Sheriff Carney had been getting more anxious by the minute when Lyle hadn't returned after almost two hours. He should have been back an hour ago, and he began to believe that his young deputy had decided to engage the outlaws in some misguided attempt to be a hero.

He finally saddled his buckskin mare and headed east, warily scanning the road and the surroundings. If there had been a shootout, it wouldn't have been too close to town, but his concern was that if Lyle was dead, then the four outlaws might be heading back to wreak havoc on Walsenburg. He'd told the mayor about the four men, and before he'd gone, he'd deputized four men and told them to watch the road.

As he continued east, he really wished that Joe had been in town.

———

On the Double EE, the Evans family had gathered for their big Sunday luncheon, but before everyone took their assigned seats, Katie asked, "Where's Ryan?"

Her question triggered Dylan's explanation of Ryan and Lynn's disappearance, which then slipped into the reason that Lynn had gone with him.

Katie then asked, "Do you know why Ryan first goaded Lynn into asking about his natural father then convinced him to leave?"

"Do we even know why Ryan decided to leave in the first place?" Erin asked.

"Bryn and I think it was because he had asked me if he could join us as a deputy marshal, but I told him that he was more valuable here. It wasn't the real reason, but I thought it was better than telling him that his temperament was all wrong for a lawman."

Gwen then said, "Our biggest concern is what Ryan will try to do to prove that he is good enough to wear the badge. I wouldn't mind so much if he didn't have Lynn with him. I really don't understand why he wanted Lynn along, either."

Bryn said, "Maybe he knows his own limitations and wants to use Lynn's expertise. Dylan has been teaching all of the boys, and Bethan too, for that matter, about tracking and everything else since they stood on their own feet and toddled around the house."

Bryn hadn't even finished his reply when Gwen understood the motive for Ryan's prodding suggestions. He wanted to push Lynn into questioning his own character, so he would join Ryan when he left the Double EE.

LYNN'S SEARCH

"What are you going to do now, Dylan?" John asked.

"Nothing. Lynn didn't want us to look for him, and I'll honor his request. He's got to find himself, John. He needs to be sure that he's an Evans and not a Riddell."

"Surely, he knows that by now," Meredith said.

"I'll let you read his letter, Mom," Dylan replied, "and you won't see anything but a young man with a good heart in his words. Ryan cast some doubt into his mind, and until that worry is washed away, Lynn won't be content."

"I suppose you're right. I just hope he doesn't get hurt."

Bryn said, "He's been trained by the best, Mom. He'll be fine."

Meredith nodded as she looked at the concerned face of her daughter-in-law. She knew that Gwen was probably just as worried as she was, even though she knew her oldest son's abilities better than anyone except Dylan.

———

Lynn and Ryan rode into Castle Rock just before noon and headed for the nearest diner. They'd skipped breakfast because Ryan wanted to get to the town quickly.

As they sat waiting at the table, the young waitress headed their way and as she passed another table suddenly hopped away as the two men at the table laughed.

She turned and glared at the pair but continued to walk toward Ryan and Lynn.

When she reached their table, Ryan asked, "Did those boys offend you, miss?"

She smiled at him then replied, "It's just a hazard of the job, but thank you for asking. What can I get for you?"

"What's the special?"

"Chili and cornbread."

"We'll have a couple of big bowls and some coffee," he replied as he smiled.

"I'll be back shortly," she said before turning and heading back to the kitchen, avoiding the two grinning men at the other table.

Lynn asked, "What were you going to do if she said that they had embarrassed her, Ryan?"

"I would have been her knight in shining armor, Lynn. I would have told those boys to keep their hands to themselves."

"It isn't your business, Ryan. She had it right when she said that it's just something that she has to put up with every day. That doesn't make it right, but it's not worth getting into a fight over."

"Did you take a look at that girl, Lynn? If I worked this right, I could have spent an extra day in town and wouldn't have to stay in a hotel, either."

Lynn sighed, then said, "No, you would have spent it in the doctor's office or jail when her angry husband found you bothering her. Didn't you see the wedding band on her finger?"

Ryan glanced back at the kitchen, then answered, "It doesn't matter if she's married or not, Lynn. I managed to bring some joy into the lives of a few frustrated wives."

"Not here and not now, Ryan."

Ryan shrugged as the waitress brought them their chili, cornbread and coffee.

He finally glanced at her left hand, but still smiled at her before watching her walk away; already regretting bringing that killjoy Lynn along.

―――――

They were mounting their horses twenty minutes later when Lynn noticed the sheriff on the nearby boardwalk as he loudly gave instructions to his two deputies. What made it unusual was that it was a Sunday and seeing the three lawmen meant that something must be causing their concern.

Ryan continued riding south as Lynn slowed Griffin to listen, catching, "…they might not be coming this way or not, but Sheriff Carney down in Huerfano County is waiting for find out from his deputy which way they're going."

One of the deputies asked, "Is he sure they're the same boys that knocked off the stage outside of Pueblo?"

"He said they matched their description."

"That's over a hundred miles from here, boss."

"I know that, but I want you to watch the train when it shows up in a few hours. I don't want those bastards to set one foot in Castle Rock."

"Can we at least get lunch first?"

"Go ahead, just be back here before the train gets here. After that we'll just wait for more news."

They were still talking as Lynn walked Griffin too far away to pick up any more information.

As he nudged his gelding into a medium trot to catch up to Ryan, he was debating whether or not to tell him what he'd heard. It would be a good three days before they could even get to Walsenburg, and the outlaws would be long gone by then. If they knew that the sheriff had identified them, they'd most likely head for nearby Mexico.

He decided to tell Ryan with the expectation that they'd never run into the outlaws anyway. He still had no idea what he could do to reveal the potential flaw in his character, but he was absolutely convinced that Ryan's need to find the four killers wasn't it. If that minute possibility of running afoul of the outlaws happened, all it would probably do would be to get them both killed.

When he caught up to Ryan as they left Castle Rock, he said, "I heard the sheriff telling his deputies that the four outlaws that held up the stage and killed the driver outside of Pueblo had been spotted down in Walsenburg."

Ryan looked at him and loudly asked, "Way down there? How far away is it?"

"About a hundred and forty miles or so. It would take us three days to get there."

"They're not there anymore, though; are they?"

"Probably not."

Ryan then grinned and said, "I'll bet that they're heading this way to pay a visit to Bryn. We'll probably spot them on the road tomorrow or the next day."

"Maybe."

Lynn kept his eyes on the empty road ahead of them as Ryan began making his plans for confronting the gang. It didn't matter what Ryan was saying because Lynn was confident that they'd never run across the outlaws. If they weren't heading for Mexico; the last direction they'd be taking would be north. They weren't about to show their faces in Pueblo.

―――

Sheriff Carney found Lyle's body in the early afternoon and was sickened when he spotted the three bullet holes. He felt responsible for the young man's death but still hoisted the body onto his horse's saddle and tied it down. He noticed the absence of Lyle's Winchester; not that it mattered.

When he led the body-draped white horse into Walsenburg, he took the back street and stopped at the mortician. He let Jim Nilsson take care of Kyle while he went to the telegraph to send his follow-up message. He hadn't tracked the four outlaws because, as he had told Kyle before he rode off, his first duty was to protect the citizens.

―――

By the time the outlaws approached Placita, John realized that they were still too close to Walsenburg, and even without any law in the town, it wouldn't be long before word leaked to the small burg and they'd be exposed.

As the outline of Placita appeared on the horizon, John shouted, "Hold up for a minute!"

Rusty pulled up and asked, "Now what?"

"I think just one of us should head into town and buy some supplies. We need to get further away from Walsenburg. We wouldn't be here for two days before they figured out that we're the ones who killed that deputy."

"Now you think about it," Rusty snapped.

"Better now than later," John replied before turning back to Mike and saying, "You don't stick out as much as the rest of us, Mike. Head into town, buy a few days' worth of food, then we'll follow the Apishapa Creek to the railroad station where we can catch the train north."

"How long before we get there?"

"By sundown tomorrow."

"Alright," Rusty said before Mike nodded and rode off to Placita.

As they watched Mike trot away, Rusty asked, "Are we still heading for Castle Rock?"

"That's the plan, but we won't get off there. We'll get off at Huntsville, about ten miles south of there. It's a small town, just a little bigger than Placita. We'll ride around Castle Rock and then head for Denver. Once we get there, we can just blend in. There are too many people in the city for anyone to pay attention to four strangers."

"All of a sudden, you're not worried about gettin' spotted now?" Rusty asked.

"Let me worry about it."

"Maybe we should split up before we get there."

"Maybe we should," John replied.

Rusty just nodded as he shifted in his saddle and watched the road.

———

Kyle rode alongside John's full carriage as they returned to Denver. In a way, he was relieved that Lynn had finally learned the truth and had a measure of understanding of why he'd gone with Ryan. When he'd left Wilkes-Barre more than six years earlier, he had been almost driven to discover the truth of his own real father. The enormous difference was that he had been told by his mother that his father had been a good man while Lynn's real father had been a monster.

He had more trouble understanding Ryan's role in Lynn's discovery and departure. He didn't spend as much time with Ryan as either Bryn or Dylan did because Ryan lived with them on the Double EE while he lived in Denver. Katie hadn't been at all surprised by the news, so he'd talk to her more when they were alone.

He was still deep in thought when he spotted a rider heading their way and soon recognized Dylan's most recent hire, Deputy Marshal Pete Towers.

He rode ahead of the carriage, then he pulled up and waited for Pete.

When the deputy marshal reached Kyle, he stopped and said, "We just got two telegrams from Walsenburg. The sheriff down there said that the four men who held up that stage near Pueblo ambushed and killed one of his deputies."

"Did he say which way they were headed?"

"Nope. I figure we'll find out soon enough. I'm on my way to tell the boss and Bryn. I figure they wouldn't want to wait until tomorrow to get the news."

"You're right. Thanks, Pete," Kyle said before the deputy tossed him a salute and rode south, soon passing the carriage with a wave.

Kyle waited for John to pull the carriage to a stop and told the curious passengers what Pete had just passed along. As the incident was so far away, none of them were particularly concerned; at least for the time being. Knowing that one of the men had a grudge against Bryn and maybe Kyle, did add significance to the news.

———

After Pete had relayed the information to Dylan and Bryn, he left the ranch to return to Denver.

Bryn was still in Dylan's house with their combined families; the older boys and girls sat in chairs while the young ones were scattered across the floor listening with the big fire warming the room behind them.

Gwen asked, "Are you going to have to do anything about this, Dylan?"

"Not yet. It they're smart, they should have hightailed it to Mexico. I need to get more information about which way they're headed before we even think about it. But it's already in our wheelhouse because they've committed murders in two counties."

"Do you think they'd come to Denver?" Erin asked.

"I'd be surprised if they did. We all know what John Coleridge looks like and he's traveling with a tall blonde-headed man named Ollie Thorsen. Between the two, they'd be easy to spot."

"You'll still be careful; won't you, Bryn?" asked Erin.

Bryn smiled at his wife and replied, "I'm always careful, sweetheart."

Dylan may not have been concerned about the arrival of the killers in Denver, but he was definitely anxious to know where they were and how close Lynn was to that location.

————

It was late in the afternoon when Ryan and Lynn stopped in the town of Monument for the night; about halfway to Colorado Springs.

After dropping off their horses, getting a room in the small hotel and having their supper, Ryan tried to convince Lynn to join him at the saloon so he could have his first beer, but Lynn declined, saying he needed to rest after the long ride.

Ryan was far from tired as he trotted to the Halfway Saloon; happy that Lynn had freed him for the night.

————

As Lynn stretched out on the thin, hard bed, he smiled as he pictured his brothers, Bethan and his cousins playing baseball while he and Ryan had been riding south. Most of the time, the adults played as well, including his mother. The first time he'd seen her swing the bat, he almost laughed, but when she then got a clean single, he had been impressed as he watched her run to the base.

He knew how fortunate he was to have such an incredible family and wished that he didn't discover any failings within himself to cause them grief. He knew that the true nature of his character would only be revealed when he had to shoot a man. If he discovered that he enjoyed it, then he knew that he'd never be able to return to the Double EE. That possibility bothered him even more than the revelation itself.

―――

By the time Ryan staggered into the room and flopped face first onto his bed on the other side of the small space, Lynn was already in deep sleep and didn't even notice his arrival.

CHAPTER 3

The next morning, Lynn had to hold his breath when he tried to wake Ryan. It took a good minute of shaking to stir him from his alcohol-induced slumber, and when Ryan finally opened his eyes, he let Lynn know that he didn't want to leave the mattress.

"We've got to leave soon, Ryan. We don't want to have to pay for another night's stay just so you can recover."

"Alright…alright. No need to be so much of a nag," Ryan said as he swung his legs out of the bed, put his elbows on his knees and then rested his face on his palms.

"What time is it?" he asked; his voice muffled by his hands.

"Almost mid-morning. I had breakfast already and the horses are saddled out front. We need to get moving, Ryan."

"Alright. Where's the privy?"

"Out back where they always are," Lynn said before he lifted Ryan from the bed and with his eyes watering, led him out of the room.

———

Ryan had no desire to put any food into his stomach, so in just twenty minutes, they were riding out of Monument heading south at a slow trot.

"Can't you make the sun less shiny?" he asked loudly as he kept his eyes down.

Lynn didn't answer as he looked at Ryan and hoped that his behavior wouldn't recur every time they stopped in a town. It probably didn't matter in Ryan's mission, but Lynn didn't want to get used to the mornings after.

Ryan's hangover began abating after the first hour in the saddle and the frequent swallows of water from his canteen, so by the time they reached Colorado Springs, they were able to stop for a decent lunch before continuing their ride.

It was when they were about two hours south of Colorado Springs that the almost boring ride suddenly and dramatically changed.

Lynn spotted the riders heading their way while Ryan was beginning to feel the aftereffects of his impressive hangover coupled with his full stomach and was almost napping.

He wasn't concerned about the four men because they were wearing chaps and had coils of ropes on their saddles. They were obviously ranch hands heading into Colorado Springs; probably to have a few beers after a hot day out with their herd. He still kept an eye on them, just because he'd learned from his father never to assume that unknown riders weren't a threat until he could read their eyes.

The four ranch hands were about two hundred yards away when Ryan finally blinked his eyes and exclaimed, "There they are!"

Lynn whipped his eyes to his left and loudly asked, "What are you talking about, Ryan?"

Ryan pulled his Winchester as he answered, "It's those killers!"

Lynn shouted, "Put that thing away, Ryan! They're just ranch hands heading into Colorado Springs. Can't you see their chaps? Besides, none of them have blonde hair."

Ryan cocked his Winchester as he replied, "They're just trying to disguise themselves. I'm not going to be caught with my pants down."

"Put the gun away, Ryan! You're wrong!"

———

The four hands from the Rocking M all noticed Ryan pull his repeater, and the oldest of them, Steve Procter, asked, "What's his problem?"

Bill Livingston, who rode beside him, replied, "I don't know, Steve, but I'm not going to let him get within rifle range to find out."

"Alright, let's head east about a hundred yards to give them the road."

"Okay, Steve," Bill replied before steering his gelding to the right as the others matched his turn.

———

"Look! They're running!" Ryan said excitedly.

"Put the gun away and let them go, Ryan. They're not the outlaws."

Lynn knew he was losing the argument even as he watched the four riders continue heading away from the road, but there was nothing he could do about it short of shooting Ryan.

They were almost due west of the ranch hands who were just sitting on their horses watching them when Lynn noticed Ryan start to change his horse's direction.

He shouted, "Ryan, just keep riding! Those men aren't who you think they are!"

He was hoping that the four men would hear his warning and understand that Ryan was just making a mistake.

Ryan turned, glared at Lynn and snapped, "Shut up! They can hear you!"

"I hope they're listening, because you sure aren't! Let them go, Ryan!"

"You're just yellow! Are you going to help me or not?"

Lynn simply couldn't understand why Ryan wouldn't listen to the obvious. *None of the four men even had his rifle out of his scabbard, so why did he still believe that they were the outlaws?*

Lynn was about to shout to the ranch hands that they weren't lawmen or outlaws and that Ryan just was confused, when Ryan made the warning irrelevant.

He whipped Boot to the left, set him at a medium trot and after bringing his Winchester level, shouted, "I know who you are! Drop your guns or I'll fire!"

LYNN'S SEARCH

Steve had no idea why he'd warned them to drop guns that they weren't holding, but shouted back, "I don't know who you think we are, mister, but you'd better just ride on!"

Ryan was within eighty yards, but none of them, including Lynn really expected him to pull the trigger. Even if they were the outlaws, there still wasn't a single muzzle pointed at Ryan.

But when Ryan kept riding at them, Bill Livingston shouted, "I'm not just sitting here while that crazy son of a bitch tries to shoot us!" then reached for his Winchester's stock.

Ryan saw his move and it confirmed his suspicions that they were truly the disguised outlaws and fired.

Lynn was stunned as he sat on Griffin in the road and watched with wide eyes as the other three ranch hands began to pull their own repeaters when Ryan fired his second shot.

Ryan was just forty yards out and preparing to fire again when Bill was the first to return fire as he sat in the saddle.

None of the bullets found their mark after Ryan fired his third shot, but then when the other three ranch hands added their combined fire, Ryan felt a .44 drill into his left upper chest and dropped his rifle before a second one punched into his upper gut on the right side, exploding his liver.

He tottered, then slowly dropped off to the right and tumbled awkwardly onto the dry ground.

Lynn finally emerged from his shock and turned Griffin to the east and started him at a fast trot, ignoring any possible gunfire as he raced to help Ryan.

None of the ranch hands even paid any attention to Lynn as he wasn't armed, but Steve Procter started his gelding forward at a walk as he slid his repeater home. The others followed behind as Lynn dropped down from Griffin and stepped rapidly to where Ryan lay sprawled on the ground.

He took a knee and rolled Ryan's body flat on the dirt and knew there was no point in trying to stop the blood as it was no longer being pumping through his body.

"What the hell was wrong with you, Ryan?" he shouted as he closed Ryan's eyelids.

Steve Proctor stepped down and approached Lynn.

"Why did he come at us like that, son?" he asked as he stood nearby.

Lynn looked up at him and replied, "I don't know what made him do it, mister. I kept telling him that you weren't the outlaws that he wanted to find."

"Was he your brother?"

"No. He was my uncle; my aunt's brother."

"You want some help bringing him into town?"

"I'd appreciate it. I'm sorry that you had to do what you did, and I'll tell the sheriff that it was all his fault and you just reacted in self-defense after he started shooting."

"I'm sorry we had to do it too, son, but he put us in a bad spot."

Lynn nodded, then stood as the other three ranch hands stepped closer.

———

LYNN'S SEARCH

Twenty minutes later, Lynn was leading Boot with Ryan's body laid across his saddle as they headed to Colorado Springs. He knew that he couldn't ride all the way to the Double EE with the body, so he'd leave the body with the mortician and send a telegram to Bryn and Kyle to ask them what he should do. Each of them was married to one of Ryan's sisters, so it was up to them where he should be buried.

None of the ranch hands talked to him much on the ride, and he appreciated the courtesy.

He had spent the time reviewing the incident that had resulted in Ryan's death and tried to think of anything he could have done differently to prevent the tragedy. He knew that he wasn't responsible but hoped that none of the family blamed him for what had happened.

Even though he knew he'd be returning to the Double EE soon, he was convinced that he couldn't stay. He'd go alone now, but he had to go because he still hadn't found his answer.

———

It was almost sunset when they reached Colorado Springs and stopped at the sheriff's office where they stepped down and walked inside.

The deputy at the desk looked up and asked, "What can I do for you, boys?"

Lynn replied, "I have my uncle's body outside on his horse. He was convinced that these men were the four outlaws that robbed the stage outside of Pueblo and killed the driver. I tried to convince him that he was wrong, but he insisted that they were and after they pulled off the roadway because he had pulled his Winchester, he attacked them.

"They didn't even have their pistols out of their holsters or their rifles free as he charged. It wasn't until he opened fire that they finally had to return fire. They did nothing wrong. It was all his fault; his and mine for not trying hard enough to stop him."

The deputy rose from the chair and passed by Lynn and the cowhands as he walked out the door. They followed and watched as the deputy sheriff examined Ryan's body, then looked at Lynn.

"What's his name?"

"Ryan Mitchell. He's my uncle."

"What's yours?"

"Lynn Evans."

"You any relation to U.S. Marshal Dylan Evans?"

"Yes, sir. He's my father."

"Why don't you take his body to the undertaker? Steve can show you where he is. Then come back and you all can write your statements. I'll have the sheriff come to the office to hear the story and review your statements, but I don't see any problem."

Steve Procter untied Boot and handed the reins to Lynn as he said, "We'll walk. It's just a couple of blocks."

"Okay."

LYNN'S SEARCH

Lynn walked with Steve down the main street of Colorado Springs and turned west at the next intersection. They slowly walked along the dirt road, almost like a funeral procession, and soon stopped at the undertaker.

Once inside, Lynn asked that Ryan's body be prepared for burial, placed in a coffin and held until he received word from his brother about what Erin and Katie wanted done with their brother's remains.

He paid for the mortician's services, then he and Steve left the mortuary and began walking back.

"I need to send a telegram on the way back."

"The Western Union office is in the other direction, but just another block."

Lynn nodded, still numb from the entire, unfathomable episode as he tried to understand what had driven Ryan to his own death. It was almost as if he was trying to commit suicide without knowing it.

They stopped at the telegraph office and Lynn sent his long telegram to Kyle because he would be the only one in Denver and would be able to reply quickly after talking to Katie.

He paid his eighty cents for the message, then said to the operator, "I'll be at the sheriff's office for another hour or so and then the Fairmont Hotel after that."

"Alright, son. I'll have a boy with the reply as soon as it comes in."

"Thank you, sir," Lynn said before he turned with Steve and headed back to the sheriff's office.

―――――

Forty minutes after Lynn left the Colorado Springs telegraph office, a messenger arrived at the home of Kyle and Katie Evans and knocked loudly on the heavy front door.

The family was having dinner with John and Meredith, and Kyle waved Katie back down as she began to stand.

"I'll get it, Mrs. Evans. You're too slow anyway."

Katie laughed and replied, "And whose fault is that, Mister Evans?"

Kyle grinned at his wife as he left the dining room and walked down the long hall to the parlor.

He opened the door and said, "Good evening, Ronnie. Got a message for me?"

"Yes, sir," he answered as he held out the yellow sheet.

Kyle handed him a nickel and accepted the telegram while Ronnie waited because Mister Williams had told him to wait for a reply.

Kyle opened the message and read:

KYLE EVANS 232 SIXTH ST DENVER COLO

TWO HOURS SOUTH OF COLORADO SPRINGS
RYAN MISTOOK FOUR RANCH HANDS
FOR OUTLAWS
DESPITE MY WARNINGS HE ATTACKED
HE FIRED TWICE BEFORE THEY REACTED
HE WAS SHOT TWICE AND KILLED
LET ME KNOW WHAT TO DO WITH BODY

LYNN EVANS COLORADO SPRINGS COLO

Kyle stared at the message, then looked at the boy and said, "I'll be right back with a reply, Ronnie."

He left the door opened and quickly returned to the dining room.

As soon as he entered, he looked at Katie and said, "It's from Lynn. He said that Ryan launched an attack on four cowhands believing them to be John Coleridge's bunch. He fired twice before they returned fire, but he's dead. Lynn wants to know what to do with his body."

Katie stared at Kyle for a few seconds before she sighed and replied, "I think he should have it brought here. By the time Lynn arrives, we can talk to Erin and decide where he should be buried."

"Alright. I'll let Lynn know."

Katie nodded as Kyle turned and headed back to write the reply.

After he'd gone, Meredith said, "I can't imagine why he would have done something like that."

"We'll just have to wait for Lynn to return before we get the full story," Katie replied.

———

The meeting with the sheriff didn't take long after he listened to the story and read their statements. By the time he received Kyle's short reply, he was in his room at the Fairmont Hotel. He read the message asking him to escort Ryan's body to Denver, then wrote a quick reply that he'd be returning on tomorrow afternoon's train.

He hadn't eaten any dinner and wasn't in the mood to leave the room as he lay on the bed and still wondered if trying to stop Ryan by just shouting at him had been enough. Maybe if he's pulled his pistol and fired a few times into the air, this tragedy could have been avoided. He spent the rest of the evening and much of the night trying to come up with other methods he might have used to stop Ryan from mounting that delusional assault. Maybe he shouldn't have even pulled him out of bed in the first place.

The only other thoughts that crossed his mind before falling asleep revolved around the question of his family's reaction to the news. He knew that his father and uncles would understand; *but what about his aunts that were also Ryan's sisters?*

He began to dread getting off that train tomorrow and seeing his two aunts, but he had to face them. He owed Ryan that, if nothing else.

———

Immediately after sending his reply, Kyle rode out to the Double EE and stopped first at Bryn and Erin's house to tell them about Lynn's telegram.

Erin seemed less surprised than Katie had been and had agreed that bringing Ryan's body back to Denver was the right decision.

They'd walked to Dylan's house and, with Alwen, Garth and Bethan present, explained what had happened. They assumed that Lynn would be returning on tomorrow's train, so they made quick arrangements to be at the station to greet him.

"Where do you want to bury Ryan?" Kyle asked Erin.

"What did Katie say?"

"She didn't think that sending him back to Omaha for burial would be welcomed by your parents, so she thinks he should be buried in Denver in the city cemetery."

Erin nodded and said, "That sounds right to me, too. Can you make arrangements tomorrow morning, Kyle?"

"I'll do that, Erin."

Garth asked, "Do you think Lynn is okay?"

"We'll find out tomorrow afternoon, Son," Dylan replied.

"Is he going to stay here now?" Al asked.

"I hope so," Gwen replied.

Kyle then rose and said, "I've got to get back and see Katie."

"How is she doing?" Erin asked.

Kyle smiled at his sister-in-law before he replied, "It's going to be a long eight weeks, Erin."

"Maybe she'll be the first in the family to have triplets."

"She'd never try to outdo her older sister, Erin. I hope she doesn't even try to keep up with you."

"I thought twins would be twice the burden of just one baby, but that wasn't true at all. Tell her to go for three and I won't mind."

"If you don't mind, I'm not going to bring up the subject," Kyle said before he stood, gave the family a short wave then left the house.

———

Outside of Apishapa Station, the four men that Ryan believed that he was facing were sitting around their campfire.

"When does that train leave?" asked Rusty.

John answered, "It's supposed to get here at 9:40 and leave fifteen minutes later. We'll be in Littleton by 3:30 tomorrow afternoon."

"And we're finally gonna sleep in a bed?" Ollie asked.

"Yeah, Ollie, we'll stay there one night so you can sleep all comfy in a featherbed."

Ollie snorted, then took a big scoop of beans and bacon.

"I just need a beer," Mike Greenburg said to no one in particular.

"Don't we all," Rusty replied, "and a lot more when we get to Denver."

"We got all this money and ain't even been able to spend much," Ollie complained.

John glanced at him and said, "Quit whining, Ollie. You can whore your way across Denver on Wednesday night and disappoint all of them."

The other two laughed as Ollie said, "I don't care if they are anyway. As long as I'm not," before he joined in their laughter.

————

The next morning, Lynn made up for his skipped meal by having a big breakfast at the hotel restaurant before returning to the sheriff's office to get his permission to leave Colorado Springs with Ryan's body.

He'd barely entered the office, leaving the chill of the late summer morning outside, when the deputy at the desk looked up and motioned him over.

Lynn took a seat and the deputy said, "The sheriff already talked to the prosecutor and he called it justifiable homicide, so you can leave whenever you want. I'm guessing that you'll be taking the train?"

"Yes, sir."

"It doesn't leave until just after noon, so you have plenty of time to arrange for the transport."

"I appreciate it, and I'm really sorry for having caused such a headache for everyone. I should have figured out how to stop Ryan from doing something that stupid."

"Your father is a famous lawman and he'll be the first one to tell you that once a man has something rock solid in his mind, you can't change it with ten sticks of dynamite. You would have had to shoot him yourself to keep him from making that run. You didn't do anything wrong, son."

Lynn nodded, then said, "That's what I keep telling myself, but it's hard to make it stick. I'd better get over to the undertaker and arrange for the coffin to be put on the train."

The deputy rose, shook Lynn's hand, then said, "Good luck, Lynn."

"Thanks," he replied before standing and leaving the jail.

The stop at the undertaker didn't take long as it seemed to be a common request, so after paying for the shipment, he headed back to the hotel's livery where he saddled Griffin and Boot, then mounted, rode out of the barn and headed for the train station where he paid for his ticket and the two horses before taking a seat on one of the three benches.

It was only 10:15 by the station's big clock, but he didn't mind waiting. He had left most of his things on Griffin as it would only be a three-hour ride to Denver. If someone wanted to steal his pillowcase travel bags, he really didn't care.

———

John Coleridge and the others were seated in the back four seats of the last of the three passenger cars on the train so they could watch anyone who entered the car.

No one had so much as given them a second glance when they arrived at Apishapa Station that morning to buy their tickets. Since boarding the train, the only other passengers to use the third car didn't seem to notice them either.

They'd kept their conversations to a minimum, to make it appear as if they weren't together, so as the train approached Colorado Springs, they were getting unusually confident about their anonymity for four men who had recently murdered a lawman.

———

As Lynn heard the whistle of the approaching train and pried his eyes away from the coffin that awaited loading onto the freight car along with other cargo.

When the undertaker's men had unloaded it from their hearse, Lynn had seen it as just that and nothing more. It was just a long pine box with a label hammered on the top lid. It could have contained sledgehammers or scythes for all anyone knew. There had been no ceremony but there had been a scrawled black cross on the top lid to identify its contents to the railroad workers.

As the locomotive's cowcatcher passed by the platform at walking speed, Lynn stood and headed for the rails.

When the train finally came to a stop, he hopped onto the middle passenger car's platform, then entered the almost empty car and plopped on one of the middle seats on the side of the car near the platform so he could watch the coffin being carried to one of the freight cars behind the passenger cars, but couldn't see them load it.

He just sat and stared at the platform as the train took on coal and water. He was familiar enough with the operation of trains that he could read the posted schedule and see where the locomotive would demand just water or water and coal; depending how long it remained at each station.

The engineer yanked the whistle three times to tell the conductor he was ready to roll and just two minutes later, he felt the lurch of the car as the couples stretched.

In just four hours, he'd meet his parents and have to explain what had happened. He hadn't expected to return so soon after leaving and wasn't sure he had provided a satisfactory answer to why he'd accompanied Ryan in the first place. He still hadn't found the answer to his troubling question and knew that he'd still have to look elsewhere. This time, though, he'd talk to his father and try to clarify why he needed to go and maybe even get an idea where it should be. He was already thinking that he might have to go where he began – Fort Benton.

————

After leaving Colorado Springs, the train continued its journey north, stopping in those small towns that either had passengers waiting to board or any that needed to disembark. It took on water at one stop and only added more coal at its stop in Castle Rock.

Lynn thought about leaving the train for a quick lunch at Castle Rock, but it was only another ninety minutes to Denver, so he stayed put as he watched some of the passengers leave the train to get something to eat or use the rest facilities.

He wasn't really paying that much attention as four men hustled across the platform and two lined up to use the privies, while the other two quickly trotted to the railroad's nearby restaurant.

Initially, he believed that his mind was just making an unrealistic connection to the four outlaws because of yesterday's confused confrontation, but when one of the two waiting to use the privy removed his hat to wipe his forehead, the man's blonde head practically glowed like a yellow halo from the bright sunshine.

That jerked Lynn's mind back into full consciousness as he stared at the two men, just before one entered a privy.

Each of them wore a pistol, which wasn't unusual in itself, but as he examined the man still waiting, Lynn saw the cruelty on the man's face that marked him as one who didn't accept society's rules. It was one of the many skills he'd learned from his father, who had told him that reading men was much more important than tracking or even marksmanship, but he hadn't believed it until now.

He moved further away from the window and continued to watch after the second privy door opened and a man exited, letting the suspected outlaw finally rush inside.

After the first man into the privy left and waited for his partner to finish, Lynn studied him more closely. He may be a blonde-headed, blue-eyed handsome man, but his eyes spoke much more eloquently of his true nature. He was furtively scanning the platform and the town as he impatiently waited.

As soon as the other man exited the privy, they both quickly left the platform to join their cohorts in the restaurant.

Fifteen minutes later, the engineer blasted his whistle, and soon, the four men shot across the platform and disappeared out of view as they headed for the only passenger car behind Lynn's.

As the train slowly began to accelerate, Lynn began to think of how he could let his father know that they were there. Even if there had been enough time to send a telegram, it was unlikely that it would arrive in time to warn his father and uncles of the gang's presence.

All he could do was to be the first one off the train and hope that he found his father and uncles before the four men saw them. He had his new Smith & Wesson Model 3 that his father had given him for his sixteenth birthday, and he was accurate with the weapon. Maybe this would be his chance to answer his lingering question after all and he wouldn't have to leave the Double EE again.

For another hour, the train rolled north, but didn't have to stop at any of the small towns, which wasn't a surprise.

Lynn was still working on a plan to stop the four men when the train's whistle startled him into looking out the window as the train began to slow.

He soon spotted a sign that read LITTLETON, and he assumed that someone was boarding the train in the town.

As the train banged to a stop, he saw an empty platform; then as he watched, the four men strode across the platform, then turned to the stock corral where they waited at the gate.

He hoped that the train would stay at the station to take on some water as he kept his focus on the four men; now convinced that they were John Coleridge's gang.

The whistle blew again just as the men mounted and Lynn had to strain to look back as he watched them leave the station riding north.

Once he'd seen them ride away, he plopped back onto his bench seat and knew that he'd just been presented with a gift. They were still heading to Denver, obviously not wanting to be seen at the big train station, but he'd arrive a good thirty minutes before they did. That should give his father and Dylan enough time to prepare for their arrival.

The road they were using was the same one that he and Ryan had used when they snuck out of the Double EE on Saturday night. Now, just four days later, he'd be returning with Ryan's body and a warning.

———

At the station, most of the Evans clan were waiting for Lynn; the only exceptions were the smaller Evans children.

Kyle had arranged to have Ryan's body brought to the big Longley Brothers Mortuary, so the hearse was waiting near the other side of the platform.

Alwen, Garth and Bethan were all at the platform's edge, dangerously close to the tracks as they peered south along the rails.

"Can you see the train yet?" Bethan asked as she looked around Garth.

Garth didn't turn to look at his sister as he replied, "Just the smoke. I figure we'll see the locomotive pretty soon."

"I hope that Lynn doesn't run away again," Al said.

"I don't know why he did anyway. Ryan must have really made him mad," Garth added.

Bethan countered, saying, "I don't think he was mad. Mom let us read his note and he sounded more confused and sadder than anything else. I hope that watching Ryan get shot down in front of him didn't make him worse."

"That's going to be some story," Garth said before he exclaimed, "There's the train!"

———

Lynn watched Denver's outskirts pass by his window as the train slowed, then took a deep breath and pulled on his hat. When his father had given him his new pistol for his sixteenth birthday, his mother had given him a genuine Stetson hat. It was a beautiful dark gray creation with a black band around

87

the base of the crown. There were many imitators already producing cheaper copies of the popular hat, but his mother had ensured that his was the real thing and he could tell by its quality.

The station soon reached the window, so he quickly stood and walked to the front of the car to be the first one off the train. There was no time to waste in giving his father the critical information about John Coleridge and his fellow murderers.

As soon as the stations wooden platform slowly passed the passenger car's steel steps, Lynn bounced onto the flat surface and almost plowed into his brothers and sister.

"Lynn, we missed you!" Bethan said as she bearhugged her oldest brother.

Lynn kissed Bethan then looked past Garth and saw his parents heading toward him.

"I have to talk to dad right away," Lynn said as he released Bethan and stepped past her.

Before Dylan or Gwen could say a word, Lynn quickly said, "Dad, don't say anything. Please. Just listen. It's important."

Dylan stopped four feet in front of him and just waited for Lynn to continue.

"Before I talk about Ryan or anything else, I have to let you know that I'm sure that John Coleridge and the other three were on this train but left at Littleton less than an hour ago and rode north."

Dylan was startled, but turned to Bryn who was just six feet to his right and said, "Did you catch that, Bryn?"

Bryn nodded and replied, "I did. How do you want to handle it, boss?"

Dylan then looked back to Lynn and asked, "Did you get a good look?"

"A very good look for quite a while in Castle Rock when they left the train. The one I watched the longest was the blonde one. He took of his hat while he waited to use the privy and there wasn't a doubt in my mind that he was one of them. I was pretty sure before that, but once he took off his hat, it was the final convincer."

"What about their horses?"

Lynn hadn't heard the descriptions before, but as he told his father and uncle what he'd seen, Dylan nodded.

"They're our boys, Bryn. Head over to the sheriff's office and let Quentin know, then swing by ours and have Thom join us. We'll concentrate on our road and set up on the Double EE. Sheriff Wheeler and his boys can cover the other southern access road."

"Okay, boss. I'm out of here," Bryn said before he turned and jogged across the platform.

Once Bryn left, Dylan said, "Lynn, your Uncle Kyle has already arranged for Ryan's body to be taken to the mortuary, so after you collect Griffin and Boot, head over to his house where you can explain to everyone what happened. Okay?"

"Yes, sir," Lynn replied, knowing his father needed to go.

Dylan smiled at Lynn as he placed his hand on his son's shoulder and said, "I've got to get moving, but I'll talk to you when we're done."

Lynn nodded as his father turned to his mother, gave her a quick kiss, but didn't say another word before trotting away.

Gwen watched him leave, knowing that he needed every minute, then looked back at her son and said, "We'll wait for you at Kyle's house, Lynn. I'm just so happy to see you again."

After she stood on her tiptoes and kissed him on his forehead, Gwen turned and began gathering everyone to return to the carriage.

Erin and Katie each smiled at Lynn before following Gwen, just as an early way of telling him that they weren't upset with him for what had happened to their brother.

Lynn watched the mass of Evans depart, then turned and headed for the stock corral.

As he did, he saw the pine crate being loaded onto the polished black hearse and wondered if they would move Ryan's body to a real coffin or bury him in the box. He didn't think it mattered to Ryan anymore.

————

After leaving Littleton, the four outlaws stopped in the town of Petersburg to talk about their approach into Denver.

"Do you want to break up now, or wait until we reach Denver?" Rusty asked.

"I've been thinking about that," John replied, "the road forks off about three miles south of town and I think that's where we split up. The one that veers east enters right in the middle of Denver and the other one comes in from the west side of town."

"Where's the ranch of your old pal, Bryn Evans?"

"It's right before the road splits, but I don't want to do anything until we're settled in."

"I got news for you, old pal, once we're settled in, anything you want to do with him, or any other lawman is your problem. I intend to spend some of my wealth as God intended."

John didn't bother replying as he finished his beer.

———

Getting the sheriff's men and his own coordinated didn't take as long as he'd expected, so Dylan, Bryn, Thom Smythe and two of the sheriff's deputies headed for the Double EE just twenty minute after Lynn had stepped off the train and rode at a fast clip for the ranch while the sheriff and two more of his deputy sheriffs and one of Dylan's deputy marshals rode for the other south road. Both groups would set up defensive positions outside of Denver, so there was no way the four killers could enter the city.

As they rode toward the Double EE, Dylan hoped that they'd have enough time to prepare before the four killers appeared on the horizon. They could have already taken the other road, but he hadn't seen anyone riding south as he looked east, so that wasn't likely. Not for an instant did he doubt that Lynn had made a mistake in identifying the killers.

When they reached the Double EE and the road ahead was still clear, Dylan pulled up and waited for Bryn and the others to reach him.

"How do you want to handle this, Dylan?" Bryn asked.

91

"They're a bit late, but I'm sure that they're still coming, so we'll take advantage of that delay. I'll ride south with Thom and set up on the other side of my barn while you and the two others stay behind the north side of your barn. When I see them pass, we'll ride out as quietly as possible with our Winchesters ready. Once they spot us, I'll fire a shot and order them to stop.

"My best guess is that they'll head for the nearest protection, which is your barn. When you get there, before you set up, warn Alba and Jack, then have them move all the children upstairs. Jack can watch from the window as a last line of defense should any of them make it that far, and I don't believe they will."

Bryn nodded, then said, "Let's get this show on the road," before turning Maddy down the access road with Denver County Deputy Sheriffs Hal Baker and Ken Tanner following.

Dylan then angled toward his barn with Thom riding alongside and watched as the two deputy sheriffs disappeared behind the barn and Bryn continued to the house.

Once he and Thom had dismounted, he held Crow's reins in his left hand and peeked down the road, still finding it devoid of traffic or even dust clouds.

When he stepped back, Thom asked, "Do you figure that Lynn coulda been wrong about those boys?"

"Not a chance. They must have stopped in Petersburg for some reason. Other than that, they should have been here by now."

Thom took his own peek then stepped back, grinned at Dylan and said, "It's just like the old days back in Omaha, Dylan. I kinda miss the wild times."

"Don't wish too hard, Thom. Wild times may be arriving in a few minutes."

Thom snickered as Dylan took his turn at the back corner of the barn and finally spotted a small dust cloud on the horizon.

"Here they come, Thom," he said quietly.

"Are we gonna ride straight out to the road, or try and get closer faster?"

"Let's walk the horses diagonally until we're spotted, then make a bull rush to the road. We'll just have to see how close we can get before they see us."

"You're the boss, Dylan."

Dylan nodded before he turned back to Bryn's house about six hundred yards away and couldn't see Bryn or the two deputy sheriffs behind the barn. The ranch looked empty and he hoped it stayed that way.

The road was almost four hundred yards from the back of the barn, and he hoped they'd be able to cut that distance in half before all hell broke loose.

—————

"Is that Evans' place?" Rusty asked as he pointed to the first set of buildings.

John replied, "We've been passing it for the last forty minutes. I think that first bunch of buildings is where his older brother, the marshal, lives. My pal, Bryn, lives in those other houses further north."

Rusty chuckled and said, "It's all nice and quiet. Maybe we oughta pay the family a visit before they get home."

John snapped, "I told you, Rusty, we need to get into Denver without any fuss!"

"I was just gettin' you riled, Johnny. I'm not in the mood for a gunfight yet anyway. Killing one lawman a week is my limit."

John turned away to keep from putting Rusty in his place. He'd be rid of the man soon and maybe he and Ollie would just split away. He didn't really care for Mike that much either. He was too chummy with Rusty.

———

Dylan and Thom had mounted when Dylan had seen them approaching and estimated that they'd pass the access road in another minute or so.

He pulled his Winchester, cocked the hammer, then turned to Thom and said, "Ready?"

"Ready, boss."

Dylan walked Crow around the southwest corner of the big barn and was gratified that he didn't see the riders, so he turned the big gelding along the southern wall and nudged him to a fast walk as Thom followed in line.

As he passed the far corner of the barn, he spotted the backs of the four men as they continued to ride north approaching the access road.

He then tapped Crow's flanks and the horse accelerated to a medium trot as Dylan angled toward the end of the access road while keeping an eye on the outlaws.

He was immensely proud of Lynn for providing not only the warning, but an accurate description. Even if there had been a tiny doubt in his mind of Lynn's claim, it evaporated the moment he laid eyes on the men.

He was almost two hundred yards away from the men when they neared the access road, yet he and Thom still hadn't been spotted, so he changed his angle slightly to the east to get behind them.

It was shortly after he and Thom made the adjustment when Mike Greenburg, who was riding behind Rusty on the left side, caught movement out of his peripheral vision and turned his head to see what it was.

The instant that Dylan saw Mike's eyes, he brought his Winchester level and shouted, "U.S. Marshal Dylan Evans! Stay where you are, or I will open fire!"

The other three outlaws whipped their heads around and saw Dylan and Thom about a hundred and fifty yards out with their repeaters ready to fire.

There was no question of stopping to chat. Each of them was well aware of the consequences of being caught alive and none wanted to hang. They also believed that they had the advantage in numbers and the marshal was out of range.

As they began pulling their rifles, Dylan and Thom continued to close the gap and as the outlaws began to turn their Winchesters toward the lawmen, Dylan took his first shot.

His .44 missed all of them, but it still had served two purposes; it triggered Bryn and the two deputy sheriffs to enter the gunfight and it caused all four of them to rush their first shots.

As Dylan levered in a fresh cartridge, Thom fired his first shot and caught Ollie Thorsen in the left thigh. The bullet slammed into the muscle and cracked into his thick femur before stopping. Ollie screamed in pain and reached for his leg, but still held onto his rifle.

The other three were focused on Dylan and Thom as they tried to keep their sights still as their horses jostled on the roadway.

Bryn and the deputies quickly closed the gap and as the deputy sheriffs rode directly toward the road to cut off any possibility of escape by the killers, Maddy carried Bryn quickly down the access road to keep them from invading his home.

Dylan was close enough now to bring Crow to a sudden stop in order to have a stable shooting platform, and Thom did the same off to his right.

Neither of them paid any attention to the incoming fire as they selected their targets and fired almost simultaneously.

Thom's second shot sliced through the thin Colorado air and drilled into Ollie again, who had managed to bring his Winchester to bear. The second hit wasn't as benevolent as the first and punched into the left side of his chest, fractured two ribs, then mauled his left lung's upper lobe before slamming into Ollie's spine.

He didn't scream this time before he rocked twice as if he was on a hobby horse, then just flopped onto his bedroll with his feet still in his stirrups as his rifle dropped to the road.

Dylan had targeted Rusty Halloran for two reasons; he believed that Rusty was the worst of the four and he wanted to leave John Coleridge to Bryn, so he would be the one to administer his final justice.

LYNN'S SEARCH

After Dylan pulled his trigger, the Winchester popped back against his left shoulder and the aerodynamic cylinder of lead spun down his barrel before exploding into the air as flame and gunsmoke boiled out behind it.

It continued its stabilizing spin for another .34 seconds until it twisted into Rusty's gut, just above his belly button. Rusty felt as if someone had struck him with a sledgehammer and reached for his stomach, dropping his repeater as he reacted to the pain.

He didn't have time to register the sensation of the warm blood that erupted from the wound when then bullet exploded his abdominal aorta and his blood pressure disappeared in the flood of blood that filled his gut.

He just rolled off to the right and fell face first into the ground, never feeling the pain that it would have created if he'd been alive when he hit.

Bryn saw two men down and had identified John Coleridge, who had finally spotted him as he roared up the access road.

If it had been anyone else, John would have ignored him and concentrated on the two closer lawmen, but it was Bryn Evans; the man who had ruined his life and had him sent to prison and he wanted payback.

He turned his gelding toward the access road and kicked him into a canter as he brought his Winchester's sights onto the hated deputy marshal.

Bryn could see the hate in John's eyes, even at eighty yards, but also saw Coleridge's sights dancing as his horse charged closer. It was as if he wanted Bryn to shoot him.

Bryn pulled Maddy to a stop and let his sights drift until they centered on John Coleridge's chest. He watched John's muzzle flash but didn't know where the bullet's path had taken it.

Then, just as John was working the lever for a second shot, Bryn saw him pull the trigger, but nothing came out of the end of his repeater.

John's horse was still racing closer as Bryn watched the ex-deputy frantically yank on the lever, but it appeared stuck.

Bryn then kicked Maddy into a trot and just as John looked up from his jammed Winchester, he caught the incredibly brief sight of Bryn's Winchester's barrel before he saw nothing at all.

While John had made his charge at Bryn, Mike Greenburg had made his own charge and raced north to try to escape into Denver.

He still had his Winchester in his hand as he looked back at the two lawmen now about three hundred yards away while the other one was still on the access road. He thought he was safe until he turned his eyes to the front and spotted the two deputy sheriffs sitting astride their horses blocking the road with their rifles aimed at him.

Mike suddenly whipped his horse to the east and left the road, racing across the rough, rocky ground to make his break. He was looking back at the two deputies who had taken up the chase when his horse struck a large rock with his left front hoof and fell.

Mike didn't know if someone had shot his horse or him as he flew from his saddle freeing his Winchester to make its own trajectory to the earth.

He was bracing for the ground's arrival when his left side met a watermelon-sized jagged rock. He bounced off the small boulder after it had shattered six of his ribs and rammed the ends into his left lung.

The pain was extraordinary when he finally came to rest on the dirt just four feet from the killing rock and wailed as the two deputies reached him.

Hal Draper and Ken Tapper walked their horses close and over the loud screeching, and Hal asked, "Do you think there's anything we can do for him, Ken?"

"We could shoot him and put him out of his misery like we'll have to do for his horse."

Hal nodded, then said, "Let's go and do that first and then come back here after we figure out what to do with him."

Ken turned his horse and Hal followed as they approached Mike's downed animal. Ken was the one to put a .44 into the suffering horse's head before they headed back to Mike Greenburg.

Dylan had watched the two deputies handle the last outlaw then waited for Bryn to reach him to ask about Coleridge.

"Is he still alive, Bryn?" he asked when his brother neared.

"I'm a bit surprised he survived, but he's not dead. I don't think he'll be awake for a long time, though. I didn't even have to swing all that hard. Between Maddy and his horse, I'll bet they were closing at fifteen miles an hour. Are the other three dead?"

"The two on the road are, and I think the one who took the spill will join them shortly. Let's get them on their horses, so we can take them into town."

"Okay," Bryn said then turned at the sound of rapidly approaching hoofbeats.

Dylan looked at the approaching riders and said, "I think that this is Quentin's jurisdiction now, Bryn. I'm sure that he'll be happy as hell to have John back in his jail again."

Bryn watched as Sheriff Wheeler drew closer and replied, "I'm sure he will. He'll probably ask to have the privilege of putting the noose around his neck, too."

————

Even before the first bullet streaked through the air outside of the Double EE, Lynn had finished the story of what had happened to Ryan.

He was glad that he only had to tell it once, but relieved that no one seemed to place any of the blame on him. He may have been tortured wondering what else he could have done to stop Ryan, but he was alone in his concern. Erin and Katie had even apologized for what Ryan had done to goad Lynn into joining him.

Everyone else had already eaten before he arrived, so Katie furnished him with some cold chicken and lemonade while he spoke.

When he ended his narrative, he asked, "Where will you have him buried?"

Erin replied, "In the city cemetery. The undertaker said it would be tomorrow at ten o'clock."

Lynn nodded but didn't ask if he could attend because he knew that it was probably expected that he be there and would have gone even if it wasn't.

It wasn't until after sunset that Bethan finally asked the question that he'd expected much earlier.

"Are you staying here now, Lynn?"

He'd expected it to come from his mother, who now sat just eight feet away looking at his eyes expectantly.

He kept his eyes on hers as he replied, "I need to talk to mom and dad later, Bethan."

Gwen knew immediately that he wasn't going to stay but would ask for their blessing before he left. She still believed that Lynn was too young to go off on his own, and even if he was with an adult, it wouldn't make much difference. She didn't say anything, but mentally began preparing her arguments.

———

Dylan and Bryn finally reached the house an hour and a half after the last shot had been fired. As he'd expected, Sheriff Wheeler had readily accepted jurisdiction for the incident, so Dylan had let him handle the bodies and the lone survivor who had returned to consciousness a lot earlier than Bryn had expected, but had an enormous egg growing on his forehead.

When they entered Kyle's house, Lynn rose and before either of them could say a word, he said, "Dad, I'm going to ride home now. I need to talk to you and mom alone when you get back."

Dylan replied, "Go ahead and we'll be back in about an hour. The information you gave us was immeasurably valuable, Lynn. We caught up with them about two hours ago outside of the Double EE. Three of them are dead and John Coleridge is in a jail cell. Lord only knows what mischief they could have done in Denver. Thank you, Lynn."

Lynn nodded, then picked up his Stetson and left without looking back. He knew that he was going to face some tough parental arguing when his parents got home, but he was ready.

Luckily, he knew that his brothers and sister would stay to hear what had happened with the outlaws, so he wouldn't have to talk about anything until it was necessary.

He mounted Griffin, and with Boot still attached, rode out of Denver heading south for the Double EE. There was a chill in the air as Griffin trotted along the half-moon lighted road, but he didn't bother retrieving his jacket from the pillowcase.

When he reached the access road, he turned to his parents' barn, then dismounted and led both horses inside. He took his time unsaddling them and brushing them down as they took big bites of the full oat bins.

He left Ryan's Winchester and his other personal items on the shelf but took his repeater and bags with him when he exited the barn. Instead of going to the house that he shared with Alwen and Garth, he walked to the big house.

All of his brothers and sisters had been at his uncle's house, so he knew it was empty.

Once inside, he walked to his old room, then set his things on the bed before lighting a lamp.

LYNN'S SEARCH

After he closed the glass chimney, he set it on the nightstand and sat down on the bed. He found that it was difficult to put into words that would properly explain his need to leave again but hoped that his father would understand. He knew that Uncle Kyle would be sympathetic to his desire to discover who he really was, but it was his father he needed to convince.

He didn't want to run again, and if they were adamant, he'd acquiesce until he turned eighteen, just under eighteen months from now on the fourth of March in '75. It seemed so far away, but he didn't want to cause any more family strife.

———

Lynn heard his parents and his younger brothers and sisters enter the house but stayed in his room; just sitting on his bed with the lamp burning on the nightstand as he waited for his parents.

He listened as his mother and father said their goodnights to Bethan, Cari, Brian and Conway, took a deep breath and exhaled sharply as he looked at the closed door.

He saw the doorknob turn, and as the door swung open, he looked up at his father and then his mother as they entered the room.

Dylan closed the door, lifted the chair and set it before Lynn's bed as Gwen sat beside her son.

They had only managed a few private minutes in Kyle's house after Lynn had gone. Each of them had already arrived at the same conclusion; Lynn was going to leave again regardless of their desires. Even Gwen had realized that any of her arguments would have no impact on Lynn's decision. Now it was just a question of timing and a few other incidentals.

Dylan looked at his son and asked, "We assume that you're still planning on leaving; is that right?"

Lynn was surprised but nodded, then quietly replied, "Yes, sir."

"Your mother and I talked about it already and we're not going to try convince you to change your mind. You're old enough now to make these kinds of decisions. Leaving in the middle of the night wasn't one of your better ones and it shouldn't be repeated."

Lynn glanced at his mother before looking back at his father and asking, "You're not going to argue with me?"

"No, but we do want to know where you'll be going."

"I want to go to Fort Benton."

Dylan gave a quick look into Gwen's startled eyes before he said, "I'll admit that's a bit of a surprise, but I can understand why you may want to go there. Just remember that the man who started all this is long dead."

"I know that, Dad. I can't explain why I chose Fort Benton as the place that I needed to be, but it is. As soon as I left with Ryan, I didn't know where we were going because it was Ryan's choice; not mine. After he died, I still didn't have my answer and I immediately realized that I had to go back to where my life began."

"What answer are you searching for?" Gwen asked.

"It's hard to explain, but I think Uncle Kyle would understand it better than most people. I have to know who I really am inside. I want to be absolutely sure that I'm an Evans and not a Riddell."

"Lynn," Gwen replied, "since the day you were born, you've been no one but an Evans. You've never shown a hint of anything malicious or cruel. That man who was my contracted husband was as different from you and your father as night is from day."

"I know that, Mom, but that's only because I've been shielded for my entire life either here on the ranch or even in school. I need to know if I'm still an Evans when I face the world on my own."

Dylan asked, "Didn't you prove that to yourself south of Colorado Springs? You didn't chase after those four ranch hands with your rifle like Ryan did. You used your mind and showed restraint. Not many men would do that."

"That was just being logical, Dad. I wasn't really tested."

Dylan silently looked at his son for almost a minute before he said, "Your mother and I need to talk about this for a while, so we'll continue talking tomorrow. Is that okay?"

"You're not going to change your minds about letting me go; are you?" Lynn asked.

"No, but we'll have a few requests and suggestions."

"Okay. Thank you, Dad," Lynn said, before turning and kissing his mother and saying, "Thank you, too, Mom."

Gwen and Dylan rose, then after Dylan replaced the chair, they left the room, closing the door behind them.

Lynn stared at the far wall and was relieved that they hadn't raised the expected objections to his departure but wondered what they would ask of him. He suspected that they would ask him to delay the journey to Fort Benton until he was eighteen, but he knew that was out of the question. By then, he may be walking up the gallows steps when his natural father's inherited urges exploded in a hellish eruption.

He couldn't wait another eighteen months. It had only been a week since he'd learned the truth about his parentage, and he'd felt as if a bomb had been ticking inside him ever since. He had to know.

————

As Dylan and Lynn snuggled tightly under their layers of quilts in the night's chill, Dylan said, "He's got to go, Gwen. I saw it in his eyes."

"So, did I. He's afraid, Dylan. I've never seen that before, but it's not the fear of imminent danger or possible death, it's a fear of the unknown."

"Tomorrow morning, we'll spend some time to make it better for him, but he's got to find his own way and his own answer."

"I know, but I'll hate to see him go. I guess all mothers feel this way when their firstborn leaves home."

Dylan kissed Gwen gently and said, "But in this case, Mrs. Evans, when your firstborn returns, he'll know that he's an Evans without a single hint of that bastard that sired him."

"I just hope that he doesn't die trying to find it."

"Sweetheart, just remember that he is an Evans and we Evans men don't die easily. We have to marry the perfect woman and have a dozen Evans children."

Gwen laughed and replied, "We stopped at six, husband."

"That is because each of them is worth two of any other children."

"Don't let Bryn or Kyle hear you say that, Dylan Lynn Evans; especially with Katie about to have their fourth."

"Maybe she'll have triplets just to catch up."

"I believe that Bryn already made that little joke and it wasn't well received by either Kyle or Katie."

Dylan pulled Gwen even closer and even though they weren't about to create their seventh, he knew she still very much appreciated the affection.

————

The next morning, the Double EE was emptied as a line of riders, carriages and buggies headed into Denver for Ryan's burial.

There had only been coffee and biscuits for breakfast and surprisingly little conversation.

Lynn rode with Garth and Alwen behind his father and Bryn while his mother drove the buggy and Flat Jack handled the big carriage. Bethan, Cari, Brian and Conway could all ride, but were riding in either of the wheeled vehicles because of their more dignified attire. All of Bryn's children were also sitting on leather seats for the same reason.

When they arrived at the cemetery, they found Kyle's family and John and Meredith already waiting.

They had barely gathered by the open gravesite when the hearse arrived.

Father Matthew Byrne stepped down from the hearse after the undertaker had descended from the high driver's seat.

The burial followed a standard ritual that had been practiced for hundreds of years in every culture around the world. They all prayed for the deceased as God's spokesman pronounced that the soul of the recently departed was now happily in the presence of God and would be waiting for his beloved family to meet them again.

None of the family spoke after the last shovelful of dirt was tossed onto the grave, and the only tears that fell came from his sisters' eyes.

As Lynn stared at the mound of dirt with its temporary marker, he still questioned himself about the bizarre situation that had put Ryan into that box under the earth. *What if there had only been three riders? Why did they decide to ride to town on a Sunday afternoon? Had God really decided that it was time for Ryan to join him and had created the whole scenario; as if it was a stage play?*

He was pulling his Stetson back on when he decided that it was just a combination of coincidence and Ryan's poor judgement coupled with a hint of his hangover. If God had really manipulated the path that each of them took, going to Fort Benton was just a waste of his time.

———

LYNN'S SEARCH

After they returned to the ranch, Lynn avoided Garth and Alwen because he could almost hear their unasked questions during the entire ride to and from Denver.

Bethan was a different problem altogether. He didn't need to dodge her because she seemed to already know what he was thinking. She probably didn't; but she had a way of looking him in the eyes and reading his thoughts and moods even more than his mother could. Garth and Al said the same thing, too.

So, after he'd unsaddled and taken care of Griffin while his father and brothers did the same for their mounts, he walked with his father to his parents' home.

As soon as they cleared the barn, Dylan said, "Your mother and I talked for a while before we left, Lynn, and when we get inside, let's just go to your room where we'll continue last night's discussion."

"Okay," Lynn replied, knowing that he wouldn't have any of his questions answered until both of his parents were present.

Dylan then asked, "How is Griffin?"

"He's great, Dad."

"Does he need new shoes?"

"Yes, sir."

Dylan nodded as they reached the front porch and clambered up the steps before going into the house.

Gwen was waiting in the parlor with Bethan when they entered, so she took her husband's hand and walked with him to Lynn's room, but let Lynn open the door.

Once inside, they assumed the same places they'd used last night and once seated, Dylan began.

"Lynn, I'm sure that you can understand why we would prefer that you wait until you're eighteen and can legally sign official documents, or at least wait until spring when the weather is on the upswing and the Missouri is running deeper, but we don't believe that you'll wait that long. Are we right?"

"Yes, sir."

Dylan nodded, then said, "Now, we would like you to wait until Monday, so you can be better prepared for the trip than you were when you rode off with Ryan. I mean, pillowcases for travel bags, Lynn? Really?"

Lynn laughed lightly when he saw his father's smile before he replied, "That did look kind of silly."

"So, is Monday alright with you?"

"Yes, sir."

"The next thing we need to discuss is your mode of transportation. I hope that you weren't planning on riding all that way."

Lynn paused then asked, "Why not?"

"Do you know how far it is to Fort Benton?"

"I know it's a long way, but not the exact distance."

"On a map, it's almost eight hundred miles, but if you ride, it'll be over a thousand. Your Uncle Kyle discovered that difference when he made his journey from Pennsylvania. He also left in late spring while you'll be leaving just before the autumn equinox and riding north, too. I won't mention that you'd be riding through Pawnee, Cheyenne, Sioux, Blackfoot and Crow lands to get there, either. I won't even mention the smaller tribes."

"Then how should I get there? They don't have a railroad."

"Not yet, but the Northern Pacific is laying track out of Minnesota already. It won't get close to Fort Benton for quite a while, though. Your best route is to take the train to either Kansas City or Omaha, then catch a riverboat to Fort Benton. It's how your mother and I got there. The river is lower now, but still navigable, so there's still steamboat traffic although the number of boats that go all the way to Fort Benton has been dropping since the transcontinental railroad was completed, so you may have to wait a few days."

"Okay. I'll use a riverboat."

"Once you arrive at Fort Benton, you have to decide quickly how long you'll stay. The cold weather arrives up there even earlier than it does here, so any riverboats stop running before it does. If you aren't gone by the end of October, you'll have to stay there until the spring."

Lynn felt incredibly ignorant as he listened to his father. He simply hadn't considered many of the obstacles that his father had already mentioned and he assumed that there were more.

"I understand. What else do you recommend?"

"We'll spend the weekend getting things set up for you, but we also have already come up with something that we need you to do when you get there."

"I'll do anything you ask, Dad."

"I know you will, Lynn, but this is a little different."

Lynn looked at his father curiously as he just smiled.

"When we left Fort Benton seventeen years ago, we had just enough time to settle things down after cleaning up the mess that Burke Riddell had created. We had to leave more quickly than expected because of a problem with a stuck riverboat. Anyway, one of the last items on our agenda was Riddell's bank. He owned it and as your mother was legally his wife, it became hers. She wasn't old enough to inherit at the time, so my name was put on the deed.

"We never really paid any attention to the bank over the years and they never contacted us, either. We had appointed a man named Walter Capshaw to run the bank as the president, but he doesn't own it; we do. We're not sure if he's still there, or even if the bank is still operating, but you can help us close that last remnant of our Fort Benton experience."

"How does that work?"

"I had to ask your Uncle Kyle about it because of the legalities involved and he said that as the owners, we still would receive any profits made by the bank over the last seventeen years after operating costs had been subtracted. We also own the bank proper, so we could sell the building and its contents."

"Do you want to sell it, Dad?"

"Absolutely. As I just mentioned, we barely even thought about it, but after we realized that you were headed there, we saw an opportunity to finally get rid of it."

"How can I do that? I'm not even seventeen yet."

"Kyle will draw up a legal bill of sale and your mother and I will sign it and he will notarize our signatures. We'll leave the sales price and the buyer blank and you'll fill them in. I'm going to give you a copy of the deed as well."

"But I don't know how much it should be, Dad."

"It really doesn't matter to us anyway, Lynn. We just want to be rid of it."

"What about all the money that they've made all this time. Do you know how much that will be?"

"We haven't got a clue, and as I just said, it doesn't matter to us at all. In fact, we don't care if we see a penny from it. Whatever you can get out of it, just use it to get a good start in your life."

"But what about my brothers and sisters? Don't you think it would be better if you just divided it six ways?"

Dylan smiled at his son and replied, "It'll be your decision, Lynn. When you return, you can do whatever you want with the money. You can talk to your brothers and sisters on Sunday."

"I'll want them each to have an equal share, Dad. There isn't going to be any big farewell party or anything; is there?"

"No. Just the usual family get together and maybe you'll finally hit a ball over Garth's head in center field."

Lynn grinned, then replied, "I doubt it."

"Kyle said he'd be bringing his maple bat to the game this time."

"The one with the bullet in it?" Lynn asked excitedly.

"Yes, sir. He told me last Sunday after you were gone that of you returned, the next game you played on the ranch would be with his bat."

Gwen then said, "We'll have some other things that we want you to do in Fort Benton, Lynn, but nothing that you might not be doing anyway."

Lynn turned to his mother and asked, "What do you need, Mom?"

"Just to contact some people that we left behind. It's more about my curiosity than anything else. I just want to know what happened to the women that went with me on the riverboat upriver who didn't come back with us. I've already started a list with their names and I'm sure that your father will add a few of his own."

Lynn nodded as he replied, "I'll bring back as much information as I can, Mom."

"Lynn, if any of them want to leave, I want you to take them with you."

"To Denver?" Lynn asked with raised eyebrows.

"Just away from Fort Benton. They can go wherever they choose, but I'm probably being overly dramatic. They probably have families by now and are perfectly happy. That place just has too many bad memories for me."

"Okay, Mom."

"Now you may as well move your things back into the house with Al and Garth. They're probably hovering by the door waiting to pounce on you by now."

Lynn smiled and replied, "Alright, Mom. I'll go and talk to them and we'll be back for lunch in a while."

"Good."

Lynn kissed his mother, then stood, walked to the dresser, opened the top drawer and began removing his hastily stored clothes while his parents left the room.

As they entered the parlor, Dylan and Gwen met the staring eyes of their other children and Bethan asked, "Well? He's leaving on Monday?"

Gwen glanced at her husband before he replied, "Yes, Bethan, he's leaving on Monday. Before then, we're going to do as much as we can to help him prepare properly."

Bethan nodded as her parents sat down to tell their other children about Lynn's plans.

―――――

After Lynn returned to the small house, he spent a good twenty minutes explaining things to Garth and Al before they finally left to join the rest of the family for a late lunch. He didn't mention the money from the bank sale yet because he had already decided that he wasn't going to mention it until he returned. If he was able to do a good job, he'd enjoy watching their surprised faces.

Now that everyone knew of Lynn's plans, the subject became the focal point of the conversation with many suggestions coming from each of them; even six-year-old

Conway had a recommendation. Everyone had laughed and Conway couldn't understand why they thought that Peanut shouldn't join Lynn as a companion. Dylan had explained that Peanut needed to stay on the ranch to keep Hazel, Wally, and the newest members of his family, Acorn and Chester, happy.

Naturally, both Alwen and Garth asked to join Lynn on his journey, but that idea was quickly quashed.

Still, many of the ideas did make the cut and Lynn had to start writing them down to make sure that he didn't miss anything.

————

By Sunday, Lynn was as ready as he could be. His father had given him three hundred dollars, which bumped his total cash to over four hundred, which should easily finance the trip.

Griffin was wearing new shoes and had a second, enormous set of saddle bags to augment his old set.

Lynn commented that they looked better than pillowcases.

In addition to all of the physical preparations, he met with his father for hours in intense, concentrated instruction about what to expect and how to react to different situations that were very different from what Lynn had experienced in the past.

With each session, Lynn realized just how ignorant he had been about much of the outside world.

That Sunday afternoon, with the entire family present, Lynn got to use Kyle's big maple bat that everyone called the .44. He may not have hit the ball over Garth's head, but he did hit one so hard that it quickly rolled past Garth giving Lynn a home run.

After the game, Lynn sat with his parents and his Uncle Kyle who gave him two copies of the bill of sale and explained how to use them. He was also given a large wallet that could protect the legal document as well as his large wad of cash.

The Denver Evans finally began preparing to head home, and as each of the left the big house, Lynn was hugged, kissed, or had his shoulder punched and hand shaken by his relatives; depending on their gender.

Lynn knew that he wasn't going to see each of them for a while, but as he looked into their eyes, he felt their genuine love and concern. He hoped that he would see them again as a true, confident member of the Evans family.

CHAPTER 4

September 15, 1873

Lynn was packed and ready to go shortly after the sun rose. The train leaving for Kansas City was scheduled to depart at 9:40, and it would be a race to make it to the station on time.

He had his parents' list of contacts and a letter of introduction in case it became necessary.

After a quick breakfast of leftovers from Sunday's big spread, he kissed Bethan and Cari, then after hugging Brian and Conway, he approached his mother.

Gwen had tried not to shed a tear when Lynn left, telling herself that he would return in just another month or so, but she couldn't convince herself enough to keep her eyes dry.

The tears were streaming across her cheeks while she embraced her son and held on tightly as she whispered, "Come home to us, Lynn. We love you so much."

Lynn was fighting his own tears as he whispered, "I love you, too, Mom. I'll be back as soon as I can."

Gwen sniffed, stepped back from Lynn and wiped her eyes and her nose with her handkerchief before Lynn bent at the waist and kissed her gently on the forehead.

He then turned to his father and said, "I'm ready, Dad."

Dylan nodded, then smiled at Gwen before following Lynn out the back door.

Griffin and Crow were being held by Garth and Alwen who were determined to ride with Lynn to the station; so, just minutes after leaving the house, Lynn was riding down with the access road his father, brothers and his Uncle Bryn, who had been waiting for them astride Maddy.

When they had arrived to pick up Bryn, Lynn smiled at the crowded front porch and waved to the second half of the Evans Double EE family which included Flat Jack and Alba Armstrong.

The five Evans riders turned north when they reached the road and set off at a fast trot to make it to the station with enough time to get Griffin aboard the stock car.

———

When they reached the depot, it was only 8:45, so the need for haste disappeared, but the time would be well-used when Lynn spotted the entire Denver side of the Evans clan waiting on the platform.

He and the others dismounted, and Lynn headed for the ticket window with his father. He pulled out his wallet to pay for the ticket, but Dylan told him to hang onto his cash and paid for the ticket and the horse transport to Kansas City.

Once that was done, the second round of farewells began as each of his cousins expressed their best wishes and hopes for his rapid return.

Lynn finally said goodbye to his grandmother, who was crying almost as much as his mother had.

The train's whistle put an exclamation point on the partings, so Lynn finally shook his brothers' hands and turned to his father.

Dylan rested his left hand on Lynn's shoulder as he shook his hand and said, "Lynn, I named you after my father because you are my son and always will be."

Lynn nodded and in a barely audible voice, replied, "I know, Dad. I'm proud to be your son and I hope that I never do anything to make you ashamed for giving me his name."

"You won't, Lynn. I'm sure of it."

Lynn embraced his father, then turned, picked up his heavy saddlebags and headed for the train, getting in the queue of passengers boarding the second passenger car.

After he took a seat, he looked out at the platform and waved to his family. They returned his wave and then watched as the train clanked and began to roll away.

Lynn watched them for as long as he could before he turned his eyes to the front of the car and let out his breath.

His journey to Fort Benton had begun and hopefully, it would finally answer that one, troubling question.

———

After Lynn's train rolled out of Denver, Dylan, Bryn and Kyle all had to go to work.

But before he and Bryn went to the office, Dylan sent a telegram to Benji Green, who was still a deputy marshal in Omaha. Dylan let him know that Lynn would be passing through town on the next steamboat that was heading north.

LYNN'S SEARCH

When Kyle arrived at his office, he was called in by his boss, Denver County Prosecutor, Walter N. Jones. He told Kyle that John Coleridge's trial was set for Friday and even though he knew that Kyle would love to be the one to convict him for his crimes, that he would be handling the case. Judge West didn't want any perceived conflict of interest to impact the proceedings and give Coleridge even a sliver of a chance to avoid the noose. The general consensus that a lot of money could be made in town if they had a raffle for the job of pulling the lever to open the gallows trap door.

Kyle agreed but would assist outside the courtroom.

―――

The next day, just before noon, the train reached Kansas City and Lynn had an inkling of just how long the trip would take. It was just six hundred miles to Kansas City from Denver, and he'd only chosen this train because the next train to Omaha wouldn't leave until the afternoon. But now, he realized that he'd added another hundred and fifty miles to the Missouri River leg of the journey. But he had arrived now and stored that piece of information for the return trip, all the while wondering what other mistakes he would make.

He exited the train and waited for Griffin at the stock corral. When he spotted his gelding, he handed the manager his claim tag and took his horse's reins, lashed his large set if saddlebags over the ones already in place, mounted and headed for the docks, which he could see as soon as he was in the saddle.

When he arrived, there were two riverboats at the wharf, but he didn't know which direction they'd be heading or when. He hoped that one was going north but didn't think he was that fortunate.

As it turned out, he was that lucky. The *Alberta* was not only heading north but going all the way to Fort Benton. She was due to sail the next morning, and as he purchased his ticket, Lynn could see the deck hands already loading the boat.

"When do I have to have my horse on board?" Lynn asked.

"Well, son, you can ask that feller right over there. The one who's yellin' at the other boys. He's the cargo master."

Lynn looked back at the boat, then asked, "When do I have to be on board?"

"She's leavin' early, so you might be smart to just stay there tonight. A few other passengers are already on board."

"Thanks," Lynn replied before taking his ticket, then walking back to Griffin.

After untying him, he led his horse to the *Alberta* and stopped near the heavy gangplank.

The cargo master eventually ceased his tirade at the two deckhands whom he considered incompetent buffoons, then looked at Lynn.

"What do you want, boy? Lookin' for a job?"

"No, sir. I have a ticket to Fort Benton and the man at the ticket window said I should ask you about boarding my horse."

"I'll have one of those morons take him aboard if you aren't plannin' on ridin' later."

"He said I could use my cabin, too."

"He ain't lied to you yet, son. What's your cabin number?"

"Thirteen."

The cargo master snickered and said, "You aren't superstitious, I reckon. That's usually the last one that we fill, but we ain't even half full on this trip."

"So, I can go there after they take my horse?"

"Yup. It's on the upper deck and has 13 painted on the door."

Lynn grinned as he replied, "I never would have guessed that. You are a wise man."

The cargo master guffawed before he slapped Lynn on the shoulder and said, "You're okay, son. What's your name?"

"Lynn Evans."

The man looked at Lynn and asked, "You ain't any kin to Dylan Evans; are you?"

"He's my father."

He then grasped Kyle's hand in his calloused paw and said, "Well, I'll be damned! Your pappy is a regular legend among those of us who sail the Missouri. It's a pleasure to meet you, Lynn Evans. My name is Abner Witherspoon and if you need anything, you just ask for it. I'll let the captain know you're aboard. You can eat with the crew, too."

"I appreciate it, Mister Witherspoon."

Abner then called over a hand and said, "Take this fine young man's horse to the stock deck and tell Willie that it belongs to Dylan Evans' boy."

The deck hand looked at Lynn, then before he led Griffin onto the *Alberta*, he asked, "What are you taking with you to your cabin?"

"I'll get it," Lynn replied before he began untying his two sets of saddlebags.

Once they were hanging over his shoulders, he pulled his Winchester from its scabbard and said, "I'm all set."

The man nodded and led Griffin across the wide gangplank and onto the deck.

Lynn turned to Abner and said, "I'll find that cabin with the 13 painted on the door and get settled in."

Abner chuckled, then gave Lynn one last slap on the back before turning to correct two other deck hands who were taking a crate out of a large net that had just been lowered to the aft deck.

Lynn was still smiling as he climbed the starboard stairs to the upper deck and found his cabin.

He closed the door, set his Winchester against the wall and lowered his saddlebags to the floor.

There were two bunks, a table, chair and a small chest of drawers in the cabin, which didn't leave much room for maneuvering. He wondered how two people could manage to coexist in harmony for the long trip upriver.

He'd been surprised that Abner had heard of his father because it had been so long ago. He knew all of the stories, of course, but hadn't expected them to live on outside of the family.

LYNN'S SEARCH

That evening, as he shared his supper with the crew, he discovered that not only were the stories still alive, either they had been enhanced over the years, or his parents and uncle had been too modest in their accounts.

Whatever the reason for the alteration, Lynn soon found himself a virtual celebrity on the boat and promised to tell them more Evans family stories as they steamed up the Missouri. He had quite a few that none of them had heard, and he was glad to have something to pass the time. He still planned on going into Omaha and buying some books, though.

The next morning, Lynn was standing on the upper deck watching the hands prepare to cast off. The heavy black smoke was pouring out of the twin stacks and the other passengers had joined him to watch the show.

He counted another sixteen passengers lined up along the rail and wondered if that was all of them. The *Alberta* could probably serve almost three times as many and he guessed that it was the wrong time of the year for most people to travel to Fort Benton. He wondered how many of them would be getting off in Omaha to take the train west.

Most of the other passengers were men of various ages and dress, but only six were armed as he was. There were four women aboard, and he marked three of them as part of one family. There was an older woman and two daughters; one about his age while the second looked to be two or three years younger. The man next to the mother was obviously her husband as he had his arm through hers, and the two young men to the girls' left were most likely their brothers.

The only other woman was in her mid-twenties and was probably being escorted by the armed man to her right.

So, his quick calculations had one family of six, one couple, and eight unattached men. He didn't expect trouble during the trip, but if there was, it would come from one of the bachelors.

As Kansas City slid past the port side, most of them continued to watch the buildings and stockyards while Lynn examined each of the single men as well as he could from the poor angle. It was one of the most strident points his father had emphasized before he left; study strangers and be ready for anything. It was always better to be prepared and have nothing happen than to be surprised if it did.

The passengers began to peel off and head to their cabins after the novelty wore off and they needed to get settled in.

Lynn stayed on the deck for another twenty minutes as the *Alberta* fought its way upriver. The Missouri may have been down from its flood stages that usually appeared in the spring and summer, but this year it seemed to be stretched out into late summer. John Wittemore had more experience with the river than anyone else in the family, even his father, and Lynn had learned of the Missouri's meandering, temperamental path from the far north that had claimed so many riverboats.

The *Alberta* seemed robust and larger than he'd expected after what his father had told him before he left. It wasn't that old, and he suspected it had only been built near the end of the war to try and cash in on the need to move so many soldiers who needed to be moved back to their places of enlistment.

Lynn finally returned to cabin thirteen and closed the door.

———

At lunch that day, Lynn ate with the other passengers rather than the crew, so he could get a better look at them. He sat down at one of the long tables and set his Stetson down on the bench seat next to him.

He was cutting a thick slice of his beef when two men sat down across from him.

"Where are you headed?" the taller, dark-haired man asked.

Lynn replied, "Fort Benton."

"That's where we're goin', too. Then me and Paco here are heading west to do some prospectin'. The name's Larry Dixon."

Lynn stuck his hand across the table and shook his big hand as he said, "Lynn Evans."

"Are you gonna be lookin' for gold like us?"

"No, sir. I just have to meet some folks up there."

"You been to Fort Benton before?"

"Nope."

Larry snickered then said, "I woulda been kinda surprised if you had 'cause you're just a kid. How old are you, anyway?"

"Sixteen," Lynn replied before taking a bite of his beef.

He didn't expand on the purpose for his trip because he didn't like what he'd read in either man's eyes. They tried to smile and put on a friendly façade, but they had calculating eyes. He didn't see any violent facets but suspected that they were evaluating him as a potential source of added capital for their venture.

Larry glanced at Paco, then said, "I figured you were a year or two older than that, Lynn."

Paco finally spoke when he asked, "Do you play poker?"

Lynn nodded, then after swallowing, replied, "Some."

"Well, maybe we can get a game goin'. It's gonna be a long boat ride to Fort Benton."

"Alright," Lynn said before scooping up a forkful of stewed cabbage.

As he ate, the two men continued to chatter about their plans to strike it rich but never talked about their past at all. Lynn used the time to scan the rest of the faces and found his eyes drawn to the older daughter of the family group that was seated at their own table on the other side of the room.

He'd had his share of girlfriends in school, but like most boys, would lost interest in one either before or after she would lose interest in him, then each would move on.

He and his brothers and sisters had each learned the basic biological reasons for reproduction at an early age when they witnessed the curious behavior of the horses and then asked their parents about it.

Over the years, his father and sometimes his mother would expand on that foundational knowledge to include ever more complex explanations that included how emotions and the need to feel affection enhanced the experience and how dangerous giving in to lust could be.

LYNN'S SEARCH

When Lynn had first been told of the danger, he, just like his brothers after him, thought it was a silly concept. *How could anything that his parents had described as being one of God's great gifts to the human race be dangerous?* It was only after they explained all of the consequences of giving into temptation that it made sense. The thought of spending the rest of his life with a girl that he may not even like that much and having to raise a child with her was almost frightening; especially to a twelve-year-old boy.

Ryan had demonstrated the truth in that lesson when he'd almost been jailed for his indiscretions.

So, he and his brothers had managed to make it through the first few years when all they could think of was girls, yet each of them knew that the urge would hardly subside that much for a long time. It would be a constant tug of war until he met the right girl and then he could let himself go.

As he looked at the girl with her family, he wondered how that worked. His father and his uncles Bryn and Kyle had all told him that each of them had never had one doubt about his choice for a wife, and he'd never witnessed any behavior to challenge that notion.

The girl had glanced his way a few times as she shared her meal with her family, and Lynn had to admit to an urge surging within him. She was a pretty young lady with blue eyes and dark blonde hair. Her sister was similar in appearance, but the older girl was impressively developed for one her age.

He finished his inspection of the other passengers when Larry asked, "How about we get that game goin' tonight?"

"Alright. I hope that it's not for high stakes, though. I don't have a lot of money and I need to buy a ticket to get back home."

"Nah. It's just penny ante. We'll roust some other feller that we met to join us. We'll just stick around after supper."

Lynn said, "Okay," then wiped the last bit of brown gravy from his plate with a slice of bread before picking up his plate, cutlery and cup and leaving the table.

When he returned to his cabin, he sorted his cash; only taking two dollars and a handful of change. He still carried the long wallet in his inside vest pocket and began to think that it might not be a good idea to keep it with him while walking around on deck after dark. So, after shoving his poker cash into his pants pocket, he removed the all-important papers that his father had given to him and slid them into his smaller saddlebags. He didn't think that they would be of any value to the men who would try to steal his things because most of them couldn't read.

The large wad of currency he stuffed into one of his socks and rolled it with the matching sock and put it in the small dresser drawer with his other five pairs. His mother had insisted that he have at least six extra pairs of socks before he left.

————

As the boat's steam engine thrummed and vibrated beneath his feet, Lynn sat at the round table with the other three players. Larry Dixon had introduced him to the third player, a man named Colt Biggby, and he didn't bother putting on a false face at all. He barely spoke but it didn't take long for Lynn to mark him as a problem.

The game itself wasn't unusual and no one cheated, at least not poorly enough to be spotted, but within an hour, Lynn was down to his last thirty-five cents.

The *Alberta* had docked at Brownsville just after they'd started, but no one was getting off the boat. When they reached Omaha tomorrow, then they'd stay for a day to add a lot more cargo before resuming their journey.

Lynn had anted his penny and accepted his cards. As he fanned his five cards, he immediately knew he was looking at a two-edged sword. He was holding a diamond flush in his fingers. He couldn't discard any cards to break up the flush and staying pat would be a signal for the others to fold. He hadn't bluffed so far and that it had come back to haunt him.

As he looked at the other faces, he noticed that the dealer, Colt Biggby, was almost smiling, so he suspected that maybe the man was a better cheater than Lynn had realized. What he couldn't understand was why he was doing it for such a small pot.

Lynn was the last to call Paco's nickel bet then each player began dropping his bad cards on the table and Colt dealt their replacements.

When Colt looked at Lynn, Lynn said, "I'll play these."

As soon as the words left his lips, he expected to hear some comment about his confidence in his hand or to watch at least one of the other players fold his cards, but neither happened. Instead, Paco raised a dime, and each of them called until the dealer raised fifteen more cents.

Lynn finally dropped his last dime and nickel into the pot and waited for Colt's bid. Lynn knew that he could have raised and pushed Lynn out of the game when he ran out of money, but he didn't. He called the bet and set his cards on the table.

"Three tens," he said as he spread them out.

"Damn!" Paco cursed as he tossed his face down onto the tabletop.

"You got me, Colt," Larry said as he laid his down without showing the hand.

Lynn glanced at their faces, and thought about folding, but wanted to see their reaction, so he spread his five cards and said, "Diamond flush. Sorry, Colt."

The other players laughed as Colt grinned and said, "Well, you got me, Lynn. I guess you're better at this game than I figured."

Lynn raked in the pot as he replied, "I got lucky in the deal; that's all."

After that hand, Lynn won the next four in a row before Paco said he was tapped out and the game broke up.

"We gotta do this again after we leave Omaha," Larry said as he rose.

Lynn replied, "Might as well. It's going to be a long trip."

"You got a lot of our money, Lynn, and we need to get some of it back," Paco said as they headed for the door.

"You almost had all of mine, Paco," Lynn replied as they reached the door and stepped onto the deck.

He watched the three men ascend the starboard stairs and began to understand why they'd let him win. They wanted him to think he was better at the game than they were and once they had the kid believing he was a good poker player, they'd up the ante until they could swoop in and take him for everything he had. Luckily, they didn't know how much he did have, and he wasn't going to let them even get a hint.

During the entire game, they'd asked innocuous questions about his reason for going to Fort Benton and his family, but Lynn had been vague in his answers. He surely hadn't told them that his father was a United States Marshal. He might save that for later on the voyage if he thought it was getting out of hand.

When he finally returned to his cabin, he counted his winnings and came up with $4.27 and left the cash in his pants pocket as he prepared for sleep.

Tomorrow he'd arrive in Omaha and he had a job to do when he arrived. When he stood silently beside Ryan's grave, he'd vowed to tell the Mitchells about their son's death and his part in it. He knew that Erin had sent them a telegram, but she hadn't included any details. He didn't know if she'd written a letter or not, but he did know that they hadn't replied to the telegram.

He wasn't sure where the farm was, but he knew that at least one of the deputy marshals that had worked for his father was still in Omaha, so he'd head there and ask. He'd have to borrow a horse too, because he wasn't going to take Griffin out of the stock deck for one short ride. He'd visit his gelding tomorrow and bring him an apple that he'd picked up at lunch. The stock manager had told him that he exercised the horses once a day during the journey by walking them around the outside of the stalls. He had joked that the other critters didn't deserve his attention.

————

The next morning after breakfast, Lynn wandered to the bow of the boat as it plowed through the muddy water of the

Missouri. The morning was brisk, if not downright cold as the wind blew from the northwest into his face. He guessed that the boat's speed added to the effect and probably even made the steam engine work harder.

He was smiling as he recalled some of the stories his father had told him of his own youth when he worked a steam engine and then served as an engineer on steamboats. Bryn had followed in his footsteps and was now doing the same job as his father as a deputy marshal, but it was their work with the steam engines like the one powering the *Alberta* that had given them the opportunity to be where they are and doing what they wanted to do with their lives. He wondered what opportunities awaited him as he embraced the chill.

He was staring at the passing landscape when he heard light footsteps nearby and turned to see the smiling faces of both sisters as they grasped the rail.

"Good morning, ladies," Lynn said as he returned their smiles.

"Hello," replied the older sister, "I'm Libby Perkins and this is my sister, Ann."

"It's nice to meet you both. My name is Lynn Evans and I'd be honored if you each would call me Lynn."

"We will and we'd both be happy if you'd address us using our Christian names as well."

"Thank you, Libby. Are you going to Omaha?"

"No, our family is heading to Yankton in the Dakota Territory. My father has been appointed as a territorial judge there. We had been living in Jefferson City, Missouri. Are you going to Omaha?"

"No, I'm heading to Fort Benton."

"Oh, my!" she exclaimed, "all the way? Why are you going there?"

"I have to meet some folks and do something for my father."

"Why are you traveling alone? Couldn't he do it?"

"He's ailing and wants to clean up some things before he passes on. I'm his oldest son, so he asked me to go."

"Don't you have brothers?"

"I have several brothers and sisters, but I'm the oldest, so I volunteered. My brothers wanted to come along, but I thought they were too young and so did our mother."

Libby laughed and said, "Mothers can be like that."

Lynn glanced back at the empty foredeck and asked, "Aren't you traveling with two older brothers?"

"We are. Jake and Billy are still asleep, or they'd be out here watching over us to keep us from getting into mischief."

"It is a dangerous place for young women, Libby, so that's not a bad idea."

"I know, but you didn't appear to be dangerous."

"I'm not; but looks can be deceiving."

Ann was staring at Lynn's Smith & Wesson as she asked, "Are you good with your pistol, Lynn?"

"I'm reasonably proficient, but I've never fired it at anything except a target and I hope I never have to use it for something more deadly."

"We really shouldn't be on this boat; you know."

"Why not?"

"My mother insisted we make the journey by riverboat instead of by train. It was quite a long row between my parents over the issue, but my father eventually gave in as he usually does. We could have been there days ago if we'd taken the train."

Lynn quickly asked, "The train goes all the way to Yankton now?"

"You didn't know that? I can understand why you may not, though. They only finished it in February."

Lynn stared at the river for a few seconds, wondering if his ignorance was going to continue to penalize him, when he heard loud footsteps on the foredeck behind him and turned to see two young men approaching.

Libby smiled at Lynn and said, "Uh-oh! It appears that our guards have arrived."

Lynn smiled as he looked at her brothers' serious faces before they stopped and the older brother said, "Papa said to come here and bring you both back to the cabin."

"Jake," Libby replied, "this is Lynn Evans and he's going all the way to Fort Benton."

Lynn offered his hand to Jake and as he shook, said, "I was telling your sister that it wasn't a good idea for young women to wander around without escort, so I'm glad to see you arrive."

"Well, we're here now, so me and Billy will make sure that they both stay safe."

"Good. It's going to be a few days before we get to Yankton."

Lynn shook Billy's hand before he turned to Libby and Ann and smiled as he said, "It's been a pleasure to meet you, ladies."

"It's been our pleasure, Lynn," Libby replied before she and her sister walked away with their brothers.

Lynn then turned back toward the north and hoped that he hadn't caused trouble for the sisters.

———

As the *Alberta* churned its way north, John Coleridge was being led into the Denver County courtroom by two sullen deputies.

The trial was almost a show trial as the only possible defense available was that John and his other men hadn't been warned and were acting in self-defense. John's attorney had explained to him that he only faced a long prison sentence in Denver County because he hadn't killed anyone; he'd just fired at lawmen. But John didn't care anymore. He knew that he was going to hang, whether it was here or down in Pueblo or Huerfano County. He just wanted to end it now and not drag it out for another month.

So, just forty-five minutes after entering Judge West's courtroom, John Coleridge was sentenced to be hanged the next morning at nine o'clock.

———

It was late in the afternoon when Omaha's outline appeared on the northern horizon. Lynn was on the upper deck expecting to spot the city and wasn't off by much in his estimate.

He was standing alone on the deck when he first spotted the taller buildings near the docks, but after the captain pulled the whistle announcing the boat's arrival, other passengers began to filter out of their cabins.

Lynn had been in the dining room when the *Alberta* had docked at Brownsville, so he wanted to watch the process as the riverboat maneuvered into position and slowed.

He waited until the sternwheeler was secured before turning to his cabin where he hung his valuable saddlebags over his shoulder then headed back to the deck and joined the queue going down the port staircase.

He spotted his three poker partners already trotting across the gangplank but didn't see the Perkins family anywhere. Either they were staying aboard until the boat it departed on Sunday or were waiting until all of the other passengers had departed.

He stepped onto the dock and began walking west into Omaha. He knew the address of the U.S. Marshal's office, so he didn't have to ask anyone.

He stepped quickly along the crowded boardwalk and soon spotted the sign hanging above the entrance.

LYNN'S SEARCH

As he entered the surprisingly quiet office, he caught the eye of the lone occupant at the desk who was perusing a newspaper that covered almost the entire desktop.

"What can I do for you?" the deputy marshal asked as he looked up from the paper.

Lynn approached him and said, "My name is Lynn Evans and my father used to be the marshal here until he was sent to Denver."

Benji Green's face lit up as he stood, shook Lynn's hand and exclaimed, "I didn't know if you'd be stopping by, but I'm glad to meet you, Lynn. Your father sent me a telegram telling me that you'd be passing through on your way to Fort Benton. How's your father doing?"

Lynn was grinning as he replied, "He's doing great and so is my Uncle Bryn and Uncle Kyle. All of the family is fine, too."

"That's good to hear," Benji said before adding, "Have a seat and talk for a little while. How long are you staying?"

Lynn set his saddlebags down and then parked himself on the chair beside the desk before answering, "Just until Sunday morning."

Benji leaned forward slightly and quietly said, "I'm in a bit of a jam with the boss right now. I should have gone with Thom when he joined your father, but my wife wasn't about to make that long trip with the kids."

"It's not so bad now; just a day or so on the train. I'm sure my dad would be more than happy to have you join him."

"You think so? Does he have any openings? I was a bit too embarrassed to ask for a favor."

139

"He still has two openings because he's so particular. I know if you wrote him a letter and let him know that you'd like a change in scenery that he'd invite you to come to Denver."

Benji was all smiles when Lynn asked, "Could you let me borrow a horse for a couple of hours? I need to know how to find the Mitchell farm, too."

Benji's smile left his face as he replied, "Why would you want to go out there, Lynn? They're not friendly to anyone named Evans."

"I suspected that, and they'll probably be downright hostile after I talk to them, but I feel an obligation to explain what happened to Ryan."

"Ryan Mitchell? What happened to him?"

"He was shot in a really strange set of circumstances and I think that they should know what happened."

"Well, I'm already in hot water with our brave marshal, who has already gone home for the day, so let's get a couple of horses saddled and I'll show you the way. You can tell me what happened while we ride along."

"Thank you, sir."

Benji stood, folded the newspaper and snatched his hat from a nearby peg before following Lynn out the door.

He locked the office and then walked with Lynn down the side alley to a small barn.

As they strode through the shadowed alley, Lynn began explaining the strange circumstances that led to Ryan's death.

LYNN'S SEARCH

He didn't include his own motives for joining Ryan, but just narrated the facts beginning with their departure.

By the time they were in the saddle and heading north out of Omaha, Lynn had shifted to his discovery of the four outlaws on the train carrying Ryan's body back to Denver.

Benji had commented about the illogical nature of Ryan's assault on the four ranch hands using almost the exact wording that Lynn had heard from his father and Bryn. He wondered if it was just lawman vernacular or Benji Green had adopted it from his father as Bryn had.

Lynn wasn't able to go into details about the shootout at the Double EE because he wasn't there but did give a reasonably accurate account of the gun battle.

When they reached the Mitchell farm, they pulled up and Benji asked, "Do you want me to come with you and back you up just in case?"

"Do you think it can get that bad?"

"I don't reckon his parents will do anything, but Jack still lives there and he's still holding a grudge against Dylan for shooting him when he tried to kill Bryn. That slug he took from your father is still stuck in his shoulder blade, but he can shoot."

"If you stay out here, I think it'll be all right. I shouldn't take too long anyway, and I won't go inside the house, so you should see anything that happens."

"Did your dad show you how to use that pistol?"

Lynn grinned and replied, "Yes, sir. I may not be as good as he is, but I'm close to my Uncle Bryn."

"That's still mighty good, Lynn. I'm nowhere near as good as Bryn was, and I'm not ashamed to admit it, either. Those two are downright spooky."

Lynn replied, "You should see my mother and sister, Bethan, on the target range. You'd be ready to turn in your pistol. When you get to Denver, ask them to have some target practice."

Benji smiled and said, "Why am I not surprised?", before Lynn gave him a short wave and started the borrowed gelding down the access road.

Lynn still didn't think it would be a serious confrontation, even if Jack Mitchell was nearby. If Erin and Katie's angry older brother was close, he'd see Deputy Marshal Green looking at him and wouldn't dare to pull his pistol, but he still would rather not see him. It was already difficult for him to make this visit but believed it to be nothing less than a confession. He hadn't suffered even a hint of reproach from anyone about his failure to stop Ryan, yet he still felt that nagging guilt that he had failed. No one else had been there, or maybe they would be able to tell him what he could have done, but he'd never know.

He slowed the horse and then stopped before the farmhouse, dismounted and loosely tied the reins around the sad, bowed hitchrail.

Lynn hadn't bothered announcing his presence because, technically, he was family.

He stepped across the porch, knocked loudly at the door, then removed his hat and waited.

LYNN'S SEARCH

After hearing loud footsteps on the other side of the door, it swung wide and Lynn knew instantly that he was seeing Jack Mitchell and not Erin and Katie's father.

"What do you want?" Jack snapped, "We're having our dinner."

"May I please speak to your father, Mister Mitchell?" Lynn asked.

"What for? Are you sellin' something?"

"No," he replied, "My name is Lynn Evans and I need to talk to him and your mother about Ryan."

Jack's eyes hardened even more as he glared at Lynn, but before he could reply, Lynn heard more footsteps behind Jack.

"Who is it, Jack?" asked Liam Mitchell.

"It's another damned Evans. He's come to rub salt into your wounds about Ryan."

Liam pulled Jack away from the door, then stepped past him to face Lynn. He may not have been as hostile as Jack had been, but he wasn't exactly jovial either.

He quickly asked, "What do you want to tell me?"

"I want to explain how he died. I don't have much time in Omaha because my riverboat is leaving on Sunday. I don't know if Katie or Erin sent you a letter or not, but I felt an obligation to tell you because they weren't there when it happened."

"And you were?"

"Yes. He had asked me to join him to find four outlaws that had already killed two men, including one deputy sheriff. He wanted to make a name for himself and prove that he was good enough to be a lawman."

"What was he to you?"

"He was my uncle. I'm Dylan Evans' son, and Erin and Katie are married to my uncles."

"Don't mention their names again, boy," Liam snapped.

Lynn noticed the almost volcanic hatred erupt in Jack's eyes and glanced down to make sure he wasn't armed.

"Why did you go with him? You wanted to make a name for yourself too, so you could impress your pappy?"

"No, sir. I didn't need to impress my father or anyone else. I had other personal reasons to go with him."

"So, how did he die? All that telegram said was that he was shot."

Lynn let his brown eyes bore into Liam's faded blue eyes and said, "We had stopped in a town the night before and Ryan had gotten drunk. I woke him the next morning and we got on our horses and headed south…"

Lynn didn't take his focus from Ryan's father as he narrated the story but didn't spare any details either. He knew that Jack probably suspected that he was lying, but Lynn really didn't care what he thought.

The tale itself took longer than he expected, and he even left out the following story of the gunfight with the real outlaws. He simply ended it with the burial at the town cemetery.

LYNN'S SEARCH

Ryan's mother had emerged and stood beside her husband about the time Lynn reached the point where Ryan had charged at the four ranch hands with his Winchester ready to fire.

When Lynn finished, he said, "I just wanted you to know how he died. I'll never understand why he didn't listen, and I really didn't expect him to fire at those men. After he ignored my warnings, I thought he was going to act like a real lawman and have the ranch hands throw down their weapons, then we could sort it all out to Ryan's satisfaction. But once Ryan pulled that trigger, the cowboys had to return fire. Ryan gave them no choice."

Liam opened his mouth to say something, but Jack snarled, "Liar! I don't believe a word you said! Ryan never even fired a gun before he ran off to be with your bastard father and the rest of your bottom-feeding family."

Lynn didn't acknowledge Jack's tirade, but simply said, "I just wanted you to know, Mister Mitchell," before he turned, pulled on his hat and left the porch.

He stepped into the saddle, glanced once more at the three Mitchells, then wheeled the gelding around and set him at a slow trot to rejoin Benji Green.

As he rode, he asked himself aloud, "How can that family possibly be related to Erin and Katie?"

When he reached Benji, he slowed and turned the horse back toward Omaha.

Benji brought his horse even and said, "That seemed a bit touchy back there. I could hear Jack all the way where I was. His pa didn't seem all that happy either. Was coming out here worth it?"

145

Lynn looked across at him and replied, "It was. I don't feel guilty about anything anymore. After meeting Ryan's father and brother, I understand why Ryan acted as he did. He was stubborn and ready to act before he thought, just like Jack does. I could see it in his father too, but I guess Mister Mitchell is getting old enough to slow down somewhat."

Benji asked, "Did you want to join me and the family for dinner, Lynn? I'd like to catch up on what Dylan and Bryn have been doing. I didn't even know that Kyle was an assistant county prosecutor until two months ago."

"I'd enjoy that. Thank you."

Benji grinned at Lynn as the Mitchell farm faded behind them.

———

After Lynn's interruption, the three Mitchells resumed their dinner, but there was no conversation as each of them reviewed what Lynn had told them and processed that information through three totally different prisms.

Liam had believed Lynn, but still blamed him and all of the Evans for Ryan's death. If Ryan hadn't left the farm, he'd still be alive and be able to help with the harvest.

Catherine Mitchell also recognized the truth in Lynn's story and understood Ryan well enough to place all of the responsibility for his death on her son. She had now lost all of her children save Jack; and he was the worst of them. Erin's loss was the first hurt, but when they'd lost Katie, she had almost given up. She had almost expected Ryan's departure, and had been surprised that he hadn't gone until well after Katie was established out in Colorado. Now, all she had was Jack, who was brooding on the opposite side of the table.

LYNN'S SEARCH

Jack, of course, was sure that Lynn was covering up for his own part in Ryan's death. He wasn't sure if Evans had pulled the trigger that sent those bullets into Ryan, but he was convinced that Lynn had been part of the conspiracy to murder him for some reason. With Ryan's well-recognized penchant for the ladies, he suspected that Lynn Evans had lost his girlfriend to Ryan and wanted revenge.

By the time dinner was ended, Jack had built an entire imaginary scene in his mind that had Lynn Evans as a gloating killer. He had also made note that Evans had said that his riverboat was leaving on Sunday, which meant that he'd be in Omaha for another whole day; a full day and a full, dark night.

———

Dinner at the Greens was a noisy affair with questions constantly coming from the adults and their children. So, what could have been a forty-minute meal lasted almost two hours.

What made it interesting to Lynn was Martha Green, Benji's older daughter. The raven-haired young lady was about a year younger than he was and quite handsome. He had been impressed with the maturity of her questions and almost considered staying in Omaha and catching the next boat, but there wouldn't be another one for over a week, and he'd been told it was the last one of the season that would go to Fort Benton.

He supposed that he could let it go without him and catch the train to Yankton and pick it up there, but finally realized that he might not leave Omaha at all and he may never know if Fort Benton held the answer to his nagging question. He could always stop on his return trip and Martha might be living in Denver by then, but he figured he may as well enjoy talking to Martha for a little while.

Alice Green seemed happy when Benji told her that he was going to write a letter to Dylan and ask him if they could join him in Denver, so Lynn felt good for making the offer. He had heard his father mention Benji Green many times over the years; expressing his wish that he could have pried him out of Omaha as he had with Thom Smythe.

––––––

When Lynn finally left their home, it was well into the night, but he headed east along the main road with the half-moon overhead which provided enough light.

He wasn't concerned about being assaulted and robbed but maintained his vigilance as he always did; another habit infused into him by his father.

He reached the *Alberta* without any issues, climbed the port staircase and headed to his cabin.

Once inside, he dropped his saddlebags, unbuckled his gunbelt, then stripped and dropped onto his bunk. Tomorrow, he'd do a little shopping which included buying at least three long books to pass the time. He didn't plan on spending too much of that time playing poker.

––––––

Saturday morning dawned cloudy and drizzly, but Lynn didn't mind as he left the boat and walked briskly to the large emporium that he'd spotted when he and Benji Green had ridden to his house.

He was wearing his dark gray slicker as he stepped across the boardwalk. He wanted to get some more toiletries while he was shopping and then just as he entered the large store, he thought of something else that might be worthwhile to have.

LYNN'S SEARCH

So, before he bought his books, soap or anything else, he headed for the leather goods section and after a few minutes of searching, found exactly what he wanted.

He took the money belt to the counter and as the clerk rang it up on his big brass cash register, he said, "You made a good choice, sir. This model has a rubber coating inside that keeps the contents dry even in a flood."

"I saw that on the poster, which is why I selected it," he replied as he handed the clerk the three dollars.

It was a lot to spend on such a small item, but Lynn thought it was worth it and the premium price that added almost a dollar to the cost over the cheaper versions that had no rubberized interior was a good investment as well. He didn't plan on wearing the belt in the bath, nor was he expecting to go swimming in the Missouri River, but he felt better knowing that the documents his father had given to him would stay legible.

He then accepted the money belt from the clerk, but didn't see the need for a bag, so he just took the receipt and headed for the books and magazines.

He only had a few books in his room on the Double EE, but now he saw an opportunity to expand that collection as he scanned the titles.

Lynn ran into a problem when he had already chosen four books and spied two other titles that tickled his fancy. He was about to put two of the others back but shrugged and added the others to the stack instead.

He left the books with the clerk before going to the grooming section and bought two bars of white soap, a new toothbrush and powder, and a hairbrush. He'd only packed a comb and regretted his choice after the first serious wind tangled his hair into knots.

He figured that he'd get a haircut on the way back to the boat when he finished his shopping to minimize the tangles from becoming a serious nuisance.

Lynn left Sadler's Emporium around ten-thirty and headed for the barber shop across the street carrying his big bag under his slicker to keep the books from absorbing any of the constant drizzle.

After leaving twenty cents at the barbershop, a well-groomed Lynn Evans headed back to the *Alberta*. There seemed to be no imminent change in the weather, so he figured he'd have lunch with the crew after he dropped off his new purchases in his cabin.

He trotted across the gangplank, then clambered quickly up the staircase to the upper deck before he walked to his cabin and opened the door.

As soon as he opened it, he stopped and looked at his things. He wasn't sure, but something was amiss. He closed the door behind him and set his bag onto the spare bunk before he took a longer look at his possessions.

Then he noticed the difference. It wasn't much, but his big set of saddlebags had been opened. He had made it his habit to always secure the two leather straps that held each bag's flap. But as a final measure of security, he had counted the number of holes that had extended past the small black buckle. He'd left two holes visible on each strap, but now, there were three on each one.

There was nothing of value in any of the saddlebags anymore after he'd moved his money-stuffed socks into the small dresser, so he quickly turned to the dresser and yanked open the middle drawer. Lynn quickly rummaged through the clothes and found his spare socks and exhaled sharply in relief when he felt the heavy bulge in the thick woolen socks. He still pulled the socks out of the drawer and extracted the thick wad of bills from their hosiery hotel before returning the socks to the drawer.

After sitting on his bunk, counting the money and finding none of it missing, Lynn set it aside on the blanket and lifted the big set of saddlebags to his lap.

He examined the straps more closely and began to think that maybe he hadn't threaded them right after all. Lynn then slipped the straps out of the buckles and opened the flap.

As soon as he saw the saddlebag's contents, he knew that he hadn't made a mistake. Whoever had rummaged through his things hadn't been very meticulous when he replaced them. He'd left Lynn's shaving kit on top of the towels, and Lynn always kept the towels on the bottom of the saddlebag to act as a cushion when he dropped the saddlebags to the floor.

After doing an inventory of his things, he didn't find anything missing. He imagined that the thief must have been pretty frustrated when he left the cabin. He also was sure that it had been at least two men. One had to be going through his things while a second watched guard. They also had to have seen him leave. He suspected that it was his poker partners, and they weren't just looking for their lost bets.

After he moved the money, deed, bill of sale and his parents' list of people to contact in Fort Benton to the new money belt, he opened his shirt and wrapped it around his stomach before buttoning his shirt to see how noticeable it was. If someone looked for it, he'd see it, so Lynn pulled his leather vest from the dresser and put it on to hide the new personal vault.

Satisfied that things were now safe and reasonably sure in the event that the sneaky visit would be repeated, Lynn left his cabin to join the crew for lunch and more Dylan Evans tales.

―――――

On the back end of the wharf behind a stack of empty water barrels, Jack Mitchell watched as Lynn left his cabin and headed down the stairs.

He estimated the distance to be about eighty to ninety yards, which was too far for a guaranteed killing shot with his rifle. He'd marked the cabin that Evans was using and thought that the best method would be to wait until he was asleep and then when the boat was quiet, just sneak aboard, open the cabin door and start shooting. He'd be able to unload his pistol before anyone else even realized what was happening, then he'd just leave the boat in the darkness and no one would even know he was there.

But for now, he'd return to the farm and would make sure that his parents watched him enter his room and then, after they were asleep, he'd make the short ride to the dock and get back before the law even thought of him as a suspect. If they showed up at all, it would be well after the riverboat sailed and his parents would provide him with an alibi.

So, just after Lynn disappeared into the big cabin on the main deck, Jack walked off the dock, mounted his mule and headed back to the farm.

―――――

After a long bull session with the crew, Lynn returned to his cabin and closed the door. He began rearranging his things now that he had the books and decided that he'd keep the saddlebags on the other bunk rather than the floor. As an added precaution, he arranged them in a particular order, so he'd know if they had been moved again.

He lit the one lamp in the cabin and tried to get comfortable so he could read, but found the pillow too small to serve as a good back support, so he grabbed his big saddlebags and set them against the wall at the head of his bunk, then laid the pillow on top before wriggling himself into a comfortable sitting position.

He read the first two chapters before he set the book aside, stood and stretched. It was almost time for supper, even though he wasn't really hungry. But he was curious about the weather, so he opened the door and looked at the gray skies. At least the drizzle had finally stopped.

With the absence of precipitation, Lynn decided to spend some time on deck and get his blood flowing, so he turned and quickly strode across the upper deck, passing the wheelhouse then turning when he reached the aft deck. He wasn't surprised to find that he had the entire upper deck to himself and made good use of the opportunity as he began to jog.

As he completed his third circuit, he found himself already winded and when he stopped after his sixth and final lap around the upper deck, he bent at the waist with his hands on his knees as he sucked air into his lungs.

Lynn finally stood and walked to the starboard side of the boat and wrapped his hands around the brass rail. He'd seen his Uncle Kyle do his exercises with his bat a number of times. It had almost become an expected display after the family baseball games when one of the young Evans begged him to do it.

Lynn smiled as he pictured his smaller siblings or cousins pleading with Kyle to do his 'bat dance'. He'd tried it himself a few times when no one was looking, but never got the hang of it. He thought it was because he had two left feet, but now he wondered if it was because he didn't have the Evans gift of coordination; at least when it came to dancing.

He'd done all right when they had a family dance with the player piano providing the tunes, but he always felt awkward, so he'd have to come up with his own way of improving his stamina.

Maybe he should just run like Uncle Bryn still did. It was when he was running that Jack Mitchell and his pal tried to kill him, but his father's timely arrival not only prevented them from succeeding, it resulted in Jack's friend's death and the bullet that still resided in Jack's shoulder blade. He had asked his father why he hadn't arrested Jack for trying to kill Bryn, and he had been told that Bryn hadn't wanted to press charges which would give Jack a chance to change his ways.

Lynn stared at the river as it flowed past and said aloud, "Well, Dad, you can tell Bryn when you see him that it didn't work. I know that he's technically my uncle, but I think he'd put a bullet through me if he had the chance. Luckily, I'm leaving tomorrow morning, and I'm not going to stop on the way back. I'd just as soon never see him or his father ever again."

He released the rail, turned and walked back to his cabin.

After closing the door and stripping off his wet shirt and boots, he sat on his bunk and thought about dressing and having dinner, but he still wasn't hungry so he picked up *Great*

Expectations, opened it to the third chapter, then leaned back on his saddlebag-pillow rest and began to read.

He didn't know what time it was when he had to light the lamp, but it didn't matter as he was engrossed in Mister Dickens' novel.

By the time he found it difficult to concentrate, he knew it was time to put the book away for the night and get some sleep. So, after sliding his bookmark in place (he'd seen other readers fold the corners of pages to identify the last one read and found it appalling), he set the book on the other small dresser, moved the saddlebags back to their spot on the other bunk, then puffed the pillow, stretched onto the bunk and pulled the blanket over him. He was too tired to even take off his socks or britches. Besides, they'd keep him warmer when the night chill arrived in earnest.

Lynn Robert Evans didn't drift off to sleep; he shot into sleep with the speed of a cannonball.

————

Jack Mitchell didn't fall asleep at all. He was excited as he sat on his bed and examined his pistol's load for the sixth time. All six cylinders of his Colt New Army were loaded and primed. As he stared at the revolver, he rotated his right shoulder, feeling the slight pop every time Dylan Evans' .44 clicked past the nearby rib.

For eight years, he'd lived with that bullet inside him and he may never be able to put one into Dylan Evans, but he'd put all six into his son. He wished he could see the great Marshal Evans' face when he was told the news that his boy had been murdered by an unknown assassin. The best part would be that he was sure that Dylan would know that Jack had been the one to murder his precious son but couldn't prove it. He was counting on the same silly sense of honor that seemed to pervade all of the Evans to keep them in Denver and just live with the pain of the loss and their frustration for not being able to have their justice.

Jack smiled as he whispered to himself, "Any other man would repay the murder with a quick revenge killing, but not the Evans. No, sir. They'll wail and weep when they find out, but they won't do a damned thing. Hell, he even sent me home after we tried to kill his brother. What idiots!"

He closed the Colt's loading gate and heard it click into place. He was ready, and now he just had to wait. He was sure his parents were already in deep slumber, but he didn't want anyone to see him on the ride to the docks.

———

It was almost midnight when he left the room carrying his boots as he made his way to the front room.

He left the house quietly, then stopped on the porch to pull on his boots before stepping carefully to the ground.

Fifteen minutes later, he was astride one of the family mules and heading south. It was still cloudy, so there wasn't much light, but the moon's glow through the clouds was enough. Besides, he'd made the ride many times and the mule knew the way, too.

It was almost one o'clock when Jack rode close to the docks and dismounted. He tied off the mule in an alley behind a warehouse and did a careful scan of the area for any movement. He didn't know if there was a night guard to keep thieves from walking off with some of the cargo, but if there was, he would be tired and bored by now and Jack could make short work of him.

LYNN'S SEARCH

He stepped around the warehouse, still searching for any signs of another human being, but not seeing anyone in the dim light.

Jack was almost giddy as he quietly walked across the dock and reached the gangplank of the *Alberta*. He still hadn't spotted anyone, so he crossed onto the main deck and headed for the port staircase.

Once he reached the bottom step, he did one last long scan of the empty deck, then began his silent climb. He wouldn't be so stealthy on his return.

He reached the upper deck and turned to the left to get to the front row of cabins. The Evans kid had gone into the middle cabin on the top deck and now, his only concern was that the door may be locked. He didn't know if riverboat cabin doors even had locks. If they did, he assumed they'd just be cheap deadbolts that could be broken free with a hard yank.

He turned the corner and smiled at the row of doors. Soon, he'd have his revenge on Dylan Evans.

Jack stepped silently to the door, then pulled his pistol, cocked the hammer and reached for the door handle with his left hand.

He grasped the iron firmly, and slowly turned it clockwise. It wasn't locked, but there may be that deadbolt, so once it reached its end of travel, he steadied his feet on the deck, took a deep breath and yanked the door as hard as he could.

There was no deadbolt, so the door flew open and slammed against the outside wall.

Jack took one quick step into the dark room, and as he pointed the revolver at the shape on the bed, said in a normal voice, "You're a dead man, Evans."

When Jack saw his head lift from the pillow and mumble, "What…", he fired at Lynn Evans' chest and quickly pulled back his hammer and fired again as his victim screamed.

————

In cabin thirteen, Lynn had jerked into a sitting position when he heard the door slam open and when that first shot was fired, he ripped off the blanket and put his feet on the floor. Even as he heard the screams of the man in the next cabin, he didn't rush, but stood and stepped to the other side of the bunk and slipped his Smith & Wesson from its holster.

He heard the rapid succession of shots as the screaming suddenly stopped and he stepped to his cabin door and slowly opened it. Running outside would likely get him killed.

————

Jack had just finished emptying his Colt and felt a wave of satisfaction as he prepared to make his escape. He was counting on the other passengers' fear to keep them in their beds, but knew his time was still short. Yet, despite that need to flee, he still wanted to savor the moment for just a little longer.

As he stared at Lynn Evans' bloody, lifeless body, he said, "Go to hell, Evans!", then began to turn away.

As he did, he caught some movement on the other side of the cabin. He'd been so focused on killing Evans, he hadn't even bothered looking at the other bunk once he'd spotted Evans sleeping, and even now, didn't think it was a problem.

LYNN'S SEARCH

For the briefest of moments, he thought that Lynn Evans had a woman in the room and that wasn't anything to cause him concern, so he continued to turn to start his escape.

He took his first step when he caught a flash of light out of the corner of his right eye followed by a roar and the immediate sensation of being kicked by a mule.

Jack then felt the familiar burn and pain as a bullet rammed into his chest, but this one didn't stop anywhere. It had been fired from just six feet away and the .44 slug exited the right side of his chest almost immediately after entering his back.

He spun counterclockwise from the impact and before he reached the deck, a second bullet drilled into his neck and Jack Mitchell sprawled onto the wooden surface, his life's blood quickly pooling beneath him.

Jack was gagging as he struggled to get air into his failing lungs but there was too much blood to let it pass.

He knew he was dying but felt the small satisfaction knowing that he had taken Dylan Evans' son with him.

Lynn had his pistol cocked as he stepped out from his cabin and spotted a dying man on the deck just eight feet away. He could hear the sickening, choking sounds as the man desperately tried to extend every second of his life.

When he was closer, he finally recognized Jack Mitchell and knew that he'd come to assassinate him as he slept but must have chosen the wrong cabin.

Lynn released his pistol's hammer as he stood bare chested over Jack Mitchell.

Jack knew he wasn't going to last much longer, but then he heard a voice from the dead say, "You should have just stayed home, Jack."

Jack slowly turned his head and looked up into the dark sky only to see Lynn Evans standing over him. He thought he had died, and Evans was with him, so he smiled. He hadn't gone to hell after all.

Lynn saw the smile and loudly said, "I don't know why you're smiling, Jack. You just killed an innocent man and you'll burn in hell for it. You went to the wrong cabin."

Jack had enough consciousness to realize his error and his small gift of fulfilled revenge was replaced with the horrible revelation that he would soon be in hell. Suddenly, he wanted to repent and not be condemned to eternal punishment.

"You…you…gotta get a priest…" he whispered.

Lynn shook his head and replied, "You don't have the time, Jack, and I'm not a Catholic."

"But…" Jack gasped before his head rolled slightly and his breathing stopped.

It was only then that Lynn turned to cabin twelve's open doorway and saw Larry Dixon standing there with his pistol in his hand.

"Who was he?" Larry asked quietly.

"His name is Jack Mitchell. He came here to kill me and chose the wrong cabin. I didn't know you were in twelve. I thought it was empty."

"It was, but me and Cole were stayin' there cause Paco's snorin' was gettin' too loud."

Lynn wasn't sure that was the real reason for their use of the neighboring cabin, but it didn't matter anymore.

"Is Cole dead?"

"Yeah. He took six hits from that bastard. He was so happy to be pullin' his trigger that he never even looked my way. I was able to get my gun and cock the hammer without him even payin' attention 'cause he was makin' so much noise."

Lynn turned to the right when he heard footsteps and spotted Captain Felix Clyde, Abner Witherspoon and two armed deckhands as they came around the corner.

"What happened?" he asked loudly.

Lynn pointed at Jack's body and said, "He snuck on deck to assassinate me, but chose the wrong cabin. He emptied his pistol into Cole Biggby and then Larry shot him."

"This is a damned mess!" the captain said as the four crewmembers approached.

"We need to notify the law," Abner said.

"I know that, Abner," the captain replied as he stared down at the body, then snapped, "This is gonna cost me a day at least."

Lynn then said, "Maybe not, Captain. I know that this is the county's jurisdiction, but I know a U.S. Deputy Marshal here and he probably could help the sheriff to move things along. The man who committed the murder is dead, so there won't be a trial. I can tell them that Larry acted in self-defense, which is the truth, and maybe you'll only be delayed by an hour or two."

"That's right! Your father is Marshal Dylan Evans; isn't he?" the captain exclaimed.

"Yes, sir. I know that their office is closed, but the sheriff probably has someone on the desk right now. Leave the body where it is, and Larry and I will head over to the sheriff's office and then I'll go talk to Deputy Marshal Benji Green. He's on call tonight anyway."

Larry asked, "What about my pistol?"

"I guess you should bring it along, but we should leave Jack's where it is. I need to get dressed, though," Lynn answered without commenting that Larry was fully dressed already for some reason.

Larry nodded, then Lynn turned and headed back into his cabin. When he sat down to pull on his boots, Abner entered and watched.

"What do you need, Abner?" Lynn asked without looking up.

"Those boys weren't supposed to be in cabin twelve."

"I know."

"They were both dressed, too."

Lynn yanked on his left boot and replied, "I noticed that as well, Abner."

"I think they were planning on some shenanigans of their own."

"Well," Lynn said as he stood, snatched his shirt and slid his right arm through the sleeve, "I don't think that they'll be a problem for the rest of the voyage."

"I reckon not, but I'm going to keep an eye on 'em. The captain is mighty upset with Harry Fenster, too. He was supposed to be on night guard duty and claimed that he was just taking a leak over the stern when the guy snuck on board. I don't figure the captain believed him."

"That's his job, Abner," Lynn said while he buttoned his shirt, then added, "I've got to get going."

Abner nodded, then left the cabin with Lynn behind him.

————

After spending twenty minutes at the Douglas County Sheriff's office explaining what had happened on board the *Alberta* to Deputy Sheriff Jimmy Kennedy, who had been snoozing at the desk when they arrived, Lynn left Larry in the jail and headed for Benji's house.

He hated to wake Benji but knew that he had to know anyway because he was on night call and his new boss would probably throw him deeper into the doghouse if he heard the news from the sheriff the next morning.

Lynn stopped before the door and held his knuckles eight inches from the thick pine surface for a few seconds before he rapped as loudly as he thought necessary to awaken Benji without disturbing the entire household.

After almost two minutes, he repeated his knock only with a more forceful impact.

He was about to begin a third rapping session when lamplight suddenly illuminated the front room, and Beni opened the door a few seconds later.

"Lynn?" he asked sleepily as he stared.

"I'm sorry to bother you, Benji, but there have been two shooting deaths on my riverboat. Jack Mitchell came to murder me in my sleep but opened the wrong cabin door and killed someone else. The other man in that cabin then killed Jack."

Benji blinked and said, "Come in and wait while I get dressed."

Lynn nodded and removed his hat as he entered then closed the door.

While Benji Green disappeared into his bedroom to dress, Lynn finally had time to think about what had happened. He had now witnessed two Mitchell killings, yet hadn't been responsible for either of them. He had felt that sense of obligation for Ryan's death; not knowing if there had been something that he could have done to prevent it but felt no guilt or anxiety over Jack's demise at all. He hoped that it wasn't his first symptom of the cold, heartless character of his natural father finally beginning to emerge.

When Benji exited the bedroom, Lynn was surprised as he thought that he had only been gone for a few seconds. Yet even as Benji walked towards him fully dressed, Lynn spotted his wife wearing a dress as she stepped out of the room.

"When will you be back, Benji?" she asked.

"You should go back to bed, dear. This may take longer than you think."

"Alright," she replied before she looked at Lynn and asked, "Are you okay, Lynn?"

"Yes, ma'am. I'm fine. I apologize for having to wake you and your family."

"That's not a problem. It's a hazard of the job."

Benji said, "Let's go, Lynn. You can give me the details while we walk back to the sheriff's office."

Lynn smiled at Alice Green before turning and following her husband out the door.

Once on the street, Lynn began providing the details of the night attack.

"You never got a shot off?" Benji asked.

"No, sir. I left my cabin with my pistol cocked, but Jack was down before I even set a foot on the deck."

"I don't see a problem with anything, but I'll be able to let the sheriff know that Jack had shown hostility toward you when you visited the farm."

"Maybe I should have taken your advice and just let it go."

"You did what you thought was right and I'll never argue the point, Lynn. It was an honorable thing to do, but you weren't dealing with an honorable man."

Lynn nodded but didn't reply. Maybe he'd unwittingly been the cause of Jack Mitchell's death after all. He still didn't feel any remorse and that caused some concern once he'd realized his part in the second Mitchell homicide.

———

By the time dawn was breaking over the Missouri, Jack and Cole's bodies were removed from the *Alberta*, and the captain had been given permission to sale.

Larry Dixon had to remain in Omaha to meet with the county prosecutor, so Paco departed the riverboat as well. It was only Benji Green's influence that allowed Lynn to remain on the riverboat.

As the *Alberta* prepared to get underway, Lynn made a quick stop at the telegraph office and sent a message to his father.

It cost him sixty cents to send:

US MARSHAL DYLAN EVANS DENVER COLO

JACK MITCHELL KILLED
TRIED TO MURDER ME IN MY SLEEP
CHOSE WRONG CABIN ON RIVERBOAT
MURDERED ANOTHER MAN
BEFORE SHOT BY CABINMATE
WILL WRITE WITH DETAILS
STILL GOING TO FORT BENTON
BENJI GREEN WANTS TO JOIN YOU

LYNN EVANS OMAHA NEB

With the message traveling along the wires to Denver, Lynn jogged back to the *Alberta*, crossed the gangplank and headed for the dining room while the crew worked.

When he entered, he grabbed a plate and utensils then piled on scrambled eggs, ham and biscuits before filling a cup with coffee and heading for his seat.

LYNN'S SEARCH

The setup in the dining room consisted of two benches that were usually used by the men traveling alone and four small tables and three larger ones for families.

Not surprisingly, as soon as he sat down, other men began peppering him with questions about the shooting, but Lynn restricted his replies to the bare facts and didn't expand on Jack's motive for the attempt on his life. The only ones who knew why Jack had tried to murder Lynn were in Omaha and Lynn thought that was where it should remain.

By the time he returned to his cabin and the *Alberta* was well away from Omaha, that failure to provide cause for the night assault began generated rumors of possible motives that usually involved women; the most common was that Lynn had been caught with the dead man's wife. Jack's body had been removed before any of them had a chance to really look at it, so the men assumed that Jack was much younger and as the stories took hold, his imaginary wife grew prettier and more well assembled, and by lunchtime, she was practically Lady Godiva and just as scantily clad.

As he sat in the dining room for his noon meal, Lynn finally had an inkling of the gossip when he was asked about Jack's wife by a young baker who was heading to Yankton.

"He wasn't even married," Lynn replied.

"Then why did he try to kill you?" the man asked.

Lynn sighed, then replied, "Because my father shot him years ago in Omaha when he and a friend tried to kill my unarmed uncle. He wanted revenge; that's all."

Lynn could see disappointment in the man's eyes as he said, "Oh. I thought it was something more salacious than just revenge."

167

"Sorry. I should have mentioned it. You can pass that word along if you don't mind. I don't get involved with married women."

The baker laughed but didn't reply.

Lynn didn't add that he still hadn't been 'involved' with an unmarried one yet either. It wasn't something that men bragged about.

The next stop was in Sioux City, Iowa and then it was a shorter run to Yankton in Dakota Territory. After that it was a series of forts and settlements until they reached Fort Benton. The boat was scheduled to arrive on the last day of September, and Lynn didn't know if it would be possible to leave before the middle of October. When he arrived, the first thing he'd do would be to check the schedules for any arriving steamboats.

———

In Denver, Lynn's telegram had arrived and created the expected stir among the family. There was no grieving for Jack's death, but much concern about Lynn; especially when he let them know he was continuing on to Fort Benton.

The only good news for Dylan was Lynn's last line about Benji's desire to come to Denver.

Dylan had to reassure Gwen that Lynn was safe and was much better prepared than he had been when he had arrived in Fort Benton seventeen years ago. Lynn was more skilled than Bryn had been when he went off to war and much better equipped to handle problems than Kyle had been when he left Pennsylvania.

Gwen understood all of the reasonable arguments, but still harbored a deep concern that she would never see Lynn again.

———

Before the *Alberta* reached Sioux City, Lynn had written a long letter to his parents explaining what had happened and why he'd gone to the Mitchell farm, which he no longer regretted.

He added several paragraphs trying to express the purpose for his trip to Fort Benton and after he finished writing the letter, he reread it twice, paying special attention to those paragraphs.

He didn't want his father to think for a moment that Lynn thought any less of him but needed to prove beyond a whisper of a doubt that there was not even a tiny vestige of Burke Riddell lurking inside him. He didn't mention what he believed would give him that confirmation because he knew his mother would worry if he wrote that he needed to put himself in danger.

He finally folded the letter, slipped it into an envelope and set it aside for posting in Sioux City.

When he returned to the dining room for dinner, he was pleased to notice that he wasn't the focus of the other men's attention so much.

After he sat down to have his dark meat and gravy, wondering what was beneath the heavy liquid, there were four empty chairs across from him, and he was grateful for the solitude.

That didn't last long when after he'd taken his first bite, which still didn't answer his food question, Libby Perkins and her sisters and brothers arrived and filled the empty chairs.

Lynn noticed their parents sitting at one of the nearby small tables but weren't looking his way.

"Hello, Lynn," Libby said with a smile as she lifted her fork.

"Hello, Libby. Why are you and your sister and brothers eating over here? There are some open big tables."

"I know, but we told our parents that we wanted to talk to you."

"I assume it's about the shooting."

"Indirectly, I suppose. It's just that they heard these rumors and I think my mother is worried that you might, um, cause difficulties."

Lynn set his knife down and said, "You're getting off the boat tomorrow, Libby. What difference does it make?"

"It didn't make any difference to me in the first place, but I think my mother just likes to gossip."

Ann giggled and said, "So, does father."

"If you heard those rumors, then they should have heard the truth in the second gossip express."

"I think that they'd rather believe the unspeakable version," Libby said with a smile.

"Well, the truth is that I had stopped at Jack Mitchell's farm the day before to let the family know how their other son, Ryan, had died with me south of Colorado Springs."

LYNN'S SEARCH

"How did that happen?" asked her older brother, Jake.

Lynn gave the briefest version of the story, which he hoped would suffice, but it didn't.

"Okay, but why would he then try to kill you? That doesn't sound bad enough to drive him to do that," Billy Perkins asked.

Lynn sighed and said, "Eight years ago, Jack and a pal of his cornered my Uncle Bryn alone on the road. He was unarmed and they chased him down to shoot him because he was going to marry Jack's sister. His friend was a man named Dennis Doyle and he'd been chasing after my Aunt Erin since she was a girl, but she didn't like him at all. My uncle fell and knew he was going to die when his older brother, my father, Dylan, arrived and shot both of them before they killed Bryn. Dennis died, but Jack Mitchell lived. He had my father's .44 in his shoulder, and I guess he wanted revenge, which is kind of stupid when you think about it."

"Why is it stupid?" asked Ann.

"Because he was the one who was about to murder an unarmed man and even after my father brought him into Omaha, he wasn't charged. My uncle gave him a second chance when he should have hanged. He squandered that chance and now he's dead."

Jake said, "That's a lot better story than you diddling his wife."

Lynn turned to Jake, saying, "He wasn't married, Jake."

Libby then asked, "You aren't married; are you, Lynn?"

"Of course not. I'm only sixteen."

"That's not a good enough reason. Don't you have a girlfriend?"

Lynn was decidedly uncomfortable talking about such things with Libby, especially with her brothers and sisters sitting nearby.

"No."

"Don't you like girls?" Ann asked.

Lynn poked his mystery meat with his fork as he replied, "Of course, I like girls. I like girls a lot, but I haven't found the right one yet; that's all."

Jake snickered and said, "I'm not waiting for the perfect girl. I'm going to find one that I like and settle down."

"Me, too," Billy echoed.

Lynn just nodded, then pushed some carrots into his mouth as an excuse to end the conversation.

Libby then asked, "Are you going to stay in Fort Benton for a long time?"

He swallowed his protective vegetables and replied, "I'm not sure. I hope to leave before the weather gets bad."

"I hear it gets really bad up here."

"I thought the winters in Omaha were bad, but Denver was colder, and I hear it's even worse where I'm headed."

"Well, maybe you could stop by on your way back," Libby suggested.

Lynn smiled and replied, "Maybe."

The rest of the meal conversation was less personal, which suited Lynn. He was charmed by Libby Perkins but knew that he wouldn't visit on the return trip; assuming he made it out of Fort Benton soon enough. She was nice, but she was still too girlish, which he found somewhat ironic. When he was in school, girlish was what he looked for among the female students.

———

The next day, Lynn spent some time with Griffin in the stock hold because he felt he'd neglected his friend. He didn't know how much he'd be using his gelding in Fort Benton but planned on getting in a few good rides while he was there even if they weren't necessary.

He ate the day's meals with the crew, who was just as anxious to hear the full story about the shooting as anyone else, even though Captain Clyde and Abner had already given them the official version.

His choice to eat with the deckhands was driven by his wish to avoid meeting Libby in the dining room. She may not have joined him at the table again, but he didn't want to risk further involvement and potential embarrassment.

———

When the *Alberta* slowed to dock at Yankton, the sun was still in the sky with another three hours of daylight, so he was able to see the Perkins when they left the boat as he stood on the upper deck.

When they stepped onto the dock, Libby and Ann both turned and searched the decks, spotted him and waved. He returned their wave and then watched the family head into Yankton.

The number of passengers still on the *Alberta* had been reduced to just an even dozen after they'd added some in Omaha. None boarded in Sioux City or Yankton, so Lynn suspected that the rest would all still be aboard when they docked at Fort Benton at the end of the month.

With Larry and Paco off the boat, Lynn didn't think that there would be any more problems for the rest of the journey, but there was always the potential for an Indian attack or some unsavory types boarding the riverboat at one of the smaller stops. He'd keep his security routine in place and avoid becoming too complacent. As his father always stressed to him; you never knew where or when trouble would arrive, and you had better be ready for it.

————

The next morning, as the *Alberta* resumed its upriver journey, Lynn settled into his new exercise regimen that was very different from either his Uncle Kyle's dance or his Uncle Bryn's running. He still planned on jogging around the upper deck, but most of his exercises would be in his cabin. He had read a book on the art of boxing while he was in school when he had a problem with a bully that never came to fisticuffs, but he recalled the basic skills that boxing demanded, including the strengthening exercises. He used that as his guide as he worked up his sweat in his cabin each day.

His father had taught him self-defense tactics, but most involved getting the opponent off-balance while maintaining his own. He also recalled Bryn's oft-told story of his last baseball game in Wilkes-Barre when he'd use a particularly painful way to make the catcher drop the ball. Every male he knew had cringed when they heard the story, and he was one of them. It was a common method that was practiced in almost every serious street fight, but the trick was to avoid it at all costs because once a knee or fist made it into your privates, the fight was over.

———

Eight hundred miles away in Fort Benton, Adele stared at her mother with her hands on her hips as she exclaimed, "We don't have much of a choice, Mama!"

Beatrice replied, "We have enough money for another three or four months, so there's time to think about this."

"Then what? You know that this was going to happen, sooner or later. At least I won't have to have men hammering at my door all night. Dan Billingsley may not be what I had hoped for when I was a silly, naïve little girl, but at least he promised to marry me rather than just hand me a dollar and walk away."

"But that's all it is, sweetheart – a promise. We've been all over this. Men like him may not seem as bad as the ones that used to pound on our door, but in a way, he's worse. At least I knew what they wanted, and it kept us fed and a roof over our heads. He won't marry you. He won't want to be seen with you in public. All he wants is to get you into his house for a little while before he tosses you out into the street. You'll probably be pregnant and much worse off.

"I've spent years trying to keep you away from men like him and the life I had to lead. Can't you at least wait a little longer?"

"But at least we'll have his backwards 'dowry' for just going to his house. Two hundred dollars could keep us going for another year."

"Addie, you've heard all the stories about him. Do you really believe that his wife's death was accidental?"

"Mama, it doesn't matter to me anymore. You can't make money now and I have to do what I can for you."

"Not this, Addie! Please, not this and not with him."

"I know that you've done all you can to keep me safe and have only wished for the best for me, but it's come to this now. Either this, or you'll have to let those men start parading into our house and you'll have to listen to what they do to me over and over."

Beatrice closed her eyes as she shook off that horrible thought, then after she opened them again to look at her precious daughter, rested her hands on her shoulders as she said, "At least wait until the end of the month. Will you do that for me?"

"He wants an answer today, Mama."

"He wants you, Addie. He'll wait."

Addie sighed, then replied, "A few more days won't make any difference, Mama. You can't work anymore and we're not going to find a gold mine in the privy hole before Monday."

Her mother closed her eyes and softly said, "I never wanted this for you, Addie. I thought you'd be able to have a good life. I had the chance and threw it away. I was even given a second opportunity to correct the first one, but I made the wrong choice again."

"I know, Mama, but that isn't going to happen. I won't even get one real choice. It's either I hope that Dan Billingsley will honor his promise, or I may as well start taking on your old customers."

Beatrice wiped her eyes, then said, "Give me to the end of the month. Please, Addie."

Adele looked into her mother's eyes and nodded. She knew it wasn't going to change anything, but there was no other way. This was her destiny; the one that was her future because of her mother's two bad choices.

She then took in a deep breath, turned and walked to her bedroom. She may have tried to put a good face on it, but she wasn't nearly as naïve as her mother claimed. She knew that Dan Billingsley was just going to use her as a kept woman until he tired of her. She'd be like a prisoner in his house while she pretended to be his wife, but she was determined to find a way to get the money to take her mother away from this place. Even if she had to kill the man to get the promised 'dowry'.

Beatrice watched her lovely daughter enter her bedroom and felt sick; and not because of the sex pox that had removed their only source of income. Her one hope after that bastard father of hers had died was that she would marry a good man then go downriver and have a happy life.

Then one of her clients had given her the pox, and she could have pretended it wasn't there and given the disease to her other visitors, but she couldn't do it. That was more than a year ago and they'd managed to get by on her savings and the few domestic jobs that Addie had managed to do.

Ever since the incident with the Donaldson boy, those jobs had stopped, and Addie had almost become a recluse in this sanctuary that wasn't even theirs.

177

Nothing had turned out well since that day she'd stepped off the *Providence* onto the dock with the other women for her contract marriage to Mike Price. The only good to come of the trip had just entered her bedroom and soon her life would be ruined as well.

She had foolishly believed that the marriage would be better for her than what she'd experienced in Kansas City, but soon discovered how wrong she had been. Then she'd compounded her error when she didn't accept Gwendolyn's offer to all of them for a chance to leave Fort Benton.

Now, her precious daughter would pay for both mistakes and there was no Dylan Evans to rescue her Adele like he'd rescued Gwen. She knew that soon after this faux offer of marriage was over, men would line up outside her door to pay for her beautiful little girl and Beatrice didn't know if she could stand to see it happen; *but what else could she do?*

———

Two hours later, Addie stood on Dan Billingsley's back porch shaking her head.

Dan glared at her and snapped, "Why not now? This is silly, Adele. I may change my mind, you know. Things aren't going to get any better for you or your mother in just a few days."

"I told her that, but she insisted. If you change your mind, then I'll just have to follow in her footsteps and let other men take me."

Dan knew he couldn't allow that to happen. Ever since he'd first laid eyes on Adele Price, he'd wanted her; and the thought of her being used as a mattress by any filthy cowhand or miner with a dollar in his hand was repugnant.

"I'll wait a little longer, Adele, but there won't be a second delay. Many young women would leap at the chance that I'm offering you."

"I know. Thank you, Mister Billingsley," she replied before quickly turning and stepping down the two steps.

Dan Billingsley greedily watched her walk down the back alley and felt the disappointment over the delay, but it also added to the anticipation.

It had been difficult and expensive to rid himself of that cow of a woman he'd married eight years ago, but now, he'd be spending his nights with Adele and she was worth it.

———

There were no major difficulties over those later days as the *Alberta* churned north and west toward Fort Benton; at least none that affected Lynn directly. There had been two fights in the dining room, but they had eventually just petered out without any involvement by the crew.

Lynn didn't feel any different as he progressed with his exercises, nor did he expect to notice any change. He was pleased with his improved breathing and stamina as he jogged around the upper deck. It was as much a time killer as anything else. He'd finished four of the six books he'd bought in Omaha as the *Alberta* cast off on the 28th of September.

The riverboat would reach Fort Benton before the end of the day where he'd begin his search for something that he didn't know even existed; much less where to find it. He just hoped that it would be in the place where his natural father had lived and died, and his true father had saved his mother.

CHAPTER 5

Lynn was standing on the foredeck as the *Alberta* bounced and rolled in its fight with the last set of rapids before reaching Fort Benton. He'd been in his cabin for the first rapids but wanted to experience this one. There was something about the power of the raging torrent that mesmerized him. He wondered how many boats had been lost on this part of the river.

The sternwheeler soon reached calmer waters, so Lynn returned to his cabin to finish his packing. He only had to put his morning cleanup items back into the big saddlebags and had decided to leave the four books he'd read on the boat. They were an unnecessary encumbrance now and couldn't fit in his saddlebags anyway.

He had his heavy jacket on and his saddlebags over his shoulders when he left the cabin with his Winchester and headed for the stock deck. He knew that Joe Ibsen wouldn't mind if he led Griffin out onto the main deck before the other animals, and he wanted to take a quick tour of Fort Benton before sundown.

He wasn't going to concern himself with the bank for a while but figured that he could ask help from someone who was on the list his parents had given to him.

They had expressed their belief that he'd be fortunate to find even half of the people on the list after more than a decade and a half, but even if he met one, he or she might be able to give him a contact who could assist him with the bank issue.

He found Griffin already saddled when he entered the stock deck and Joe was grinning at him as Lynn approached his gelding.

"I figured I'd be seein' you before we even docked, Lynn. Griffin is ready to go, and I think he's gettin' mighty tired of this damned boat's rockin'."

Lynn rubbed Griffin's neck as he said, "I imagine all of the critters weren't happy when we hit those rapids."

"You're right about that, but I don't care about the ones that we eat; just the ones we ride."

Lynn laughed, then slid his Winchester into Griffin's scabbard before tossing the saddlebags into place and tying them down.

"I already tightened the cinches, Lynn, so don't worry about fallin' on your behind when you put some weight in that stirrup."

Lynn accepted the reins and said, "I trust you, Joe."

"You're the only one, Lynn," Joe replied, then shook Lynn's hand and said, "Good luck, son, and watch out for the sheriff."

Lynn was surprised because no one had said anything bad about him before, so he asked, "What's the problem with the sheriff?"

"Oh, I heard some grumbling the last couple of trips up here, but nothin' really loud. I'm just lettin' you know that you might not wanna trust him all that much."

"Thanks, Joe. Have a good trip downriver."

"We've got a couple of days to get the old girl ready to head back, and we're plannin' on enjoyin' ourselves while we're here, too. We got a lot of steam to blow off."

Lynn grinned at Joe, smacked him on the shoulder and led Griffin out of the stock deck and around the front of the main cabin before waiting for the crew to set the gangplank in place.

As he waited, he scanned Fort Benton and wasn't sure what to make of it. It was a good-sized town now and he'd heard that the population was close to three thousand, if one added the army and the Indians.

There was a wide range of buildings; some were quite impressive, but most were average in construction and others were borderline shacks.

The streets were busy with wagon, horse and pedestrian traffic, but nothing screamed out at him that this was the place to find his answer. He hadn't expected to have an epiphany but harbored a secret belief that he might be inspired when he found Burke Riddell's house; the place where he had been conceived.

He knew where it was and what it looked like, but that was seventeen years ago. It could have burned down, and at the very least it must have been repainted. He may have had that hidden expectation but wasn't overly anxious to find the house either. He wasn't ready for the disappointment or the much more likely sensation of overwhelming disgust.

He was still inspecting the town when he was startled by the loud thump as the crew dropped the heavy gangplank onto the dock.

Lynn led Griffin to the gangplank and waved to the crew as he crossed onto the wharf and once on the solid ground of Fort Benton, he mounted Griffin and felt human again.

Lynn knew that the big gelding wanted to run, but this wasn't the time. He needed to get a room and board Griffin, but even before he did either, he had to send a telegram to his parents to let them know he'd arrived.

So, just three minutes after climbing into the saddle, Lynn dismounted, tied off his reins, then entered the telegraph office.

It wasn't a big setup like the one in Omaha, but there were two full sets of equipment. He assumed that one was a backup because there was only one operator on duty. He guessed that the boy playing jacks on the far side of the room was the messenger.

The man wasn't sending or receiving any messages, so when Lynn entered, he smiled and said, "Howdy. You just get off the boat?"

"Yes, sir," Lynn replied with his own smile.

"Lettin' your girl know that you got here, I reckon."

"Sort of," Lynn answered as he stepped up to the wide counter and slipped a blank sheet of paper from the stack.

He wrote:

U.S. MARSHAL DYLAN EVANS DENVER COLO

ARRIVED AT FORT BENTON
EVERYTHING GOING WELL
HOPE TO BE DONE SOON
SORRY ABOUT OMAHA SITUATION
LOVE TO MOM AND FAMILY

LYNN EVANS FT BENTON DAKOTA TERR

He handed the message to the operator who glanced at Lynn before taking the sheet and after counting the words, said, "Sixty-five cents, Mister Evans."

Lynn paid the fee, then waited as the telegrapher tapped it out before he handed the paper back to him to him with a smile.

As Lynn left the office, he wondered why the telegrapher hadn't commented on the recipient of the message that he'd just sent. He expected that the name 'Dylan Evans' would have inspired at least a few questions; especially when it had been preceded by the title 'US Marshal'.

He let it go, then mounted Griffin and turned him west to find a hotel and a livery.

After he watched Lynn leave, Ernie Crook waited for a few minutes, then turned to Gill Feeley and said, "Gill, go down to the sheriff's office and tell the sheriff or Deputy Granger that I need to talk to him."

"Yes, sir," Gill replied as he scooped up his jacks and rubber ball, dropped them into their brown cloth sack, then tossed it into the corner before racing out the door.

LYNN'S SEARCH

Ernie quickly wrote down a copy of Lynn's message. He had done much more than recognize the recipient's name, he spotted the opportunity to get a bit of a bonus.

———

Lynn walked Griffin down the main street, passed one hotel but still rode west before he reached the third block and noticed a nicer hotel yet continued his ride of exploration. He passed the bank, then a pair of saloons, the county courthouse and a Lutheran church. He turned north at the next intersection and found a residential area and then after another block, turned west again. The houses were getting nicer and bigger as he walked Griffin along and soon reached the western edge of Fort Benton.

His wasn't sure which of three of the houses was Burke Riddell's place, but none of them seemed eerie or different in any way; just as his logical mind had expected, but his soul had begged to find.

He wheeled Griffin around and headed back toward the center of town and the commercial area. The regular businesses were there, of course, as well as the expected whorehouses and more churches to offset the sinning. So far, Fort Benton didn't seem out of the ordinary at all.

He headed for the larger of the two hotels he'd spotted and pulled Griffin to a stop out front. There was a large livery next door, which was handy, if not a bit malodorous for the hotel's guests and imagined that the livery was built after the hotel was already there.

He walked Griffin to the livery's large doors, then stepped down and led him inside.

"Howdy!" the liveryman shouted when he spotted Lynn.

"Afternoon. I need to board my horse for a few days."

The tall, gaunt man walked across the barn floor with a big grin as he said, "That's what we're here for. You just get here on the boat?"

"Yes, sir," Lynn replied as he handed Griffin's reins to him.

"Name's Mike O'Hara, but you can probably guess what all the folks call me."

Lynn grinned as he replied, "Slim?"

Mike laughed before replying, "Yep. It's kinda obvious; ain't it?"

"Well, if you were a real Irishman, they'd be calling you 'Red'."

Slim snickered before shaking Lynn's hand and saying, "I may not have the hair for it, but I'm as Irish as they come."

"My name's Lynn Evans, and everybody calls me Lynn."

Slim was still grinning as he said, "That's sure a good name you're wearin', Lynn. You ain't related to Dylan Evans, are ya?"

"He's my father," Lynn replied.

Slim's mouth dropped open as he continued to pump Lynn's hand.

When he finally snapped it closed, he said, "Well, don't that beat all! How's your papa? Is your mama that cute little gal he took outta here?"

LYNN'S SEARCH

Lynn finally released Slim's thin hand and answered, "Yes, sir. Gwen is my mother and for my entire life, I've heard the stories about what happened here, so I wanted to see it for myself."

"Well, I'm honored to meet ya, Lynn. Your folks were the finest people I ever knew. Your papa cleaned up this town in just a few days and made it all good before they left. It kinda went downhill after a while, but we all kinda figured it would."

"I need to get a room and visit a few people before I do anything else. My mother and father gave me a list of folks to contact when I arrived."

"Well, I can probably help you with that, Lynn. I know most of the folks in town and you won't wanna go askin' the sheriff."

"The stock manager on the *Alberta* said the same thing, but he didn't have any specifics. Is he crooked?"

"Yep, but he's got his ways, so nobody can raise a stink."

"I'm glad that I stopped to talk to you first. You can be my guide to Fort Benton until I figure things out."

"I'd be right pleased to help. You got that list of folks?"

"Sure," Lynn replied as he slipped it from his jacket pocket and handed it to Slim.

He'd removed it from his money belt before he left his cabin because he didn't want anyone to know about the private bank under his shirt. Now, he also intended to keep quiet about the bank sale until he met Walter Capshaw.

Slim said, "Well, Lou Dennison is still here, but he ain't the mayor anymore. He's runnin' his store with his wife and two boys. Capshaw is still in charge over at the bank, but we all reckon that his chief clerk, a feller named Dan Billingsley, is really pullin' the strings."

"How so?"

Slim looked up from the list and replied, "We figure he musta caught old Walter doin' some shenanigans with the books and threatened to tell your pa about it."

"Who knows that my father and mother still own the bank?"

"Not many even paid attention back in the day when they made Capshaw the bank president. Most folks figure he owns it."

"No offense, Slim, but how did you figure it out?"

"I was in the meetin' when your papa divvied things out. I had a mortgage on this livery that I coulda never paid off because of the interest that that bastard Riddell was chargin' me, but in one day, your folks wiped it off the books.

"I had to see Walter about gettin' the deed, and I was joshin' him about bein' the big bank owner when he said your folks still owned it, and he just ran it. He seemed okay with it, but I guess after a few years. he got a bit greedy and Dan Billingsley caught him. I'm kinda guessin' about all that, though. Billingsley sure does seem to have a lot more money than he oughta."

Lynn was close to confiding to Slim about the pending bank sale but held off for the time being and just waited for more information about the other people on the list.

Slim continued as he worked his way down the page, saying, "Three of the ladies on your mama's list have passed and three left town years ago. Only Beatrice Price is still here, but I don't reckon you'll want to see her."

"Why not?"

"She kinda fell on bad times after her husband, Mitch, died a few years back. She became a working girl, if you know what I mean."

"That doesn't matter, Slim. I can still talk to her; can't I?"

"I reckon you can, but she's not workin' anymore 'cause she's got sex pox, and you won't wanna go there."

"I'm not planning on taking her to bed, Slim, and I'm not going to get sick by just talking to her."

Slim shrugged and said, "Well, don't say I didn't warn ya, Lynn. But if you still wanna talk to her, she lives at #12 Oak Street. That's the third street west of here."

"I suppose there's the obvious reason that you know the address."

"Well, she was a mighty handsome woman in her day, but she's kinda tired now."

"Is there anyone else on my father's list?"

"The Injun feller, Joseph Walking Bear, went back to his village after he stuck that knife into Burke Riddell, but his nephew, Charlie Red Fox is in town. He's a deputy sheriff, if you can believe it."

"Does your crooked sheriff use him to sneak up on folks and stab them in the dark?"

Slim giggled, then replied, "Nah. Nothin' like that. Charlie was made a deputy by ol' Cap Johnson after Charlie stopped scoutin' for the army. The new guy, the crooked one, his name's Paul Martin, tried to get rid of him, but the mayor didn't want to make the army or the Crows mad, so he wouldn't let him do it. Charlie doesn't do much, but he's a good man, even for an Injun."

"My father thought that Joseph Walking Bear was one of the best men he'd ever met. Is Charlie his only deputy?"

"Nope. He's got another one named Tex Granger. He's a giant galoot, about four inches taller than you and probably sixty pounds heavier. He can be a bastard, and he ain't that smart so that makes him worse. He's kinda easy to rile, too."

"That's good to know. I'm going to drop my stuff off at the hotel and maybe go visit Mrs. Price to get that out of the way. I promised my mother that I'd do it and maybe she can tell me more about the journey from Kansas City."

"Well, stop by later and tell me how it went."

"I'll do that, Slim," Lynn said before unstrapping and removing his two sets of saddlebags.

Before he left, he asked, "Is it okay if I leave my Winchester with you, Slim? I don't want to lug it around town."

"Sure thing. I'll keep it in my sleepin' room in back."

"Do you ever get used to the smell, Slim?"

Slim laughed then answered, "It's the sweetest smell in all the world, Lynn."

LYNN'S SEARCH

"I guess it's better than a pig farm," Lynn said before he waved and headed for the door.

Slim waved back as he led Griffin to an empty stall. He hadn't mentioned Mrs. Price's daughter because he didn't believe she was still at the house. He'd heard gossip that she was living with that snake in the grass, Dan Billingsley.

Lynn was very pleased with the wealth of information that Slim had provided but was more interested in Slim's reaction when he'd introduced himself. It was what he'd expected from the telegrapher when he'd handed him the message. He'd only told Slim his name, yet the liveryman had immediately asked if he was related to the famous Dylan Evans.

Yet the telegrapher had actually read his father's name without any reaction whatsoever. Even if he was new to the town, Lynn expected that anyone who lived in Fort Benton for more than a few months would know the name.

For now, he'd just store that piece of information with the rest, but after hearing Slim's assessment of the sheriff, he thought it may have even more value.

He reached the Rangeland Hotel and climbed the steps to the hotel's porch.

After opening the door and entering the lobby, Lynn made a quick scan of the large room, just because it was a Marshal Dylan Evans-infused habit, then headed for the check-in desk.

"I'd like a room, please," Lynn said as he reached the desk.

"Very good, sir. Our rates are a dollar a night for a single bed. Is that acceptable?"

"That's fine."

The clerk took a key from the board, then handed it to Lynn.

Lynn accepted the key, smiled at the clerk, then looked at the tag to get the room number and headed down the hallway for room 116.

———

Deputy Sheriff Tex Granger looked at the message and asked, "Where did he go?"

"I'm guessing he's either at the Rangeland or the Brewster House, Tex. It shouldn't be hard to find him."

"I'll go and show the boss. He ain't gonna like this."

"I shouldn't think so, but he's just a kid; a tall kid, but still a kid."

Tex looked at the telegrapher, snorted, then turned and marched out of the room, slamming the thin door behind him.

"Idiot," Ernie Crook mumbled under his breath before returning to his seat by the key set.

Gill Feeley glanced up at Ernie after he scattered his jacks on the floor and wondered what why the sheriff might be worried about Mister Evans. He seemed like a nice man, and despite what Mister Crook had just said, Gill didn't think Mister Evans was a kid at all. He'd known that the telegrapher did a lot of things that he shouldn't be doing, but Gill couldn't tell anyone, not even his parents about it. He'd not only lose his job as a messenger; he was sure that his father would lose his cashier position at the bank.

———

LYNN'S SEARCH

Lynn had put his clean clothes away in the room's lone dresser and had filled his old pillowcase with his dirty laundry. He'd drop them off at the Chinese laundry he'd spotted on his short ride on the way to visit Mrs. Price. He didn't think the visit would take long, but he hoped to get more information.

He wondered if there would be any harm if he went inside her house. He wasn't concerned about his reputation as such because he'd be leaving soon. He was just a little concerned that if he was seen entering or leaving her place, it might have an impact on the rest of his visit.

So, just fifteen minutes after entering the hotel, Lynn was leaving with his bag of dirty laundry hanging over his shoulder.

He stepped onto the boardwalk and turned west. The Chinese laundry was on the same side of the street, so he didn't have to worry about traffic until he crossed the first intersection.

The stop at the laundry didn't take long, and the small Chinaman behind the counter didn't ask his name, but simply accepted his laundry, handed him a claim ticket and told Lynn he could pick his clothes up tomorrow afternoon.

Lynn stepped back onto the boardwalk, then let his eyes absorb the main street's traffic for a minute before he headed west again.

The cross streets were marked by having the street's name painted on the walls of the closest building, so after a few more minutes, he turned down Oak Street to find #12.

———

Sheriff Martin said, "Okay, Tex, why don't you head down to the Rangeland Hotel and see if he checked in there or the

193

Brewster House. Stay in the lobby until you see him, get a read on him and come back here."

"Okay, boss," Tex replied before turning and leaving the office.

Charlie Red Fox watched as Tex left but didn't say anything. Something was going on, but he'd been kept in the dark as usual. As far as the two white men were concerned, he was just a piece of furniture; and not as valuable as the chair that he called home most of the day.

He was aware of the sheriff's shady dealings, but had no power to stop it, even if he wanted to. But as far as Charlie Red Fox was concerned, as long as Sheriff Martin only cheated other white men, he couldn't care less.

But this was different from his normal schemes. Something bothered the sheriff and he knew that whatever or whoever it was, it had been triggered by a telegram.

————

Lynn arrived at #12 and stopped in the street as he evaluated the house. It wasn't a big house and it had seen better days, but he'd seen worse on his tour of the town.

He stepped down the cobblestone walkway where grass was sprouting between the cracks, then stepped onto the porch.

Lynn rapped on the door loudly and waited for Mrs. Price to arrive, hoping she didn't assume that he was there as a customer.

LYNN'S SEARCH

He heard footsteps from the other side of the door, then it swung wide and he thought he'd been struck by lightning as he stared into a pair of dark blue eyes.

Standing before him was the prettiest girl he'd ever met, and she was definitely not Mrs. Price.

Adele had been prepared to launch a vitriolic salvo at the man who had arrived to satisfy his lust, but even though her eyes registered a man standing before her, she was just as dumbstruck as Lynn as she looked back at him.

For an incredibly long thirty seconds, each just stared unblinking at the other before Lynn finally stammered, "Um…um, I…I need to talk to Mrs. Price? You…you aren't her. Could I see her…please?"

Adele did blink before, in an explosive return to normal thought, she snapped, "You ought to be ashamed of yourself! How dare you come here in the middle of the day? Leave this porch right now!"

Lynn found his own mind somewhere in the cavern of his skull and put his palms out in front of himself and quickly replied, "I'm not here to, um, visit Mrs. Price, ma'am. I just want to talk to her about my mother."

Adele had her right hand on the door's edge and was about to slam it home but stopped. She obviously had never met the young man standing before her, but it was what he'd said that had kept her from loudly terminating the brief conversation.

"What do you mean that you need to talk to her about your mother?"

"My mother was a cabinmate of Mrs. Price on the *Providence*; the riverboat that took them from Kansas City to

Fort Benton seventeen years ago. She asked me to find each of the seven women who had traveled with her but stayed behind when she left."

Adele's heart began to pound as she quietly asked, "What is your mother's name?"

"Gwendolyn. She was Gwendolyn Driscoll when she was with Mrs. Price on the boat, and Mrs. Price was Beatrice Spencer."

"What is your name?" Adele asked as she stared into Lynn's brown eyes.

"Lynn Evans. My father is Dylan Evans."

"Come in, Mister Evans," Adele said robotically as she stepped aside.

"Thank you, ma'am," Lynn replied.

As he stepped past Adele and removed his hat, Lynn wondered what she was doing here. If Mrs. Price was a prostitute, then the natural assumption was that the girl was one as well, but her reaction was a definite denial of that possibility.

As Adele closed the door, her mother appeared from the hallway and stopped when she saw Lynn beside Adele, wondering if her daughter had decided to reject Dan Billingsley's offer after all.

Before she could ask anything, Addie looked at her and said, "Mama, this is Lynn Evans. Gwen is his mother and Dylan Evans is his father."

LYNN'S SEARCH

Beatrice felt her knees weaken, so she braced herself against the wall before she took a breath and unsteadily walked to the closest chair and sat down.

Adele saw her mother trying to comprehend what she'd just been told, so she turned to Lynn and asked, "Would you have a seat, Mister Evans. I believe that my mother would like to talk to you."

"Yes, ma'am," Lynn replied as he walked to a chair and slowly sat.

At least now he understood why the girl was in the house, and not only that, he had a good idea of her age. When he'd first seen her, he'd thought she was around eighteen, but that wasn't possible if she was Beatrice Spencer's daughter. She had to be no older than he was. She had to be much closer to his own age, so she couldn't be older than seventeen.

He finally was able to concentrate on the girl's mother even as the pretty young lady took a seat in the chair beside her.

Lynn felt hot in his heavy coat, but didn't take it off before he said, "Mrs. Price, before I left Denver, my mother asked me to find each of the women who had stayed behind when she and my father left. I was told that you're the only one still here, so I made it my first priority to see you."

Beatrice sighed and asked, "How is Gwen?"

Lynn smiled and said, "She's perfect. I'm the oldest of her children, but I have three younger brothers and two sisters back in Colorado. We have my cousin, Alwen, living with us, too. He's almost my age."

"Is your father well?" she asked quietly.

"He's been a United States Marshal for a long time now and we live on my Uncle Bryn's enormous ranch southwest of Denver. He's a deputy marshal and has a large family as well. He raises horses there, too."

"Why did you come here? Why didn't your father or mother come with you?"

"I wanted to see where it all started, ma'am. Once I told my parents that I was going, she asked me to check on you and the others and they gave me another job that I'll handle in a few days."

"Then you're returning to Denver?" Beatrice asked, suddenly seeing the gold in the privy after all.

"Yes, ma'am. My mother also made another request. She asked me to return with any of the ladies who wished to leave Fort Benton."

Adele turned quickly to see her mother's reaction to his offer.

Beatrice was speechless. It was as if God had spoken to her just days ago when she'd pleaded with Adele to postpone her arrangement with Dan Billingsley. Now, her fervent prayers had been answered in the form of Lynn Evans.

"Would you just take my daughter with you, Mister Evans?" she finally asked.

"I'd be willing to do that, ma'am, but I know that my mother would be much happier if you came along. I'm sure that you have a lot of stories to share and I know that she has more than a few herself."

"I'd love to see Gwen again, but I don't believe that I'd be welcome. Do you know what I am now?"

"Yes, ma'am. I was told that I shouldn't come here, but I'll honestly tell you that it makes no difference to me or anyone else in my family. I'd much rather have you come back, if for no other reason than to act as a chaperone for the long trip."

Beatrice lightly laughed at the irony of his suggestion, but then said, "We don't have to make this decision right away; do we?"

"No, ma'am, we don't. But before I head back to my hotel, is there anything I can do for you?"

Beatrice glanced at Adele then replied, "Not at the moment, but can we talk for a while?"

"That's why I'm here, ma'am, and please call me Lynn."

"Thank you, Lynn. No one calls me Beatrice, I'm Betty and this is my daughter, Adele. I'm the only one who calls her Addie, but I'm sure she wouldn't mind if you address her in that fashion."

Lynn turned to Adele who smiled and said, "I'd be pleased if you'd call me Addie, Lynn."

"Thank you, Addie. Now, where do we start?"

Betty replied, "Before we begin to reminisce, I believe it's much more important for you to understand the current situation."

"I already got the impression that the sheriff isn't an honest man; is that what you mean?"

"That's only part of the problem, and not even my biggest concern. If you heard about my sordid life, then you know that I can no longer earn money."

"At the risk of sounding crude, Betty, I was curious about one aspect of what Slim told me. He said that you were no longer seeing men because you had contracted a contagious disease."

"Yes. That's why I cannot earn money any longer and no one is about to hire a retired whore as a housekeeper or a nanny."

"What piqued my curiosity is that many working women know that they are diseased, yet continue to work, believing that the men deserve it."

"I can't do that, Lynn. As soon as I discovered my affliction, I had to stop. I didn't work in a bordello; I used this house. I was ashamed of myself knowing that Addie was just twenty feet away listening to what I was doing, but I had no choice."

"You have a good heart, Betty, and it's a sad thing that our society did to force you into that life."

Addie said, "You sound like a preacher, Lynn. How do you even know such things?"

"You forget that for all of my life, I've lived with lawmen. So, it wasn't a day that passed without some tragic story. My father and uncles each had the same views about what society calls 'the oldest profession'. Some women do consider it a profession and to me, they deserve to be called whores.

"But many other women, and I believe that you're one of them, are forced into that life because of circumstances.

Looking at Addie, I'm guessing that she was one of those contributing factors. You had to provide for her."

Betty nodded then said, "I married her father on the same day that all of us were contractually married in the courthouse by that phony judge. My husband, Mitch Price, was all right for a year or so, then after Addie was born, he took to drink. With each visit to the saloon, he became more violent. When I became pregnant again, he was furious."

She paused, took a breath, then continued, saying, "I lost the baby at four months and never conceived again. I'm sure both were the result of that beating. He never hurt Addie, but he wasn't exactly a good father either. That went on for seven horribly long years before he finally didn't return one night. I didn't discover for three days that he had drunk himself to death, and when I learned about it, I'm not going to lie and say that I missed him.

"But we needed food and to pay the rent on the house, so I married a man named William Trappe, but it wasn't a real marriage. It was just that he moved in and provided for me and Addie for a few months before he left. After that, it was one man after another for a year or so before I finally admitted to myself what I had really become and started charging by the visit."

Lynn had watched Betty's eyes as she spoke and didn't see one tear slide across her cheek, but her eyes revealed a deep shame and anger as she spoke of the men who had used her.

Then she quickly said, "Many of them wanted Addie, but I refused to let them even go near her. I bought a heavy bolt for her door that she drops in place from the inside."

Lynn said, "I'm sorry for what happened to you, Betty. I really hope that you and Addie will return with me."

"Then there's something else you need to know," Betty said.

"About a month ago, a man approached Addie and asked her to marry him. He's much older than she is and there was a rumor about how his wife had died, so I told her to ignore him. But he persisted to the point of becoming obsessive and reminded her of our financial situation and promised to give us two hundred dollars as a sort of dowry.

"She agreed to marry him, but both of us know that he'll never do that. He'll sneak her into his house and use her as a kept woman until he either tires of her or she becomes pregnant."

Lynn was startled, but looked at Addie briefly before turning his eyes back to her mother and saying, "You can forget about the arrangement, Betty. I can give you the money with no strings attached, but I'd rather get you both out of Fort Benton."

"I don't need the money, Lynn, not if you can take Addie away from here. I'm just telling you so you'll understand that if he finds out, it may put you in danger."

"I'll be all right, Betty. Who is this man, anyway?"

"His name is Dan Billingsley, and he's the chief clerk at the bank. Everyone knows that he really runs the place and has the money and power to get his way."

"Slim told me about him, but I thought he was just some bowler hat-wearing man in a dark suit who did some embezzling on the side."

"I'm sure that's how he started, and he's not as big as you, but he has his ways. If he believes that you'll be taking Addie away from him, he'll try to stop you."

"I'll be careful, Betty. How soon was this arrangement supposed to start?"

"Last week, but we were able to delay it until the 30th."

Lynn quickly realized that he couldn't bring them back with him on the riverboat that wouldn't arrive for a week and said, "The *Alberta* will be returning the day after tomorrow. I know the crew, so I know you'll be safe. I can get you and Addie tickets and give you enough cash to get all the way to Denver on the train."

"But you'll be coming with us, won't you?" Addie asked.

"No. I have things that I need to do here. I'll probably leave on the next boat, so I'll only be a week or so behind you."

"You'll be in trouble for doing this, Lynn," Betty said.

"Maybe, but I need to stay for a few more days, and I'd feel a lot better if you were both on that boat when it sails. It would make my mother happy to see you again, Betty, and Addie needs you to be with her."

Betty glanced at her daughter, then nodded as she said, "Alright, Lynn. We can pack tomorrow, and you can make the arrangements then stop by and let us know what to do."

Lynn smiled as he replied, "Good. Tomorrow night, I'll probably move you both to your cabins on board the *Alberta*. If we manage it right, no one will even know where you went."

"I'm not worried about myself, Lynn. I'm terrified for Addie."

"I know. In a couple of weeks, you'll both be on the Double EE and you'll be talking to my mother."

"I hope so. Can you take some time to tell us about her and your family?"

"It's one of my favorite subjects," he replied, then began telling stories that began when his parents had left Fort Benton.

———

Tex sat across from the sheriff and said, "He checked in at the Rangeland, boss, but he left right after. Eddie said he was carryin' a sack."

"A sack? What kind of sack?"

"He said it looked like a pillowcase full of clothes."

"That makes sense. What does he look like?"

"Eddie said he was tall, maybe three inches shorter than me, but a lot skinnier with dark hair and eyes. He's just a kid, boss."

"He's Dylan Evans' kid, Tex, and that could be a problem."

"Why?"

"Aside from the fact that his old man is a U.S. Marshal and can come up here and start trouble for us, he's also the real owner of the bank."

"The kid owns the bank?"

Paul Martin rolled his eyes before replying, "No, his father owns the bank. Most folks think that Walter Capshaw owns it, but he was just made the bank president when Dylan Evans left here seventeen years ago. He's the one whose name is on the deed."

"How did you find that out? You weren't here back then."

"You don't need to know how I did; just that the kid's father owns the bank."

"Why is he here, do you reckon?"

"I'm not sure. I know he can't do anything about the bank 'cause he's just a kid. He can't be older than seventeen because he didn't exist when his father left. But I do see the potential to pull some cash out of our good friend Dan Billingsley."

Tex stared at the sheriff, trying to understand what he was planning, but knew he'd have to wait to hear what he would say next.

"I'm going to head over there in a little while and let him know about the kid. He'll figure out pretty quickly that Evans is too young to do anything about the bank, but I'll suggest that the kid is here to do some preliminary work and will probably just telegraph his father."

"That'll scare him?"

"Of course, it will. He knows that I own Ernie Crook, so only I'd be able to keep him from sending the message. He might try to get rid of the kid, but that would be incredibly stupid. I'd just mention that I'd have to send a telegram to his daddy to let him know about the death and it'd bring Dylan Evans and a bunch of deputies up here in a flash."

Tex grinned and said, "That's pretty smart, boss."

Sheriff Martin leaned back and replied, "I think so. One more thing, Tex; did Eddie say if he was packing iron?"

"Yup."

"Okay. Head back over that way and try not to be noticed. Or at least pretend you're not looking at him. I want to know what he's doing here."

"Okay, boss," Tex said before leaving the sheriff's private office.

As he passed a napping Charlie Red Fox, he snorted then exited the jail and headed for the Rangeland Hotel.

Charlie wasn't asleep, but he'd listened to their entire conversation and it bothered him. If the sheriff was just planning on killing another white man, Charlie would enjoy the show; but the sheriff was plotting to stop Dylan Evans' son from doing whatever he had come to do, and that was altogether different.

He still wouldn't do anything, but he'd pay even more attention to what they said. His family had a debt to Dylan Evans' family when the River Warrior had allowed his uncle, Joseph Walking Bear, to avenge the rape and death of Singing Willow. His uncle still considered Dylan Evans to be a brother, and Charlie couldn't let Sheriff Martin harm Lynn Evans. He may not be able to actively help the boy, but he'd be able to give him a warning and any other kind of support that would thwart the sheriff and that two-faced banker friend of his.

———

Lynn hadn't explained the driving need for his decision to come to Fort Benton, nor had he mentioned the papers in his money belt. He didn't want to burden anyone with that information, not even Betty or Addie Price; especially not them.

They may be leaving soon, but that was another day away and the more Betty had explained, the more concerned he became.

He'd only been in the house for forty minutes when Betty said, "I think you should go back to the hotel now, Lynn. I wish we could talk more, but I believe that the sheriff knows you're here now and is probably already looking for you. Everyone believes that he gets any important telegrams before the legal recipient does."

"That explains the operator's reaction when he read the message. Can I return after dark to talk longer?"

"You should come in the back door, which is how you should leave right now. I'll leave it unlocked."

"Okay. Do you want me to bring anything when I come back?"

Betty glanced at Addie then asked, "Could you bring some sugar?"

Lynn nodded as he smiled and replied, "Yes, ma'am."

He then stood, picked up his hat and waited for Betty and Addie to rise before he followed them down the hallway to the kitchen.

As Betty unlocked the back door, Lynn looked at Addie, who was already staring at him and felt a smaller version of the earlier lightning strike. He stared back into her dark blue eyes for a few seconds longer before he turned and walked to the open door.

"I'm glad I stopped by, Betty," he said after stopping at the threshold.

"You'll never know how happy we are that you did, Lynn," Betty replied.

Lynn chanced one more glance at Addie, said, "I'll see you both later," then pulled on his hat and stepped out into the late afternoon sun.

After she closed the door, Betty turned to Addie and as she walked toward her daughter, asked, "What do you think?"

"I wish he wasn't staying here by himself, Mama. We should wait and go with him."

"No, dear, he's right. I believe we'd be a distraction if not create more trouble for him. I'm sure that you are already causing him to lose his focus."

She glanced at the closed door and replied, "I'm finding it difficult to think of anything else now, too."

———

Sheriff Martin rapped on the heavy door and waited for Dan Billingsley.

As he waited, the sheriff thought how ironic it was that he was going to use the return of an Evans to Fort Benton to blackmail a man living in this house.

He didn't know the details of Burke Riddell's demise because there were so many different versions of the story floating around the town, but the common thread was that he had met his death just a few hundred yards from where he was standing now. Burke Riddell had lived here, and Dylan Evans probably confronted him here. Now, he'd be using the famous man's son as a threat to confront its current occupant.

He was still smiling at the irony when the door opened and Dan Billingsley asked, "What do you need, Paul?"

"I've got some information that you might find interesting, Dan. Mind if I come in?"

Dan didn't reply, but just left the door open as he turned and headed into the parlor.

Paul Martin closed the door behind him as he removed his hat and entered the room.

As he was sitting down, Dan asked, "What do you have?"

"Do you know who just arrived in our fair town?"

"Obviously, he's someone that would interest me, or you wouldn't be here. Who is he?"

"His name is Lynn Evans and guess who is father is?"

Dan noticeably blanched before doing a quick calculation and replying, "He can't be seventeen years old, Paul. Why would he be here?"

"That was some mighty quick cyphering, Dan. That was my big question, too. I don't think he's here for a nice vacation; especially at this time of year. Personally, I figure he's doing some background investigating for his old man. And there's something else that might interest you about his father."

"And that is?"

"He's a United States Marshal."

"Strangely enough, Sheriff, I already knew that, and I'm surprised that you didn't know that before the kid arrived."

"I haven't been here that long to care, Dan. Now on the other hand, you have a really good reason to care about it; don't you?"

"Walter probably has a bigger concern than I do. Everyone around here thinks he owns the bank."

"Yeah, but what if our old pal Marshal Evans comes up here with his own accountant? He'd spot those irregularities before he took his hat off."

"Then I'd just point out that the embezzlement was ongoing long before I arrived, and Walter would be marched off to prison."

"And the marshal would ask why you hadn't reported him. You can't claim to be ignorant and it wouldn't take long for them to figure out you've got a lot more money than you should have."

Dan had been trying to bluff the sheriff since he first heard the Evans name escape his lips; but that hadn't worked. He knew exactly why the sheriff was telling him; the only question was how much it would cost him to make the problem go away.

"Alright. I'll admit to his arrival being a problem. I'll take care of it."

Sheriff Martin smiled and said, "You can't do a thing about it without my help, Dan. You can't touch the kid, or his father will show up here with a whole herd of deputy marshals and somebody might let him know what happened to his precious little boy."

"And you're the one who'd have to let him know about the boy's disappearance. Is that right?"

Paul just shrugged as he grinned.

"Has he done anything since he arrived? How did you find out he was here so quickly?"

"He sent a telegram to his father in Denver to let him know that he had safely arrived. Since then, he got a room at the Rangeland and dropped off some dirty laundry. He's out wandering the town right now, but I've got Tex watching for him."

Dan stared at the confident sheriff and knowing that the pumped-up lawman had the upper hand infuriated him. Ever since he'd worn that badge, he thought he was the real power in Fort Benton. Then somehow, he'd discovered the situation at the bank, and he'd been paying blackmail money to the sheriff ever since.

Now, the man had him over a barrel and knew it. He knew that he had no choice but to give in to whatever scheme the sheriff was plotting, but once the kid was safely eliminated from the scene, Dan would eliminate the Paul Martin threat once and for all. He'd been getting greedier since he'd solved the problem with his fat wife, and Dan wasn't about to give him another dime once the Evans issue was behind him.

He was so incensed about being a victim of the sheriff's blackmail that he even forgot about Addie Price. He had been anxiously preparing to bring her into the house on the first of October, but this problem would delay his pleasure.

"What do you propose to do about him, Paul?"

"Right now, all we do is wait until we find out what he's doing here. I won't trust Tex to do anything more than watch him, but I'll talk to him myself tomorrow. I wouldn't be surprised if he stops at the bank, either.

"Once we find out the purpose for his visit, I'll decide the best way to handle it. I won't let him send any telegrams without reading them first, and I won't let any of his mail leave here either."

"Okay. I'm just going to wait until you find out what he's doing. If he shows up at the bank, then I'm sure that Walter will panic and tell me what he wants. I don't know how that man ever possesed the backbone to start embezzling."

"He is a bit of a sissy. Now you, Dan, you've got the makings of a real nasty feller under that fancy suit. I'm surprised that you haven't stolen every penny out of that bank and send Capshaw floating down the Missouri like your beloved wife."

"That would be stupid, Paul, and I'll never do anything stupid."

The sheriff stood, then as he pulled his hat on, said, "Adele Price," before he laughed and left the room.

Dan Billingsley remained sitting as he fumed at the sheriff's parting remark. He thought he'd been discreet about his plans for Adele, but he should have guessed that the damned sheriff would have found out. It was another reason for him to rid Fort

Benton of the man; but only after he'd help to eliminate the more urgent problem – Lynn Evans.

———

Lynn was on high alert as he threaded through the back alleys of Fort Benton. He didn't want to pop out on to main street too soon and run the risk of bumping into the sheriff or his big deputy.

He'd been surprised that Betty had described the bank clerk as being the biggest danger. He'd never met a banker who seemed to be a threat but wanted to meet Dan Billingsley when he had the chance. The bank was closed now, but he'd make a point of it tomorrow. He absent-mindedly patted his money belt, knowing that the deed and two copies of the bill of sale might be his best weapons. If he wasn't careful, they could give the head cashier what he probably wanted even more than he desired Addie.

He was deeply disturbed when Addie described how the man had been harassing her, and not solely because the actions themselves were so objectionable. The man's behavior was obsessive and the rumors that he'd had his wife murdered so he could possess Addie made him much more dangerous. Lynn thought the man was insane and crazy men aren't predictable.

It made getting her and her mother onto the *Alberta* the single most important task before him.

He turned back onto the main street, but just before reaching the boardwalk, he stopped and surveyed the scene. He spotted a big man sitting on one of the two benches and was certain that he was looking at the deputy sheriff. The only way the sheriff could have known about his arrival is from the telegram he'd sent to his father. He didn't believe for a moment that Slim would have said anything.

As he looked at the giant lawman, Lynn pulled the message that he'd written from his pocket and examined his own words. There was nothing that explained his purpose for being in Fort Benton, so he had no idea why the sheriff would have sent his deputy to wait for him.

He shoved the paper back into his coat pocket, then figured the best thing to do was act as if he didn't know the man. He'd also need to come up with a reason for his presence in Fort Benton but would need to operate on the assumption that they knew more than they should. It was an odd situation, but all he could do would be to roll with the punches.

He turned back down the alley and instead of backtracking, he headed east again. He figured that as long as they didn't know where he was yet, he'd take advantage the time to visit Captain Clyde on the *Alberta*. He may not be on the boat at the moment, but someone had to be in charge, and he knew all of them.

————

Ten minutes later, he bounded across the gangplank and spotted one of the stevedores, Al Borden, sitting on a crate near the door to the engine deck.

Al saw him coming, waved and waited for Lynn to reach him.

"Howdy, Lynn. Tired of Fort Benton already? You comin' back with us?"

Lynn grinned as he replied, "Maybe so, Al. Is the captain aboard, or is he partying in town with the rest of the crew?"

LYNN'S SEARCH

"You know the captain is married to *Alberta*, Lynn. He's downstairs in the engine room right now. He's worried about a leak or somethin'."

"Thanks, Al," Lynn said before he opened the door to the engine room and began the climb down to the dark abyss.

When he reached the deck, he turned and headed for the iron beast that drove the *Alberta*, where he could see Captain Clyde leaned over a big wheel.

He stopped when he was close but didn't say anything as the captain inspected something. He knew that if he startled the captain, he'd smack the back of his head on the heavy shaft just above him.

When Felix Clyde was finally satisfied that there wasn't a leak after all, he slipped away from the engine and was startled to see Lynn standing just six feet away.

He grabbed his chest and exclaimed, "Lordy, Lynn! You scared me half to death!"

"I figured if I called your name with your head stuck in that tangle of iron, you'd crack your noggin on the shaft."

Captain Clyde grinned and replied, "You're probably right. What brings you back on board, Lynn? Are you coming back with us?"

"No, sir, but I do want to ask for a big favor. I don't want to be seen buying tickets, but I need two tickets to Omaha."

"What's the problem?"

"My mother asked me to find some women who had been with her when she came to Fort Benton almost eighteen years

C. J. PETIT

ago. She gave me a list of the seven who remained in Fort Benton rather than join her and my father when they left. Six of the women are already gone, one way or the other, but the last one, a lady named Beatrice Price, is still here. She desperately wants to leave, but there is an issue with a man who is obsessed with her daughter, Adele. I need to help them get out of Fort Benton. My parents gave me enough money to handle it, but I need to get them aboard without the man knowing they're gone."

"Hell, Lynn, I don't care about any damned tickets. I got plenty of empty cabins on the way back, and I'd be tickled pink to be able to help."

"I really appreciate it. Can I sneak them aboard tomorrow night? You're casting off on Wednesday morning; is that right?"

"Yup. As soon as the sun comes up. I'll get a couple of cabins ready. I'll even give them thirteen and fourteen. Twelve still has a few blood stains that the carpenter hasn't gotten around to scraping off."

"I won't be too late; just a couple of hours after sunset. Just to let you know, Mrs. Price has had a bad time of it for the past few years; bad husband and worse times after that. She's endured a lot of humiliation and pain to protect her daughter, and you can probably guess what she had to do to keep Adele safe. Adele is about my age and is a very pretty girl, which is why this man is obsessed with her."

"I kind of figured out it was something like that. Are you smitten with this young lady?"

"I only met her a couple of hours ago, Captain."

"That ain't an answer and the time doesn't mean much. I'll assume that your answer is 'yes', and I'll be sure that the crew all understand that she's your lady and is to be respected. I hope that none of them spent any time with her mother, but I'll ride herd on them about that, too."

"Thanks, Captain. I'll be giving them some letters for my parents and Deputy Marshal Green in Omaha. I need to stay here until I find some answers, but hopefully I'll be following you in a week or so. Do you know when the next boat is coming upriver?"

"That'll be the *Princess of Ohio*, and she should be here in about ten days or so. You'd better get your answers by the time she shoves off because she's the last boat of the season. You won't see another one until springtime."

"I hope it doesn't take that long, but I'm really grateful for your help," Lynn said before shaking the captain's hand.

"Any riverboat captain would be glad to help Dylan Evans' son, and I'm proud to be the one to help you, Lynn. I think you'll be making your own legends before you leave."

"I'll never come close to matching my father's well-deserved reputation, Felix, but I'm forever grateful to be his son."

"I'll be waiting for your ladies to arrive tomorrow night, Lynn."

Lynn nodded, then turned and headed for the ladder.

When he stepped back onto the deck, the sun was in his eyes as it neared the horizon.

He knew that the general store was closed, so he turned to Al Borden and asked, "I don't suppose that JoJo is still aboard. That would be too much to ask. I need to grab some sugar."

Al snickered before replying, "You got that right. JoJo was off the boat as soon as he put away the last pot. Abner is down in the cargo hold, though, and he can get some for ya."

"Thanks, Al," Lynn said as he headed toward the bow, then turned along the front of the main cabin and entered the cargo hold doorway.

He didn't see Abner Witherspoon when he reached the main cargo hold, so he shouted, "Abner?"

"Back here!" came Abner's loud reply.

Lynn walked quickly around a stack of crates and after passing bales of furs, spotted the cargo master with a clipboard in his hand.

"What brings you by, Lynn?"

Lynn gave him a shortened explanation, knowing that the captain would fill in the gaps later, then asked, "I just needed to pick up some sugar, but JoJo is in town."

"Why didn't you just head into the storeroom and grab some, Lynn?"

"I guess it would feel too much like stealing."

Abner laughed as he set his clipboard down and said, "Let's go upstairs."

As they headed back to the main deck, Lynn answered his questions, but felt a growing sense of urgency to get back to the hotel. He didn't want the deputy to report to his boss that he was unable to track Lynn down or spotted him on the *Alberta*. That might lead the sheriff to become suspicious of his motives; and it was much too soon to raise any kind of alarm. He still didn't understand why anyone would see him as a threat, but they obviously did, and he needed to get Adele and her mother on the *Alberta* before he discovered that reason.

Once they reached the galley, Abner led Lynn into the storeroom where he grabbed one of the empty coffee tins that JoJo used for grease, then scooped sugar from a nearby barrel until the tin was filled with sweet granules.

After popping the top onto the tin, he asked, "Do you want anything else, Lynn?"

"Do you think I could get one of the tins of tea and another of the condensed milk?"

Abner rubbed the stubble on his chin as he scrunched his face and replied, "I think that might be askin' too much, Lynn."

Lynn flushed red as he quickly said, "I'm sorry, Abner. Thanks for the sugar."

Abner burst out laughing as he swatted Lynn's shoulder, then said, "I'm just pullin' your leg, Lynn. You're just too damned honest sometimes."

He grabbed a tin of tea and another of sweetened condensed milk before snatching a cloth bag and dropping them inside. As he held its mouth open, Lynn slid the tin of sugar into the bag before taking it from Abner.

"Thanks, Abner. I'd like to spend some time talking to you, but I've got to sneak off the boat before anyone in Fort Benton sees me."

"What's goin' on, Lynn?" Abner asked as he and Lynn started to walk out of the galley.

"I wish I knew, Abner. It's just that the sheriff seems to be interested in me. What's got me wondering is that the only way he could know who I am is from the telegram I sent to my father as soon as I arrived. I've only been in Fort Benton for a couple of hours and I feel as if I've been here for a month."

"Well, if you need any help before we leave, I'm sure that you could get the entire crew to give you a hand."

"Thanks, Abner. And thanks for the sugar, tea and milk."

As they stepped onto the main deck, Abner replied, "Anytime, Lynn. You take care."

"I will," Lynn said before waving to Al Borden and then trotting to the gangplank.

He hadn't seen anyone watching the boat when he left the galley, so he didn't waste any time on the dock before heading back to the same back alley he'd used to reach the wharf.

He wasn't sure if the deputy would have had the patience to stay on the bench, but he'd know soon enough.

After two blocks, he turned up a side street and soon reached the main street, just a block from the hotel and was relieved to see the big deputy still lounging on the bench. As he crossed the street, he was curious to the deputy's reaction to his delayed reappearance.

LYNN'S SEARCH

Tex Granger was woolgathering as he stared at the middle of the road. He was close to drifting off when he shook his head and spotted Lynn on the boardwalk just thirty feet to his left.

He hadn't been given specific instructions by the boss, but he had been told to find out why Evans was here, so just a second or two after seeing Lynn, he awkwardly rose to his feet and turned to face him.

Lynn was wearing his most innocent poker face when he saw the ogre-like deputy rise but kept walking to the hotel's entrance that was now mostly blocked by the man's bulk.

He smiled at Tex and as he began to walk around him, Tex asked, "You just got here; didn't ya?"

Lynn stopped and had to look up slightly to reply, "Yes, sir. I just got off the *Alberta* a little while ago. Are you the sheriff?"

The thought tickled Tex's fancy, so he grinned as he replied, "Nope. I'm still just a deputy, but the sheriff likes to know about any strangers in town. Why did you come all the way to Fort Benton?"

"I wanted to see the town. My parents always talked about it, and I've been kind of badgering them to let me come here. It's a lot different than the way they described it, though."

"How long are you stayin'?"

"I'll probably take the next boat downriver."

Tex figured that he had enough information, so he said, "Well, I've got to get back to the jail," then simply walked away.

Lynn turned to watch him leave and had to agree with Slim's assessment of the man's mental faculties. If his job was to check out strangers, then his first question should have been to ask the newcomer for his name.

When a lawman poses that question, the stranger's eyes provide a lot more information that whatever name he offers, yet Tex Granger hadn't bothered to ask because he already knew the answer.

Rather than go to his room, Lynn thought it would be a good idea to have an early supper. He was planning on spending a longer time with Betty and Addie, so he turned back around and headed for Ziggy's Diner.

————

"He said he's just visiting out of curiosity?" Sheriff Martin asked with raised eyebrows and a raised voice.

"That's what he said, boss," Tex replied.

Paul Martin sighed, accepted the responsibility for not giving Tex exact instructions, then said, "That's okay, Tex. I'll take care of Mister Evans from here on in. If I need your help, I'll let you know."

"Alright. Did you go see Billingsley?"

"I did, and he knows that there's nothing he can do but sweat because I hold all the cards. I'll talk to the kid tomorrow and see if I can get him to open up some more."

Tex was relieved that the boss wasn't mad at him. When he'd first told him that he'd talked to the kid, he seemed about ready to shoot him.

"Well, I'm gonna head over to the *Lonely Widow* for a while, boss."

"Enjoy yourself, Tex. See you tomorrow."

Tex rose then smiled at his boss before turning and leaving his private office and quickly stepping through the front room, not paying one bit of attention to Charlie Red Fox.

―――――

Betty and Addie were already packing as the sun's refracted light turned the sky a deep red.

"How much do you think we should take with us?" Addie asked as she stacked her clothes on the top of the scuffed dresser that tilted slightly to the right because of a broken footing.

"We don't have much, Addie, so we can pack it all. We won't take any food and we surely won't be packing anything to remind us of this place."

"Do you really think we'll be welcomed at his father's ranch?"

"Yes, I do. You never met Gwen or his father, of course, but I spent more than two weeks with both of them on that riverboat. I got to know Gwen quite well, and I'll admit to teasing her about her infatuation with Dylan Evans. To be honest, almost all of the women were in love with the man. It was a measure of him that he only cared for Gwen, even though she was the smallest and youngest of us all. He could have had his way with a number of us, including me, but he just spent hours talking with Gwen.

"When he took her away from that bastard, Riddell, we all cheered; and then when he returned a few days later and almost single-handedly cleaned up the mess, many of the townsfolk expected that he'd just take over, but he just left with Gwen and the women who wanted to leave. Any man who would so easily reject the opportunity to gain power and wealth is an incredibly unique person."

"Mama," Addie said as she turned to look at her mother, "What did Burke Riddell look like?"

"He was tall with dark hair and eyes, but I didn't see him very often before he died. He wasn't even in the courtroom when each of us was matched with our contract husbands. Why do you ask?"

"I'm probably thinking about things that don't matter, but I was wondering about Lynn. You described his father as tall with brown hair and hazel eyes. Is that right?"

"Yes," she answered, suddenly realizing where Addie was going with the questioning, "but Gwen had brown eyes."

Addie nodded slowly before saying, "Never mind, Mama. It doesn't matter. It's just that he seems older than me, yet that's impossible; isn't it?"

"Yes, dear. You were conceived just days after that mass wedding."

She nodded again but didn't say anything more as she continued to empty the drawers. After Lynn had gone, she'd found herself in a fantasy world where they were happily married and had their children laughing and playing nearby. It had been that image of their children that had prompted the review of the timing of her birth and his arrival into the world.

LYNN'S SEARCH

She knew that it didn't matter at all to her who had fathered him with Gwen, but after she'd realized that it was possible that Lynn was really the result of Burke Riddell's few nights with his mother, she surmised that Lynn was here to find the truth of his conception.

As soon as she'd come to that conclusion, Addie knew that she could never ask him to confirm it. She just hoped that if he did discover that Dylan Evans wasn't his natural father, he wouldn't so angered and despondent by the revelation that he wouldn't return to Denver. If he didn't, then Addie wasn't sure that she'd stay in Colorado. She desperately wanted her new dream to become a reality.

———

It was dark enough to suit Lynn, so he left his room and rather than go out through the lobby, he walked to the back of the hallway, passed through the back door that gave the guests access to the privy, then stepped out into the night.

As he made his way along the dark alley, he hoped that they didn't lock the door when it was late knowing that their guests would use the room's chamber pots.

He was wearing his heavy coat, gloves and his Stetson as he walked quickly past the backs of the buildings carrying the bag from the *Alberta*.

When he'd left the Price house, he'd noticed the paucity of items on the pantry shelves. He knew that they'd be well fed on the boat, so he hadn't asked for anything more, but thought that some tea would be welcome.

He had to cross the main street, so he turned south and walked between two buildings, unsure of their purpose. As long as one wasn't a saloon or bawdy house, which were the

225

only businesses open at this time of night, he shouldn't be spotted.

Once he made it across the street, he slowed and made his way following the route he'd taken when he left.

When he reached the back door, he rapped three times and not ten seconds later, the door opened, and he quickly stepped inside. It was as if he was a thief, or maybe one of Betty's old customers.

Addie smiled at him as he removed his hat with his left hand and handed her the bag with his right.

"Thank you for the sugar, Lynn," she said.

"There's some tea and a tin of condensed milk inside, too," he replied as he stuffed his gloves into his coat pocket.

"Tea?" Betty asked quickly.

Addie handed the bag to her mother, who quickly extracted the items and hurried to the cookstove.

Lynn removed his jacket and hung it on a peg near the door before he and Addie headed for the table.

"You're all set to leave on the *Alberta* tomorrow night," Lynn said as he sat, "We'll leave about this time and they'll have your cabins ready for you. The boat will depart just after dawn the next morning."

"But you're still staying here?" Addie asked.

"I have to, Addie. Tomorrow, I'll write a few letters, and I'll write some instructions about what to do when you arrive in Omaha."

"Omaha?" Betty asked as she set the coffeepot on the stove.

"On my journey here, I discovered that I could have saved a whole day if I'd taken the train to Omaha instead of Kansas City. Besides, I know a deputy marshal in Omaha who can help."

Betty joined them at the table before she asked, "Did you see anyone after you left?"

"I ran into Deputy Granger, but he just asked some general questions that didn't matter. I'm not going to do anything until after the *Alberta* is well on its way."

Addie asked, "What are you going to do, Lynn? What is keeping you here?"

Lynn tried to look away from those piercing dark blue eyes but couldn't escape their grasp.

"Aside from the tasks that my parents requested of me, I hoped that by coming here, I could discover something about myself that I have to know."

"Can you tell me what it is?" Addie asked quietly.

Lynn was suddenly embarrassed to admit his true bloodline. He was sure that Betty had met his natural father and Addie had probably heard all of the tales of the man's malevolence. She'd look at him with fear and disgust and he couldn't bear to see either emotion in her eyes.

"It's not important right now, and I may never find the answer anyway. What is important is that we make all the arrangements to get you to Denver."

Addie nodded, believing that Lynn still held out hope that Dylan Evans was his real father. She wasn't about to initiate that line of conversation if he didn't want to talk about it.

Lynn then reached into his pants pocket and pulled out a thick wad of currency which he set on the table.

"This is to buy your train tickets in Omaha and anything else you might want while you're there. I still have more than enough left because my mother thought she'd be financing the journey of as many as seven women and their children."

Betty stared at the stack of cash and wondered if she'd earned that much in her years satisfying those grunting men.

Without counting the money, she slipped it from the table and pushed it into her dress pocket. The amount was unimportant, but she knew that Lynn wasn't going to let them leave without it and didn't want to waste the time arguing.

"How long will you stay tonight?" Addie asked.

"At least long enough to share your tea, Miss Price," Lynn replied with a smile.

Addie smiled back and asked, "And what if I decide to have eight cups of tea, sir?"

"Then I'd wait until you returned from your third trip to the privy, ma'am."

As Addie laughed, Lynn smiled as he watched her face transform; her eyes dance and her laugh lines appear. He was relieved that the subject of his parentage hadn't resurfaced.

Addie may not have had eight cups of tea, but Lynn still lingered long after their teacups were empty as they talked about the extended Evans family and Betty explained more about the situation in Fort Benton.

Addie also added much more detail about Dan Billingsley, which Lynn was glad to know, but then, he was startled by an innocent remark.

Betty said, "What made it worse for me when Addie told me that Dan Billingsley wanted her to live with him was that I knew she'd not only become a kept woman but would live in Burke Riddell's house."

Lynn gulped before asking, "Which house is it, Betty?"

Addie noticed his discomfort, but her mother simply replied, "It's the big gray house at the corner of the main street and the last cross street going west. I don't know the address."

Lynn just nodded as Betty continued, "He bought the house about three years ago. He and his wife had been living in a smaller house just four houses down from ours."

Eager to change the subject, Lynn asked, "What about the rumors that he murdered his wife?"

"In May, his wife, Wanda, just went missing. Dan said she must have stowed away on a riverboat, but he didn't bother looking for her."

"So, she could be having a good time in St. Louis?"

"No, her body was found about eight miles downriver a few days later by a passing riverboat, which kind of backed up his story."

Lynn nodded, but had to agree with those who believed the rumors that it hadn't been an accident or case of a disenchanted wife.

After another half an hour of less morbid conversation, Lynn knew he had to return and get some sleep. He wasn't going to do much tomorrow during the day other than picking up his laundry, but knew he had to be alert for the dash to the *Alberta* tomorrow night. The story about Dan Billingsley's likely dispatch of his wife only added to his concern.

So, ten minutes after saying goodnight to Betty and Addie, he entered the back door of the hotel and snuck back into his room.

When he finally made it to the bed, he lay there for another hour thinking about what might happen after Addie and her mother were on their way. He was almost certain that Dan Billingsley would suspect that he had something to do with Addie's disappearance, and that might trigger a reaction he had never anticipated when he had arrived.

CHAPTER 6

The next morning, Dan Billingsley sat behind his desk tapping a pencil on the oak surface. He was in a foul mood after the sheriff's visit and then having to spend another night alone in his bed. He'd been eagerly anticipating having Adele fulfill his fantasies, but the unexpected and unwanted arrival of Lynn Evans had delayed that unimaginable pleasure.

He didn't believe that the kid would do anything to jeopardize his cozy and rewarding setup at the bank; at least not for a while. If the sheriff wasn't able to prevent the kid from returning to his father, then Dan had his own escape plan in place. He'd wire the money from his account here to his account in St. Louis, then leave on a riverboat with Adele. He also had a significant amount of cash hidden in his house in the unlikely event that he wouldn't be able to access the account.

There was one other major player in this situation that ensured that nothing would happen soon, even if the kid left to go tell his father that something was amiss. The river traffic would soon end, and the feared Marshal Evans couldn't get there before the spring arrived and the riverboats began sailing again.

Still the mythical qualities that the sheriff had bestowed on Dylan Evans still gave Dan pause in his confidence that he was safe until the weather warmed, and the Missouri flowed freely again in 1874. It would be just like that damned Evans to make the long ride from Colorado, and Dan didn't want to take the risk.

When Walter had passed by his desk a short time ago as he headed to his fancy office, Dan had to avoid asking him if he knew that Evans was in town, leaving off the kid's first name just to watch the horror on the man's face. But he'd held off because he still needed Capshaw. Only the owner of the bank could replace him, and Dan had as much interest to avoid revealing the owner's name as Walter did.

As he continued to rap the pencil on the desk, he'd glance at the door whenever someone entered, hoping that it was Evans who had walked in. At least then he'd know why the kid was here.

———

The kid had slept in, so by the time he rolled out of bed then made a hasty exit through the same back door that had allowed him to make his stealthy trip to see Betty and Addie, he returned to clean up for the day.

After a close and blood-free shave, Lynn dressed warmly in expectation of the morning chill. It was cold enough in his room, so he wouldn't have been surprised to find a few inches of snow outside. Betty had claimed that she'd seen snow as early as late August, which Lynn knew was probably true, but still hard to believe.

With some free time, Lynn figured he'd visit Griffin and talk to Slim for a while before he had his late breakfast. Then he'd go to Dennison's General Store to buy some necessary item before he picked up his clean laundry on the return trip. He didn't expect to be interrogated by the deputy again.

———

Twenty minutes later, Lynn was rubbing Griffin's neck as he asked, "Does the sheriff get along with Dan Billingsley?"

"I ain't sure if you'd call 'em drinking buddies, but I reckon that they scratch the other feller's back."

"That's what I figured. Do you have any idea why the deputy spent so long outside the hotel waiting to talk to me? He didn't exactly interrogate me when he found me, either."

"I saw him out there and I guess the sheriff told him to see where you were."

"Do you have an idea why he'd be interested in me?"

"I did some thinkin' about that, and the only thing that popped into my noggin was the bank. Now, I'm sure that Dan Billingsley knows who owns it and that means that the sheriff does, too. Maybe they reckon you're here to take over."

"I'm only sixteen, Slim. I can't even buy a beer."

Slim snickered before replying, "They'll sell you a bottle of rotgut whiskey around here, Lynn. If I didn't know better, I'd figure they mighta guessed you to be nineteen, but that ain't possible."

"It's not, and I'm sure that they can do the math…although Tex probably can't get past five because he doesn't know he had fingers on both hands."

"Ain't that the truth!" Slim exclaimed with a loud snort.

"Well, I'm going to head over to Dennison's to buy a couple of things and then pick up my laundry."

Then, as Lynn turned, Slim said, "Don't forget that I've got your Winchester in here."

Lynn looked back and said, "I won't," but as he left the barn, he wondered why Slim had felt the need to remind him.

As he headed for the general store, Lynn patted the right side of his coat to make sure the Smith & Wesson was still there. He hadn't fired the pistol in almost a month and knew he wanted to get some target practice before much longer. After Addie and Betty were on their way tomorrow, he'd take Griffin out west and run some .44s through the Winchester and his pistol. He had two full boxes of the rimfire cartridges, and that should be plenty. He still didn't believe that things would rise to the level of gunfire.

As he crossed the street to Dennison's General Store, he glimpsed the sheriff striding towards him, but acted as if he hadn't noticed him.

The sheriff had been waiting outside his office for almost two hours watching the hotel and had seen Lynn enter the livery. He wished he could have overheard the conversation, but figured he'd find out soon enough.

When he saw Evans leave, he stood and timed his pace to converge with the kid's arrival at Dennison's door, and managed a reasonably friendly countenance as he drew closer.

Lynn smiled at him, but as he turned to pass the sheriff to enter the store, Sheriff Martin said, "Son, I haven't seen you around here before. What's your name?"

"Lynn Evans, sir."

"Did you arrive on the riverboat yesterday?"

"Yes, sir."

"Are you going to stay in town for long?"

"I'll probably be heading back to Denver on the next riverboat."

"What brings you to Fort Benton?"

"My parents were here a long time ago and they talked about it a lot, so I asked if I could see it before I went back East to college next summer."

"It's getting kind of late in the year, son."

Lynn grinned and scratched the side of his neck with his right index finger as he replied, "That's my fault, Sheriff. I, um, I spent too much time with my girlfriend and, well, my father thought it was a good time to leave Denver before her parents found out what we were doing."

Paul Martin laughed, then said, "You said your parents were here a long time ago. Your father wouldn't be Dylan Evans; would he?"

"Yes, sir. I'm trying to keep that quiet because he's a famous man down in Denver and I'm trying to be myself. That's why I'm going all the way to Pennsylvania to college. I'd appreciate it if you kept my name quiet. I don't want my father to think I'm taking advantage of his name."

"I can understand that. What's your father do now?"

"He's been a United States Marshal for quite a while. He was assigned to Omaha, then moved to the Denver office."

"Really? That is impressive. Well, if you need any help while you're here, don't hesitate to stop by."

"Thanks, Sheriff, but I'm going to just spend a few days exploring and then catch that riverboat back to Denver."

"Good enough," the sheriff said before turning and heading back down the boardwalk.

Lynn watched him leave and slowly let out his breath. He had really stuck his neck out by breaking the cardinal rule about answering a lawman or a lawyer's question; don't provide any more information than necessary. As soon as he said that he was going to college in Pennsylvania, he realized that he didn't know of a single college in the state. If the sheriff had asked which one, he would have said the University of Pennsylvania and hoped that it was right. If he'd then asked where the campus was located, Lynn would have been in real trouble.

He entered the store and wandered the aisles, not really looking at the stock, but finally bought a pair of heavy fur gloves to augment his leather gloves and a thick woolen scarf.

He paid for the items without spending any time to talk to the young man at the counter, assuming he was one of the original mayor's sons.

Lynn half-expected to find the sheriff or his gorilla-like deputy waiting for him but was relieved to find them absent as he crossed the street to get his clean laundry.

He stopped at the diner for what turned out to be an early lunch rather than a late breakfast before finally returning to his room. He could have spent some time wandering the town or even going to inspect the outside of Dan Billingsley's house; the place where he had been conceived, but he didn't want to bump into the sheriff, deputy or the chief clerk. He didn't want anything to interfere with getting Addie and her mother on the *Alberta.*

————

"What do you think he's going to do after we're gone?" Addie asked before she took a sip of her tea with sugar and condensed milk.

"I don't know, but I'm concerned that he's headed for trouble. Maybe before we get on the boat, he'll tell us the reason that he's here."

"I think I know the answer, Mama. I believe that Lynn suspects that Burke Riddell is his real father and he came to try to find evidence of it."

"You think that Dylan and Gwen would keep that from him for all these years?"

"Maybe they didn't know, Mama. It's likely that they were together soon after he took her away from here, so when she found she was pregnant, she wouldn't know who the baby's father was."

"If that's so, Addie, then how could he hope to find evidence that he is Burke Riddell's son after almost twenty years?"

"I don't know, Mama. Maybe it's a spiritual thing; a sudden revelation if he goes into Mister Billingsley's house."

"Well, when he comes tonight, I don't want you to say anything. I'll ask but in my own way. I'd hate to get him upset."

Addie looked down into her teacup and said, "That's what scares me the most, Mama. What if somehow, he finds his answer and is so upset that he won't return to Denver? I know that I've only known him for a short time, but when I first saw him, I felt a shock race through me. I know he felt it, too. I could see it in his eyes. After that, when we talked, it was as if I already knew him."

"It's very early, sweetheart. After we get to Denver and he returns, you'll be able to spend more time with him to be sure."

Addie smiled at her mother and said, "I'll be waiting for him to return, but I won't be patient."

Betty nodded and took her last sip of tea. She had seen the reaction in each of them and then, after he returned and spent another two hours with her, Betty was amazed at how well they had meshed. She just hoped that Addie wouldn't have her heart broken if he didn't return.

She'd spent so long trying to protect her daughter from the horrors that she knew would be thrust upon her when she became the beautiful young woman she is; but now that those dangers would soon be gone, they were replaced with a very different set of motherly concerns.

———

When the sheriff returned to his office, he didn't say anything to Charlie Red Fox as he strode past the desk and entered his office.

After tossing his hat on his desk, he dropped loudly into his chair and pulled a cigar out of his drawer. After lighting it and blowing a large cloud of blue smoke to the ceiling, he leaned back and thought about what the kid had told him.

Either the boy was a damned good poker player, or he was exactly what he claimed to be. His story had many very believable aspects; the issue with the girlfriend and his desire to break free from the shadow of his famous father being the two most noteworthy. But the sheriff still wasn't ready to buy the whole tale; hook, line and sinker.

But it was a start and there was no rush. He'd have Tex do his rounds a few more times a day and he'd pay some visits to the businesses as he usually did. Just because there was an Evans in town didn't mean he would let any of his clients miss a payment.

He'd head over to visit Dan Billingsley after supper to ask if the kid had shown up at the bank. He didn't believe he had, but it was possible.

Sheriff Martin tried to make a smoke ring, but never could get the hang of it. He blamed his thick moustache for his inability to master the trick but wasn't about to shave it off. He considered it to be his trademark.

————

After he'd written his letters to his parents and to Benji Green, Lynn had tried to do some reading to pass the afternoon but kept having to turn back a page or two after missing a piece of the plot, so he finally closed the book and set it on the nightstand.

With reading no longer a viable waste of time, he pulled his heavy saddlebags over and opened the bag with the ammunition.

He set a box of .44s on the bed and took his gunbelt from the bedpost and began filling the cartridge loops with spare ammunition. He usually left them empty because they could be a nuisance when sitting, but now he figured that he could live with the annoyance to have the extra shots. Once all the loops were filled, he cracked open his Smith & Wesson and filled the last chamber before returning it to his holster.

As he looked at the pistol and its fourteen total rounds of .44 cartridges, he began to question what had driven him to believe it was necessary.

He had no doubt that the sheriff was concerned about his presence; probably because he was worried about Lynn reporting the sheriff's malfeasance to his father. Still, he couldn't imagine the sheriff would do anything as stupid as getting into a gunfight with him over such a tenuous idea. Besides, the sheriff must know that if anything happened, U.S. Marshal Dylan Evans wouldn't accept the sheriff's findings. On the other hand, the deputy was stupid enough to do something like that, but Lynn didn't believe that Tex Granger would do anything at all without the sheriff's direction.

So, why did he load his pistol with the sixth round? Why carry the extra cartridges?

Finally, Lynn shook his head to clear his mind and hung his gunbelt back over the bedpost before returning the box of remaining .44s to his saddlebags.

He then walked to the small desk in the corner and took out another sheet of paper from the saddlebags to write the instructions for Addie and her mother.

As he wrote, he smiled as he realized that's how he thought of them now; not as Mrs. Price and her daughter, but as Addie and her mother.

The instructions were fairly simple:

- Take the *Alberta* to Omaha where they should seek out U.S. Deputy Marshal Benji Green and give him his letter.

- Send a telegram to his mother in Denver letting her know that they were in Omaha and would be coming to visit.

- Either take the train right away or wait if Benji Green and his family are going so you can travel with them.

He'd thought about having them disembark in Yankton to take the train to Omaha, but it wouldn't be that much longer to stay on the boat, and he'd feel better knowing they were being escorted by the entire crew until Benji could look out for them.

When he'd suggested that they wait to travel with the Green family, he recalled how close to derailing his plans to come to Fort Benton after meeting Martha. She was a handsome, intelligent young woman, and so was Libby Perkins, now living in Yankton; but there was no doubt in his mind that Addie was the one. He just hoped that after she'd headed downriver, he'd be able to see her again as Dylan Evans' son.

He set the pencil on the desk and let his focus return to the sheet of paper. There weren't many other things he could add, but when he got to their house after dark, they could spend a few minutes to review the short list and make any necessary modifications. Lynn folded the sheet and set it on top of the two letters before he returned to the bed and stretched out.

With all of his preparations behind him, Lynn felt it was acceptable to let his mind wander back to his new favorite subject – Adele Price. Many times since he returned to his hotel last night, he had relived that first instant when he'd seen her and felt that lightning rip through him. He'd never experienced anything like it in all of the times he'd been with

241

other girls, and the all-too-short amount of time he'd spent with her later that night did nothing to lessen her effect on him.

But he couldn't hope to have what he now considered a normal Evans life until he was convinced that he was an Evans and not a Riddell. He just hoped he'd have his answer soon.

————

"Do you know what is making me so nervous, Mama?" Addie asked.

"Yes, Addie, I understand, and I'm sure that Lynn will be on the next riverboat."

Addie paused before replying, "That's not what has me nervous, Mama; at least not at the moment. The closer we get to sunset I just feel as if Billingsley will appear at the back door and try to take me away. We're so close to leaving, it's as if I'm standing on the gallows trap door watching the hangman as he has his hand on the release lever while hoping for the governor's pardon to arrive."

"I'm sure that he won't come before then, Addie. It's just three hours to sunset and soon we'll be walking with Lynn to the dock."

Addie sighed and said, "Once we're on the boat, then I'll start worrying about Lynn returning to Denver in earnest."

"Can you think of anything we missed?"

"No, Mama. I just want that sun to leave for the day."

————

Dan Billingsley left the bank, still annoyed with the world. The Evans kid hadn't shown up and as far as he knew, Walter didn't even know the boy was here. It was the only pleasant part of his day when he imagined seeing Walter's face when he was introduced to Lynn Evans.

But that introduction would light the fuse to the powder keg that was buried in the bank's ledgers. He knew that Walter, despite his embezzling, was not capable of standing up to scrutiny. As soon as he found out that Evans was here, he'd probably confess, beg forgiveness and point his accusing finger at his chief clerk.

If that happened, Dan would have to depend on the sheriff and that goon of a deputy to eliminate the problem. He could handle Walter, but if things got out of hand with Evans, then he'd have to handle things himself.

As he strode west toward his big house, he glanced south along Oak Street and briefly considered bringing Adele home with him, but it was daylight and he couldn't be seen going there. Then, with the Evans issue still hanging over his head, he doubted if she'd be warming his bed until it was solved.

He decided to pay a visit to the sheriff to ask about the kid's activities. If he hadn't gone to the bank; *what had he been doing all day?*

That same question had just been asked to Tex Granger.

"Not once?" the sheriff asked, "you haven't seen him all day?"

"Nope. You musta seen him last over at Dennison's."

243

"I don't like this one bit. If he's out exploring the town, one of us should have seen him."

"Maybe he took a ride out west. That's what I woulda done if I was him."

"Maybe. I should have checked on his horse, but I was sure I'd see him again after he left Dennison's."

"What did he buy there?"

"Just some gloves and a scarf, or something. Nothing that really stuck out."

They were still talking when Dan Billingsley entered the outer office and without saying a word to Charlie Red Fox, passed down the hallway.

He left the door open, then stopped next to Tex; dwarfed by the enormous man.

"Did you find out anything?" Dan asked.

"I talked to him for a couple of minutes and he said he just came to Fort Benton because his folks talked about it so much and he wanted to see it. He mentioned some girlfriend issue back home and that he was heading off to college next year."

"Do you believe him?"

"I'm not so sure. Either he's a lot better poker player than you'd expect out of a kid his age, or he's telling the truth. He said that he was trying to get out of his famous daddy's shadow, too. It all makes sense, but I really will feel a lot better when he's gone."

"Well, he didn't show up in the bank today, and I'm concerned about how Capshaw will react when he learns that Evans is here. More than likely, he'll break down and start begging for forgiveness."

"If that happens, just let me know right away and I'll take care of it."

"You already have a plan?" Dan asked with raised eyebrows.

"It's not complete, but it'll buy us time. If the kid shows up in the bank, you be there when he's talking to Capshaw. If Walter does what we both expect him to do, then you accuse him of lying. You're better at it than he is. Then you have Evans drag him down here to let me investigate Walter's accusations. You'd come along, of course. That'll get everyone here and we'll see how it plays out."

Dan wasn't satisfied with the 'playing out' aspect of the plan, but it was better than anything he'd come up with.

"Alright, Paul, but I'll have a backup plan ready if this one blows up."

"You do that, and maybe you can get that girl in your house sooner than you figured," the sheriff said as he grinned.

Dan contained his outrage as he calmly replied, "Adele isn't going anywhere and maybe when this Evans surprise is over, I'll let you spend some time with her mother."

Tex snickered loudly, as Dan wheeled and marched away, then looked at his boss's face and stopped.

After the door slammed, Paul Martin snarled, "That fancy bastard is really getting on my nerves. After Evans is handled,

245

one way or the other, I'm going to let Billingsley know who's really in charge around here."

As Tex nodded, the sheriff continued, saying, "I've got enough dirt on him to get him hanged. He won't get a chance to lay a finger on Adele, much less anything else."

Tex didn't know if he should laugh or not, so he played it safe and just continued to nod.

———

Dan reached his house and slammed the door after entering, then threw his coat and hat on the parlor couch as he headed for his office.

Once inside, he walked to the liquor cabinet, grasped a crystal bottle of Kentucky bourbon and a matching glass, then took a seat at his desk.

He was still fuming when he heard footsteps and wished he had closed the door.

"What is it, Mrs. Butterfield?" he asked as he poured the liquor.

"I was just wondering if you were dining at home tonight, Mister Billingsley. I haven't started cooking yet."

"No, you can go home. Thank you," he said without looking up.

Ruth Butterfield could see he was in a foul mood, so she didn't reply before she turned and headed back to the kitchen where she donned her coat and hat, then left the house to make supper for her husband.

Dan took a long sip of the whiskey, then set the glass back onto the desk's dark, polished maple surface. He'd had to hire Mrs. Butterfield after he'd had arranged for his annoying wife's unpleasant departure. She only spent a few hours each day tidying up the place and would cook dinner for him a few times a week, but she was just temporary until he could get Adele Price into the house. He'd come close to ending her employment last week, but then Adele had forced him into this annoying delay.

Now that damned Evans kid was pushing him, and he didn't like it. Mrs. Butterfield's appearance escalated his already seething anger and resentment, but he calmed himself as well as he could, knowing it should only be for a few more days.

He took another sip of his bourbon, then when he set the glass on the desktop, he smiled. This was the same desk that the hated Burke Riddell had used. He may even have been sitting in this chair and having a glass of whiskey as he prepared to go upstairs and have his way with the Evans kid's mother.

He was still smiling as he lifted the glass to his lips again, then froze for a few seconds before lowering it back to the desk, standing and slowly walking out of the office.

As he crossed the carpet in the parlor, he exclaimed, "That's why that kid is here! Of course! He doesn't know who his father is!"

He reached the staircase and trotted quickly up the stairs to the second floor.

He wasn't sure which of the bedrooms Riddell had used, and wasn't sure if it mattered, so he opened the door to the first bedroom and stepped inside.

Dan hadn't spent much time at all on the second floor of the house since he'd bought the place, but now he scrutinized the room as he imagined Riddell brutally taking the sainted Gwendolyn.

As he let his mind work, he understood that to be reasonably sure that he was correct about Lynn Evans' purpose, he'd need to know the kid's birthdate. If he was born after April of '57, then his theory would be so much garbage. But there was that magic month of March that would confirm it.

He wasn't about to mention it to anyone but stored it away as a potential way to get to the kid if he posed a threat. Discovering that your father was a monster like Burke Riddell would be devastating to a boy who grew up believing that his father was a hero.

Dan lingered for another few minutes staring at the bed before he turned, left the room and closed the door behind him.

———

Lynn left his room as the sun neared the horizon to get his supper at Ziggy's Diner. He could have walked another block to the much larger Tucker House restaurant but didn't want to waste the time; he just wanted to fill his stomach.

He hadn't seen the sheriff or Deputy Granger on the way to the diner and hoped that they were satisfied with his story. He'd settled on the University of Pennsylvania and assumed it was in Philadelphia in case the sheriff asked but vowed never to make that mistake again.

As he settled into his seat at the table, he began reviewing all of the errors he'd committed since leaving Denver and was embarrassed that he could have almost filled a page.

After placing his order for the special, which turned out to be meatloaf, he wondered if he was about to make the biggest mistake and not getting on the *Alberta* with Addie. It was too late to change his mind now anyway, but his sense of pending disaster was growing. He simply had no idea of the direction from which it would arrive.

―――――

Lynn left the diner as the sun began to set behind him, still didn't see the sheriff anywhere and headed back to his room to wait for the darkness to take charge.

As he passed the Main Street Saloon, he didn't bother looking through the big glass window, but if he had, he would probably have seen Tex Granger staring back at him.

Tex normally frequented the Nugget and Dust Saloon, down the road, but the boss had stationed him in the Main Street to watch for the Evans kid. So, as he sat at the table near the window with his fourth beer, he was almost startled to see Lynn stroll past the window just eight feet before his eyes.

He quickly tossed the remaining brew down his throat, grabbed his hat and stepped quickly to the batwing doors. He slowed as he exited, then turned to the east to see Lynn walking toward the hotel.

Tex maintained a decent following distance and when Lynn entered the Rangeland, he stopped and waited.

His instructions were reasonably clear this time, so he wanted to be sure that Evans was going back to his room for the night. He expected that the kid was almost there, so he strode the rest of the way to the front of the hotel, then peeked through the window.

He saw the kid walking down the hallway, open his room's door and go inside. Satisfied that he'd done right this time, he smiled, then turned and headed west again. The boss had told him to only bother him if Evans did something out of the ordinary and going back to his room was ordinary.

———

Lynn hadn't seen Tex, but he knew that the deputy had been following him. Deputy Granger may have been following at what he considered a decent distance, and that may have been true if it had been a normal-sized man, or if he wasn't following a young man who had a lifetime of training by one of the best lawmen in the country. But Lynn's awareness and the loud thumps made by the big man's boots on the tired wood of the boardwalk had alerted Lynn to Tex's presence just two steps after the deputy had left the saloon.

As he turned to enter his room, Lynn had taken one quick glance at the door to see if the deputy had followed him inside and was relieved that he hadn't deposited himself in the lobby.

Lynn was still planning on using the back door, but if the deputy was sitting in the lobby, he'd probably spot Lynn leaving his room. That would require a window exit which posed many more risks.

———

So, just an hour later, Lynn stuck his head into the hallway and stared at the visible part of the lobby to be sure that the big deputy hadn't returned before sneaking out, closing his door quietly, then slowly walking to the back door.

He scanned the dark surroundings before stepping into the cool night air and began walking west.

Lynn was trying to concentrate on his environment as he quickly made his way along the alley but had to fight off the intruding thoughts about Addie. This would be the worst time to make his next mistake; he needed to get them safely and quietly onto the *Alberta*.

He stopped before the main street as he listened to the noises coming from the three saloons, then just calmly cut across the street and entered a side alley.

It seemed as if the walk took two hours, but he knew he'd only left the hotel ten minutes earlier when he arrived at the back door of the Price house.

He rapped once on the door and it was immediately yanked open. He didn't see who had opened it as he rushed inside and heard it close behind him.

He was reaching to take off his hat when Addie said, "I'm glad that you made it, Lynn."

He smiled as he removed his hat, looked into her dark blue eyes and replied, "I wish it was for a different reason, Addie."

"Me, too."

Betty then asked, "How long before we leave?"

"Not long. I just want to go over my short instructions and see if we need to modify them."

"We're all packed, so we can leave whenever you're ready."

Lynn smiled at Betty and replied, "That's good. Let's sit down and I'll explain what I think you should do."

As they headed for the kitchen table, Addie asked, "Do you mean when we get to Denver?"

"Before then," he replied as he sat down.

Addie took the seat closest to Lynn as her mother sat across the table from him.

Lynn pulled the two letters and instruction sheet from his jacket pocket and set them on the table.

"One of the letters is for my father and the second is to the deputy marshal in Omaha that will be joining him soon."

He paused for any questions, but when none were asked, he said, "After you arrive in Omaha, see U.S. Deputy Marshal Benji Green. He should still be there, but he's probably already preparing to move to Denver with his family, so you may want to travel with them. When you arrive, send a telegram to my mother to let her know that you're coming. I wrote the family's address on the bottom. It's pretty easy to remember; the Double EE ranch outside of Denver."

"How long will it take for us to get there?" Betty asked.

"It depends on the boat, the weather and the river's current, so I'd guess less than two weeks. The downriver trip is much shorter because the boat isn't fighting the current. I only discovered when I was on the *Alberta* coming up here that the railroad goes all the way to Yankton now, so if you want to get off there, you can take the train to Omaha and save a few days."

"We'll think about it on the way."

Lynn nodded as he slid the sheet and letters to Betty, who slipped them into her large plaid purse.

Addie then asked, "Can we just talk for a little while before we leave?"

"I had planned on it," Lynn replied, "I want the road traffic to be almost gone anyway."

Addie asked, "What are you going to do after we leave?"

"I have to do another job that my parents asked of me and then I need to spend some time here to answer some personal questions."

Addie then glanced at her mother, who said, "Addie asked me a question this morning, so I was curious. She asked me if she was much older than you, and I couldn't answer. You look older, but that would be impossible. May I ask your birthdate?"

Lynn looked at Addie, smiled and said, "You go first, Addie, then I'll give you mine."

Addie smiled back before saying, "March 11th, 1857."

Lynn then asked, "What time?"

Addie looked back to her mother, who answered, "It was 4:10 in the morning."

After Addie returned her dark blue eyes to Lynn, he said, "Then your mother was right, Addie; I am older than you are. I'm exactly six days, thirteen hours and forty minutes older."

Addie laughed then said, "You did that calculation quickly, sir."

"I've always had a head for numbers, but I surely don't have any ambitions to be a banker or an accountant."

Even as she laughed, Addie had confirmed her theory for Lynn's trip to Fort Benton; he was trying to learn the identity of the man who had helped to create him. She looked into his smiling brown eyes and wished she could tell him now that it didn't matter and ask him to join her on the riverboat, but knew it wasn't her place to tell him. It was his question to answer and his decision about how to deal with what he found.

For the next hour, they talked about what to expect on the downriver journey and what they would find in Omaha and Denver.

When Addie asked about his family, Lynn felt as if they were all in the room watching him, so he let the warmth fill him as he answered.

"You know about my parents, but I haven't talked about my brothers, sister or cousins much, so I'll tell you about them now."

For the next twenty minutes, he described each of his younger brothers and sisters after starting with Alwen, who was just a month younger than he and Addie. He accurately described each sibling's appearance and without hesitation, told Addie that each of the boys, including Alwen, who was his deceased Uncle Colwyn's son, was more handsome than he was.

He didn't explain that it was because they were all true Evans while he was almost an imposter, but it was how he had thought of himself, especially after that night with Ryan when he'd had his suspicions confirmed.

Addie had listened as Lynn extolled both the physical and character virtues of his brothers and cousins and wondered why he thought that way. She hadn't met any of them, of course, but doubted any could match what she saw in Lynn.

LYNN'S SEARCH

She would have asked him, but time was running against them, and just as Lynn finished talking about Kyle and his family in Denver, he said, "I think that we should go now."

Betty rose and replied, "I'm ready."

Lynn and Addie both stood, then he pulled on his hat, stepped to the back of the kitchen and grabbed the two heavy bags while Addie and Betty donned their coats and hats.

After they picked up their smaller bags, Betty walked to blow out the only lamp when Lynn stopped her, saying, "Let it burn itself out, Betty. That way if anyone looks at the house, they'll think you're still here."

"It's pretty low on kerosene anyway, so it won't be long," Betty replied before walking to the door.

————

As they walked silently through the dark back alleys, Lynn had Addie at his right and her mother on his left. He could sense their tension as they headed for the docks and with each step felt the urge to stay on board the *Alberta* with them.

The only sounds came from the saloons, but they didn't see the light coming from the establishments as they passed.

It was only when Lynn could see the outline of the *Alberta* against the night sky that he relaxed.

"There's your boat," he said to Addie in a low voice.

Addie just nodded as she looked over at Lynn, wishing she could convince him to come with them. She had a feeling that once she was in her cabin, she'd never see Lynn's face again.

255

They stepped onto the thick wood of the dock and Lynn could see shadowy figures on the deck.

"There's your welcoming committee," Lynn said as they approached the gangplank.

"That you, Lynn?" a voice asked from the *Alberta*.

"It's me, Abner."

When they reached the gangplank, Lynn let Abner take Betty's hand to cross onto the deck before another deckhand helped Addie across. Lynn followed with his heavy bags and stopped once he was on the deck.

"We'll head up the port staircase," Abner said as he took Betty's bag.

The other deckhand, who he'd finally recognized as Jimmy Tubman, one of the stokers, took Addie's bag and they all headed for the stairs.

Once on the upper deck, Abner and Jimmy brought the bags into cabin thirteen, then waved and headed back down the steps before Lynn lugged the other two bags into cabin fourteen.

After he dropped them onto the floor and stepped back outside, Betty asked, "Which one is ours?"

"They're both yours. How you use them is up to you. Just stay inside until the boat is away from the docks. The captain and the rest of the crew know you're here, so they'll bring you breakfast."

Betty then stepped forward, hugged Lynn, kissed him on the cheek and said, "Thank you for all you've done for us, Lynn. I'll tell your parents what a fine son they have."

"They have a many fine sons and daughters, Betty."

She nodded and stepped back to let Addie say her farewell to Lynn.

As much as each of them wished they didn't have to say goodbye, each understood that it was necessary.

Lynn turned to Addie, wrapped his arms around her and simply whispered, "Goodbye, Addie."

Addie felt his warmth through their heavy coats and whispered, "Please return to Denver, Lynn. Whatever you find here won't matter to me."

Lynn was stunned by her soft declaration but didn't ask for any clarification as he looked into her dark blue eyes.

Instead, he simply nodded, then stepped back, smiled at her and then turned to her mother and said, "Goodbye, Betty."

"Goodbye, Lynn," she replied before he took one last glance at Addie, turned and headed for the port stairway.

As he stepped down to the main deck, he assumed that Addie had realized his reason for staying in Fort Benton after her mother had asked for his birthdate. It was no longer a secret and he could have told her before they left, but he thought that she may say something close to what she'd just told him. If she had, then it would make his decision to stay even more difficult.

He reached the main deck, waved to Abner and Jimmy and hustled across the gangplank.

_____

After entering cabin thirteen and closing the door, Betty sat on one bunk and Addie took the other; the same bunk that Lynn had used since leaving Omaha.

"May I ask what you told him?" she asked.

"I just asked him to return to Denver and I didn't care what he discovered here."

Betty knew that it would only hurt Addie if she continued on the topic, so she said, "Light the lamp and we'll start unpacking. I think it's better if we do as Lynn suggested both stay in this cabin."

"So, do I," Addie said as she stood to light the lamp.

_____

Lynn made it back to his room without anyone noticing, and after closing the door, removed his hat and coat, then hung his gunbelt over the bedpost.

He stripped to his skivvies, then slipped beneath the blankets. It was probably only around nine o'clock or so, but he wanted to sleep until after the _Alberta_ sailed. He knew he couldn't see Addie again and stay in Fort Benton. He just hoped that he would see her again in Denver, but still had no idea how he could destroy that niggling demon that drove him to Fort Benton.

CHAPTER 7

The sun hadn't quite enveloped the landscape with its harsh rays when Captain Clyde leaned over to the speaking tube and shouted, "Ahead one third!"

After hearing his order repeated, he turned to the pilot and said, "Get us into the river, Pete."

Pete Gilliard nodded and as he felt the sternwheels begin to push the *Alberta* away from the wharf, he spun the big spoked wheel a full turn clockwise before catching it again.

The bow pushed aside the waters of the Missouri and the sternwheeler pulled away from Fort Benton to begin its long journey back to St. Louis.

———

Addie felt the boat shudder and Betty said, "I haven't felt that since I arrived on the *Providence* almost eighteen years ago."

Addie finished her coffee and set the cup on the tray as she replied, "Captain Clyde said that there was only one more riverboat coming here this year. He said that if Lynn didn't find his answer before it left, he'd be stuck there until spring."

"He may never find it, Addie. I don't know how he'd ever really know which of them is his real father."

"That's why I had to tell him that it didn't matter to me."

Betty picked up one of the four books that they'd found in the cabin and said, "Well, at least we'll have something to read. Some kind soul left them behind."

"I think this was Lynn's cabin, Mama."

"Did the captain tell you that?"

"No, but I can almost feel him here and these books are all titles that I wanted to read; almost as if he knew that I'd need them."

"He didn't even know we existed when he left the boat, Addie."

"I know."

————

Even as the *Alberta* was beginning its downriver journey, six hundred miles away, the *Princess of Ohio*, was entering the river to continue its battle with the Missouri's current as it headed northwest.

————

Lynn had heard the *Alberta's* steam whistle announcing its departure an hour earlier, but he had only made a quick dash to the privy since then.

As much as he wanted to start his search for the answer to the question that had driven him to Fort Benton, he wanted to take some time to let the riverboat get further down the Missouri. He'd seen the remains of three sunken riverboats on his long journey upriver and wanted the *Alberta* to be far enough downriver so if it foundered, the passengers and crew wouldn't return to Fort Benton.

He'd already planned on getting in some target practice and decided that it would be a good chance to let Griffin run too. His last request from his parents about the bank would have to wait until tomorrow if not the day after. After all he'd heard about the chief clerk, he was concerned that seeing Mister Capshaw might create a stir, and he wasn't ready for it.

After having breakfast, he headed to the livery where he saddled Griffin while Slim went to his room for the Winchester.

He really wanted to tell Slim about Addie and Betty's departure, but didn't want it slipping out, even accidentally, so he picked a different topic; one that he'd neglected earlier.

"What do you think of Mister Capshaw?" Lynn asked as he tossed his saddle over Griffin's back.

"I don't talk to him much, but he's okay."

"Is he married? Does he have a family?"

"His wife, Prudence, died havin' a their third about six years ago, then his other two young'uns fell to the measles the year after that. He ain't remarried."

"How does he get along with Mister Billingsley?"

"He's the one who hired him, and they seemed to get along okay for a while, but I don't reckon they're exactly pals anymore. That Billingsley acts like he's the boss."

Lynn nodded, then stepped into the saddle and said, "I'll be back in a while, Slim. I'm going to ride west and do some target practice."

"Good luck with this wind, Lynn," Slim replied as he looked up with a grin.

Lynn waved and walked Griffin out of the big barn, turned west and set him to a medium trot.

As he rode past the jail, he noticed Tex Granger sitting on the bench outside the door, so he waved.

Tex returned his wave and then stood as he watched Lynn heading out of town.

After he saw the kid pass the last house, he turned and entered the office.

Once outside the town, Lynn let Griffin loose.

The tall mahogany gelding shot along the roadway that continued all the way to the Pacific Ocean leaving a large cloud of dust in his wake.

Lynn forgot about his concerns as exhilaration overtook him feeling Griffin's power beneath him and the already strong west wind rush past his face.

After a mile he slowed Griffin in stages until he was moving at a slow trot. He could hear the gelding's heavy breathing and realized that he'd neglected his friend for far too long.

Except for the strong westerly wind, it was almost like an early summer day with temperatures already approaching seventy.

He glanced back to the town to see if anyone had followed him but found it clear of anyone leaving Fort Benton. Once he knew he was alone, he kept Griffin at the same comfortable pace as he hunted for his temporary shooting range.

———

LYNN'S SEARCH

Even as Lynn was scanning the east for trailers, Addie was looking west from the upper aft deck of the *Alberta*. The boat had just passed through the first of the treacherous rapids and would soon enter the second, more violent stretch of angry water. Addie decided to take advantage of the calm river in between, anxious to be free to leave their cabin at last.

"This is going to be an awkward trip. We know all of the other passengers, and almost all of them are men," she said.

Her mother replied, "No more uncomfortable when we were in Fort Benton, Addie. At least we have the crew as a shield. They won't bother me, but I'm concerned about you."

"I'm all right, Mama," she replied with a smile, "the cargo master said he's passing the word among the passengers that I'm Dylan Evans' future daughter-in-law."

Betty turned to look at Addie but held her tongue, hoping that Addie wasn't getting too far ahead of herself. As much as she hoped that Addie would realize her new dream, her own dreadful experiences had made her more pessimistic about life.

―――――

Her prospective father-in-law was sitting in the main office with his deputies, including his brother.

"Just in case some of you boys have your heads buried in dark places and haven't noticed, I've been busy recruiting a new member of our little family of lawmen. He's not some youngster with fire in his eyes and a lump of coal in his skull; he's an experienced lawman who is known quite well by some of you.

263

"Benji Green should be telling his boss sometime today or tomorrow that he's leaving Omaha to come here. I'm sure that Marshal Edgar Claggett, our esteemed colleague, will provide Benji with a resounding sendoff."

Thom Smythe laughed before exclaiming, "Unless Benji gives him a resounding kick in the butt first!"

"When is he coming, boss?" Deputy Marshal Boris Barkov asked.

"He thinks they'll be leaving by the twentieth of the month."

Pete Towers then asked, "Do you want any of us to go up there and give him a hand?"

"No need, Pete. Al and Garth have already volunteered to take the train to Omaha for some reason."

"Just trying to get away to have a good time where nobody knows who their daddy is?" Jesse Vandenberg asked with a grin.

"I can understand how you might think that way, seeing as how you're the closest one in this room to his wild teenage years, Jesse. I think the real reason is that they want to go back to see some of their Omaha friends."

Bryn said, "Female as well as male, I assume. Isn't Martha Green about the same age as Lynn and Alwen?"

"A bit younger, but when we lived in Omaha, neither of them paid much attention to her."

"Things change, Marshal," Bryn said with a slight smile.

"I just wish I knew what is going on in Fort Benton. I guess all we can do is wait for another telegram or maybe a letter."

Thom said, "He's gotta get out of there soon, boss. There aren't as many riverboats heading up that way anymore."

"I keep telling Gwen that all parents have to face this sooner or later, but I'll admit that even I wish it was later and under different circumstances."

"I don't think you have anything to worry about, boss. You've been training that boy since he was in diapers and all he's doing is checking the place out."

"I know, Thom, but not knowing what's going on eight hundred miles away is frustrating. All we can do is trust that all he'll do is shake a few hands, then get on the last steamboat leaving Fort Benton."

Bryn nodded, but understood the reason for his brother's concerns; and it wasn't getting rid of the bank. Each of the adults in the family realized that there was a chance that Lynn would never return if he didn't find the answer he sought.

———

"He's out west target shootin'," Tex said.

"That's all right; it's just something to keep him busy. I'm still convinced that he's really here for an innocent visit."

"Are you gonna talk to him again, boss?"

"I will, but not today. If I start pestering him, he'll get suspicious."

"Did you want me to go talk to Slim? He spent a long time in there getting his horse."

"I'll go and talk to him in a little while. I want to ask my questions in a way that won't make him think that I'm interested in the kid."

Tex nodded in agreement, realizing that it was better this way.

————

As Lynn slid his Winchester into its scabbard, he was satisfied with the last six rounds he'd fired. It had taken him two shots to adjust to the new lower altitude before he began putting his bullets where he wanted them to go. He didn't want to use too many of his cartridges, even though he still didn't believe that he'd need them. It was another of his father's axioms; always assume that you'll need more ammunition because it doesn't do any good to wish for it when you're empty.

He pulled his Smith & Wesson Model 3's hammer loop and faced his target about sixty feet away. Pistol shooting was a very different method from his rifle technique. He'd learned how to balance his timing and accuracy rather than to rush and miss.

Once he'd settled on his target, an innocent Ponderosa pine, he suddenly drew his pistol, cocking the hammer as he brought it level, then let the muzzle steady for just a fraction of a second before firing.

He quickly slid the hammer back and squeezed the trigger a second time and then repeated the action once more. Each shot had that small delay to let the pistol steady on the target.

LYNN'S SEARCH

As the gunsmoke began to waft away in the strong wind, Lynn walked to the tree and was gratified with the pattern of new holes in the trunk.

He slipped the pistol back into his holster, then walked back to Griffin to get his Winchester and cleaning kit to remove the corrosive residue as quickly as possible.

In the bank, Dan Billingsley was reviewing the receipts from yesterday's deposits, withdrawals and loan payments and matching them to the ledger entries but wouldn't have even noticed an egregious mistake. He simply didn't like having to depend on the sheriff to deal with the Evans kid. He'd been in town a couple of days yet hadn't set a toe into the bank. He simply couldn't understand a different reason for his arrival, but the sheriff hadn't discovered his true purpose yet.

What was infuriating was that he knew he couldn't do anything about it. The sheriff's caution to Dan about taking care of the kid was very real and he couldn't see a different way out of the dilemma.

He then glanced down the short hallway to Walter Capshaw's office and wished he could just march into that room and tell him that Evans was here and wanted to see the books. He knew it would ignite the fuse and force the sheriff to act, but there was also the chance that the kid really wasn't here about the bank at all. It had been so long that maybe Dylan Evans had forgotten all about it.

It was just one more frustration to add to his growing list. *When would the kid do something?*

Sheriff Martin left the jail and glanced west to make sure that Evans wasn't returning yet and after seeing the empty roadway, headed east along the boardwalk.

Slim was lugging a heavy sack of oats from the backroom storage area when he spotted the sheriff entering the gaping doors and immediately assumed that he was here to ask about Lynn Evans. The sheriff used Ralph Thompkins' livery and only visited his when he wanted something. He never understood why the sheriff hadn't asked him for any under-the-table payments for added protection and knew that Dennison didn't have to pay anything either, but most of the other merchants did.

"Morning, Slim," Sheriff Martin said affably as he stepped across the barn floor.

Slim set the bag on the floor and replied, "Mornin', Sheriff. What can I do for ya?"

"I'm thinking of moving Lucky out of Ralph's livery and was wondering if you had room for him."

"Sure thing, Sheriff. I've got a couple of open stalls for regular customers."

"That's great. I thought you might have been full up because after the Evans boy showed up. That's a mighty fine animal he's riding."

"Yes, sir, he sure is. He said his pa gave it to him. You know who his pa is; don't ya?"

"Of course, I do, Slim. It's my job to know those things. I can even tell you that he's out west of town taking some target practice right now."

"That's what he's doin', Sheriff. He sure seems like a right nice boy."

"I agree with you, Slim. I talked to him for a few minutes yesterday and I thought he was really polite. I think he gets it from his father. I never met the man, of course, but from what the folks say, he was a regular hero."

"He wasn't some big high-fallutin' feller tryin' to make a name for himself. He was a real hero; a man who just wanted to do the right thing."

"Maybe the boy is the same way. Maybe he's here to set things right. What do you think?"

Slim grinned and replied, "Nah. He's just here to look around where his folks got together, but he's kinda disappointed. He told me it wasn't what he figured to find and was gonna head out on the next riverboat."

"That's kind of sad; isn't it, Slim? Imagine coming all this way and finding nothing but a regular town with regular, boring folks."

"I reckon we all get disappointed sooner or later."

"I'll drink to that, Slim," the sheriff replied before adding, "Well, I've got to get back to the office. I'll let you know about Lucky."

"See you around, Sheriff," Slim said before lifting the bag of oats from the floor.

As he watched the sheriff leave, Slim smiled. He didn't know what was worrying the sheriff, but he was none the wiser after his visit. He didn't expect to see the sheriff's gelding anytime soon, either.

———

Sheriff Martin was already behind his desk when Lynn entered Fort Benton with his clean and reloaded guns. As he passed Dan Billingsley's house, he slowed Griffin to study the structure, knowing who had resided there more than seventeen years ago.

Finally, he pulled his gelding to a stop on the west side of the house, knowing it was close to the spot where Joseph Walking Bear had plunged his knife into his natural father.

He knew which window was in his mother's bedroom and it was that window that drew his focus. His father had told him the story in great detail; how he'd seen that one room illuminated when he had gone to the house in the fading light. The window was no different than the others on the second floor as he looked at the house; but knowing what had happened behind that glass sent a shiver up his spine.

He stayed mesmerized by the window for almost a minute before he finally yanked his eyes from the house and nudged Griffin to a walk. Even though he'd seen the house on that first day and hadn't given it any notice, associating that house and that particular room with the long-ago events had an enormous impact on him.

Deep inside his soul, he was suddenly certain that his answer was waiting for him not only in that house; but in that room. He couldn't imagine the circumstances that could possibly get him into the house, but he was convinced that was where he would finally discover if there was any Burke Riddell hidden deep within him.

As he passed by the bank, Lynn didn't give it a second thought. After what he'd experienced as he stared at that window, the bank sale meant nothing. He would do as his parents asked, but only after he'd found his answer.

When he reached the livery, he dismounted and led Griffin inside where he spotted Slim leaning against a stall sideboard just looking at him.

"How did your shootin' go?" he asked as he stood.

"It took a couple of rounds to adjust to the altitude, but after that it was good."

As he led his gelding into his stall, Slim walked behind him and said, "The sheriff paid me a visit when you were out there."

Lynn began stripping Griffin and asked, "Can I guess that he asked you about me?"

"Yep. He kinda beat around the bush a bit, but I reckoned as soon as I saw him walkin' through those doors what he was really wantin' to know."

Lynn hung the bridle on a peg, looked at the liveryman and just let Slim continue.

"It sounds like the sheriff can't figure out why you're here and reckoned that I might have an idea. I told him you were just visitin' on account of your folks bein' here and you were kinda disappointed 'cause you didn't find much. I even told him that you was headin' out of here soon."

"That's not far from the truth, Slim," Lynn replied as he slipped the Winchester free.

"I don't wanna know if you got another reason, Lynn. I could make a slip and get him mad at ya."

Lynn stopped unsaddling Griffin, then turned to Slim and said, "To be honest, Slim, I'm not sure that I'll find what I'm looking for anyway. But I can tell you that it doesn't involve the sheriff and it's just not important to anyone but me."

"Well, don't tell me any more about it. We can talk about your horse, though."

Lynn grinned, then as he resumed unsaddling Griffin, began a very comfortable conversation about his equine friend.

———

"What did Slim say, boss?" Tex asked.

"About the same thing the kid told me. He even said that Evans mentioned that he was leaving soon because he was disappointed."

"So, we ain't gonna do nothin'?"

"That's the idea. If he just wanders around and then gets on that riverboat that's arriving next week, then we let him go. In a way, that's the best thing that could happen because he'll get back to his father and tell him that Fort Benton is just a boring town."

Tex chuckled as he smiled at his boss. Just waiting was a good thing.

———

"Now I don't want you two to go anywhere outside of Omaha," Gwen said as she sat before Alwen and Garth.

"Where else would we go, Mom?" Garth asked.

"I don't want you to visit the Mitchells or any of my sisters because all that might do is cause trouble."

Alwen asked, "Why would seeing our aunts and cousins be a problem, Mom?"

Gwen sighed then replied, "Maybe not the kind of trouble that Lynn found after visiting the Mitchell farm, but I think it might cause a stir."

Bethan was sitting beside her mother on the couch and was more than mildly annoyed that she hadn't been allowed to go along. She was fourteen; for God's sake! She was also at least as proficient with a Winchester or a pistol as either of her older brothers. She bristled at being treated like a girl, even though she did admit to certain advantages to her sex. Her mother had instructed her well in how to manipulate the human male without appearing to be a domineering witch.

Bethan was very much a Western young woman. There was little on the ranch that she couldn't do, and even at fourteen, had already attracted the attention of many of the boys in school. But as each of them became better acquainted with her, Bethan's confidence and honesty invariably drove them away.

At first, Bethan had been stung by their reaction and confided in her mother. Gwen had not only soothed her wounds but had reinforced Bethan's determination to stay true to herself. She'd explained to her daughter that if a boy expected her to be more genteel or subservient, then he wasn't worth spending any time with anyway. The clinching point in her advice was when she pointed to Bethan's father and her two Evans uncles. None of them would have tolerated a wife who was nothing more than a sweet house mistress.

Now, as she listened to her mother warn her brothers about their behavior when they arrived in Omaha, she hoped that when she was sixteen, she would be able to go off on her own adventure.

———

As the day ended, the *Alberta* was docked at a settlement almost eighty miles downriver and Addie and Betty were having dinner by themselves at a small table. Obviously, the word about who would be waiting for them when they reached their destination had made its impact on the other passengers.

———

Four hundred and eighty miles downstream, the *Princess of Ohio* was also docked and most of the crew were in Mandan as the engineer worked to repair a problem with the boiler. It wasn't serious, but he knew that the captain didn't want to lose a day on their already tight schedule.

———

Lynn had settled in for the night and felt isolated and almost useless as he lay on his bed. He felt as if walls were closing in around him and there wasn't a door to let him escape. He didn't know what the sheriff was doing that made him so suspicious but assumed that his interest was because Lynn's father had jurisdiction anywhere in the county, which included the sheriff's domain. Lynn thought he'd assuaged the sheriff's concerns after their talk, but obviously he hadn't.

He couldn't tell the sheriff that he didn't care about the lawman's illegal activities because that would probably send him floating down the river like Mrs. Billingsley.

LYNN'S SEARCH

After a lot of thought, Lynn finally decided that all he could do was to keep going as he had today until a few more days before the *Princess of Ohio* arrived. Then he'd quickly take care of the bank issue, get on the boat and head back, even if his question remained unanswered.

―――――

So, the next morning, Lynn began following a boring, time-consuming routine to put the sheriff at ease; not realizing that his decision to keep things calm would have no effect whatsoever on the firestorm that would soon be ignited; an inferno that would be sparked by two totally separate incidents.

―――――

That first routine day, Thursday, the 2nd of October, passed without incident or any significant changes other than growing frustration for the sheriff and Dan Billingsley.

The *Alberta* continued her downriver path while the *Princess of Ohio* churned its way upriver but were still hundreds of miles apart when they had to dock.

Lynn had another day of target practice and done more exploring around the town but not much else.

In Denver, Garth and Alwen were preparing to leave on tomorrow morning's train to Omaha.

As Lynn slipped into his bed that night and Addie and Betty rested in cabin thirteen on the *Alberta*, Dan Billingsley lay on his bed seething while Sheriff Martin sat at the bar at the Main Street Saloon having a beer.

No one expected anything different to happen on Friday, but the next day would be anything but routine.

CHAPTER 8

Friday, October 3, 1873

The *Princess of Ohio* left Mandan just after sunrise and by the time Lynn was walking to the diner for breakfast, she was already forty-five miles upriver.

The *Alberta* had also gotten underway when the sun broke over the horizon and had pushed sixty miles further south thanks to the following current.

Lynn had stopped by Dennison's and bought two more boxes of .44s for his Winchester and pistol before heading out for his target practice.

It was midafternoon when the first spark ignited the chain of events when the engineer on the *Princess of Ohio* noticed that his boiler's pressure was still rising. He glanced at the governor's relief valve, saw that it was still spraying clouds of steam and couldn't understand why the pressure was going up.

He picked up a small sledge and began to rap different valves and connections, then would check the gauge to see if it had at least steadied, but it kept nudging ever higher. It wasn't in the danger zone yet, but he knew that he had to stop it soon or shut the engine down.

The sternwheeler was making good speed as it pushed aside the muddy waters of the Missouri River, and as much as he hated to slow the boat down, he had to let the captain know.

He opened the speaking tube and shouted, "Captain, we're building up too much pressure! I'm going to have to slow the engine!"

He leaned closer to the tube to hear the captain's reply over the pounding cacophony of the steam engine and even as he reached for the throttle to bring the RPMs down, he heard the captain's question.

"Is it in the danger zone yet?"

The engineer yelled back honestly, "No, sir. Not yet, but it's climbing fast!"

The engineer blanched when he heard, "If it hits the red, slow it down, but not until then."

He slapped the cover over the tube then turned looked at his stokers and shouted, "You boys get out of here! I'll see if I can figure out why it's building pressure and if I can fix it, then I'll come and get you."

"Just slow her down, Ed!" Lenny Jefferson yelled.

"I'm not the captain!" he shouted back, then as the stokers headed out of the engine room, glanced once more at the terrifying needle as it quivered ever higher.

He knew the odds weren't good that he'd find the reason for the problem, but it was his engine and he had to try to fix it.

Lenny and Don Jones had barely reached the main deck when the boiler exploded.

The entire stern of the *Princess* was ripped apart sending debris flying hundreds of feet in all directions.

Within seconds, shocked and horrified passengers and crews scattered across the foredeck as whatever remained of the *Princess of Ohio* began to slip beneath the water.

On the land, the massive detonation had only been heard by assorted critters and Sioux as the nearest settlement was forty miles away.

Within ten minutes, all that remained of the riverboat was a section of the bow that had been shoved into the western shoreline by the blast and one of the two smokestacks that had somehow remained sticking upright out of the river, almost acting as a grave marker.

The surviving eleven crewmembers and eighteen passengers had made it to shore, but many were injured and burned.

Within an hour, the healthier survivors had managed to salvage enough supplies to keep them alive for a few days, but they all knew that their boat was the last one that would make the journey that year and they were stranded in Lakota Sioux land.

Their only hope lay in the expected arrival of the *Alberta*, which the first officer, the highest-ranking crewmember, had told everyone should have left Fort Benton a few days earlier.

———

The *Alberta* was still more than two hundred miles north of the site of the wreck and would make one more stop before they reached the survivors.

———

As the drama on the Missouri River unfolded, a much different fuse was lit in the Bank of Fort Benton later that afternoon.

Dan Billingsley was at his desk, reviewing a loan application when he heard someone clear his throat in front of him.

He looked up, saw Harry Feeley looking down at him and snapped, "What do you want, Feeley?"

"You said to let you know about any overdue rent payments, Mister Billingsley. This one is only a couple of days late, but I thought you should know," he replied as he held out a small notepaper.

Dan was about to tell him to take care of it himself, when he just snatched the paper from his clerk's hand and said, "Go back to your cage, Feeley."

Harry Feeley wasn't about to spend another second near Dan Billingsley, especially when he knew the importance of that account. It seemed that everyone knew about the chief cashier's plan to keep Adele Price as his personal whore, but Dan still seemed to believe that it was a secret.

Dan tossed the loan application into the flat box on his desktop and looked at the note.

He maintained his outward decorum, but as soon as he saw the name, he was enraged. He assumed that Beatrice Price must have believed that she was no longer obligated to pay her rent despite the fact that her daughter was still living with her and not him.

He slowly stood, then with measured dignity, took his hat and overcoat from the nearby coat rack, then walked across the bank's lobby and was pulling his hat on as he stepped outside.

He dropped his placid façade as he marched along the boardwalk. He'd been denied his pleasure by that damned Evans' arrival and now that woman had the gall to act as if he had to pay her rent. Dan was determined to let her know that the rent was due and maybe, while he was in the house, he'd just show Adele what to expect when she moved into his place.

————

Dan was furtively glancing about him as he made his way through the back alleys heading to the Price house. Ironically, he was following almost exactly the same path that Lynn had taken just a few nights before when he had escorted them to the docks.

He was still seething as he stepped onto the back porch, and after making sure that no one was looking, pounded on the kitchen door.

His right shoe was tapping on the dry wooden surface as he waited for either Beatrice or Adele to open the door. After a minute, he banged even louder on the pine surface as his fury engulfed him.

He knew they had to be inside and were probably trying to hide from him, and as they were just renters anyway, he finally just opened the door and stepped inside.

"Get out here, Mrs. Price, and bring Adele with you!" he shouted as he crossed the kitchen floor.

He passed into the hallway, then began searching the rooms.

He was opening and slamming doors as he found each one vacant, and it wasn't until he reached Adele's bedroom that the reason that the rent hadn't been paid struck him.

Dan entered the bedroom and noticed the open, empty drawer then walked to the closet and noticed it was devoid of clothing as well.

"Son of a bitch!' he swore under his breath, "*Where the hell did you two go?*"

He turned and stormed out of the room, down the hallway and quickly exited the house before he stopped in the back alley and tried to calm down. *Where could they have gone?* He knew that Beatrice had no friends after she began taking paying customers, and once she was diseased, not even the most deprived man would take her in. If it was just Adele who was missing, at least he could understand it; *but both of them?*

He started to head to the bank, then realized that it would close soon, so he changed his direction. He needed to ask the sheriff if he'd heard anything about Adele.

————

Lynn was riding back into town when Dan Billingsley popped out of the back alley and turned west onto the boardwalk. As passed the jail, he wasn't paying particular attention to the banker, and as he'd never met the man shouldn't have even given him a second look. But it was the fancy overcoat and bowler hat that drew his interest, so he just turned to give him a quick onceover and found the man's eyes trained on him.

Dan didn't know Lynn by sight, but as soon as he'd seen the tall young stranger on his mahogany gelding, he was sure that he was looking at the already despised Lynn Evans.

After the two men made their quick assessments, Lynn quickly turned his eyes back to the front and continued riding to the livery.

Dan took one last glance back at Lynn and then leapt to the conclusion that somehow, Evans was responsible for Adele's disappearance. He didn't know where he'd hidden them, but he was determined to find out.

He stormed into the sheriff's office, ignored Charlie Red Fox and headed down the hallway.

When he turned into the smaller office, he found the sheriff talking to his ogre of a deputy and both sets of eyes turned to look at him.

"What do you need, Billingsley?" the sheriff asked.

"I need to talk to you privately."

"Tex, you go and wait outside."

"Okay, boss," he replied as he stood as straight as possible then looked down at Dan, grinned, and left the office.

After he'd gone, Dan closed the door and took the seat that the deputy had just vacated.

"I went over to Mrs. Price's house to collect her overdue rent but found it empty. She and Adele have gone, and I think that Evans is behind it."

Paul grinned as he asked, "Now, how did you come up with that brilliant conclusion?"

"Where else could they go? Nobody would go near that pox-ridden whore and they didn't have any money to leave on their own, either."

"How do you know that? She might have been saving up for all those years on her back just so she could spring her and her daughter out of town."

"Trust me, Sheriff, I know she didn't have any money."

"Is that why Adele agreed to move in with you?"

Dan didn't bother arguing the point, but replied, "I just want to know where he put her. Don't you have any ideas?"

"I doubt if he snuck them into his room over at the Rangeland, but I suppose he could have gotten another room and brought them in the back way at night. But that's assuming your cockamamie idea is right."

"Can't you do a kind of search to find her?"

"Her? You mean them; don't you?" the sheriff asked with a grin.

"I'm not playing games anymore, Sheriff. That boy is causing me trouble and I want this all to go away!"

"I told you before, Billingsley, we aren't doing anything that is going to bring his father racing up here with a bunch of deputy U.S. marshals. I'm sure your little girl will show up soon enough. She's got to eat; doesn't she?"

Dan glared at the smirking lawman and decided that he'd do things his way now. He had his escape plan in place and if he had to kill the kid, he'd still be able to take that last riverboat down to Yankton and catch a train east with his money. By the time Marshal Evans was able to investigate the loss of his precious baby boy, he'd be in Ohio.

"Never mind," he snapped, then stood, opened the door and hastily left the office.

Sheriff Martin may have been smirking, but he'd seen the look on the banker's face and knew that he was now a loose cannon. After hearing the outer door slam, he just waited for Tex to return.

After Tex sat down, Paul said, "That idiot is going to do something stupid about that girl, Tex."

"Do you want me to stop him?"

The sheriff thought about it, saw the silver lining if Billingsley acted rashly and slowly shook his head.

"No. Let's see what happens; but I want you to head over to the bank and keep an eye on him. I don't want him causing trouble; at least not yet. We may have to get rid of the kid ourselves before he does something stupid that we can't fix."

Tex nodded, then stood and left the small office, not quite sure of what the sheriff wanted.

After he'd gone, Sheriff Martin began to hope that the girl wasn't found. If he could nudge Billingsley into trying to kill the kid, then he'd be in control of the situation.

Paul smiled as he visualized an enraged Dan Billingsley pointing his pistol at the unsuspecting Evans kid and pulling the trigger. He'd have Tex shoot the banker in self-defense and it would all be over. He'd send a telegram of regret to Marshal Evans and then he'd have a nice conversation with Walter Capshaw to let him know that Billingsley may be gone, but the payments would not only continue, but would double.

———

After seeing Dan Billingsley enter the main street from a side alley, it wasn't difficult for Lynn to guess where he'd been. That first night, when Betty had told him that Dan Billingsley was expecting to have Addie move into his house by the end of September, he had anticipated that the banker would get antsy by the time October arrived.

Suddenly, he realized that his planned routine had morphed into a potentially explosive situation. Once he'd realized where Billingsley had been, he knew where he was going. If he was headed for the bank, as he should be even at this time of day, then he was going the wrong way. He was either going to his house, or more likely, heading to see the sheriff.

As he stepped down outside the livery, he began to look for a way to avoid the unavoidable; a dangerous confrontation with Dan Billingsley, the sheriff or both of them.

He led Griffin into the barn and didn't see Slim anywhere, so he began to unsaddle his horse as he continued to think.

There were still so many unknowns swirling around him that the frustration he'd felt earlier was returning in spades.

He could understand why Dan Billingsley might suspect that he had something to do with Adele's disappearance; if for no other reason than the coincidental timing of his arrival with her disappearance. Whether Billingsley knew that she and her mother had taken the *Alberta* probably didn't make any difference but blaming him for it could send the banker out of control.

It was his relationship with the sheriff that was still sketchy. Slim had said that everyone suspected that Billingsley had murdered his wife, yet the sheriff really hadn't investigated her death, supposedly because of the lack of evidence.

That meant that the sheriff was at least guilty of covering up the crime, if not an active participant. And that meant the sheriff and his big deputy were more of a threat than he'd first realized.

But even when he accepted the premise that the sheriff and deputy were partnered with Billingsley, he couldn't see it starting with the murder of the cashier's wife.

Slim said Billingsley bought Burke Riddell's house years earlier, and Lynn couldn't see how a cashier could afford to buy such a lavish place. Maybe he'd worked a shady deal on the previous occupant, but then there was the more likely explanation that he had been embezzling from the bank. The only obstacle to cooking the books would be Walter Capshaw, who would have to review the ledgers.

Lynn guessed that once Billingsley had the sheriff on his payroll using some of his embezzled funds, he'd be able to intimidate the bank president into looking the other way.

Suddenly, his frustration was replaced with a heightened sense of danger. If Billingsley was paying off the sheriff, then no wonder they wouldn't want him around.

He rued his decision not to get on the *Alberta* with Addie. At least he could head back and tell his father all that he'd found, but it was too late now. The primary purpose for coming to

Fort Benton was now almost insignificant. He had to survive long enough for the *Princess of Ohio* to arrive.

So far, the only trustworthy person he'd found was Slim, and Lynn wasn't about to ask for his help other than to give him information.

Lynn finished stripping Griffin, then thought he'd just head back to the hotel, but didn't want to just leave his Winchester without telling Slim, so he hung his saddlebags over his shoulder and with his Winchester in his left hand, headed for the hotel.

―――――

Dan had been so angry at the entire world after leaving the jail that he didn't want to go back to work but headed for his house instead. He'd calm down with a nice glass of bourbon and then think about what he should do about Evans. He'd need to check his pistol to make sure it was loaded, too. He was getting tired of having to depend on the sheriff and that oaf of a deputy. He was as much a man as either of them, and was smarter than both of them combined.

When he entered the house, he startled Mrs. Butterfield, who was dusting his liquor cabinet.

"I won't need you for the next three days, Mrs. Butterfield," Dan said as he entered the office, not noticing the empty glass on the sideboard.

Dora smiled at him, slid before the sideboard and picked up her glass, then replied, "Of course, sir. I'll just leave you to your privacy."

Dan was already heading for the desk and paid no attention to her as she left.

He'd told her three days, but hoped that if everything worked out, she wouldn't need to return at all after the weekend.

———

As Lynn walked along the boardwalk, he spotted Tex Granger on the other side of the street heading his way. He didn't acknowledge the deputy but continued to the Rangeland Hotel and walked inside.

Tex stopped when he saw Lynn with his repeater, and quickly realized that whatever the sheriff expected was happening, so rather than go to the bank to keep an eye on Dan Billingsley, he spun on his heels and headed back to warn his boss.

———

Dan Billingsley had his Colt Model 1873 in his hands with the hammer half-cocked as he checked the load. He'd just bought the cartridge pistol in April and had only fired it twice but had been impressed with the revolver. The bourbon had calmed his volcanic rage to just a seething anger which allowed him to spend more time thinking and less time cursing Lynn Evans.

He still believed that the kid had something to do with Adele's disappearance but managed to avoid thinking about the kid's reason for helping her in the first place.

As he released the pistol's hammer, he tried to rationally determine where he could have hidden her. The sheriff's smarmy comment about her having to eat was actually a good starting point. She and her mother had to not only eat but satisfy all of the other basic human needs. If he watched the kid, then he'd find Adele soon enough.

———

As Lynn was setting his things in place in his hotel room, Tex blew past Charlie Red Fox and marched into the sheriff's office.

"What's wrong, Tex?" Paul Martin asked as he saw his deputy's anxious face.

"You were right, boss. I was headed to the bank and saw the Evans kid with his Winchester. I think he's gonna go shoot Billingsley."

"Sit down, Tex. I don't think he's going to shoot anyone; at least not yet."

Tex was staring at the sheriff as he slowly took a seat.

"He ain't had his rifle with him before, boss."

"I think that it's just a coincidence. He doesn't have a reason to go after anyone. Besides, he's just a kid."

Tex quietly said, "I killed two fellers before I was fifteen."

Paul didn't tell him the difference between a fifteen-year-old Tex Granger and a sixteen-year-old son of Dylan Evans, but said, "Now, he might not have a reason yet, but after you left, I did some thinking that we might be able to get things going in a way that won't get us in trouble with the kid's father."

"How can we do that, boss?"

"Right now, Billingsley is stewing over the loss of his sweet Adele and is blaming the kid for it. I can understand why he might believe that, and I intend to use it to our advantage.

There's one other thing that I've been thinking about since Evans arrived; it's about the real reason he's here."

"It's not about us or Billingsley?"

"Nope. I think he's here to find out if he's really Dylan Evans' son or he's the spawn of the reviled Burke Riddell."

"*What?*" Tex asked with wide eyes.

"It makes perfect sense when you look at it from his point of view. Why would a sixteen-year-old kid come all this way on his own? It surely isn't to enjoy the scenery. I almost bought his story, but then I did the simple arithmetic and I'll bet if you ask him his birthday, it will be nine months after his mother arrived here. His sainted parents never told him that he was Burke Riddell's son and he finally figured it out. He's here to find out if it's true or not."

"Can he do that?"

"He might if he finds an old timer who was here when Riddell married his mother; an old timer like Slim. He could ask the right questions and get his answer."

"Okay, so what difference does it make who his pappy is?"

"If you thought your father was your hero all your life and suddenly, you suspect that he might have been lying to you and he wasn't your father after all, then wouldn't you want to know?"

"I never knew my pa."

"It's okay, Tex. I think I'll go pay a visit to Dan Billingsley after the bank closes and get him stirred up a bit. If things play out as I suspect they will, we'll have to shoot Billingsley or the Evans kid; whoever is left standing."

"What do you want me to do, boss?"

"Right now, we'll just wait for a little while, then you can go have your supper, then come back here. I should have a better idea of what to expect."

Tex just nodded, but still had a lot of questions.

Fifteen feet away, Charlie Red Fox had far fewer questions, but knew that he'd have to warn River Warrior's son.

————

On the banks of the Missouri, four hundred miles southeast of Fort Benton, the survivors of the *Princess of Ohio* disaster were working to set up a campsite using the shattered remains of the riverboat. They were sure that the Sioux had heard the explosion and would at least come to investigate its cause. They had six pistols and two Winchesters, but knew it wasn't enough to stop the Indians if they were intent on finishing them off.

But knowing that their presence wasn't a secret, at least allowed them to build a fire to stay warm. They were also counting on the Sioux having no incentive to make an attack. They had little in the way of supplies and weren't planning on living there, either. But that hope provided little comfort for what promised to be a long, cold night. Their only real hope was that the *Alberta* would arrive before the Sioux.

————

The *Alberta* was docked a little over a hundred and eighty miles away and no one on board had any idea that the

Princess of Ohio was mostly under the waters of the Missouri River.

Addie and her mother had settled into a reasonably comfortable routine on the boat, and despite Betty recognizing two of the passengers as past clients, hadn't had any problems.

They spent much of their time in cabin thirteen where they either read or talked. Most of their conversations were about what they would find when they arrived in Omaha and then Denver, but Addie's half of the talks were always centered on Lynn. She wasn't concerned about how she and her mother would be received by the Evans family, but focused her worries on whether or not Lynn would return. It had only been a few days since they'd parted, and had only shared a few hours of time together, but she desperately wanted to see him again.

Betty wasn't surprised at all by Addie's instant attraction to Lynn because her daughter had lived such an abnormal life as compared to other girls her age. She didn't say anything but wondered how Addie would react when she met the other Evans boys. Lynn had joked that they were all better looking than he was, and although Addie had claimed that it didn't matter, Betty suspected that it would matter once she met them.

But Omaha was at least a good week away. Captain Clyde had told them earlier that day that they were making very good time as the current was faster than they'd expected and joked that as long as they didn't hit a fallen tree or a sand bar, they'd arrive in Omaha well before their schedule.

There had been a close call when they'd narrowly avoided a boulder when they'd passed through the second set of rapids, but since then, the *Alberta* had stayed in the center of the wriggling Missouri and hadn't even bumped into any floating logs.

"Do you want to go straight to Denver or travel with the deputy marshal, as Lynn suggested, Mama?" Addie asked as she lay stretched out on her bunk.

"I think we have to wait until we arrive in Omaha, dear. The deputy may already be gone, but if he and his family are ready to depart within a few days, I'd rather just wait."

"I think so, too," Addie said.

Betty smiled at her daughter and said, "Just in case Lynn suddenly arrives on the next riverboat, Addie?"

Addie smiled back at her mother and said, "That will be a while, Mama. We haven't passed the last one that's going north yet, so it wouldn't be back to Omaha for at least ten days after we arrive."

"But you wouldn't mind waiting; would you?"

"No, Mama. I wouldn't mind waiting. I wouldn't hesitate to stand on that dock for the entire time, either."

Betty was still smiling at Addie and hoped that she wasn't really planning on waiting.

The sun was setting while Sheriff Martin sat across from Dan Billingsley sipping some of his fine bourbon.

"You don't know where she is?" Dan asked.

"Nope. But I've been giving it some thought, Dan, and I think you might be right about the Evans kid hiding her somewhere."

"You do? That's quite a shift from what you told me earlier; and rather rudely, I may add."

"I know, but it got me to thinking about it. It makes a lot of sense when you get past the other stuff we were concerned about. What if he spotted her and was smitten? If she or her mother cried about what you were planning to do with her, then the kid pretends he's his heroic father and decides to rescue Adele like his daddy rescued his mommy."

"But where could he hide her?"

"Like I said to you before; she has to eat. We watch the kid and we'll catch him bringing food to her and her mother. Maybe he'll spend some private time with her, too."

Sheriff Martin was pleased to see the fire reappear in Billingsley's eyes as he snapped, "That boy had better not set one finger on her!"

"Now, calm down, Billingsley. Don't get all riled over something that hasn't happened; or at least we don't know if it has."

"*Calm down?*" Dan exclaimed, "*How can you say that?*"

"Don't go off half-cocked, Billingsley. If you can't wait for us to find out where he's hiding her, I'll just head over to his hotel and have a chat with him. You're too worked up to do it."

"You'd better lean on him hard, Sheriff," Dan snarled as he glared at the sheriff.

Paul knew he'd pushed Billingsley far enough but needed to add that final piece.

"One more thing, Dan. I figured out why he's really here."

Billingsley snorted and replied, "That he's trying to find out if Burke Riddell is his real father? So what?"

The sheriff was surprised that the banker had already come to the same conclusion, but said, "Because it's what I intend to use to push him into telling me where he hid your little girl, Billingsley. If I can convince him that Riddell was his real father and that Dylan Evans has been lying to him all this time, it might even turn him against the marshal."

"I don't care what you tell him. Just find out where he took Adele and then let me know."

"I'll let you know, but you'd better hang onto that pistol, too. He might decide to keep the girl and get rid of you. She's probably been filling his ears with tales about you and once I start asking him about her, he might come visiting."

"I'm not worried about a damned kid, Sheriff. Just find out where he hid her."

The sheriff drained the crystal glass, set it on the desk, then rose pulled on his hat and left the office without another word. He'd set the first part of his plan into motion and now had to get the kid ready. He'd talk to Tex before heading to the kid's hotel room. What happened in that room would be the most critical part of the plot; he had to somehow convince the kid to visit Dan Billingsley.

———

After he'd had his supper, Lynn headed back to the hotel. He hadn't seen the sheriff or the deputy in the fading light but wouldn't have been surprised to find one or the other waiting in the lobby as he passed through.

He barely swung the door to his dark room open when he spotted a seated figure against the wall opposite the bed. He began to reach for his pistol, but quickly identified the figure, even though he had never met the man.

He closed the door as Charlie Red Fox just looked at him.

Lynn removed his hat, then sat on his bed before asking, "You're Charlie Red Fox."

"I am."

"You are Crow; yet are a deputy sheriff."

"Yes."

"Why are you here?"

"To warn you. The sheriff intends to have you confront Dan Billingsley, then after one of you kills the other, he will shoot the survivor."

"Is this because of Addie Price?"

"It is the excuse the sheriff is using to anger Billingsley enough to act, but I think the sheriff sees a way to rid himself of the banker and you without suspicion."

"What do you think I should do?"

Charlie shrugged then replied, "It is not for me to tell you. This is your fight now. I have warned you of the danger, so now you will not be surprised."

"Slim told me that you are Joseph Walking Bear's nephew. Is that why you're helping me?"

"Yes. I will help if I can, but I cannot fight."

"I understand and I appreciate your help."

As Charlie rose, he looked across at Lynn and asked, "The sheriff said that you are here seeking to find if Burke Riddell is your birth father. Is this true?"

"No. My parents told me about it before I left. I suspected it long before then, but it didn't matter until it was confirmed."

"Then why did you come?"

Lynn sighed, then answered, "Because I need to know if part of that monster lurks inside me. If it's there, then I cannot return to my family. I don't know what I'll do, but I can't go back."

Charlie huffed, then said, "Bah! You think too much. We are who we are and not our dead ancestors. If you had been like the vile man who hurt your mother and done other evil things, then you would not even be here. You should have gone back on the boat, but I don't think you have time to wait for the next one."

Lynn didn't agree with Charlie, but said, "I know."

Charlie turned and headed for the door but stopped and asked, "Did you hide the girl and her mother?"

"I put them on the riverboat. They're hundreds of miles away by now."

Charlie nodded, said, "At least something good has happened because you came," then opened the door and disappeared into the dark hallway.

Lynn rose, lifted the lamp's chimney, then struck a match and set the wick aflame.

He finally took off his hat and coat and hung them on the pegs on the wall near the door before taking a seat on the one chair in the room and looked at his Winchester leaning against the opposite wall near the bed.

Charlie's warning wasn't as shocking as it would have been the day before, but it was still unnerving. Knowing that three men were planning on killing him may have provided him with time to prepare but didn't do anything for his state of mind.

He sat on the chair for another ten minutes, trying in vain to try to find a way out of this debacle, when there was a loud knock on the door and he almost fell out of the chair.

He loosened his gunbelt's hammer loop, then slowly walked to the door, ready to draw if someone was standing there with a pistol; even if he wore a badge.

Lynn gripped the knob, twisted it and carefully pulled the door wide.

Sheriff Martin smiled broadly at him and said, "Evening, Lynn. Mind if I come in?"

Lynn was more than mildly suspicious with the sheriff's friendly greeting, but replied, "Of course, Sheriff," then stepped aside to let him pass.

The sheriff hadn't noticed the free pistol at Lynn's side, and by the time Lynn turned, he'd slipped the leather strip back over the Smith & Wesson's hammer.

"Go ahead and take the chair, Sheriff. I'll sit on the bed."

As the sheriff sat down, he tried to keep his pleasant façade as he evaluated Lynn.

"What brings you by, Sheriff?" Lynn asked as he lowered his behind onto the bed.

"Do you know Dan Billingsley? He's the chief cashier over at the bank."

"No, sir. I haven't been to the bank and, to be honest, I've only talked to a few people since I've been here, and two of them wear badges."

Paul Martin chuckled, then said, "I figured you hadn't, but he seems to be mighty upset with you."

Lynn raised his eyebrows as he asked, "Why would he be upset with me? I don't even know what he looks like."

Sheriff Martin was studying Lynn's eyes as he said, "He thinks that you had something to do with the disappearance of a girl that he wanted."

"A girl? I haven't even been to a bawdy house since I've been here and after what happened in Denver, I'm not about to do anything to make my father that upset again."

Paul hadn't seen any level of obfuscation in the boy's eyes, but said, "He's really mad, Lynn. You might want to go down to his house and calm him down. I tried, but I don't think anyone can do it except you."

"Can't you just tell him that I didn't have anything to do with his girlfriend? I don't want to face a crazed man if I don't have to."

The sheriff then said, "I'll tell you what, Lynn. I'll go and get Tex and we'll go with you. He won't try anything with us in the house and you'll be able to convince him that you had nothing to do with it."

Lynn knew that he shouldn't agree to go with the sheriff; he may as well begin his climb up the steps to the gallows. But when the sheriff had said that they'd be going to that house where he had been conceived, it triggered an almost mystical belief that this was finally going to provide him with his one chance to have his answer.

"Alright, Sheriff. Do you want me to leave with you?"

"No. I've got to drag Tex out of his watering hole. So, just come on down to the jail in about thirty minutes and we'll go over there."

"I hope you're right, Sheriff. I don't want any trouble."

"Neither do I, Lynn," Paul replied as he stood, smiled at Lynn, then turned and left the room.

After listening to the sheriff's footsteps fade, Lynn whispered, "I hope I'm doing the right thing, Dad. Charlie warned me that they would try to kill me, but if I don't go, then I believe that I'll never find my answer. I don't know why I even feel this way, but it's there. You always said to follow my instincts, and I'm not sure that this is one, but I have to go."

He then pulled his pistol, made sure all six cylinders were filled, then slid it back into his holster. He'd never been in the house but tried to imagine how the meeting with Dan

Billingsley would play out. He suspected that the banker would probably be in his office, where he could be half hidden behind a heavy desk. He'd have a cocked pistol hidden close to his hand, or maybe even on his lap under the desk.

No matter where the banker was, having Sheriff Martin and Tex would be behind him was the biggest problem. He didn't know how good they were with their pistols but assumed each of them was very proficient. He knew that he couldn't get both of them without taking a hit, and that was only after he'd eliminated Dan Billingsley, who would have to make the first move.

It was an almost impossible situation that he'd be facing in less than an hour, and he had to think first before acting. He wasn't sure that Billingsley wasn't already waiting for him and suspected that he may not even be mad at all. It had made sense when the sheriff had questioned him, but if Charlie was right, then they were probably just setting him up and using Addie as an excuse.

That also meant that there would be no reason to try to placate Dan Billingsley. They could shoot him as soon as he entered the house and make up whatever story they wanted.

After waiting for the proscribed thirty minutes, he stood, pulled on his hat, but left his coat hanging in place. He didn't want any hindrances when he had to pull his pistol, and it really wasn't that cold anyway.

Lynn took a deep breath, blew it out, then opened the door.

As he passed through the lobby, he could smell the smoke from the four lamps before he reached the door and wondered why he'd never noticed it before.

Once outside, he stopped on the dark boardwalk and scanned the roadway. There was some light traffic, but nothing unusual.

As he began walking, he released his hammer loop. If the sheriff asked, he'd tell him that his father had told him to always be prepared when dealing with a jealous man; which was one of the many lessons he'd learned.

———

Sheriff Martin didn't have to hunt for Tex because he had told him to wait for him in the empty jail. He'd used the extra time to trot down to Billingsley's house to let him know that he'd convinced Evans to talk to him and that he and Tex would be behind the kid. He didn't have to explain why they'd be there.

After the sheriff left, Dan set up in his office, making sure that the kid didn't see the cocked Colt that was now laying in his partially open center drawer.

When the sheriff returned to the jail, he didn't notice the absence of Charlie Red Fox because he didn't notice when he was there either.

While Lynn had been sitting on his bed, explaining to his distant father why he was putting himself in danger, the sheriff was explaining how this would work to Tex.

"He's really goin' in there?" Tex asked.

"He balked at first, but after I told him that we'd back him up, he agreed."

Tex snickered, then said, "That boy is sure stupid."

"He's naïve and trusting, Tex, but he's far from stupid. Now, when we get to the house, I'm not going to knock. Dan's expecting me to come back after talking to the kid, so I'll just open the door and you walk in behind the kid. I'll make a show of telling Billingsley that Evans is here to talk to him and to just listen."

"Is he goin' straight there, boss?"

Sheriff Martin was so accustomed to hearing those kinds of questions from his deputy that he didn't usually get annoyed, but this time, he did when he snapped, "No, Tex! He's going to sprout wings, fly down to Colorado, get his marshal daddy and the rest of them, then they'll all fly back here."

Tex was embarrassed by the sheriff's sarcastic reply but didn't say another word. He knew that he wasn't as smart as the sheriff but didn't like having it shoved in his face like this.

Paul Martin then said, "He'll be here in a couple of minutes. Be friendly because he's got to trust us."

Tex just nodded as he looked past the sheriff's left ear; not wanting to see his face.

Lynn entered the jail and found the sheriff and Tex already standing in front of the desk.

"Ready to go and talk to Dan Billingsley?" the sheriff asked with a smile.

"I hope that's all it is," Lynn replied before turning around and stepping out onto the boardwalk.

Tex glanced at his boss then followed him out the door, closing it behind him.

The three men walked west under the light of an almost full moon. Lynn made sure that he was on the far right so neither the sheriff nor the deputy would notice his untethered pistol.

As they stepped along the wooden walkway, the sheriff said, "I think he might have calmed down since I talked to him earlier, Lynn. He was drinking some of his favorite bourbon when I got there and was on his third glass before I left."

"That might make him more hostile, Sheriff. Drunk men don't think very well."

"He might be passed out, Lynn. I'll go in first and let him know that you're here under my protection. I'll make sure that he isn't armed before you talk to him."

"Thanks, Sheriff. I appreciate it."

Lynn doubted every word that left the sheriff's mouth and even as the shadowed outline of the hated Riddell house appeared in the moonlit distance, he was already formulating a way out of this. It wasn't much of a plan; but given the low odds of his walking out of the house alive, it was better than nothing.

They turned down the cobblestone walkway and headed for the big porch. Lynn glanced up at the house but knew that he'd be unable to see the window of his mother's room from the front. He could see the south wall of the room, and almost heard it calling to him. If he lived through this, he knew that he'd have to go there. That was where he'd find his answer.

They stepped onto the porch and Lynn stopped a few feet short of the door and watched as the sheriff knocked three times. Without hearing a response, Sheriff Martin opened the door and gestured for Lynn to enter.

Lynn was nervous about having Tex Granger behind him but stepped over the threshold and followed the sheriff into the foyer while Tex closed the front door.

"Billingsley," the sheriff shouted, "I brought Lynn Evans with me to talk to you. Don't do anything but talk! Do you understand me?"

Lynn finally heard Dan Billingsley's voice when he loudly replied from his open office, "I understand, Sheriff. I'm better now, but I still want some answers."

Sheriff Martin turned to Lynn, then smiled and said, "You'll be okay."

Lynn nodded, then glanced at the sheriff's holster, saw his unrestricted Colt, then stepped toward the office. He didn't expect the sheriff or Tex to pull their pistols yet but would wait for the masking sound of his conversation with Dan Billingsley to pull and cock their revolvers. He just wasn't going to give them a target.

He walked to the open door, saw Dan Billingsley behind his desk with an almost contorted face as he tried to mask his still smoldering anger, then calmly stepped inside.

Before either he or the banker could say a word, Lynn reached over and quickly closed the door.

Sheriff Martin was taken by surprise when he watched Lynn slam the door because it was so unexpected and hinted that the kid had gotten wind of the plan somehow. He was certain that Billingsley hadn't told him, and that left only one other person who could have warned him – Tex.

LYNN'S SEARCH

He didn't know why his deputy would have turned on him, but maybe he'd insulted him once too often, so he turned to look at Tex and noticed that he hadn't been surprised at all when Evans had closed the door, which confirmed his growing suspicions. He didn't say a word but stepped back slightly and watched the closed door and listened.

———

Inside the office, Lynn stared at the banker and said, "The sheriff told me that you're mad at me over some girl."

Dan's poor excuse for a mask slipped from his face as he snapped, "Don't lie to me, Evans! I know that you hid her somewhere. Where is she?"

"Who are you talking about? I've only been here for a few days."

"Don't play coy with me, kid! You know I'm talking about Adele Price. You'd better tell me where she is right now, or you'll be sorry!"

Lynn had noticed the open center desk drawer when he'd entered the room and now, the banker's right hand was resting inside. He didn't have much time and that door wasn't going to stay closed much longer.

He kept his eyes focused on the banker and his hand close to his pistol as he said, "She and her mother are about six hundred miles away by now, Mister Billingsley. I put them aboard the *Alberta* before she set sail and they're safe."

Dan blinked as he heard Lynn's calm admission and stammered, "You...you bastard! You don't have the right to send her away!"

Even before he finished screaming, Dan gripped his cocked pistol and began to yank it out of the drawer.

Lynn saw the expected motion and immediately pulled his Smith & Wesson, while the banker's index finger wrapped around his Colt's trigger as he was pulling it free.

Lynn saw the flash of steel in Dan Billingsley's right hand and as he was cocking his hammer, the Colt's hammer that Billingsley was pulling from his drawer snagged on the edge of the desktop.

As Lynn's sights settled on the banker, Dan's index finger was jerked back when the hammer caught on the desk and the hammer snapped back down, setting off the .45 cartridge in its chamber.

The loud roar of the pistol in the enclosed space was soon replaced by the scream of pain from Dan Billingsley as splinters from his damaged desk drawer pierced his left thigh above his knee while the slug of lead creased the outside of his leg.

Outside the office, the sheriff believed that his plan had worked despite the door being closed. He'd heard Dan's shouts followed by the shot and scream, but just wasn't sure who'd fired the pistol.

He had his cocked pistol in his hand as he took two long strides to the door and threw it open without entering.

As soon as Dan had accidentally discharged his pistol, Lynn stepped off to the side, expecting the sheriff and Tex to burst through the door. He had his gun leveled at the space when it flew wide.

The sheriff spotted a very much alive Dan Billingsley wailing in pain behind his desk, but didn't see Evans, so he quickly backed away from the door.

Tex then yelled, "Go get him, boss!"

Paul whipped his pistol around to point at Tex and snarled, "That's just what you want; isn't it? You want me to go in there and get ambushed. You set this all up with Evans!"

Tex stared at the sheriff in disbelief. He had his cocked pistol in his giant right hand, but it was pointed at the floor.

"I ain't even talked to him but once," he replied in stunned disbelief.

"You told him what I was going to do, Tex, so I want you go into that room and prove me wrong."

Tex shifted his attention from the sheriff's glare to the open door. He could see Dan Billingsley, who was still crying and gripping his left leg, but knew that Evans was somewhere in the room with his pistol ready to fire.

He turned his gaze back to the sheriff, released his Colt's hammer and said, "I ain't goin' in there, boss. He'll kill me."

Paul Martin glared at his big deputy, pointed his muzzle just four feet from his eyes and calmly said, "If you don't go in there, I'll kill you myself."

Tex simply couldn't believe that the sheriff, his boss and perceived friend, would pull that trigger, so he called his bluff. He rammed his pistol into his holster, then turned and began to walk back to the foyer.

The sheriff couldn't risk having Tex's gun at his back if he had to deal with Evans, so he aimed at the back of the big man's head and squeezed his trigger.

Dan was still in anguish over his wound and was already plucking splinters from his leg as he watched the sheriff shoot Tex and almost vomited as the bullet ripped into the deputy's head and then blew most of his forehead across the foyer as the misshapen slug of lead plowed through the front of his skull.

When Dan stopped wailing in shock, Lynn knew what had just happened without witnessing the results of that one shot after hearing what the sheriff's warning to his big deputy. It also meant that the sheriff was now alone outside the office and waiting for him to show himself.

He looked over at the banker, and although Lynn knew that he still had his Colt somewhere close by, judged that Dan Billingsley was not an immediate threat and he'd have to figure out how to get a clean shot at the sheriff.

Sheriff Martin was in a similar dilemma. He knew that he couldn't enter the office without getting a bullet in his own head and had to figure out a way to get a clean shot without exposing himself.

He closed his eyes briefly to recall the inside of the office, then began to quietly step away. He had to carefully avoid tripping over Tex's massive body but soon reached the front door. He slowly turned the knob and tiptoed onto the porch, leaving the door open.

Lynn found that he was surprisingly calm considering his precarious situation, and as he stood with his pistol pointed at the open office door, he let his eyes roam around the room. He ignored Dan Billingsley who was weeping as he continued to pull splinters from his leg but noticed the window on the east side of the room and thought about using it as a way to get out of the house.

He was still looking at the window when a light breeze flowed into the room and lifted the edges of some papers on the desk.

It took a few seconds for Lynn to understand that the only place wind could enter the closed house was through the open front door. He knew that Tex had closed it behind him when they had arrived and that he had never reached it before loudly thumping to the floor, so the only reason it could be open now was if the sheriff had left the house.

Where the sheriff might go was secondary as Lynn slowly moved to the doorway, glanced outside and didn't see the sheriff; just the sprawled, bloody mass that had been Tex Granger on the floor before the open door.

He didn't hesitate to study the scene but stepped quickly but quietly into the parlor and soon passed Tex's body as he entered the foyer. He stopped at the front door's threshold for a few seconds to listen for any sounds that might indicate where the sheriff might be waiting but didn't hear anything. It was still a risk, but he was reasonably sure that the sheriff wasn't expecting him to exit the front door. So, he stepped onto the porch, and quickly scanned the empty moonlit yard, not finding the sheriff's shadow.

Once outside, he was tempted to rush down the steps onto the open ground to seek some measure of protection but took an extra few seconds to try to think like the sheriff.

The sheriff's best tactical move would be to find a clear shooting angle and eliminate Billingsley and himself; the only two witnesses to the murder of Tex Grange. The only place the sheriff could get the shot would be through the window that he'd almost decided to use as an escape hatch.

Lynn turned, and with his left shoulder close to the outside wall, began to step along the porch, heading for the southeast corner.

———

Sheriff Martin had reached the window, but worried about being seen by either Dan Billingsley or Evans, so he slowly took off his hat and then stuck it in front of the glass and waved it.

After three passes, Paul lowered his hat to the porch and then slowly moved toward the middle of the porch. Once he was facing the window, he sidestepped until his gunsights were aligned with the glass and he peered into the office. He could see Dan Billingsley shaking as he did something with his left leg, but he couldn't see Evans.

He shifted one step to his right and then stepped closer to widen his view.

The liquor cabinet had just come into sight when he heard Lynn Evans shout, "Drop the gun, Sheriff!"

Paul knew that his options were gone if he surrendered. He didn't doubt that Billingsley would try to salvage his own skin and give him up, so there wasn't any need to spend time deciding what to do before he turned to bring his Colt in line to shoot Evans.

Lynn hadn't expected Paul Martin to comply, but in that brief moment before the sheriff began to turn to face him, Lynn hesitated because he'd never shot a man before.

LYNN'S SEARCH

The sheriff had no reservations when he picked up Lynn in the moonlit porch just fifteen feet away and fired before he even stopped turning.

Lynn knew that he'd made one more mistake even before he saw the sheriff's Colt flash. But even before the sound of the pistol died behind him, Lynn fired his Smith & Wesson. He didn't even know if he'd been hit because he'd never been shot before, but there was no doubt that his .44 had found its mark.

The bullet had spun out of Lynn's barrel and crossed that short gap in an instant before drilling to the sheriff's chest on the left side. Because he was still turning counterclockwise, the bullet ripped into his left lower lung, tore off the top half of his heart and then continued into his lung's right middle lobe.

Sheriff Martin never knew how he died and probably didn't care as he spun awkwardly to the porch and flopped onto his back.

Lynn slowly approached the sheriff's body and stared into his white lifeless eyes. He had hoped to feel sick with remorse if he'd had to kill a man, but he felt nothing, and it bothered him.

Still, there were more things to do inside the house of horrors.

He picked up the sheriff's pistol and slipped it into his waist, scanned the streets but didn't see anyone coming, which surprised him, then began walking back to the front door.

When Lynn had shouted to the sheriff, Dan Billingsley had instantly forgotten about his leg wound. He knew that he couldn't stay in the office any longer, so he grabbed his pistol then hobbled for the open office door.

Then, as he heard the gunshots outside the window, he stopped, walked to his liquor cabinet, and grabbed his decanter of bourbon before continuing his limping escape.

He knew that he couldn't go out the front door and thought about heading down the hallway to the kitchen, but that would only delay the inevitable. He had to get Evans first and blame this all on him. There were no other witnesses to prove otherwise and he had all of the power now.

Dan suddenly had an inspiration, set down the bourbon on the sideboard and quickly scrambled toward the staircase. He was moving as fast as he could as he climbed to the second floor.

Lynn entered the front door and spotted Billingsley when he turned into the first bedroom. As he stood beside Tex's corpse, he felt the strong magnetic pull of the staircase. The only light in the parlor came from the lamp in the office, but it didn't matter as Lynn headed for the bottom step.

He hadn't felt any fear since his talk with Charlie Red Fox right up to the moment when he'd killed Sheriff Martin and then hadn't felt guilt or remorse. Now that one lingering fear that had driven him to Fort Belton was very much alive. His lack of emotion after shooting the sheriff triggered a growing belief that he had no soul or compassion and could almost hear Burke Riddell laughing from the depths of hell as he climbed the stairs.

Dan Billingsley sat on the floor behind the bed with his Colt pointed at the door. He knew that the kid wouldn't be stupid enough to walk through it unless he could goad him into making a mistake and he believed he had just the incentive to make him walk to his death.

Lynn may have been concerned about his lack of remorse, but he still wasn't about to make that final mistake and walk through the open door. He had made enough noise coming up the stairs that he was sure that Billingsley knew he was coming, so he still needed a way to get to the banker without getting shot in the process.

The room was probably even darker than the hallway, and Lynn knew that his silhouette in the open doorway would be an easy target.

He shifted his Smith & Wesson to his left hand then pulled the sheriff's Colt from his waist.

He stood about ten feet from the doorjamb, cocked the Colt's hammer and pointed it at the wall.

"Come out of there, Billingsley!" he shouted.

"Come in and get me, Evans!"

"I'm not that stupid. I won't shoot you if you toss your pistol out the door."

"Of course, you'll shoot me, Evans. Or should I call you Riddell? Didn't your mommy tell you that Burke Riddell took her in this very room? She probably said that she hated him for it, but I'll bet she loved every second. She couldn't spread her legs fast enough for your real father; that heartless monster who spawned you."

Lynn gritted his teeth after the taunt. He didn't care if Billingsley called him Burke Riddell's bastard, but saying those

315

things about his mother infuriated him, and it took every bit of concentration to maintain his reasoning mind.

"The name is Lynn Evans, Billingsley, and my parents explained my birthright, so it doesn't matter what you say. Just slide the gun across the floor and you'll live. You haven't done anything serious enough to get you hanged yet."

"You're wrong about that, Riddell. I killed my wife to get to that tasty little girl you took from me. The sheriff knew about it and he's been blackmailing me ever since. So, you see, I do have to worry about getting hanged and I'm not about to give up."

When Billingsley reminded Lynn about his twisted plans for Addie, he felt his anger boil again, but took a deep breath to push the anger back before he yelled through the wall, "I'm giving you one last chance to toss out your pistol!"

Dan huddled near the foot of the bed, using the mattress to support his gun hand as he steadied his sights on the open door.

"You're a coward just like your real father, the big yellow Burke Riddell. You're too afraid to come through that door."

Lynn ended the conversation when he kept the Colt at waist level and pulled the trigger, sending a .45 through the wall before quickly sidestepping two feet to his right and firing again.

Dan Billingsley's sights were still on the open doorway when the wall exploded and a .45 ripped through the bed's quilts and mattress just five feet from his head.

"Son of a bitch!" he cursed as the second .45 blasted through the bed even closer.

He began to drop to the floor when the third missile blew through the wood and after exploding through the bedding, caught the top of his left shoulder.

Dan screamed again as his Colt dropped to the floor and his blood began to soak his jacket.

Lynn heard the scream and didn't think it as an act but approached the open door with caution before he spotted Dan Billingsley on the floor. He was grabbing at his left shoulder, and as Lynn entered, he could see blood dripping onto the polished floor.

Dan looked up at Lynn as he approached with the sheriff's Colt still cocked and snarled, "Are you gonna shoot me now, Riddell? Come on! Do it! You're your father's son!"

Lynn stared at the unarmed banker, then slowly released the Colt's hammer, slipped it back into his waist and said, "You're right, Billingsley. I am my father's son. The same man who taught me never to fire at an unarmed man, even if he had horns."

Lynn then pulled Dan Billingsley to his feet, marched him out of the bedroom, then walked him down the stairs to get a bandage on the wound.

As they reached the bottom landing, Lynn was startled to see Charlie Red Fox silhouetted against the frame of the front door.

"Charlie?" he asked.

"I told you that I would help, but not fight. I am here to help now."

"Thank you, sir. You're the only lawman in Fort Benton now."

"Until they get a white sheriff," Charlie replied as he approached Lynn and Dan.

Neither spoke while Lynn helped Charlie to staunch Dan Billingsley's wound as the banker moaned.

As Lynn had pointed his pistol at the Dan Billingsley, the murdering husband who had planned to take advantage of Addie's love for her mother, Lynn had felt the powerful urge to pull the trigger as he listened to the man's vitriol. But even as that momentary revulsion struck, he heard his father's voice; his real father's voice, reminding him that there was never any excuse for shooting an unarmed man. It was at that decisive moment, as he stood in the bedroom where he'd been created, when he finally had his answer. He was Lynn Robert Evans and would never doubt for a moment that Dylan Evans was his only father.

Now, he would help Charlie with the aftermath of the confrontation, then tomorrow, he'd talk with Walter Capshaw and get rid of the bank.

In a few days, he'd be on the *Princess of Ohio* and be heading home to his father, his family and Addie.

————

While Lynn escorted Dan Billingsley to get his shoulder wound sutured, Charlie Red Fox said he'd hunt down Mayor William Minden to tell him what had happened and then arrange for the two bodies to be removed from the house.

As Billingsley was walked to the doctor's office, he was furious with himself for his loss of control and confessing to killing his wife in front of Evans. He had thought that the kid would just shoot him and end it so whatever he said didn't matter. But that hadn't happened, and now he faced hanging. The image of dropping through that trap door chilled him much more than the almost instant death provided by a bullet.

With his fury dissipated, he returned to rational thought and would focus his mind on a way to avoid the noose.

The only one who'd heard that confession was alone with him now and he hadn't done anything other than shoot an unarmed desk and could blame the sheriff for everything else.

So, Dan Billingsley decided to use a tried and proven method to avoid punishment; he'd talk or bribe his way out.

"I shouldn't have said those things, Evans," he said as he hobbled alongside Lynn, "I was just saying them to get you mad. Your father would tell you that a confession like that can't be used in a court. Can't we come to some kind of arrangement?"

"Oh, now you mean my father, the United States Marshal?"

Dan was even more irritated with himself for his insults but slowed his pace to give himself more time.

"Yes. Your father in Denver. I'm sure that you want to see him and the rest of your family soon. The sheriff told me that you planned on leaving on the last riverboat for the year."

Lynn didn't reply, so Dan continued, saying, "Listen, Evans, there's nothing to gain by taking me to trial. If you want to leave right away, a trial could take a week or so and then you'd be stuck here over the winter. If you sent Adele away, don't you want to go and find her?"

Lynn didn't bother to reply, but the thought of missing the *Princess of Ohio* and being almost imprisoned in Fort Benton for six months did bother him. He hadn't been trying to be modest when he'd told Addie that he thought his brothers were all handsomer than he was. He also thought each had a better character than his.

If she was going to live with Alwen and Garth on the Double EE for six months, it was likely that she might even be married before he left Fort Benton. If that happened, he knew he couldn't go back. As much as he liked his brothers, the thought of seeing Al or Garth with Addie was devastating.

The long pause told Dan that he'd found Evans' weakness; the kid was smitten with Adele and wanted to go after her. Now he just needed to add a touch more incentive.

"You know, Evans, there doesn't even have to be a trial. I mean, what difference does it really make? The sheriff killed Tex and then you shot him in self-defense. If you just leave me with Doctor Hamilton and tell that Indian deputy that you're not going to press charges. I'd even make a generous wedding gift for when you find Adele. How does three thousand dollars sound? You could build her a nice house and all the clothes she'd ever want. What do you say?"

Lynn was about to tell him to forget it and yank him to a faster pace when the offer of a bribe reminded him of the legal papers that he still had in his money belt and the rumors that Slim had passed about embezzlement at the bank.

"Where could you get that much money, Billingsley? Does Capshaw pay you a lot as a cashier?"

"Your father made him president of the bank, Evans, and he's afraid of his own shadow. When the sheriff asked me to investigate Capshaw for embezzling, I found large

320

irregularities in the books and the sheriff threatened to arrest Walter and notify your father. It was blackmail; pure and simple. Walter agreed to pay what the sheriff demanded, and the sheriff gave me a substantial reward for providing the evidence."

"So, you're just as guilty as Capshaw and the sheriff, and I imagine that Capshaw's embezzling stopped but yours didn't."

"Even if that was true it would be impossible to prove, Evans. You may be good with that pistol, but those ledgers are impeccable because I made them so."

Lynn asked, "If I accepted your offer, would it drain your account, Billingsley? I'd hate the thought of leaving you destitute."

Dan smiled slightly, knowing he had won, then replied, "Not entirely. I'll still have a reasonable nest egg. Do we have an understanding?"

"Not if you continue embezzling from my father's bank."

Dan didn't see any harm in agreeing because he'd have a few days to make another plan of escape with his much larger balance.

"I have no need to do it any longer, Evans, so I'll even turn the books over to Walter Capshaw again. How's that? Do we have a deal?"

They had reached the doctor's office when Lynn stopped and turned to face Dan Billingsley.

"No, Mister Billingsley, we have no deal, arrangement or agreement. I'll take you inside and stay with you while the doctor treats your wound. Then, Acting Sheriff Charlie Red

Fox and I will escort you to jail where you'll be tossed into a cell and await trial for the murder of your wife, embezzlement, and attempted murder."

Dan was about to loudly voice his displeasure when Lynn yanked his left arm to almost drag him up the porch steps, forcing Dan to emit a piercing shriek of pain instead.

———

It was well into the night when Dan Billingsley was finally left in his cell and Lynn was able to tell Charlie about the banker's offer. Lynn suspected that Billingsley was right about one thing; he'd probably miss the *Princess of Ohio*'s departure. It had been a real temptation to just hand the cocky bank cashier over to the doctor and walk away. He didn't care about the money, but to let a man like that even have the remote chance of walking free again was reprehensible.

As he finally returned to his room around midnight, the survivors of the *Princess of Ohio* disaster lay huddled around their campfire while the passengers and crew of the *Alberta* rested at a small settlement ninety miles up the Missouri.

CHAPTER 9

For the first time since he'd arrived at Fort Benton, Lynn was up before the sun appeared over the horizon. He still had one more job to do for his parents and now had even more to discuss with Walter Capshaw.

When he walked to Ziggy's for breakfast, he didn't see anything out of the ordinary which surprised him somewhat. He'd expected to see huddled groups whispering about the shocking events that had transpired at the notorious home that had been owned by the equally notorious Burke Riddell, but everything seemed routine.

That changed when he entered the diner and he immediately heard conversations about gunfire and the rumor that the sheriff and his deputy were both shot and killed by Dan Billingsley, no less.

His name hadn't been mentioned at all, so he was grateful to be able to just have his breakfast in relative peace before leaving to head to the jail.

When he entered, he found Charlie Red Fox talking to a short, round man that Lynn didn't know; which was hardly surprising in itself.

"Lynn, this is Mayor Minden. He wants to talk to you."

Lynn pulled his hat as he walked across the office, taking a glance at Dan Billingsley who was sitting on his cot in the first cell.

"What can I do for you, Mayor?"

The mayor glanced at Charlie, then said, "We'll use the sheriff's office, Mister Evans."

Lynn nodded then followed him down the short hallway and after he entered, the mayor closed the door before stepping past Lynn and taking a seat behind the desk.

As Lynn settled into the chair, the mayor cleared his throat and said, "Charlie told me what happened last night, and I want to assure you that you are not to blame for any of it. The fault lies solely with the sheriff and Dan Billingsley."

Lynn was waiting for the 'but' and it arrived on schedule.

"But even though I'm sure that Dan Billingsley deserves to be punished and possibly hanged for his crimes, my concern is what will happen to the bank when word of the embezzlement gets out. Folks will pull their money out and the bank will fail. They need to have confidence in the institution. Do you understand my dilemma?"

"Yes, sir. What do you propose?"

"I'd like to keep the embezzlement issue quiet, but Billingsley has threatened to expose the issue if he goes to trial. Do you see my concern?"

Lynn had almost told the mayor about the deed and bills of sale in his money belt, but quickly realized that the mayor's worries were very real, and the ownership of the bank didn't matter if Dan Billingsley talked.

"Yes, sir, I do. But even if there is no trial, his threat would still give him power that he doesn't deserve. He'd be able to effectively blackmail the entire town."

"I'm aware of that and the only solution that comes to mind is if he was to be banished; sent into exile."

Lynn blinked, then raised his eyebrows as he asked, "Exile? How can you do that? He'd just come back sooner or later."

"Perhaps, but if he leaves on the last riverboat then he couldn't return until the spring at the earliest and that will give us time to restore the bank to a solid foundation. He won't have much money when he leaves, and that delay will remove his incentive to return."

Lynn could still see problems with expecting Billingsley to just accept his poverty and willingly board the *Princess of Ohio* with a smile but didn't have a solution that was any better.

"But he'll stay in jail until the boat leaves?"

"Of course. Right now, the story flowing around town is that the gunfight was about Adele Price and it's a much more salacious rumor than embezzlement."

Lynn flinched, but just replied, "I won't mention it to anyone, Mayor, and I assume that you've already asked Deputy Red Fox to do the same."

"Yes, and I do appreciate your cooperation, Mister Evans."

Lynn nodded, then rose, opened the door and left the small office with the mayor walking behind him.

As he passed the cell, he looked at Dan Billingsley who had the smug appearance of a man who'd gotten away with murder; as he probably had.

He waved at Charlie Red Fox before heading outside and pulling on his hat.

It was time to finally meet Walter Capshaw. The bank was only open for three hours on Saturdays, and although Lynn wasn't sure of the time, suspected that Mister Capshaw might be in his office even before the doors opened.

Lynn walked quickly along the boardwalk and then diagonally cut across the main street, weaving his way through traffic until he stepped onto the opposite boardwalk and soon reached the Bank of Fort Benton.

The doors were open, so he walked inside and stopped in the lobby, scanned the big room and spotted the small hallway on the right, which he assumed led to Walter Capshaw's office.

Still, he headed for the teller window and had to wait for a farmer to make a deposit, which gave him time to mentally edit his offer to Walt Capshaw.

The farmer left, so Lynn stepped forward, smiled at the teller and asked, "Excuse me, I need to speak to Mister Capshaw."

The teller surprised him when he said, "You must be Lynn Evans; Dylan Evans' son."

"I am, and how did you figure that out?"

"My son, Gill, is a messenger boy for the telegraph office, and he overheard the telegrapher tell Deputy Granger that you were in town. He asked me who you were, so I expected that you might be by to see Mister Capshaw sooner or later. I'm just surprised that it's taken you this long."

"I had other things I had to do first," Lynn replied, then asked, "May I please see Mister Capshaw?"

"Oh, yes. I'm sorry. Just follow the small corridor. His is the only office in back."

"Thank you," Lynn replied as he turned and walked past Dan Billingsley's vacant desk and entered the hallway.

He rapped on the open door and finally had his first look at Walter Capshaw.

"Mister Capshaw?" he asked as the banker looked up at him.

"Yes. May I help you?"

Lynn entered the office, closed the door, and approached his desk, noticing the bank president's already nervous face; probably after hearing the news of his head cashier's arrest after the gunfights at his house. He must have been worried that Billingsley would tell the mayor about his embezzling.

Lynn stood before the desk and replied, "I'm Lynn Evans, the son of Dylan and Gwen Evans, and they asked me to see you about the bank."

Walter stared blankly at Lynn for fifteen long seconds before he quietly asked, "Dylan sent you?"

"Yes, sir. May I sit down?"

"Oh. Yes, of course."

Lynn sat down and said, "I'm sure that you've heard about Dan Billingsley's arrest."

"Yes. It's a horrible thing. I knew that he wasn't the most honorable man, but I was shocked that he had it within him to shoot the sheriff and his deputy."

C. J. PETIT

"I was there, last night, Mister Capshaw. Dan Billingsley didn't shoot either of them. Deputy Granger was shot in the back of the head by Sheriff Martin, and I shot the sheriff after he tried to shoot me. Your head cashier is in jail for murdering his wife and other charges."

Walter swallowed hard before quietly asking, "What other charges?"

"Embezzlement for one. When I was escorting him to the doctor's office for treatment of his gunshot wound, he told me quite a bit after trying to bribe me."

"But you aren't even a lawman. How old are you?"

"I'm sixteen, but you forget that I spent a lot of time being trained by the best lawman I know; my father."

"Is that…is that why your father sent you here?" he stammered, "because of the embezzlement?"

"No. I only heard rumors about it a couple of days ago and then had it confirmed last night by Dan Billingsley. My parents don't know anything about it."

"But you know. What are you going to do?"

"Before I decide anything, Mister Capshaw, tell me how this mess began."

Walter sighed, then with his eyes focused on the desktop, began his confession. It may have been difficult for him to start, but once he began talking, the incredibly tension that had gripped him for years was released and the facts flooded the room.

Lynn heard him explain that he'd only begun embezzling small amounts to help his wife who was having a difficult pregnancy, but Dan had caught him and had blackmailed him into taking a much larger embezzlement. Naturally, Dan had been the only beneficiary of the continuing activity and had assured Walter that Dylan Evans would never know because he didn't even care about the bank anymore.

When he finished, Lynn said, "I was told that you began embezzling because you figured that it had been so long since you'd heard from my parents and you believed that you owned the bank."

"Those were little tidbits of gossip spread by Dan to keep me from exposing him. After I realized that the sheriff was his ally, I knew that I had no alternative."

"Why didn't you just leave?"

"And turn the bank over to Billingsley? That would have been the ultimate betrayal. Your father is the only one who could replace me and if I voluntarily left, then I'm sure Dan would have made his case to your father and been in charge. Once I discovered that the sheriff was his cohort, I was terrified that he might try to have me assassinated, but Dan told me that as long as I behaved myself, he preferred to be the power behind the throne."

Lynn studied the man for a few seconds, then said, "I just left the jail after talking to the mayor. He wants to send Billingsley away on the last riverboat of the year, so he doesn't destroy the confidence in the bank with talk of embezzlement. What do you think?"

"I don't know what to think. This is all such a shock to me."

"I'm still not sure that trying to exile Dan Billingsley will work, but we have other things to talk about, Mister Capshaw."

"Your father will want me fired now; won't he?"

"No, I don't believe he would even if he was here. You made a mistake and then were put in an impossible situation. I would have acted differently, but I'm not a banker. I may not know a better solution for Billingsley, but I can help the bank and you."

Walter lifted his eyes to look at Lynn and asked, "How could you help? You're just a kid."

"Before I left Denver, my parents gave me two tasks; the first was to find each of the women who had accompanied my mother to Fort Benton seventeen years ago and if any wished to leave, to escort them away from town. The only woman still here was Beatrice Price, and I arranged for her and her daughter's passage on the riverboat that brought me here.

"The second task was to get rid of the bank. They don't want it and they had a legal bill of sale drawn up in Denver, had a copy made and then both notarized. All I need to do is fill in the name of the buyer and the amount."

"Is that what you intend to do?"

"Yes, Mister Capshaw, and I'd like to write your name on the bill of sale. The only question is the amount of the sale."

"The bank itself is worth about five thousand dollars and I'm sure that if your father asked an attorney to write the bill of sale, then he'd know that he was entitled to the net profits made by the bank since he left. I don't have that much money, Mister Evans."

"I would have been disappointed if you had, Mister Capshaw. Let me ask you this. What is Dan Billingsley's account balance?"

"The last time I checked, it was just short of forty-five thousand dollars. It's almost half of the bank's total assets."

Lynn did some hurried calculations, then said, "Mister Capshaw, that account may be frozen until an arrangement is made with the bank owner; currently my father who is hundreds of miles away and has no interest in coming back to Fort Benton. However, if I sell the bank to you for twenty-four thousand dollars of Mister Billingsley's funds, then you'd be able to transfer the remainder of that account to the bank's operating account. Is that right?"

Walter stared at the tall young man sitting across from him and slowly replied, "Yes. That's right."

"Is that an acceptable offer, Mister Capshaw? You'll be the owner of the bank for a total of twenty-four thousand dollars which will be wired to my father in Denver."

Walter's relief was overwhelming as he nodded as Lynn unbuttoned his shirt to remove his money belt.

As he completed the two copies of the bill of sale, Lynn had no idea how to get the large sum transferred via the telegraph, but obviously Walter Capshaw did.

The transaction itself didn't take long, and after completing the bill of sale and returning his copy to his money belt, he followed the new owner of the bank to the teller's window.

Lynn could see a newfound confidence in Walter Capshaw when he filled out a draft, then told his teller that he would be back shortly and beckoned Lynn to follow him.

After they entered the telegraph office, and Walter was explaining the transfer to the operator, Lynn took the opportunity to fill out a short accompanying message to his father.

He smiled as he carefully wrote each letter in bold print rather than scrawled cursive.

Walter turned to him as he reached the telegrapher and said, "It's on its way to your father, Mister Evans."

"Thank you, Mister Capshaw," he replied, then handed the telegrapher his message and said, "I need this sent, too."

The telegrapher looked at the message, nodded and turned to tap it out on his key set.

As the operator's practiced finger danced on the key, Lynn listened to the dots and dashes, each grouping making up a letter or number until it formed a word.

The message wouldn't mean much to the man sending it or the ones relaying it all the way to Denver. It was only special to him and the final recipient.

When he finished sending the telegram, the operator handed it back to Lynn and said, "Forty cents."

Lynn handed him the silver, then accepted the receipt for the enormous voucher that had been transmitted just before his message.

After leaving the office, Walter asked, "What are you going to do now?"

"I'm going to wait anxiously for the *Princess of Ohio* to come steaming up that channel, then a day or two later, I'll leave Fort Benton and have no desire to return."

"When you see your father again, tell him I'm very grateful for all that he did then and what you did now. And be sure to let him know that I think he should be proud of his firstborn son."

"He always has been, Mister Capshaw," Lynn said as he smiled at the new bank owner.

_____

Feeling incredibly light, Lynn practically floated down the boardwalk as he headed for the livery. He wanted to take Griffin out for a long ride.

When he entered, he wasn't surprised to find Slim almost bursting at his seams wanting to ask about the shootout.

As he saddled his gelding, Lynn provided most of the details of the gunfight, but left out anything to do with the bank. As the mayor had mentioned; gossip about sex is always more interesting than funny business with ledgers.

_____

By the time Lynn was riding west out of Fort Benton, the *Alberta* was making a good twelve knots going downstream and the pilot had been able to keep the sternwheeler in the center of the channel which had been remarkably free of debris.

By noon, they were just forty miles away from the wreck of the *Princess of Ohio.*

333

_____

After he returned from a long and pleasant ride, Lynn left Griffin with Slim, then headed to the jail to talk to Charlie Red Fox. He had a few more days to spend in Fort Benton and decided he'd learn more about what had happened since is parents left.

When he walked into the office, Charlie was behind the desk writing something and Dan Billingsley was snoring loudly in his cell.

Charlie didn't even look up when Lynn entered, so as he removed his hat, Lynn asked, "Did you recognize me by the sound of my footsteps?"

Charlie still didn't look up as he replied, "That is a foolish thing to say. I just don't care who comes in because whoever walks through that door won't talk to me anyway."

Lynn tossed his hat on an empty chair and sat down.

"Why is our ex-banker friend sleeping at this time of day?"

"The doctor gave him laudanum for his pain. He is a coward and deserves the pain, but I cannot take it from him."

"I wish there had been a trial. The man deserves to hang."

Charlie finally looked up as he said, "I heard him tell you about killing his wife. He should not live."

"You heard that? How long were you there? I didn't see you when I went out to the porch."

"Long enough."

Lynn didn't ask if he would have prevented the sheriff from shooting him, but said, "He's going to be on the *Princess of Ohio* with me for almost two weeks. I wonder if he's going to try to kill me on the way."

"Perhaps you should let him swim first."

"It'll be hard to resist the temptation," he replied before asking, "Charlie can you tell me a history of what happened in Fort Benton after my parents left?"

Charlie glanced back at his prisoner, then said, "Just the important things."

For two hours, Lynn sat in the jail listening to Charlie with Dan Billingsley's snoring as a backdrop.

————

In Omaha, Deputy U.S. Marshal Benji Green and his family were starting to pack for their trip to Denver.

Alwen and Garth had arrived and had been a welcome help to the heavy workload, and spent most of their time with the family, even though they shared a room at the Herndon House.

It hadn't taken long after they were reintroduced to the younger Greens that Alwen took serious note of a very different Martha from the girl he'd known before leaving Omaha.

He knew that Martha had harbored a serious crush on him when they'd been in school, but after that first day, he hoped to rekindle that flame that he'd never reciprocated.

Benji and Alice Green weren't oblivious to the budding romance, so they made sure that at least one of them was around when Alwen and Martha were together.

Garth was a bit jealous but deferred to his older brother making the excuse that she was too old for him anyway.

They planned on leaving for Denver on the 20th of the month and would be arriving late the next day.

Romance aside, it was a busy household as everyone prepared to pull up their roots and head west.

————

It wasn't until late Saturday afternoon that a messenger arrived at the Denver offices of the United States Marshal.

Bryn was talking to Pete Towers when he spotted Jack Templeton enter and asked, "Bad news, Jack?"

"I've got two messages for the marshal, but they're marked personal, so I have to give them to him."

Bryn expected that they were from Lynn, so he turned and shouted, "Marshal, you have two personal telegrams!"

Dylan was reading a report when he heard his brother's shout and instantly thought that they were from Lynn and probably were bad news.

He shot up from his chair, rammed his left thigh into the corner of his desk in his haste, then cursed under his breath, before he hobbled out of his office and entered the main room.

Jack handed him the telegrams and waited.

Bryn watched his brother's face while he handed the boy a nickel.

Dylan opened the first one, then blinked and looked at Bryn and said, "It's a voucher for twenty-four thousand dollars from the Bank of Fort Benton."

"I'm surprised that they were still there, much less had that much money."

Dylan didn't reply as he quickly opened the second.

He read:

US MARSHAL DYLAN EVANS DENVER COLO

BANK SOLD
BEATRICE PRICE ENROUTE WITH DAUGHTER
WILL LEAVE ON NEXT BOAT
YOU ARE MY ONLY FATHER

LYNN EVANS FORT BENTON DAKOTA TERR

Dylan stared at the telegram, fully understanding the last, most meaningful line, then handed it to Bryn.

"He's coming home, Bryn. I'm sure he'll have a lot to tell us when he gets here, too."

"That's a lot more than you expected; isn't it?"

"The money is his and he's already asked that it be divided equally among his brothers and sisters, but I'm proud of him for handling it so well and I know that Gwen will be just as relieved as I was when I read that last line."

"You'll have to explain that one later."

"We'll talk on Sunday when we all get together. I'm sure that Gwen will be happy to know that Beatrice is coming, too."

"I'm surprised that he didn't add much detail."

"That's my fault, I suppose. I told him to be careful what you put across the wire because you never know who's reading it. Besides, he'll be home about the same time that Benji and his family arrive."

"That, big brother, will be an interesting time."

"I don't believe that we can imagine how interesting it will be until he gets here, Bryn."

————

The *Alberta* should have docked at Fort Jacobson, but they'd made such good time and there was a full moon, so the pilot recommended that they keep going and reach Mandan a day ahead of schedule.

So, as the sun was almost ready to begin painting the sky pink, the sternwheeler rounded a bend and the lookout on the upper deck spotted a fire on the western shore ahead.

"There's a fire ahead, Captain," he shouted as he turned to the wheelhouse.

Captain Clyde had been talking to the pilot when he heard the lookout, then looked forward and spotted the fire.

He left the wheelhouse and stepped to the rail of the upper foredeck then stood next to the lookout.

The steamboat kept plowing closer and soon, the captain spotted the sickening sight of a smokestack rising from the river.

He trotted back to the wheelhouse and said, "It looks like the *Princess* is down up ahead, Pete. Let's slow her down so we can pick up any survivors," then he turned to the speaking tube, pulled off the cap and shouted, "Ahead one third, but be ready to reverse!"

"Aye, aye, Captain. Ahead one third," the engineer's voice echoed from the metal tube.

———

"It's the *Alberta*!" yelled stock manager Tom Rostowski as he pointed at the approaching steamer.

The others all stood and began to cheer knowing that they'd soon be rescued.

It took some fine maneuvering to get the *Alberta* moored closely enough to the wreck to allow the survivors to board and not get the rescuing craft join her sister on the bottom; but less than two hours after finding the sunken riverboat, the *Alberta* was able get all of the survivors on board, but had to stay anchored to the location as the sun set.

The added passengers needed accommodation, so Addie and Betty moved their luggage out of cabin fourteen to make room.

As they rearranged cabin thirteen, Addie said, "Lynn won't make it now. He's going to have to stay there until spring."

"I know, Addie, but I'm sure that he'll be anxious to return when he can."

Addie nodded, but her worry that Lynn may find the answer to the question of his true birth father and not come back at all had been growing each day that the *Alberta* had taken her further away from him.

Now, he wouldn't be returning for another six months, if he did come back and it sent Addie into an even deeper depression that she'd felt when she was about to move into Dan Billingsley's house.

———

"I wish Lynn had told us more," Gwen said as she stared at the short telegram.

"He'll be coming home in a couple of weeks and let us know what happened."

She looked at her husband and said, "Betty can tell us how things were when she gets here, but the fact that he didn't come with her bothers me. He was supposed to escort her to Denver. Something kept him there."

"He stayed to find the answer to his question that drove him there, sweetheart. And judging by his last sentence; he found it. He'll be fine."

"He'd better be. This is so odd for me; having only one son in the house."

"Get used to it, Gwendolyn. They're all growing up. Soon, none of them will live here, but they'll bring our grandchildren to visit."

"Good grief, Dylan!" she exclaimed, "I'm only thirty-three and you're making me a grandmother!"

Dylan wrapped her in his arms, kissed her, and as he slid his hands across her behind, whispered, "You don't feel like a grandmother, my love."

"Prove it," she whispered back as she let the telegram flutter to the floor.

―――――

It was late afternoon when the *Alberta* finally docked at Mandan

Within an hour, two telegrams were on the wires; the much longer one heading to St. Louis to the *Princess of Ohio*'s owners detailing the loss and the names of those who perished in the disaster, and the second to Fort Benton notifying the dock supervisor of the sinking. It would be his job to pass along the information to those who were expecting the shipments of cargo.

As they had on other stops, Addie and Betty remained on board rather than go into town.

They had already decided to leave the boat in Yankton and take the train to Omaha. The sight of the *Princess*'s carcass and the woeful state of her survivors had been the deciding factor.

―――――

Lynn found it difficult to find sleep that night, which surprised him because there was nothing but boring routine awaiting him until he disembarked in Yankton.

He was spending those waking hours on his bed thinking about Addie, but beneath those pleasant, yet worrisome thoughts, was the frustration knowing that Dan Billingsley was escaping justice. He may leave Fort Benton apparently destitute, but Lynn suspected that the shrewd banker had a significant hidden cache of currency somewhere just in case he'd been caught. He'd leave Fort Benton and probably head to another town and set himself up again.

He knew that he couldn't shove Billingsley over the rail of the riverboat on its way south, but maybe the man would try something, and Lynn could provide justice after all.

Even as Lynn finally slipped into sleep, the message that would change everything was slowly being relayed from Mandan.

CHAPTER 10

Sunday, October 5, 1873

Lynn's day began no different than Saturday had started, with a quick trip to the privy, a morning wash and shave, then dressing before leaving the hotel to get his breakfast.

He had just taken a seat at Ziggy's when he overheard a diner telling his companion, "She went down around Mandan."

He froze and slowly turned to look at the man, horrified to think that the *Alberta* had sunk, and Addie might have drowned in the accident.

He rose, walked quickly to the other table and asked, "Excuse me. I couldn't help but overhear you say something about a boat sinking. Do you know have any details?"

He looked up at Lynn and replied, "Only that she was the *Princess of Ohio* and her boiler blew a few days ago. Survivors were rescued by the *Alberta*."

"Thanks," Lynn said as he turned, walked back to his table, snatched his hat and left the diner.

He'd been incredibly relieved to know that Addie was safe, but then realized that he'd lost his only way out of Fort Benton until spring.

As he yanked his hat on, he wanted to scream but just let out a low, "Son of a bitch!" as he headed for the jail.

He didn't know what they would do with Dan Billingsley now, but even as he stepped along the dusty main street, he tried to think of an alternative way of getting home.

There were roads that he could take but he knew that it would take him a lot longer and have many more risks. The smart thing was to send a telegram to his father and wait out the winter, but he had no desire to spend another six months here. The weather wasn't bad at all right now and it would be another month before it turned bad, so he wanted to get home before it did.

He had an idea, but he'd talk to Charlie Red Fox about it. He'd promised to help, and Lynn knew that he could. The only question was whether or not Charlie would give him the assistance, or just tell him that he was being a fool; which he knew was true.

When he entered the sheriff's office, he didn't pay any attention to Dan Billingsley who was still sleeping, but not snoring.

"Charlie, did you hear about the *Princess of Ohio*?" he asked as he took a seat.

"No one talks to me. What happened?"

"I just heard that her boiler blew outside of Mandan and the boat sank."

"Then you will stay."

"No, I won't sit here for the winter, Charlie. I'm going home. I just want you to help me."

"You are making a mistake."

"I know, but I have to go. I just don't want to ride eight hundred miles."

"You will walk?" Charlie asked with a slight smile.

"No. I want to take a raft or a canoe down the Missouri."

Charlie's eyebrows shot up as he said, "That is even more foolish than walking. Only a lovesick boy would think of doing such a thing."

"I'll admit that I am attracted to Addie, but I simply don't want to stay here, Charlie. I need to build a raft or find a canoe."

"Have you used a canoe?"

"My brothers and I had one years ago and used it in the Missouri, so I'm used to paddling."

"There are rapids here and you will be lost before you get far."

"I've seen them and I'm willing to take the chance."

Charlie stared at Lynn, saw the determination in his eyes and knew that even if he didn't help, the boy would make his own way and a canoe was much better than a raft.

"I will get you a canoe and supplies for your journey, but I still think you are a fool."

Lynn nodded, but smiled as he replied, "I may be a fool, Charlie, but I'll make it."

Charlie smiled back as he said, "Maybe so. See me tomorrow. I will send word."

"Thanks, Charlie. I've got to start preparing myself," then looked at the cell and asked, "What about him?"

Charlie glanced at his prisoner and said, "He is my problem."

Lynn rose, shook Charlie Red Fox's hand, then left the jail. It was a Sunday, so he couldn't start buying his supplies for the journey, but he needed to talk to Slim.

———

"*You're rowin' all the way to Omaha?*" Slim exclaimed.

"Just to Yankton where I'll pick up the train. I figure I can make it in just ten days or so."

"How'd you figure that? Even a steamboat takes a couple of weeks."

"That's because they have to stop overnight to avoid obstacles. I'm planning on staying on the river as long as I can and just pulling to the shore to get some sleep and answering nature's call. I should be able to keep going for at least sixteen hours each day. Even if I only drift with the current, that'll be about five miles an hour or eighty miles a day."

"I'm with the Injun deputy on this one, Lynn. That's a mighty foolish thing to do."

"I agree with both of you, Slim. But what I'll need you to do is to take care of Griffin and my saddle over the winter and then arrange to ship him to me in Denver when the first steamer arrives in spring. I'll leave you enough money to cover the boarding and shipping."

"I'd offer to buy him from ya, but I reckon he's too important for you to let him go."

"He was a gift from my father, Slim, and I'll never let him go. I'd appreciate it if you could take him out and let him run when you can, too."

Slim grinned as he said, "Now there's somethin' to look forward to doin'. He's a mighty handsome feller, Lynn."

Lynn stroked Griffin's neck as he replied, "He is much more than that, Slim. He's a champion."

Lynn then pulled a hundred dollars out of his money belt and handed it to Slim.

"That should cover it, but if it's short, just ask Mister Capshaw for the difference."

"Why would he pay up?"

"Just tell him it's for my horse and he won't bother asking why."

"Okay, Lynn. When do you reckon to be leavin'?"

"Tuesday or Wednesday morning. I want to get used to using the canoe before I hit those rapids."

Slim shook his head but didn't remind Lynn what a stupid thing he was doing; mostly because as foolish as it sounded, he wished he could do it.

Lynn returned to his room, sat at the small desk and began to write a list of supplies he thought he'd need before he began calculating how long it would really take him, assuming he made it at all.

———

It didn't take Charlie Red Fox long to arrange for the canoe and supplies for Lynn. He rode east out of Fort Benton and soon reached the Crow encampment outside of the army fort. He explained what he needed and the reason to his cousin, who snickered, but said he'd have the canoe and supplies ready by Monday evening.

As he rode back to the jail, he thought that as foolish as what Lynn was attempting to do wasn't nearly as absurd as the white man's law that allowed a man like Dan Billingsley to live. Lynn may have suspected that the embezzling banker had a large cache of his stolen money hidden away, but Charlie not only knew that he did have the currency, he also knew where it was. If Billingsley walked free, he'd still be a wealthy man and cause more pain.

Charlie Red Fox could not allow either to happen. Justice should be the same for white men as it is for anyone else.

———

The Sunday get together on the Double EE was filled with conversation about the voucher and the pending arrival of Betty and her unnamed daughter. Sprinkled in with the talk about Lynn and speculation of what had happened in Fort Benton, was the added anticipation of the arrival of Benji Green and his family.

But it was the much quieter and more private talk that Dylan and Gwen had with the adult members of the Evans clan that was the most emotional.

"He was worried that he'd suddenly become another Burke Riddell?" Bryn asked with wide eyes.

"I know it sounds difficult to understand," Dylan replied, "but you have to realize that he's still sixteen and unsure of himself. I know that he suspected the truth of his parentage for some time, but it didn't bother him until Ryan goaded him into asking us. Once we explained it to him, we both thought that it still didn't matter until he disappeared with Ryan and had that mess south of Colorado Springs.

"When he returned after that debacle and told us that he needed to go to Fort Benton, he explained why he had to go. We tried to talk him out of it, but I knew that if he didn't go with our permission, he'd go anyway. I have no idea what happened up there to give him his answer, but he's no longer worried about it. I just wish he'd gotten on that boat with Betty Price and her daughter."

"I wonder what the daughter is like," Erin said, "if she had been conceived right after Beatrice was married, then she'd be Lynn's age. That could have been interesting."

Katie smiled and added, "Not interesting enough for him to join her. I think we should have another family shindig for the Greens and Betty and her daughter even if it's not a Sunday. We'll all want to meet the mysterious, unnamed daughter."

"Maybe you ladies consider that a priority, Mrs. Evans, but I'd rather meet Benji again. We could use another good deputy in the office."

"Leave it to you men to ruin a perfectly good romantic fantasy," Erin said with a light laugh, "but we can always speculate about Martha Green and Al."

Dylan glanced at Gwen before saying, "Why did you bring that up? Alwen never said a word about Martha, even when we lived in Omaha."

"Martha had a crush on him, Dylan, but Al didn't notice. Now that she's probably a handsome young woman, he will definitely notice," Gwen replied.

Dylan just looked at the other adult males, then shrugged. He hadn't noticed any of it and doubted if they had either.

————

Monday morning found Lynn in Dennison's buying the supplies on his list. There couldn't be much because of the limited volume of space, so each one had to be critical. He bought matches, a wool blanket, and a small reel of cord. He didn't buy any more ammunition or tins of food, but bought a large bag of salted jerky, some smoked pork and another of hardtack for nourishment. His most important purchase was a fishing kit. It contained six hooks and some fishing line, but it was just what he needed.

After paying for the order, he returned to his room to pack. Despite the still moderate weather, he was glad that he'd bought the heavier gloves and scarf. He stuffed his new items into the large set of saddlebags and by the time he'd finished, both sets were bulging. He was satisfied that he could make it to Yankton with what he had with him, so he left his room to go see Charlie Red Fox. It wasn't noon yet but was anxious to find out if Charlie was able to get a canoe.

After leaving the hotel, he was scanning the traffic for his path to the other side of the street when he spotted a hearse parked in front of the jail.

He ignored the wheeled vehicles and horses as he trotted quickly across the street and slowed when he neared the sheriff's office.

LYNN'S SEARCH

Lynn had to wait as two men carried a blanket enshrouded body out of the jail before he was able to enter the office.

Once inside, he saw Charlie Red Fox and the mayor listening to Doctor Hamilton, who'd treated Dan Billingsley's shoulder wound.

None of them paid attention to Lynn as he quietly approached, and heard the doctor say, "It's not your fault, Charlie. He just took too much. I warned him about it, but men like that can't take any pain at all. Looking back, I should have just let him suffer."

Charlie just nodded, then the mayor noticed Lynn and said, "Well, we may not have been able to put Billingsley on trial, but God certainly rendered His judgement."

Lynn didn't want any more information about the man's sudden death, so he simply replied, "I imagine he's been judged by the Lord and is roasting in hell as we speak."

"Amen to that," the obviously relieved mayor said before he and the doctor turned and left the jail.

Lynn wasn't about to ask Charlie Red Fox if Dan's death was accidental, so he asked, "Will I have to build a raft, Charlie?"

"No. I have asked my cousin to bring a canoe and supplies, and he said that he will have them by sunset. He will leave it on the south riverbank in the trees near the dock."

"Thank your cousin for me, and thank you for your help, Charlie Red Fox. I wish that you could take over as sheriff. You're a good man and the town hasn't had any luck finding good men to fill the job."

"They would never let a Crow be sheriff. If the new one is bad, I will not stay. This town will fail soon anyway."

"Why do you think that will happen?"

"The new northern railroad is passing far south and once it is done, no one will come here. White people no longer follow the river; they follow their iron rails."

"I, for one wish, this place good riddance. If you see fit to burn down Riddell's house before you go, then you'd be doing us all a service."

"I may visit that house tonight."

Lynn didn't think that he'd burn it down but wouldn't be surprised if he did, either.

Lynn shook Charlie's hand and said, "Thank you for your help, Charlie."

"Despite your foolishness, I wish you well and hope that you find your woman."

Lynn smiled, said, "So, do I," then turned and left the jail for the last time.

The hearse was gone and all he needed to do now is send a telegram to his father to let him know that he was leaving in the morning and should be back by the last week in October.

After sending the message, he had a big lunch and was planning on eating an even bigger supper. He planned on climbing into that canoe before daybreak.

―――――

After Lynn had gone, Charlie left the jail and headed for the Riddell/Billingsley house with no intention of setting it ablaze. After giving his prisoner a large dose of his medicine, he knew that the house would be sold soon, and he didn't want the new owner to have the banker's stolen money. It belonged to the previous bank owner – the River Warrior.

———

Lynn was still belching as he lay on his bed; his two overstuffed saddlebags and his Winchester on the floor nearby. He was more than a little anxious about tomorrow. He hadn't paddled a canoe in years, and he knew that the Missouri River up here was much different than the one that was practically placid as it passed by Omaha.

Still, the excitement overweighed his anxiety. If everything worked out, then he'd be reunited with his family again in a couple of weeks, and then he could spend more time with Addie, assuming she hadn't already been smitten by Alwen or Garth. He fully expected each of his brothers to be awed by Addie and would easily fall in love with her, just as he had. He admitted that it had been the driving reason for taking this reckless journey.

———

Lynn knew that he had only slept for a couple of hours, but when his eyes snapped open, he couldn't return to sleep, so with the moonlight filtering into his room, he dressed, then hung his weighty saddlebags and the new blanket over his shoulders, picked up his Winchester, and left his room.

He crossed the lobby, leaving his room key on the unmanned desk and not caring about the three days' rent he'd be leaving behind, left the hotel and stepped into the chilly October air.

He looked at the bright moon overhead that was now waning and began walking toward the docks. He had no idea when the predawn would arrive, but there was enough moonlight to make it almost unnecessary.

After passing the docks, he continued along the southern bank of the Missouri, listening to the sounds of the night. He entered the trees and after winding his way around the trunks found the canoe a lot faster than he had anticipated.

He had expected to find a small, two-man craft, but this was a lot larger and had painted markings along both sides of what he thought must be the bow.

He reached the canoe and before loading his supplies, noticed that there were already some supplies and a big fur inside. He was grateful for Charlie Red Fox's consideration, but didn't want to take the time to find out what he'd provided for supplies, so he set his Winchester on what looked like a bearskin, then laid his saddlebags on the bow end of the canoe before getting behind the stern and pushing it slowly into the river.

The current was moving pretty swiftly and yanked the canoe sideways faster than he'd expected, so as soon as he gave it one last shove, he quickly hopped inside and let the river take him away.

As the canoe began to drift, Lynn took one of the two paddles that had been left inside and began to give it direction as he added some forward momentum to the river's flow.

He was pleased that his paddling skills hadn't left him as he began a rhythmic stroke that he'd have to maintain for days. It had to be smooth and not overly aggressive. He had to keep the same, steady pace.

As he paddled, he guided the canoe toward the center of the river to avoid unseen obstructions and to take advantage of the fastest current.

His exhilaration was tempting him to rush, so he needed to calm himself for those first few minutes.

He figured the best way to keep a steady, but not fast, rhythm was to let his mind sing an imaginary song, but most of the tunes that he knew were too upbeat, so he finally settled on Stephen Foster's, *I Dream of Jeannie with the Light Brown Hair*. He didn't know many of the lyrics, but it didn't matter; only the rhythm was important. He did, however, replace Jeannie with another two-syllable lady's name.

———

It was another two hours before the sun almost exploded in front of his eyes, illuminating the swirling waters of the Missouri River before him.

He knew that he was now moving northeast but didn't know how far he'd gone or how close he was to the rapids.

If he'd managed six knots for the first two hours, then he'd only be a little more than twelve miles downriver, so they should be another three or four hours ahead. He expected to hear them before he saw them and hoped he didn't panic when he saw the raging waters that had bounced the *Alberta* so violently on her journey to Fort Benton.

He looked down at the bearskin's thick fur and wondered what was concealed beneath. Despite his curiosity, he knew he'd have to pull off the main channel and stop to find out and wasn't about to do that before it was necessary.

Lynn kept his eyes scanning the shoreline on both sides of the river for any signs of Indians. He didn't believe that they'd pay too much attention to him even if they spotted him. His father had told him of the harmless confrontation that he and his Uncle Kyle had on their journey to Denver, so he was reasonably certain that even if they spotted him, they would pose no danger.

As part of his planning for the expedition, he had debated about stopping at any of the settlements along the way. If he had enough supplies, then he wouldn't have the need to stop and had decided to bypass them unless he had a problem with the canoe. His other concern about stopping at the settlements that he'd have to leave his canoe and most of his supplies on the nearby shore if he went into the fort or town, and there would be a good chance that he'd return to an empty canoe or no canoe at all.

The canoe itself, despite its size, wasn't proving any more difficult to paddle than the one he'd used as a boy. Maybe it was because he was proportionally the same size back then. Whatever the reason, he was very comfortable as he propelled the light watercraft along the surface of the Missouri.

––––––

Lynn's first stop was in mid-morning when nature demanded that he pull ashore. He'd attempted to empty his bladder from the canoe but had almost capsized the boat before deciding that it was better if he stood on the riverbank.

After relieving himself, he took a few minutes to satisfy his curiosity and lifted the bearskin. There was a large leather pouch, so he picked it up and before he flipped open the flap, he knew what was inside from the smell and wondered why he hadn't noticed it before. It must have been blocked by the bearskin. It was a good amount of pemmican and although he wasn't overly fond of the taste of the batch he'd tried in Colorado, he knew it was highly nutritious and would satisfy his hunger. Still, he knew that the recipe for pemmican varied widely among the tribes, so he jabbed his index finger inside and tasted it; finding it quite pleasant after all. He still didn't know what the Crow had used to make it but laid it back on the bottom of the canoe and picked up the second, smaller leather pouch. This one had no smell, so he opened the flap and spread the sides apart, then stared with wide eyes at the thick bundle of currency.

He had no idea of how much was inside or why it was even there but suspected that it had something to do with Dan Billingsley simply because of the size of the stack.

He began fingering through the bills and finally found a small white sheet of paper and slipped it from the banknotes.

He assumed that it had been written by Charlie Red Fox as he read:

This belongs to your father. It would be wasted when the house burns.

He shoved the note back into the pouch, then after he set it the money-filled sack onto the floor of the canoe, he opened his jacket, unbuttoned his shirt and removed the waterproof money belt. He wasn't sure it would be able to hold all of the money but began to arrange the bills and put them into the money belt. As he did, he began doing a rough count and by the time the money belt could accept no more, he'd already managed to put almost thirteen thousand dollars inside, and there were still another twenty or so bills in the small leather pouch.

After sealing the money belt, he slid it around his waist, buttoned his shirt, clambered back into the canoe, and slid it back into the river.

As he paddled along to his silent rendition of, *I Dream of Addie with the Dark Blue Eyes*, he developed a method of eating without losing headway.

So far, his decision to leave Fort Benton via a canoe wasn't looking foolish at all, but he expected it to change when he reached the first set of rapids.

———

"Another personal telegram for the marshal," Mark Templeton said as he stepped close to the desk.

Boris Barkov said, "Just go on back, Mark. He's in his office."

The boy nodded then trotted past the desk.

Kyle was talking to Dylan about setting up accounts for the children with the money Lynn had sent when Mark arrived with his message.

"This just came for you, Marshal," he said as he held it out.

Kyle gave him his tip again this time as Dylan ripped open the sealed message.

He stared at the telegram with a confused look then handed it to Kyle as he asked, "Does this make any sense to you?"

Kyle read:

US MARSHAL DYLAN EVANS DENVER COLO

PRINCESS LOST
WILL NOT WAIT FOR SPRING
LEAVING TOMORROW VIA CANOE
SHOULD ARRIVE BY END OF MONTH

LYNN EVANS FORT BENTON DAKOTA TERR

"I don't get that first line at all. Who is the princess and how did he lose her?"

"I have no idea, but whoever she is or whatever the reason, it sounds as if he'd planning on paddling a canoe all the way to Omaha. That's a long way to go, Kyle."

"You've made that trip, Dylan, do you think he'll be able to do it?"

"It's not that bad after those rapids, but a sixteen-year-old traveling alone down that river is a bit spooky."

Kyle grinned and said, "I was sixteen when I started walking across Pennsylvania."

"When you think about it, each of us left home around that age and we did all right."

"We did more than just all right, Dylan. But I'm not in the least bit ashamed to admit that it if wasn't for you and Bryn, I wouldn't be where I am now."

"We can't forget what Gwen, Erin and Katie have done for us, either. I wonder if Lynn's princess will be his rock after he finds her again; assuming that he does."

"Are you going to send a telegram to Fort Benton to ask what happened?"

Dylan thought about it for a few seconds, then shook his head as he replied, "No, Kyle. He's already gone and all we'd get is their version of what happened. All we can do is wait until he arrives. But I am going to send one to Benji and the boys up in Omaha to let them know he's on his way."

"Maybe Betty's daughter is the princess and she can tell us what is going on."

"It could be. Let's head out and get that message sent."

———

Lynn had been scanning the river ahead for the rapids, but his first indication that they were close was the sudden increase in the speed of the current and soon heard the distant roar of the turbulent water.

He maintained his steady rhythmic oar strokes as the water began tossing the canoe, trying to twist it sideways. He was already having difficulty keeping the bow pointed downriver and knew that there was much worse ahead.

Then the white water appeared as the Missouri plowed past rocks and boulders in its centuries long effort to wear them down to sand.

Lynn began changing to a more hectic stroke, shifting the paddle to one side or the other to keep the canoe from being capsized as the wild water splashed around him and the canoe raced past the dangerous rocks.

He knew that if the thin-skinned canoe so much as scraped one of the boulders, it would be lost, and he'd probably join it in a watery grave.

LYNN'S SEARCH

He fought the river's violence for what seemed like hours but knew it had only been minutes. Each second that the canoe remained afloat was a victory, but the war wasn't close to ending.

He could see smoother water ahead and thought he was free, but the river had one last trick up its sleeve, when the last enormous boulder on his right created a giant eddy on the other side that yanked the canoe into a spin when it struck the outer edge of the whirlpool.

Lynn felt like he had when his father had held his hands and spun him in a circle, but this wasn't nearly as much fun as the canoe rotated quickly clockwise in the strong, circling current of the eddy.

He saw the boulder reappear in his vision which meant he was facing upriver, so he used that as a guide and just as it left his view, he dug his paddle deeply into the swirling water and pulled as hard as he could to launch his vessel out of its trap.

The canoe surged forward just a few feet but caught the fast current of the main channel and was yanked downstream, away from the eddy.

Lynn continued to paddle until he reached smoother water, then pulled the paddle onboard as he breathed heavily from the effort.

He quickly searched the bottom of the canoe for leaks, but only saw the waves of the inch or so of water that had splashed aboard from the rapid's anger.

He glanced back at the rapids that now seemed so tranquil and knew that the second, longer violent water obstacle was still waiting for him.

After he regained his air, he resumed paddling, but wondered if he should attempt the next rapids if he reached them before sunset. It would be a gamble, but once he was safely past those rocks, it would be just a normally dangerous passage with floating obstacles that could punch a hole in his boat's skin or men who wanted to punch a hole in his own.

At least he didn't have to worry about shoals or sandbars like riverboat pilots. His canoe's draft was measured in inches, not feet.

―――――

Alwen asked, "Lynn is taking a canoe all the way from Fort Benton?"

"That's what your father says," Benji replied, "but the rest of the telegram has me wondering."

"You mean the 'princess' thing?" asked Garth.

"No, I think I know what that is, but I'll go and check in a little while. I think Lynn meant the *Princess of Ohio*. That was the last boat to leave for Fort Benton about a week or so after Lynn left on his boat."

"Do you think she sank?" asked Alice.

"I'll go down to the docks and find out. Do you boys want to come along?"

Garth quickly replied, "Sure," as he popped to his feet.

Alwen glanced at Martha, then said, "I'll wait here, if that's okay."

Benji glanced at his wife, winked, then said, "Let's go, Garth."

―――――

It didn't take a lot of investigation before Benji found that he'd been right, so after getting as much information as possible from the dock manager, he and Garth stopped at the closest Western Union office to pass the news on to Dylan.

As they walked back to the Green's half-empty house, Garth asked, "Do you think Lynn's girlfriend and her mother are going to be here before we're supposed to leave?"

"I got the impression that they'll be here before then, but if they aren't here yet, we might wait a day or two. How do you figure she's his girlfriend?"

Garth shrugged and replied, "I don't know. It just sounds like a good story."

Benji snickered and looked over at the boy and felt a bit sorry for Garth being younger than Lynn and Alwen. But at least after they both had been corralled, Garth would be able to have his pick, and Benji thought that any young lady who caught him would be one very lucky girl.

―――――

The human princess was getting more anxious with each turn of the *Alberta*'s big sternwheel. They were getting close to Yankton and would soon leave the riverboat to board a train to Omaha. Then the next day, she hoped to find news about Lynn. She was sure that by now he must have heard about the sinking of the *Princess of Ohio* and would be stranded in Fort Benton. He surely would have sent a telegram to his parents, and maybe they notified the deputy marshal in Omaha who would join them on the trip to Denver.

Her biggest worry was still that Lynn would become despondent when he discovered the truth about his natural father and not return at all. The loss of the last riverboat out of the town might be the final straw.

She'd tried to mask her anxiety from her mother but knew that she'd failed. At least her mother hadn't tried to convince her to forget about Lynn and if he really cared about her, he'd be willing to wait until the spring.

But there was the new worry that had arrived just after they'd picked up the wreck survivors, but she hadn't mentioned it to her mother yet.

Even as she stood on the aft upper deck looking upriver, she wondered if there was any way that she could get back now. It was so frustrating to know that hundreds of miles of railroad tracks were being laid every day now, but none could get her close to Fort Benton.

She continued to stare north in the fading light and said softly, "I don't care who your father is, Lynn, and don't wait for spring. Find a way home and I'll be waiting for you."

———

The second set of rapids had arrived sooner than he'd expected and once the canoe was in the grip of the fast water, his human decision was overpowered by the river's demand.

Yet even as he first entered the rapids, Lynn felt a greater level of control as he guided the canoe around the maze of boiling water and boulders. He had to start making those direction changes long before the canoe's bow reached the obstacle, so with his eyes now focused more than fifty yards downstream, he was able to avoid potential disaster without panic.

When his canoe finally slid into smooth water, Lynn didn't celebrate or even smile as he resumed his melodic paddling.

He'd been on the river for more than twelve hours now and knew he'd need to make another stop soon. He'd planned on continuing into the night, but the first day had drained him and he needed to rest and have something more substantial to eat.

So, as the sun dipped behind him, Lynn steered his canoe to the eastern bank and slipped it into the mud.

Twenty minutes later, Lynn had removed his gear and supplies, turned the canoe over to empty the accumulated water, and then set up a rudimentary campsite another fifty feet from the river where the ground was dry.

He ate two handfuls of the thick, gooey pemmican before washing it down with water and then chewing some hardtack.

As he sat on his slicker he stared at the passing river and tried to estimate how far he'd traveled today and how much longer he'd be on the river. He figured that the rapids and faster current on both sides had given him a boost, but he'd only know where he was when he reached the next settlement.

"I wish they had that railroad built already," he said aloud before he tossed some hardtack into his mouth.

———

Lynn started Wednesday's leg even earlier than he had the day before, pushing the canoe into the water well before the

365

predawn. He'd fallen asleep early, which helped, but he was stiffer than he had expected when he awakened.

Now, just as the predawn arrived, his muscles were loose again as he paddled with the main current. He may not have known his exact position but knew that he'd have to pass a settlement soon because the riverboats needed a place to dock overnight.

He finally spotted the fort and dock around midmorning and didn't even think of stopping. He did move the canoe to the opposite side of the river in case any of the inhabitants thought he was a marauding Crow and took a shot at him.

Lynn laughed as he passed the settlement but marked its name and recalled how long it had taken the *Alberta* to reach the stop on its journey to Fort Benton after leaving Yankton.

It had taken them twelve days to get this far and now, he was going downstream and didn't have to stop anywhere. He could even continue after dark, so as the settlement disappeared around a bend, Lynn felt a surge of satisfaction when he realized that he could be just eight days away from Yankton.

———

Dylan shook his head and said, "We got that all wrong, Bryn. Lynn's message was referring to the *Princess of Ohio*, the last riverboat of the season. That also explains his decision to try to canoe his way back."

"It explains his use of the canoe, Dylan, but it doesn't explain why he felt it was necessary to leave so soon instead of waiting until spring."

"I can understand why he'd want to leave. Gwen and I never wanted to see that place again, and whatever Lynn found there, I'm sure that he feels the same way."

"So, no more princess bride for Lynn?" Bryn asked with a grin.

"Knowing the Evans boys' tendency to rescue our brides, I'm not ready to give in yet. But at least this answers some of the questions."

Kyle said, "I heard that Bryn didn't exactly rescue Erin, but Gwen was the one who arranged everything."

Bryn looked at Kyle as he said, "You should talk, Mister Prosecutor. You married Erin's little sister and don't pretend that Gwen had nothing to do with that, either."

Kyle laughed as he put out his palms in surrender, knowing full well that Gwen's influence had changed all of their lives beginning with Dylan.

———

Lynn decided to keep going as long as he could after sunset and experimented with just drifting. It was disconcerting when the canoe began to turn sideways and he could no longer look ahead, so he resumed paddling as he tried to come up with a way to at least keep it heading downstream if he was only resting.

There was a distant memory tickling the back of his mind, but even as he recalled a seafaring tale and the use of a sea anchor to keep the ship from foundering, he knew it wouldn't work in a river because it would be traveling at the same speed as the canoe.

He'd need to find another way, but the sea anchor idea did let his mind explore a different, but similar method.

If he used some of his cord to hang something behind the canoe and let it touch the bottom, then the pull on the cord would keep him going straight.

Of course, it could and probably would snag, but when it did, he'd cut the cord if he couldn't free his river anchor then make another. He'd lose speed of course, but if he was going to be sleeping anyway, then it was actually a positive.

He never would have considered it if the riverboats were still running, but then, if they had been, he wouldn't be in the canoe in the first place, he thought as he snickered.

As he examined his stores for something to use as his anchor, he had to find something that was less likely to snag that was not very heavy; it just had to bounce along on the bottom. So, he needed something round that weighed around a pound or two.

Not that he even considered it, but that eliminated his Smith & Wesson. But even as he smiled at the idea, he looked at the box of .44 cartridges and then went from there.

First, he emptied out the pouch that still contained the remaining currency and stuffed it into his jacket pocket. Then he dropped in a few cartridges, bounced the pouch in his hand and added a few more. When he felt it was right, he took the reel of cord and began to form the small leather pouch into a rudimentary ball. When he was satisfied with the more-or-less round ball, he tied off the cord and dangled it before his eyes.

He was grinning as he said aloud, "You wouldn't want to hit this baseball with your maple bat, Uncle Kyle. Besides, it already has its own bullet."

The canoe was already drifting sideways when Lynn began lowering the homemade anchor to the river bottom. He finally felt it strike the mud about sixteen feet down and then wrapped the cord around his chest rather than the canoe. He wasn't going to leave it this way but wanted to see if it worked.

When he felt the cord tug on his chest, the canoe slowly straightened but continued downriver, albeit at a much reduced speed.

He wasn't sure how slow it was going now but could feel the anchor tugging at his chest as it bounced along the floor of the Missouri.

Lynn kept the cord around his chest for another twenty minutes before he hauled his anchor back on board and then affixed the cord to his heavy saddlebags.

He didn't need it now, but he'd try it just before sunset. He'd have to go ashore once more before then, but if this worked, he'd be able to float along after dark and gain even more time.

––––––––

In the cool, almost windless night, Lynn discovered that his canoe anchor worked reasonably well. During his brief stay on the riverbank, he created a short bed on the floor of the long canoe. If it had been the two-man canoe he'd expected, it wouldn't have been possible, but the length of the war canoe made it possible to stow his supplies and gear and still have enough room to lie down; using the stern end of the canoe as a pillow.

As the canoe floated downriver, the anchor would tug as it caught bottom debris, making the canoe bounce fore and aft, but Lynn was now able to eat and rest while still making progress.

Twice during that quiet night, he'd had to clear his bullet-laden anchor from snags. After the first time, he recalled that his father had once mentioned that bullets were waterproof and a pistol could even be fired underwater, so he assumed that there was a chance that his .44-filled sea anchor could hit a hard snag and he'd lose it after killing any catfish nearby.

He awakened from his longest nap with the predawn and was confused by his surroundings. It was as if he'd floated off the face of the earth and entered a cloud.

After rubbing his eyes and sitting in his still rocking and floating canoe, he understood why it would have seemed that way.

There wasn't a hint of a breeze and the river was steaming thick wisps of fog that hid anything more than thirty feet away. It was an eerie sensation, but it didn't change his overwhelming need to get ashore where he could stand up and empty his screaming bladder.

After barely making it to the muddy bank and answering nature's call, Lynn took a few minutes to have some pemmican and hardtack. Before restarting his journey, he scanned the landscape and wondered if there were any Sioux nearby. He was sure he was in their territory now but doubted if they knew he as there.

Forty minutes later, as he paddled down the Missouri that was so calm it looked almost like a pond or lake, the sun's disc appeared almost directly before him through the thick fog. He assumed that he was in one of the countless long, looping riverbends and was heading east at the moment. It was an other-worldly experience as the slap of his paddle made the only sound as he pushed his canoe through the water.

LYNN'S SEARCH

It wasn't until midmorning and the river curled back to the south that the fog finally began to lift as it lost its battle with the sun. The world slowly revealed itself and the dreamlike part of his long journey evaporated.

———

After midday, clouds began moving in and Lynn donned his slicker in preparation for the pending rain. It would be a cold, miserable rain if it arrived and all he could hope for is that it would hold off dousing the Dakota Territory and empty its load on Minnesota.

He wasn't that lucky as the first chilling drops arrived just an hour after the clouds appeared. It may not have been a downpour, but with the rain came a drop in the reasonably comfortable temperature.

Lynn continued to paddle his canoe down the center of the river as water streamed from his Stetson. He'd pulled on his old leather gloves, but it was his only concession to the colder air.

For two hours, Lynn continued his rhythmic paddling before he finally decided that he'd have to put ashore if he found a spot with some big trees that could provide for cover.

He was searching the bluffs to the east when he spotted what looked like a cave, so he turned his canoe to the left and soon slid the bow onto a sand bank.

It was awkward to get the canoe pulled onto the shore far enough so that the rising river didn't yank it away, but once he thought it was safe, he grabbed his Winchester, picked up his smaller saddlebags and headed for the cave.

As he drew closer, he found that it wasn't a real cave, but just a gouge in the side of the low bluff that may grow to be a real cave or simply collapse back to just a dimple in the earth. But for now, it would give him someplace dry to wait out the rain.

It took him three trips to move all of his things into the hole, then after he turned the canoe over to empty the water that had accumulated, he began gathering wood for a fire.

It took a while to find enough reasonably dry wood to get the fire started, but once it was healthy, he could use the rain-soaked branches to build its strength.

Even with the heat from the nearby flames, Lynn felt chilled as he sat on the bearskin huddled beneath his wool blanket. He was chewing on some jerky as he watched the rain drum on the tight skin of his canoe and hoped he wasn't getting sick. He'd only been really sick once in his life. When he was nine, he'd come down with mumps and was bedridden for a few days. The worst part was that he had to stay isolated from his brothers and sisters.

As he sat in the glow of the fire, he wondered if there was some Evans guardian angel that watched over them. He had friends who'd died as youngsters and yet not one of his siblings or cousins had contracted a fatal disease or been killed in an accident. What made it more unbelievable is that all of the adults in the extensive Evans clan were still healthy. Considering that his father and Uncle Bryn were lawmen made it even more extraordinary. He knew that his mother had lost a child, but he couldn't recall any tragedies other than Ryan's death, which was his own fault.

Now he just hoped that he wasn't the first to break the streak; especially now that he was getting closer to seeing Addie again. He glanced south at the rainy river and wondered if she and her mother had reached Omaha yet. If they had, then Addie could be in Denver the next day and would meet Alwen and Garth.

Sick or not, that thought made Lynn determined that he'd have to drag the canoe back into the river soon.

———

Three hundred and forty miles south, the *Alberta* was docking at Fort Randall; the last stop before Yankton. The rain that had driven Lynn into his hole hadn't reached them, but it was still cloudy and chilly.

Betty and Addie were in the almost empty dining room having coffee after their supper. The only other occupants of the room were four passengers playing poker at a nearby table.

"We'll be in Yankton tomorrow, Mama. We're still taking the train to Omaha; aren't we?"

"Yes, dear. I'm just wondering whether or not to send a telegram to Deputy Marshal Green to let him know that we'll be arriving on the train. He may not be there."

"It wouldn't hurt, Mama. We haven't been there before, and it would be nice to have someone join us."

"You're right. I'll send a telegram when we get to Yankton."

"Could I send one to Lynn? I want him to know that we're safe."

"You wouldn't be there to receive a reply, Addie. Let's wait until we get to Omaha first."

373

Addie nodded, then said in a low voice, "See that man on the right; the one who is dealing the cards?"

Betty glanced to look at the poker players, then asked, "What about him?"

"He was one of the men from the wreck and he makes me nervous. It seems that whenever we're on deck or in here, he's nearby. When he looks at me, I feel more than just uncomfortable; I feel afraid. I've never felt that way before. I always thought I was able to protect myself."

"Let's go back to our cabin," Betty said as she set her cup down.

As they stood, Betty glanced back at the poker table and noticed that only the player who worried Addie looked their way.

After reaching cabin thirteen, Betty closed and locked the door as Addie lit the lamp.

"Do you want me to tell Captain Clyde, Addie?"

"I don't think he could do anything, Mama," she replied as she sat on her bunk, "we'll be getting off tomorrow and then hopefully, we'll be in Omaha tomorrow night."

"Until then, we'll just stay together. I don't believe that he's going to actually do anything. He hasn't even talked to you; has he?"

"No. You're probably right, but I wish Lynn was here."

Betty patted her daughter's knee and said, "I'm sure that you do, sweetheart."

LYNN'S SEARCH

―――――

Back in the dining room, Pepper Taylor tossed in his worthless hand and thought about that girl he'd been watching ever since he got on board after that damned wreck. She was the only good thing about this whole month. He'd hoped to get her alone, but that proved difficult on the confines of the *Alberta*. Ever since he'd noticed her, he'd hoped that she and her ever-present mother would go into a town, but they had never left the boat. He'd heard from the crew that she and her mother were going to Omaha, so either he acted fast or hope that they'd finally leave the boat to visit the larger town of Yankton.

As he automatically picked up his new cards, he felt a combination of frustration and excitement welling within him. It had to be soon, and that girl would be the best of them all. He just needed to get her away from her mother; one way or the other.

―――――

The next morning was downright cold as Lynn hopped into the canoe then pushed out into the swollen river.

The only good thing to come from the rain was that the current seemed faster, which might make up for the delay that the heavy precipitation had cost him. He was a bit ashamed of himself for having huddled in the cave rather than sticking it out and staying on the river. He doubted if any Sioux warriors would have run from the rain and they didn't have waterproof rain slickers. At least he wasn't as cold as he'd been during the rain. He'd kept the fire going and everything was dry when he'd resumed his journey.

Now he was paddling at a slightly higher pace as he'd become adjusted to the repeated motion and thought he'd be able to maintain the higher speed.

When he felt the morning sun on his face, Lynn felt a renewed sense of purpose and his spirit was uplifted to the level it had been on the first day he'd set out.

———

The *Alberta* pulled away from the Fort Randall docks two hours after Lynn had resumed his journey and would begin to pull away from him once it built up speed.

As they sat in their cabin on that last day on the sternwheeler, Betty and Addie busied themselves by packing for their departure.

Now that she was aware of the man who was watching Addie, Betty was even more vigilant and protective of her precious daughter. For years, she'd done all she could to keep men away from her, and now, just when they were so close to a new and better life, she wasn't about to fail.

Although neither of them was armed with a firearm, Betty still wore her small dagger strapped to her thigh. It had saved her more than once from rough customers and she knew that she wouldn't hesitate to use it to keep Addie safe.

Addie didn't know about her mother's hidden weapon, but after she'd begun to notice the man's interest, she'd slipped a steak knife from the dining room into her purse. She wasn't sure that she could use it but having it there was reassuring.

It didn't take long to have everything ready, so they just sat on their bunks and talked until the noon meal; probably their last on the *Alberta*.

Betty said, "When we get into Yankton, we'll check the train schedule. As it's the end of the line, I imagine that trains arrive in the evening and leave in the morning."

"So, do we stay on board until the morning?"

"I'd rather that we find a hotel and stay there. We can have a porter move our things from the hotel to the station, too."

Addie nodded and said, "I'd rather get off his boat as soon as possible now anyway, Mama."

"I can understand that, dear. Don't worry about that man. I'll be with you and he's leaving with the *Alberta* in the morning and we'll be on the train to Omaha and then onto Denver."

Addie smiled as she replied, "I wonder what it's like. Lynn talked about his uncle's big ranch as if it was a paradise on earth."

"It sounded like it was that way more because of his family than the ranch."

"I just hope that he returns to the ranch and his family. There's nothing for him in Fort Benton just like there was nothing for us."

"I know that, dear, so all you can do is hope that he discovers that even if he finds the proof of his real father."

"I don't know why his parents didn't tell him. What struck me as odd was that he still seemed to almost revere his mother and father, despite his suspicion that he wasn't Dylan Evans' son."

"Did he actually tell you that when I wasn't there?" Betty asked.

"No. I couldn't ask him about it because I didn't want to hurt him. What other reason would have sent him to Fort Benton? He kept saying that he had another purpose that made him stay. What else could be so important to him?"

"Maybe we'll find out when we meet his family. I'm sure that Gwen will tell me."

"Won't that be awkward? I mean, if they didn't tell him, how can you ask her?"

"We'll see, Addie. In a little while, we'll have our last free meal on the boat, then tonight, we'll have to pay for our supper in a restaurant," her mother replied with a smile.

She hadn't seen Gwen since she was a teenager and wondered how much she might have changed over the years. Lynn had described his mother through a son's loving eyes, but even with that bias, she sounded as if she had just matured, but her personality hadn't changed.

If it hadn't, Betty couldn't imagine Gwen not telling her son how he'd been conceived. Then there was always the much more likely possibility that even she wasn't sure. She still recalled the young Dylan Evans and knew that she as well as most of the other women would have welcomed him into their beds and was sure that Gwen had almost begged him to at least give her the ability to believe that if she did get pregnant, the child would be Dylan's and not that monster, Burke Riddell.

While they waited for lunch, Addie was also deep in thought, but not about Lynn's parents; she was only thinking of their oldest son.

Ever since they'd spotted the wreck of the *Princess of Ohio*, she had been trying to conjure up some way to head back to

378

Fort Benton, but knew it was pointless. But with their almost imminent arrival in Omaha, she departed from the useless river passage and wondered if there were stagecoach routes running that far north.

For long, silent minutes, Addie tried to picture the wide landscape between Omaha and Fort Benton and eventually concluded that she'd either have to wait in Denver for Lynn or wait for the spring to arrive and take the first riverboat north to find him. If no one would escort her, that wouldn't change her decision. She'd have Lynn's father, uncles or brothers teach her to shoot and she'd be her own escort.

The only thing that was certain was that she was going to spend the rest of her life with Lynn Robert Evans.

————

As the sun rose ever higher and the air's thermometer followed suit, Lynn navigated the canoe past another settlement without anyone even noticing him.

He was now so dedicated to pushing himself that he was leaving a noticeable wake behind his long thin craft. With the stronger than expected current, he was now moving south at almost seven knots. He knew he was going faster but didn't realize how much boost he was getting from the river.

As noon passed, he tossed his bullet anchor into the river and after it settled, he began to eat the last of the pemmican. He'd also adapted a kneeling method for turning the Missouri River into a flowing privy, which enabled him to reduce the number of his stops.

Lynn Robert Evans was on a personal mission now and focused his eyes downriver; almost seeing the imaginary *Alberta* as she steamed ahead of him. He knew that the riverboat was hundreds of miles away, but he still let his mind see the smoke from her funnels in the southern horizon. The vision pulled him just as Burke Riddell's house had drawn him inside. But this urge wasn't to discover something that could have ruined his life; this was to reunite with the young woman that would become his life.

———

During lunch in the crowded dining room, Betty and Addie felt safe with so many people about. Although there were two other women aboard, they still dined alone.

After returning to their cabin, Betty said, "I didn't see him anywhere. Did you?"

"No, but I wasn't really looking for him, either."

"Well, I was, but I didn't spot him. We're almost to Yankton now and I'm getting more excited with each mile."

Addie smiled at her mother, but the absence of the troubling man bothered her. If she'd spotted him, then at least she would know where he was; but now he could be lurking anywhere. Yet she also believed that she was being excessively worriesome and once they were in Yankton, then they'd be all right.

———

Alwen asked, "When are we leaving, Mister Green? Everything is packed."

"We'll leave on Monday, the thirteenth."

"What about Lynn or the princess and her mother?" Garth asked.

"That's why we're holding off. The *Alberta* is scheduled to arrive on Saturday, so we'll meet Mrs. Price and her daughter at the station. We'll all stay in your hotel and board the morning train to Denver on Monday."

"But Lynn is still on his way in the canoe. Who is going to be waiting for him?"

"He'll just get on the first train to Denver, Garth. Anyone who can paddle a canoe almost that far isn't going to have a problem getting on a train."

Garth nodded but wasn't pleased. He really wanted to talk to his brother about what had happened. Even with the limited news, Garth suspected that Lynn had some very interesting stories to tell. At least he'd be able to ask the princess when he met her.

———

The *Alberta* slowed to dock at Yankton as the sun set and by the time the big paddles stopped turning, it was growing dark.

Betty and Addie didn't ask for any help as they lugged their homemade baggage across the gangplank and stepped onto the dock.

"It feels good to be standing on something that isn't moving," Betty said with a smile as she and Addie crossed onto solid ground.

As they entered Yankton, they headed for the hotel that was closest to the railway station. The station was easily spotted, even in the fading light, because of the tall tower used for replenishing the locomotives' water tanks.

Addie glanced behind them several times before they reached the hotel and was relieved when she hadn't seen anyone following them.

————

Pepper Taylor had almost missed them when they'd disembarked because they'd never gone into any of the towns since he'd been aboard, but after he had casually swung past cabin thirteen, he saw the open door and peeked inside. When he found it empty, he hurried to the dockside of the upper deck and caught sight of Betty and Addie as they carried their bags into Yankton.

He lost sight of them in the dark street, but it didn't take long for him to figure out that they were going to take the train to Omaha rather than stay on the boat. He'd taken the train to Yankton before boarding the ill-fated *Princess of Ohio*.

So, after a few minutes, he trotted down the starboard stairway, crossed the deck and entered the town. As he walked toward the railway hotel, which was probably their choice of accommodation if they were taking the train, he felt the excitement of the chase. This was even better than anything he could have planned on the boat.

He had stayed in Yankton for a few days waiting to board the riverboat, so he knew the town reasonably well. The closest eatery to the railway hotel was three blocks west heading toward the river.

Pepper was sure that they hadn't eaten supper on board, so they'd probably be leaving the hotel soon after getting a room, and then they'd walk to the diner…in the dark.

He passed along the boardwalk, not noticing any of the passersby as he searched for his perfect location.

Just a block west of the railway hotel, he turned into the dark alley between an already boisterously loud saloon and a closed hardware store. It was perfect.

Once inside the almost black space, he turned and then slipped his Colt from its holster but didn't cock the hammer. Now he just needed to wait. He knew from past experience that this would be the hardest part as his excitement and arousal would make him fidgety, but it also added a touch of danger that made it even better.

————

Betty and Addie didn't put their things into the single chest of drawers in the room because they would be leaving on the 10:10 train to Omaha in the morning.

They just had their purses as they crossed the hotel lobby to have dinner in the diner they'd passed on the way to the hotel.

————

Pepper had periodically glanced at the hotel entrance about fifty yards away, and each time, his anticipation grew but the girl and her mother hadn't appeared.

He didn't know how much longer he could hold his patience in check when he peeked around the hardware store just as Betty and Addie stepped onto the boardwalk.

He leveled his revolver but didn't pull the hammer back; not yet. He needed the terrifying effect that the simple metal sound created.

Betty was on the street side as she walked alongside her daughter on the empty boardwalk. The noise from the saloon ahead almost made her decide to move to the other side of the street, but they'd pass it soon and the diner was on this side, so they continued past the dark hardware store.

"What will you order for dinner, Addie?" Betty asked as they reached the alley.

"I..."

Addie reply was interrupted by the click of a pistol's hammer being cocked before a voice said, "Both of you come in here, or I pull this trigger."

Addie was just three feet from the muzzle and froze as Betty whipped her head to her left and recognized the man holding the gun as the survivor who had been scaring Addie. If he'd been pointing the pistol at her, Betty would have just laughed at him and continued walking; but he had those sights aimed at Addie and she couldn't risk her daughter.

"What do you want?" Betty asked, just to gain some time. She knew what he wanted and had to stop it.

"Shut up and just come in here. Both of you."

Addie glanced at her mother but didn't say anything as she turned toward the alley and knew that her mother was waking beside her as they entered the dark space and the man slowly backpedaled.

They were twenty feet into the blackness and still walking as Betty tried to think of a way to protect her daughter. Addie was all that mattered to her now.

As Addie stared at the shadowy figure before her, she was trying to think of a way to get the steak knife from her purse without notice, but that pistol was still too close to make it possible.

The man finally entered the moonlit ground behind the hardware store, but the saloon's wall continued on Betty's right.

The man stopped, then shifted the pistol toward Betty and said, "I don't need you around, lady, and nobody's gonna care about a gunshot."

Betty quickly said, "Wait! You don't want to risk being hanged for murder. I already told Captain Clyde that we were worried about you and if anything happens to us, they'll come searching for you."

Pepper wasn't sure if she was bluffing or not, but said, "You're a liar. You hardly ever left that cabin. I kept an eye on you since I got on the boat."

Betty had been bluffing and not well, so she resorted to her most practiced skill and quickly set her purse on the ground before taking off her coat and laying it on top of the purse.

"You can take me, and I won't say a word to anyone."

Pepper laughed and said, "Why would I bother with you when you got this vixen of a girl standin' right there?"

Betty kept her eyes on his as she slowly began to unbutton her dress.

Pepper was still going to rape the girl before killing them both, but as he watched Betty, he didn't see the harm in some added excitement. She sure did know how to get a man ready, too.

Betty saw the growing lust in his eyes but knew that she was still just buying time. She needed to get to the dagger strapped to her thigh before the bastard pulled the trigger. She had no doubt that he had been right when he said no one would even notice the gunshot over the noise from the nearby saloon and that gunshot would arrive the instant he was no longer interested in what she was showing.

Addie suspected that her mother was just stalling for time, and as she noticed the sex-crazed beast greedily watching her mother's show, she saw her chance and slowly opened her purse.

Betty had reached the last button on the upper part of her dress, exposing the inner curves of her breasts as Pepper began to lick his lips while he stared at her.

Addie slid her hand into her purse and gripped the knife, but having that cocked pistol still pointed at her, even though the shooter's eyes were focused on her mother, kept her from pulling it free. He was still six feet away and she'd never reach him before he pulled the trigger.

Betty knew that she was almost out of time, so as she kept her eyes on the obviously excited gunman, she took hold of her skirt and slowly began to lift it like an opening curtain. As her legs were exposed to the cool night air, they erupted in goose pimples, but Betty continued to lift them higher.

She was almost to her knees when the man suddenly ripped his eyes from Betty and looked at Addie.

He exclaimed, "You do it now! I want to see your titties!"

Addie stood there with her right hand on the knife handle and didn't know what to do. If she complied, then she'd have to drop the purse and lose her one chance to stop him.

The instant Betty had seen him shift his attention to Addie, she quickly moved her skirt just a few inches higher, then in one motion, grasped the leather wrapped dagger handle and ripped it from its sheath as her skirt fell to the ground.

Pepper saw the flurry of motion to his left and made the momentary mistake of thinking that the girl's mother was ripping off more clothing to keep him from having the girl.

By the time he realized that she had a blade in her hand, it was too late.

Betty plunged her dagger into Pepper's left upper arm, making him drop his pistol as he screeched in pain. His Colt didn't go off as it bounced onto the hard dirt, but as soon as he felt the dagger cut into his arm, he yanked away, pulling Betty's dagger from her hand.

Betty stumbled off balance but didn't fall as Pepper bent at the waist to regain his pistol.

Addie then dropped her purse as she stared at Pepper Taylor's exposed torso, lifted the steak knife above her head and shoved the six-inch blade into his back. The tip of the knife passed through the jacket and shirt, then punched into his right lung's middle lobe, slicing blood vessels as it cut into his chest.

Pepper screamed again, forgot about anything other than avoiding another stabbing and raced into the pitch-black alley with Addie's knife stuck in his back.

As the women watched him run away into the darkness, Addie stepped close to her mother and hugged her in stunned relief. Betty began to cry as she held onto her daughter, knowing how close they had come to death. Neither expected him to return; not with his wounds and without a pistol.

———

After his short, stumbling run, Pepper reached the boardwalk and was finding it hard to breathe as he shuffled into the nearby saloon with blood already dripping from under his jacket.

As soon as he entered the crowded barroom, he wheezed, "They tried to kill me! They stabbed me and tried to kill me!"

As he began to lose his strength, Pepper dropped to his knees and sat on his heels with his head bowed, almost as if he was in prayer.

Deputy Sheriff Avery George was playing poker with his best friend Dave Immelmann and two other drinking buddies when they saw Pepper awkwardly stagger into the saloon. He tossed down his cards and hurriedly ran to the bleeding man.

Dave and the other two followed Avery as he quickly reached Pepper and couldn't miss the knife sticking out of his back.

"What happened?" Avery asked quickly.

Pepper knew he wasn't going to live much longer and wanted to use his last breath to condemn the women who had murdered him.

He kept his eyes on the saloon floor as he gasped, "Two women. They…they lured me into the alley next door tellin' me they were both gonna show me a good time…"

He paused when he had to take in what little air he could before wheezing, "…and when one of 'em…began undressin'…the other one took my pistol and…and…stabbed me. They were gonna rob me."

Avery knew the man wasn't going to make it and asked, "Are they still there?"

Pepper felt his life leaving him, so he just nodded before he collapsed onto his face.

Avery looked up at Dave, then stood and said, "Let's go and find those whores!"

————

After a few seconds of shared relief, Addie said, "Get dressed, Mama, and I'll get his pistol. We need to talk to the sheriff about this."

"You're right, Addie. Let's get out of here," Betty replied before she picked up her dagger, slipped it into its sheath, then quickly buttoning her dress. It had been such a close thing and she wondered if they shouldn't just keep the pistol. It probably wouldn't matter if they did or not because neither of them even knew how to shoot the damned things.

Addie picked up her purse, then headed for the pistol lying on the ground eight feet away.

As Betty donned her jacket and picked up her purse, Addie retrieved the cocked pistol and walked back to her mother.

"Mama, do you know how to put this hammer back?" she asked as she held the Colt out to her mother by the barrel.

Betty slid her purse onto her left arm as she took the revolver's grips in her hand and stared at the hammer, making sure that the muzzle was pointed at the ground so if it went off, she wouldn't shoot Addie.

"There must be a catch somewhere," Betty said as she examined the pistol.

———

Avery and Dave were in front as the four men turned into the black space between the saloon and the hardware store and they soon spotted Betty and Addie in the moonlight sixty feet away.

Betty finally said, "I can't figure it out, Addie. We have to see the sheriff anyway, so let's just let him do it. I just have to hold it carefully."

Addie replied, "All right…", then heard footsteps to her right, and turned as Betty looked up.

Avery and Dave had their pistols drawn, but only Dave had his cocked when they neared the end of the alley.

Avery saw the cocked pistol in Betty's hand and set his sights on her as he shouted, "Drop the gun, lady, or I'll fire!"

Betty was startled, but dropped the cocked pistol's muzzle even lower as she loudly replied, "I don't know how…"

Dave saw the movement and without hesitation, fired at Betty from twelve feet.

Betty was shocked when the brilliant flash lit up the darkness for an instant and before the echo of the gunshot reached her ears, she felt a hammer blow to her chest and spun counterclockwise; her purse and the unfired Colt flying away from her.

"Mama!" Addie shouted as she sprang to her mother and reached her just as she tumbled to the ground.

"Jesus!" Avery shouted as he quickly holstered his pistol, glared at Dave who was frozen with his smoking Colt still held level.

Addie rolled her mother onto her back as tears flooded her face and knew that she would never hear her mother's voice again once she saw her vacant, staring eyes.

In an instant, Addie transformed from a shocked, grieving daughter to an outraged, revenge-filled demon as she lunged for the nearby pistol to shoot the bastard who had taken her mother from her.

As he saw Addie stretch across Betty's body for the cocked pistol, Avery quickly crossed the last few feet and snatched it from the ground just before her fingers reached the grips.

Addie's eyes were afire as she looked back at Deputy George and screamed, "Give it to me! Let me shoot the bastard!"

"You've already done enough killing for the night, lady. Now stand up."

Addie wasn't about to leave her mother, so she just stayed kneeling beside her mother's body as she glared at the man who had taken the instrument for her revenge.

The deputy again said, "I said stand up. I'll have my friends take her body to the morgue, but you're coming with me to the jail."

Addie's anger reached volcanic levels as she screamed, "Take me to jail? For what? We were attacked and almost raped and killed, then you and your murderous friends come here and shoot my mother and now you're going to take me to jail? I'm not going anywhere with you and I'm not leaving my mother!"

Avery stared at the defiant young woman and growled, "I'm Deputy Sheriff Avery George and I'm arresting you for murder, lady. Don't make me have to use force to drag you to jail. Either stand up and walk with me or I'll yank you kicking and screaming to your cell."

"I'm not leaving my mother!" Addie shouted.

The other two poker players had walked around the statue-like Dave Immelmann and stood behind Avery.

Avery finally released the Colt's hammer and handed it to one of them before saying, "Jimmy, you and Luther take the woman's body to Freeman's, but don't do anything with the body in the saloon until Sheriff Aubrey takes a good look at it."

"Okay, Avery," Jimmy Blucher replied as he slid the pistol under his belt.

Addie was still glaring at the deputy when he grabbed her left upper arm, stood her up and wrestled her back down the alley.

Dave had finally holstered his pistol and followed Avery as he marched Addie into the darkness.

Addie stopped struggling after just a few seconds as her anger morphed back into inconsolable grief when she realized that her mother, the rock of her life, was gone. She'd been stolen from her by men who were protecting another man who had tried to rape and murder her.

For as long as she could remember, her mother had protected her from men like that. Now, she'd died trying to protect her and Addie had no one.

She had no tears left as she walked mechanically with the deputy across the street and soon found herself being pulled into a building, led across a dark room and pushed into a cell surrounded by iron bars.

Addie didn't care anymore as she wandered to the back of the cell and sat on the hard cot. She stared into the low light and felt empty and alone. Her beloved mother was dead, and she was the only one who cared.

———

After leaving Addie in the cell, Deputy George found Sheriff Bernard 'Burner' Aubrey at his home and gave him a rundown on what had happened.

"He shot her?" the sheriff asked with wide eyes.

"It wasn't his fault, boss. She had a cocked pistol in her hand and after I told her to drop it, she looked at us and was going to shoot."

"A woman was going to shoot a pistol at four armed men?" he asked.

"She and her daughter had just murdered a man, so she probably knew she was going to hang. What did she have to lose?"

Sheriff Aubrey grabbed his hat from his hat rack, then turned to his wife and said, "I'll be late, dear. Don't wait up."

"Alright," she replied before he kissed her on the cheek and left the house.

As they walked to the saloon, Deputy George filled in the details, including the murdered man's dying declaration.

When they entered the saloon, there was a crowd of men around the body, so the sheriff had to clear them away as he examined Pepper Taylor's corpse.

"Anybody know his name?" he asked the onlookers.

"He was one of the survivors off of the *Princess of Ohio*," answered an *Alberta* crewmember, "his name was Pepper Taylor."

The sheriff grunted, then took a few seconds studying the body and found a second knife wound on the arm.

Then he stood and asked, "How many of you heard what he said when he came in?"

None of the others would admit to hearing a word, especially the men who would be leaving when the *Alberta* sailed in the morning. They knew if they were witnesses, they'd be stuck in Yankton and lose their pay.

After no one responded, the sheriff turned to his deputy and said, "Have the body taken to the morgue and have the doc do an autopsy. Tell him I want one on the woman, too."

"There's no need to do one on her, boss. She was shot by Dave Immelmann in self-defense and there were three witnesses."

Sheriff Aubrey looked at his deputy and replied, "Four witnesses, Avery. You're forgetting the daughter. I want the autopsy."

"It's gonna cost the county some money, boss."

"They can afford it. Just get it done and come back to the jail when you're finished."

"Yes, sir," Avery replied as the sheriff left the saloon.

Sheriff Aubrey was grumbling under his breath about the mess that his deputy's drinking buddy had created with his hair trigger response. It was bad enough to have a murder that had been committed by women to ruin his night, but to have it compounded by a second killing of one of the accused murderers was going to be a serious mess.

When he reached his jail, he entered and saw Addie still sitting on the cot staring at the far wall.

He took off his hat, walked to the cell, and after taking down the key ring, unlocked the door and stepped inside.

Addie knew he was there but didn't even look at him as he pulled up the only chair in the cell and sat down.

"What's your name, miss?" he asked.

"It doesn't matter. That bastard killed my mother. She was all that mattered to me and she's dead now for no reason at all."

"According to witnesses, she had a cocked pistol in her hand and was preparing to fire."

Addie laughed lightly before replying, "Neither one of us could figure out how to let the hammer down and you think she was going to shoot it? That's absurd, but you only see and hear what you want to believe, and that gives you an excuse to pat your friend on the back for protecting the four men who came to kill her."

Burner looked at the pretty young woman's hard face and tried to imagine her as a murderer but couldn't see it; even as angry as she appeared to be. This was no act; the girl wasn't pretending to be disgusted with the world.

"I'm not trying to protect anyone, miss. At least tell me your mother's name. We need to have it for the death certificate and her grave marker."

Addie finally turned her eyes to the sheriff and replied, "Her name was Beatrice Louise Spencer Price and she was born on April the seventh, 1841 in Kansas City, Missouri. She died today in Yankton, Dakota Territory when she was murdered by a trigger-happy friend of your deputy."

Sheriff Aubrey took out a small notepad from his shirt pocket along with a stub of a pencil and wrote down the information.

"What's your name?"

"Adele Gwendolyn Price. I was born on March 11, 1857 in Fort Benton, Dakota Territory."

After writing it down, the sheriff asked, "Will you tell me your side of the story?"

"It doesn't matter what I tell you, Sheriff. You're going to believe whatever you want anyway and, frankly, I don't care anymore."

LYNN'S SEARCH

"Miss Price, if you don't at least tell me what happened, you could be facing a charge of murder."

Addie's eyes narrowed as she snapped, *"For what? Trying to keep that bastard from killing my mother before he raped and killed me?* If that's how you define murder here in Yankton, then you may as well skip the trial and march me up the gallows' steps because I did stick that son of a bitch in the back and I'd do it again if I had to."

"Tell me what happened, Adele," the sheriff said softly.

"I already did and I'm not going to bother wasting my breath anymore."

"Don't you want to find justice for your mother, Adele?"

Addie didn't respond as she resumed staring at the far wall. She suspected that the sheriff was just there to see if he could get a confession from her using the friendly ploy. Well, she'd confessed and now she no longer cared what they did.

After not getting an answer, the sheriff slid his notebook and pencil back into his pocket, then stood and left the cell, clanging the door closed behind him.

As he sat behind the desk and began to write his initial report, he felt mildly nauseated knowing what was most likely to happen given the girl's attitude. With all of the hard evidence and the dying declaration of the murdered man, she would probably be charged with manslaughter at the very least; if not murder.

Dave Immelmann wouldn't face any penalty for killing her mother as his deputy and their friends would back up his claim, and there was a very real possibility that she might get her wish and walk up those gallows' steps after all.

He hoped that once the girl was past her shock and grief, she'd come to her senses and fight the charges. He had no doubt that what she'd said in her outrage was right, but she had no one to back up that story.

———

By the time Avery George was returning to the jail to report to his boss, he'd talked to Dave, Jimmy and Luther to get their stories straight and consistent. It was only a minor change anyway; that the woman had pointed the pistol at Dave, who had to fire first in self-defense.

When he entered the jail, he found the sheriff at the desk writing and the girl laying on the cot with her back to the office.

"All taken care of, boss," he said as he took off his hat and sat down.

The sheriff handed him a small sheet of paper as he said, "Take this back to Ed Freeman. It's the woman's name and vitals for her death certificate."

"Do you want me to watch the prisoner tonight, boss?" he asked as he took the note.

"No. She's not going anywhere. Just go home after dropping that off and I'll see you in the morning and you can write your report. Have Dave Immelmann, Jimmy Ralston and Luther Bausch stop by as well to write their statements."

"I'll let 'em know," Avery said as he stood, then pulled on his hat as he left the jail.

Sheriff watched his only deputy leave and sighed. This was turning out to be the worst day of his career as a lawman.

LYNN'S SEARCH

Lynn's anchor was still working well as the canoe bobbed along with the current still heading south in the moonlight.

He'd almost lost it earlier when it had been caught on a nasty snag and he was close to cutting the cord when it popped free and a muddy log momentarily surfaced before sliding back beneath the water like a snapping turtle's giant head.

That was three hours ago and as he looked overhead at the stars spread across the sky, he wondered what Addie was doing right now. She might be on the upper deck of the *Alberta* looking at those same point of light in the heavens, or she might be sleeping in her cabin.

He knew that in a few days, she and her mother would be in Omaha and then Denver. He also had calculated that his use of the river anchor had cut down the gap between them considerably, and now he guessed that he was just two or three days from Yankton where he could board the train to Denver.

Then he'd find Addie who hopefully would be waiting for him. He should send another telegram at the next stop, but the intense need to keep going and to avoid losing his canoe made him decide against it.

"Unless someone puts a telegraph station in the middle of the river," he said aloud before laughing, "maybe one day, they'll even figure out how to send telegrams on canoes."

He was still chuckling as his faithful floating home rode the Missouri's current south. He'd only been on the river for four days and nights but was less than three hundred miles from Yankton as he fell asleep.

CHAPTER 11

Addie had been escorted to the privy by the sheriff before breakfast had been delivered to her cell by a waitress from the diner where she and her mother had expected to share a pleasant supper. The deputy had brought all of their luggage from the hotel and put it in an adjoining cell as she ate.

Addie had decided that she wouldn't shut down but would only go through the motions of living. She wouldn't talk to them because there was no point anymore. She was convinced that they were all conspiring to protect the deputy sheriff's murdering friend and nothing she could say or do would make any difference.

The only reason she wanted to talk would be to ask where her mother would be buried and if she'd be allowed to be there. She suspected she wouldn't be permitted to go anyway, so even that probably didn't matter.

As she finished eating, the combination of anger and despondency pushed Addie into a grudging acceptance of her fate. No one cared about her mother's death and no one would care what happened to her.

Lynn would be in Fort Benton until the spring and by then, he'd probably forget all about her too.

———

The *Alberta* had departed from Yankton at daybreak and by the time Deputy George and the others were writing their statements, she was already thirty miles downriver.

―――

The Green family had moved into the Herndon House and were on the same floor as Garth and Alwen. Altogether, they occupied four rooms of the hotel, and Al and Martha managed to spend some of it alone in the lobby; or at least out of the watchful eyes of Martha's mother.

If Al and Martha were in the lobby, Garth usually found someplace else to go. Most of those visits were in the offices of the United States Marshal just four blocks away. During their many shared meals with the Green family, Benji had shared his opinion of the politically savvy marshal who had replaced Dylan; and none were very complimentary. So, when Garth visited the office, he hadn't been surprised when the small man who replaced his father never introduced himself.

The deputy marshal he talked to most often was the newest and youngest hire, Elbert Hoskins, who went by Bert. He was eight years older than Garth, but he enjoyed talking with the young lawman. Bert asked a lot of questions to verify many of the Dylan and Bryn stories that seemed difficult to believe.

By that Friday morning, Garth thought that Bert might want to follow Benji Green's path and come to Denver but would need to talk to his father before even suggesting that it was possible.

―――

Lynn watched as yet another settlement passed by on the western shore this time, and even waved at a man fishing from the dock.

401

He smiled when he remembered that he had a fishing kit in his packs and hadn't even thought about trying to use it. His original plan was to take a more reasonable pace, sleep on shore and even make campfires to roast his fresh fish. But once he got underway, he felt the same drive that he'd had when he needed to go to that house. He wondered if it was a character flaw or a common trait among the young.

Regardless of the reason for his accelerated pace, he was so used to the tempo that there was no reason to slow down. He would get a better idea of his location when he passed Fort Randall, which he expected to do in the next day. Then he'd be at Yankton the following day. He marveled that he had been able to make the trip in less than a week, which was less time than the *Alberta* would have taken, but the he'd kept his canoe on the river for most of the nights, too.

Lynn imagined the two very different watercraft acting like a giant accordion; he'd gain on the riverboat at night, then the gap would expand during the day, but each day, that distance would lessen. He spent a few hours that day just calculating the relative speeds to try to get an accurate estimate of today's gap, but finally thought it was irrelevant anyway.

————

After he read his deputy's and his friend's statements, Sheriff Aubrey took his report, their statements, and left the jail. He was a bit concerned about leaving his deputy alone with the prisoner, but he really had no choice.

He stopped by Freeman's to pick up the death certificates but knew the autopsies wouldn't be finished until the afternoon. Armed with all of his paperwork, he then headed for the office of the county prosecutor, Hiram Lefkowitz.

He wasn't sure what the prosecutor would make of the case but hoped that he'd just say that there was too much conflicting evidence and decide not to prosecute at all. After all, the murdered man wasn't a local and neither was the accused. Then there was the other sticky aspect of the case – Dan Immelmann's killing of Mrs. Price.

He'd been bothered by the four statements because they were all used similar wording and none of them varied in the slightest. That was a sure indication that they had coordinated their stories, but he wouldn't be able to prove it. With the girl's continuing silence, whatever they wrote or said would be the only story any jury would hear.

When he was admitted to the prosecutor's office, he wasn't surprised that the attorney had already heard most of the story.

As he took a seat, he slid his report, the statements and the death certificates across the desk.

"You're bringing me a real mess, Burner," he said as he began reading.

"You only know part of it, Hiram. The girl isn't talking, but I wrote what she did say before she went silent. It's in my report."

The prosecutor snorted as he continued reading. He quickly flipped one page after the other until he reached the death certificates and noticed a comment written on Beatrice Price's form.

"She had a dagger strapped to her right thigh?" he asked as he peered at the sheriff over his glasses.

403

"The girl admitted that she'd stabbed Taylor but the knife that she used was still embedded in the body. I didn't find out about the dagger until I talked to Ed Freeman. When I examined it, I found some blood on the handle, and I assume that she had stabbed Mister Taylor on the arm."

"Did the daughter explain why her mother had the dagger or why she even had the knife that she left in Taylor's back?"

"No, but as I wrote in my report, she claimed that Taylor had tried to rape and kill them, so I imagine they had armed themselves when they thought he might have been stalking them."

"I'd buy that argument for the murder weapon because it looked like a common steak knife; but a hidden dagger? Women don't just pick those up at a general store, Burner. The only women who would carry a sticker like that work on their backs to make a living."

"I know."

Hiram sat back and asked, "What's your take on this?"

"I'd like to be able to tell you that those two women did just what Taylor said in his dying declaration, but I can't see it. They arrived on that steamboat last night and checked into the railway hotel, so I assume they were planning on taking the train this morning. Why would they lure a man who had been on the same boat with them to try to rob him?"

"You found almost two hundred dollars in their purses, Burner. Maybe they needed money for the train ticket."

Sheriff Aubrey didn't like the way this conversation was headed but had to admit to himself that he could understand the prosecutor's logic. He was already building a case and was testing it for holes.

"Avery George isn't the most reliable lawman I've ever known and if you read their statements, you can see the obvious coordination. I think that Dave Immelmann panicked and fired. If he hadn't killed Mrs. Price, I think we'd get a much better picture of what really happened."

"Then you'd better get that girl to talk, Burner. Even without these statements and testimony, the evidence and the man's dying declaration are overwhelmingly against her. I have no alternative but to charge her with murder."

"Can you give me a few days to get her to talk, Hiram? She's just in the swamps over her mother's death. I think she'll talk in a day or so when she recovers from the shock."

"Alright. I'll set the trial for next Friday. Maybe the threat of hanging will loosen her tongue."

"I hope so, because I don't want to have to testify at her murder trial."

"I'd rather not prosecute either. Trying to get a jury of men to convict a young woman is difficult at best, especially if she's pretty. Is she pretty?"

"Pretty doesn't do her justice, Hiram."

"Well, let's hope she gives me enough reason to drop the charges before Wednesday. I'd rather that she just boarded a train and we could let this whole mess fade away."

Sheriff Aubrey nodded, then stood and left the office to get back to the jail to try to convince the girl to talk.

———

When he entered his office, he was relieved to find Deputy George just sitting at the desk while Adele Price still lay on her cot with her back facing him.

Avery looked up as the sheriff hung his hat and asked, "What did he say?"

"The trial is set for Friday. He's charging her with murder."

As he spoke, Sheriff Aubrey watched the cell to see if Adele had any reaction but was disappointed when she didn't even flinch.

"How come it's not any earlier?"

"She is entitled to a lawyer, Avery; or have you forgotten that?"

"No. I just…well, never mind."

"Go over to Doc Christenson's and ask when those autopsies will be done. If it's just an hour or so, hang around and then bring them back with you."

"Okay, boss," Avery said as he vacated the desk, donned his jacket, then pulled on his hat before leaving.

After the door closed, Sheriff Aubrey walked to the cell bars and said, "Miss Price, you need to tell me what happened. The prosecutor might even drop the charges if you tell your side of the story. I firmly believe that it wasn't anything like what Taylor claimed in his dying declaration."

Addie listened to the sheriff and thought he sounded sincere but didn't believe that anyone else would believe her.

She knew that if she started talking and they asked why her mother had that dagger, she'd have to tell the truth. Once they knew that her mother had been a prostitute, the leap to robbing murderer wasn't difficult to believe. Then there was the other, repulsive thought about talking about the dagger in front of strangers.

Addie wasn't about to tell them what they probably already suspected about her mother. Her mother was a soft-hearted woman who sacrificed everything for her, and she wasn't about to sully her memory just to save herself.

So, even as the sheriff almost pleaded for her to talk, Addie knew she never would.

———

An hour later, the deputy returned with the autopsy results and was accompanied by James Farrington, her defense attorney.

She never bothered to acknowledge the man as he began telling her of the consequences of her silence. When he asked her if she would accept a plea bargain of manslaughter to avoid the noose, she still didn't respond.

Finally, Mister Farrington turned to the sheriff and said, "I'll go back to my office and start writing some form of defense, but if she's not willing to even talk to me, there's little I can do to help."

"I understand, Jim. I have a few days to see if I can talk some sense into her."

"Good luck," he replied before leaving the jail.

Addie heard the door close behind him and didn't regret her decision. They could all go to hell for all she cared. She knew her mother wasn't burning in the fires, despite her sad life. She'd spent her time in a hell called Fort Benton. At least now, she was finally at peace in heaven where she belonged.

As she faced the wall just four inches from her eyes, Addie finally felt the withheld tears slide across her cheeks. She hadn't wept for her mother since she'd knelt over her body in that alley, but now, the thought of her mother at peace gave her the release that had eluded her.

She didn't even whisper as she prayed for her mother while laying on her side in what would be her final home.

———

Saturday passed slowly for Addie, but despite the sheriff's continued appeals, she didn't say a word. She still functioned as a living human being, and even was escorted to the hotel where she and her mother had planned to stay so she could take a bath. But the hours passed, and Addie stayed silent.

She had even begun to believe that she was a murderer after all, despite the terror of the moment. She could have just shoved the knife into his behind which would have stopped him, but not killed him. She had rammed that blade into his chest where it would surely end his life.

Maybe she should hang.

———

On Sunday, just before noon, Lynn passed Fort Randall and he knew that in just another day or so, he'd reach Yankton. He celebrated the event with the last of the pemmican and tossed the greasy pouch into the water for the bottom dwelling catfish to clean its last bits of nourishment.

———

Later that same day, Benji Green and Garth waited on the Omaha docks as the *Alberta* drifted closer to the wharf to tie off. The rest of the Green family and Alwen were waiting at the hotel for Benji and Garth to return with Mrs. Price and her princess daughter.

"Do you see them?" Benji asked as he scanned the passengers waiting on the decks.

"There are two ladies on the upper deck, but neither of them is young enough to be the princess."

Benji snickered and said, "After we know her name, I hope we can stop referring to her as the princess."

"We can blame Lynn for that. He should have been more exact when he sent that telegram."

Then as they watched the docking riverboat, Garth said, "I want to stay here until Lynn arrives."

Benji looked at him and said, "That might be a while, Garth. Besides, what if he takes the train from Yankton and passes right through Omaha? You wouldn't know he was in Denver until we sent you a telegram."

Garth replied, "I'm going to wait for at least another week. Somebody has to be here when he arrives."

"You're only fifteen, Garth."

"Lynn isn't even seventeen yet and dad let him go by himself all the way to Fort Benton. Besides, Bert Hoskins is here, and we get along."

"Well, we'll talk about it when we get Mrs. Price and the princess to the hotel."

Garth didn't reply as he watched the crew set the gangplank in place and the passengers began to queue to leave the *Alberta.*

After the last passenger had crossed onto the dock, Garth asked, "Where are they?"

"I don't know, but let's go and ask the captain or one of the crew to find out."

He couldn't have known that none of the crew had made the connection between their lady passengers and the two unnamed whores that had tried to rob Pepper Taylor.

When they reached the gangplank, Benji showed his badge to one of the crewmembers and said, "We're supposed to meet Mrs. Price and her daughter, but they didn't get off the boat. Are they still there?"

"No, sir. I think they got off at Yankton. A lot of folks do now that the railroad got there."

"Thanks," Benji replied, before he and Garth turned around and left the dock.

"I guess that Mrs. Price didn't expect anybody to be waiting for them here. They probably rolled right through Omaha early this morning and we didn't even know it."

"So, tomorrow you'll be taking the train in the morning and get to Denver the day after Mrs. Price and the princess get there."

"Yup. If we keep calling her daughter the princess, then maybe we should start calling her the queen," Benji said with a snicker.

Garth smiled at Benji as they continued walking to the hotel. He may not meet the princess or the queen mother, but he was determined to stay to greet his brother, the prince.

———

As Addie lay on her bunk in the darkening sky, Lynn spotted the lights of Yankton on the horizon and whooped. He'd made it!

But even as his trusty canoe approached the beckoning docks, he began to change his mind about taking the train from Yankton.

He'd become so accustomed to the constant speed of his travel that he figured that if he stopped at Yankton, then unloaded his canoe, got a room at the hotel and then had to wait for the train, which may not even leave until after noon, he wouldn't really be gaining much time.

By the time the train pulled out of Yankton, he'd be past Sioux City where it would have to stop.

His decision made, he waved at the empty Yankton docks as he sailed past and disappeared downriver.

Two hours later, Lynn felt it was time to get some sleep, so it was time to deploy his homemade river anchor that had served him so well.

He picked up his ball-shaped anchor, tossed it over the stern and waited for the line to go taut and he would feel the resulting bounce as the stern of the canoe dipped into the water.

This time, however, there was no bounce when the anchor hit the riverbed. As the .44-stuffed leather ball rapidly sunk toward the bottom, the cover struck the rusted iron strap of a discarded broken wagon wheel that jutted up from the mud.

As fate would have it, the iron's jagged edge sliced through the soggy leather before it stuck the edge of one of the rimfire cartridges. What should have been a harmless impact turned into a display of underwater fireworks just nine feet below his canoe's hull.

As the cord blew out of the water, Lynn felt the canoe shake as the cartridges ignited in a rapid domino effect. The mud quickly swallowed any bullets that shot downward and the water quickly slowed any that headed for the surface.

But slowing didn't mean stopping for a lone .44 that angled forward and punched a hole in Lynn's canoe right between his legs.

As the bullet lost the last of its energy and arced back down to the bearskin, an eighteen-inch high geyser of cold river water gushed from the hole and Lynn quickly slammed his right foot on top of the leak to minimize the flow as he grabbed his paddle and turned the canoe to the eastern shore just sixty feet away.

The water was still bubbling under his boot's sole as he rammed the paddle into the water to get the boat onto the muddy bank before it sank.

LYNN'S SEARCH

The current was shoving him downstream as the canoe's bow began to rise from the added weight from the water at the stern end.

Lynn was paddling furiously as the water on both sides of him rose ever closer to the top of the canoe.

Just when he thought he might lose the battle, the canoe's raised bow slid onto a muddy landing and he dropped the paddle into the canoe and bounded forward onto the bank.

He slid and almost fell as he reached the ground but regained his balance and began to pull the canoe ashore. It was a lot harder with all the water, but he managed to get his now useless canoe onto the muddy shelf.

"Well, I guess I should've taken the train after all," he said aloud as he looked at the stricken canoe.

He knew he might be able to do a temporary repair on the skin, but he wasn't that confident in his ability to make it strong enough to last the rest of the trip, so he began removing the things that he'd take with him; his two sets of saddlebags and his Winchester. He'd leave everything else with the canoe and start walking back toward Yankton.

Once he reached level land, he stopped and looked southeast, wondering if it wouldn't be better to head for Sioux City. He wasn't keen on the idea of heading in the opposite direction, but as he stood in his wet britches in the dark, he finally figured that at least he knew where Yankton was, and Sioux City was probably at least double the distance to travel. Its name alone added to his decision to return to Yankton; knowing that he would have to spend more time walking through Sioux territory.

Lynn tugged on his Stetson, then began walking northwest, keeping the Missouri on his left shoulder. He estimated that he could reach Yankton before midnight if he didn't stop, and he had no intention of stopping.

———

Lynn had been off in his estimation, despite his keeping a steady, rapid pace because he wasn't able to walk in a straight line. He'd had to wind his way around trees and other obstacles, then he had to climb some of the bluffs that bordered the river and then slow down when he descended them to avoid falling.

The added difficulties didn't affect his determination to get to Yankton as he wanted to get on that train. He wasn't even going to bother getting a room when he arrived in the town. He'd just head to the train station and wait for the ticket conductor to open his window. He might get some breakfast if he had the time before the train departed, though.

As he made his way to Yankton, he rubbed his chin and grinned, knowing he must look like a trapper or miner by now. He'd skipped shaving for the past few days and despite his quick hand baths whenever he stopped, was sure that he wasn't pleasant to be around, either.

He pressed on through the night, thinking of Addie and where she might be by now. She and her mother had to be in Denver and would be talking to his parents about Fort Benton. Alwen and Garth would probably be staring at Addie with lovesick eyes as she talked. *How could they not be in awe of her?* That thought added an extra jolt of energy and kept him moving at the fast pace.

The return to Yankton that he had expected to take just three or four hours took seven, and just as he saw the first

414

buildings appear, he also noticed the sky lightening with the predawn.

Once he had his goal in sight, he slowed to a normal stride, knowing he'd have plenty of time to reach the train station.

It was still predawn when Lynn reached Yankton and headed for the tall water tower. When he stepped onto the empty platform, he walked toward the shuttered ticket window and had to put his eyes close to the posted schedule to be able to read the print.

The train to Omaha wasn't scheduled to depart until 10:10, so he had a lot more time than he had anticipated. He still wasn't about to get a room at the hotel for just four or five hours, but he'd have a serious breakfast and maybe he'd go to the barbershop and get cleaned up before he returned to the station. He hoped that Addie might still be in Omaha waiting for him, but almost giggled at the foolish thought.

He leaned his Winchester against one of the benches, then shrugged off his two sets of saddlebags before taking a seat and looking east at the slowly lightening sky. He'd head over to the nearest diner for breakfast as soon as the sun peeked over the horizon and then see about that shave and bath.

———

Twenty minutes later, Lynn walked past the railway hotel, then a hardware store and a saloon before he spotted a diner. He followed a man who was even scruffier than he was into the place, took a seat and set his things down before taking off his hat and waiting to be served.

———

415

He knew that he'd eaten too much as he left the diner and stepped out onto the boardwalk. There was a lot more street traffic now as he stood and searched for a barbershop, hoping that he would open early.

As he scanned the town, he wondered about the Perkins family whom he had met on the *Alberta* on his way to Fort Benton. It seemed like ages ago but had only been a month. He was smiling when he thought of Libby Perkins and was glad that he hadn't decided to stay in Yankton to get to know her better. She couldn't hold a candle to Addie nor could any other girl or woman.

He spotted the barber pole on the other side of the street and west three blocks, so he trotted across the street, hopped onto the opposite boardwalk and strode toward the barbershop.

He arrived just as the barber was unlocking the door.

"Morning," he said as he smiled at the young man who was obviously in dire need of his services.

"Morning. I'm glad to be the first one here. I need the works; a shave, haircut and a bath."

"Well, son, you've come to the right place," the barber replied as he opened the door and let Lynn enter.

"Let me fire up the boiler to get the water heated. Just have a seat and we can get started on your haircut."

"Yes, sir," Lynn said as he set his saddlebags and Winchester on the wall away from the door and hung his coat and Stetson on the coat rack.

LYNN'S SEARCH

He sat down in the luxurious red leather barber share and thought he might fall asleep before the barber returned, but he managed to keep his eyes open.

The barber floated a cotton apron across Lynn's chest and tied it around his neck before taking his clippers in hand.

"How short do you want it?" he asked.

"Just regular, I guess. I let it go a bit."

The barber grinned as he began working and said, "I wish my hair grew as fast as you young fellers' hair does."

Lynn just let the barber talk and work as he trimmed his thick black locks and carefully held his face still when the barber stropped his razor, then lathered his beard with soap and began to scrape off the tough stubble.

Twenty minutes later, Lynn was luxuriating in a bathtub of warm water as he scrubbed away the grime from his trip.

He would have spent more time in the bath but had to get back to the station and buy his ticket, so after just ten minutes, he dried himself and donned some clean clothes.

He walked back out to the front of the shop looking nothing like a trapper or miner.

Another customer was in the barber chair as Lynn reached into his pocket to pay the barber.

The man looked at Lynn and asked, "You stayin' for the big trial on Friday?"

"Nope. I'm taking the morning train to Omaha and then going home to Denver."

"You oughta hang around for a few days, son. This is gonna be a real humdinger. We ain't never had a murder trial with a woman facin' the noose."

"I've heard of a few back in Omaha, but not many," Lynn said as he handed the barber thirty cents and then added a dime for a tip.

As the barber thanked him, out of curiosity, Lynn asked, "How did that happen?"

The man snickered and said, "These two whores tempted some feller into an alley to rob him and then stabbed him. I reckon they figured they could get away with it, but he made it to the saloon and told the deputy and some of the boys what happened before he fell over dead with a knife in his back. When they found those whores, one had the dead man's pistol in her hand, so one of the deputy's pals shot her dead. Now the other one's not saying a word and is gonna hang for it, too."

"Sounds like an open and shut case," Lynn said as he donned his jacket and pulled on his hat.

"That's what the prosecutor figures, too."

Lynn was picking up his saddlebags when the man said, "The young whore is supposed to be a real good looker, too. From what I hear they were tryin' to get money to get out of town. They just got here, too."

Lynn had just plucked up his Winchester when he asked, "They just arrived?"

"That's what I heard. Came in on a riverboat with the feller they shoved that knife into."

Lynn stood gaping at the man; if he'd just said the whores had just arrived on the riverboat, then it wouldn't have been so obvious, but to say that one was a young, good-looking woman cemented his stunned belief that Addie was facing trial for murder.

He didn't say another word as he hurried from the barbershop and as soon as he reached the boardwalk realized that he didn't even know where the jail was.

His mind was a bubbling cauldron with a variety of potential scenarios and he was almost terrified worry as he scanned the buildings for the sheriff's office.

The town was coming to life as he decided to walk east toward the biggest building, which he assumed was the courthouse.

He soon found the sheriff's office, opened the door and entered where he spotted two men wearing badges at the desk. The one standing was older and probably the sheriff and the younger one behind the desk was most likely his deputy.

But Lynn didn't pay them much attention as he kicked the door closed behind him and stared at the human shape in the cell behind the desk.

He was sure that it was Addie, but she was either sleeping or just trying to hide her shame as she lay with her back facing him.

Sheriff Aubrey looked at the well-armed young man laden with two sets of saddlebags and asked, "What do you need, son?"

Lynn began walking slowly forward with his eyes locked on Addie as he replied, "I need to talk to your prisoner."

"Not with that Winchester in your hand or that pistol at your hip. What's your name?"

Lynn reached the desk, laid his Winchester on the desktop, then shrugged his saddlebags loudly to the floor before beginning to unbuckle his gunbelt.

"My name's Lynn Evans, and I need to speak to your prisoner."

Addie knew that someone had come into the jail, and she assumed he was Mister Farrington making another plea for her to cooperate in her own defense. Even after Lynn had said his name, she hadn't paid any attention.

"You any relation to Dylan Evans?" the sheriff asked with raised eyebrows.

"He's my father," Lynn replied as he stepped around the sheriff and the desk and soon reached the iron bars.

Sheriff Aubrey and Deputy George both watched Lynn and listened for what he was going to say to Adele. The sheriff hoped that he'd get her to start talking while his deputy prayed for her continued silence.

Lynn stared at her back and quietly said, "Addie? It's Lynn. Tell me what happened."

Addie heard his voice and wasn't quite sure it was really Lynn. It might be the sheriff or Mister Farrington trying some ploy to get her to blurt out something stupid. But then she realized that no one knew about Lynn, and despite the impossibility that he could be just feet away, Addie finally turned to look at him.

LYNN'S SEARCH

When her blue eyes finally registered that it truly was Lynn standing on the other side of the bars, her heart leapt with joy and relief, but in an instant, the intoxicating impact of seeing him evaporated and was replaced with confusion and surprising distrust when she realized that he'd asked her to explain what had happened. *How could he possibly be here? Why did he ask her to talk? Had the sheriff somehow brought him here?*

She didn't stand but swung her legs to the floor and sat on the cot as she waited for him to speak again.

Lynn had expected to see her face light up before she rushed to the bars and cry out of relief and happiness, but she didn't even acknowledge him at all other than sitting up and looking at him. *What had they done to Addie? What had happened to Betty?*

"Aren't you going to talk to me, Addie?"

Addie softly asked, "How did you get here, Lynn?"

"I took a canoe, but it sank a few miles south of here, so I had to walk to Yankton to get the train. I only heard about your trial a few minutes ago. Tell me what happened, Addie."

Addie looked past Lynn at the sheriff and that damned deputy and shook her head.

"Not with them here."

Lynn glanced back at the sheriff before asking, "Why can't they be here? They're the law here, Addie."

Sheriff Aubrey said, "If you're Dylan Evans' son, then my deputy and I will step outside while you talk. Just open the door when you're finished."

Avery shot a hostile glance at the sheriff, who missed it, before Lynn said, "Thank you, Sheriff. I appreciate the courtesy. You can take my Winchester and pistol with you if you'd like."

"I still have those repeaters and shotguns on the rack, Mister Evans," Sheriff Aubrey replied before he grabbed his hat and waited for his deputy to do the same.

Lynn may not have noticed the deputy's reaction to his boss's offer, but Addie had because she'd been watching him closely.

As soon as the door closed, Addie stood and walked hurriedly to the bars.

"Did you really take a canoe all the way down the Missouri?" she asked quickly as she gripped the bars.

"I only stopped to take short breaks. After the first two days, I even figured out a way to sleep and drift on the current."

Addie then asked, "Why did you leave so quickly? Did you get in trouble for sending me and my mother away?"

"No. I handled that issue with the sheriff and Dan Billingsley just two days later, but I had to leave. I didn't want to stay until spring without you, Addie. It sounds stupid, but I was worried that once my brothers saw you, then I'd lose you."

Addie managed a smile, but then lost it as tears welled in her eyes as she said, "They killed my mother, Lynn."

"Tell me what happened, Addie. Why couldn't you talk in front of the sheriff?"

"I didn't want them to know what my mother did before we left Fort Benton. They probably already have an idea, but I'm not about to get on that witness stand and have to shame her before all these strangers, Lynn. I won't."

"So, tell me what happened. Please, Addie."

She wiped her eyes then began her story when she had first realized that Pepper Taylor was practically stalking her like a mountain lion hunting a small doe. Once she started, the horrible events that followed their arrival in Yankton poured out in a verbal avalanche.

Lynn listened and knew she was telling the truth, but when she said that the deputy's good friend had shot her mother even though the pistol's muzzle was pointed at the ground, he understood why Addie was reluctant to talk where the deputy could hear.

After she finished her rushed narrative, she asked, "What can you do, Lynn? You're not a lawman and I'm still not going to talk to them."

"The sheriff trusted me enough to talk to you in private and I'm not your lawyer. I think I can talk to him alone and at least get an idea how to help."

Addie looked into his dark brown eyes and knew that if she couldn't trust Lynn, then there she may as well give up all hope.

"Alright. But be careful around that deputy. He gave the sheriff a nasty look when he offered to let us talk privately."

Lynn nodded, then said, "We have a lot to talk about when you're out of here, Addie."

"I know, but now I have a reason to be free."

"Addie, I don't want you to change your behavior until then. Keep quiet and act as if you're angry."

"I am angry, Lynn. I'm angry and ashamed for having killed that bastard, and I know you'll tell me that I shouldn't feel any guilt for doing it, but I do."

"I would have told you just that, Addie, but when we talk, I'll explain why I had to stay in Fort Benton. I really wanted to get on the *Alberta* with you, and I feel just as guilty for your loss by not being here with you. That murdering bastard wouldn't have dared to do what he did if I was near. Just stay quiet and we'll have a long time to talk after you're out of here."

"Okay. I'm sorry I was so sullen when I first saw you, Lynn. I was just confused, and my head wasn't working right. I had become incredibly suspicious of everyone and thought you were some kind of trick to make me talk."

"I can't claim to understand how you felt, Addie, so now just let me see what I can do."

Addie smiled as she nodded before Lynn gently touched her fingers that were wrapped around the bars, then turned and headed for the door.

———

For the first couple of minutes after leaving the jail, Avery kept straining to hear what they were saying inside but realized that all he heard were muffled words.

Then he asked, "Who's Dylan Evans?"

"I guess that you're too new here to know, but that's his father and he's a legend among the lawmen and the men on the riverboats that ply the Missouri. He was the United States Marshal for Nebraska Territory for years, and now he's in charge of the Denver office."

"His father is a U.S. Marshal?"

"One of the best and I understand that young man in the jail has an uncle who is a Deputy U.S. Marshal and another who is a Denver County prosecutor. I don't recall their names, though."

"You think he's gonna try and use them to get that girl outta there?"

"I'd be surprised, but I wouldn't hold it against him. Did you see his face when he saw her? That boy is in love."

Avery could care less about the romance as he chewed on his lower lip. He hadn't worried about any legal ramifications for the modified statements before, but if a U.S. Marshal arrived to investigate, it could cost him more than his badge.

When Lynn opened the door, the sheriff and deputy entered, and as he closed it again, the sheriff asked, "How did it go?"

"I spent most of the time explaining how I got here in the first place. I can see how it would be hard to believe that I could canoe all the way from Fort Benton in just a week."

"You really did that?" the sheriff asked as he hung his hat again.

"Yes, sir. It took a lot out of me, though, so I really need to get a room and rest for a little bit. I'm going to drop off my gear at the hotel, but I can tell you about the journey as we walk."

"I'd like to hear it," Sheriff Aubrey replied, easily understanding the real reason for the invitation.

No young man as infatuated as he seemed to be with Adele Price would even thing about going to the hotel immediately after talking to her. He was sure that she had told him the story and why she wouldn't tell them.

After buckling his gunbelt around his waist, Lynn replaced his saddlebags over his shoulders, grabbed his Winchester and headed for the door with the sheriff behind him.

Once the door was closed, Lynn asked, "Is Addie safe with your deputy?"

"We won't be gone long enough for him to even think about doing anything. Why do you ask?"

"I think you know, Sheriff," Lynn replied as they crossed the street.

"Did she tell you what happened?"

"Yes. And I understand why she refused to talk about it. It's about her mother's reputation more than her fear of your deputy and his friends."

"Her mother was a prostitute; wasn't she?"

"She went to Fort Benton with my mother as a contract wife. My father was the engineer on the riverboat that carried them from Kansas City. She became pregnant with Addie right away and when her husband died a few years later, her mother accepted another prospective husband who never even married her. Then she had a succession of men who promised her marriage, but eventually her reputation was so tarnished that she did the only thing left to her to provide for her daughter. A true measure of her honesty was when she found that she was diseased with pox and refused to see any more clients. That put Addie into an even more precarious condition.

"When I arrived, I had instructions from my mother to find any of the other contract wives that were still in Fort Benton and if they wanted to leave, I was to escort them out of town. I put Addie and her mother on a riverboat and gave them more than enough money for train tickets to Denver. That's why the story of them robbing that man were even more ludicrous. If anything, he would have robbed them after forcing them into the alley under gunpoint. He had planned to kill Addie's mother, then rape and kill her. I'll give you the details later, but I'm absolutely convinced that Addie and her mother were the true victims.

"Your biggest problem now is your deputy and his friends. Addie told me that her mother had the muzzle pointed down when your deputy ordered her to drop the pistol. She was worried that it might go off because neither she nor Addie knew how to release the hammer. She was starting to ask your deputy how to do it when the man standing beside the deputy shot and killed her."

"Dave Immelmann was the shooter and all of their statements claimed that her mother had aimed the pistol at them, which would make it a legitimate case of self-defense."

They'd reached the hotel when Lynn stopped and said, "I just want to be able to take Addie away from here, Sheriff. Can I talk to the prosecutor?"

"We can talk to him this afternoon. I know that he's looking for any excuse to drop the charges. Trying to get a jury to convict a handsome woman is tough enough, but I believe that he'll be convinced that you're telling the truth."

"I hope so, but will that create a problem for you after your deputy hears that the charges were dropped?"

"I don't think so, but maybe I shouldn't have told him that your father is a U.S. Marshal. He seemed unpleasantly surprised by the news."

"I'm a bit surprised that he didn't know about him. He and my Uncle Bryn made quite a run up to Fort Randall on a salvage tug."

"I've heard all the tales, too, but Avery has only been in town a couple of years now. His father is a sheriff in Iowa, so I figured he'd be a good hire to replace my old deputy who moved on to Sioux City."

"If the prosecutor drops charges, maybe we should keep it quiet until the train is ready to leave tomorrow. I could just pick her up and escort her directly to the station then board the train."

"That might be the best solution. May I call you Lynn?"

Lynn smiled, shook the sheriff's hand and replied, "I'd be honored, sir."

The sheriff grinned and said, "Call me Burner. My real name is Bernard, but nobody would dare call me that."

"I can understand that, Burner. I'll get a room first, but can I just go and talk to the prosecutor or do you want to come along?"

"Stay in the hotel after lunch and I'll come and get you. I'll have Avery take a late lunch, so he won't be in the jail alone with your girlfriend. She is your girlfriend; isn't she?"

"I hope so, but I've only spent a few hours with her before I put her and her mother on the boat."

"Sometimes that's all it takes. I knew the moment I met my Winnie's eyes that she was the right one. She told me that she knew, too."

"My father and uncles all say the same thing. My father was eighteen when he met my mother and said that despite her small size and pigtails, he knew right away that even though she was under a contract marriage, he'd never look for anyone else."

"Well, we're taking too much time talking about things that don't matter right now. You get your room, and I'll see you in a few hours."

"Thanks for being a good lawman, Burner. My father says that there aren't enough of the good ones, and I'm sure he'd count you as one of the best."

"Now you're just sucking up, Lynn," the sheriff said as grinned, then turned and trotted back across the road.

Lynn was relieved after talking to the sheriff but felt a bit of anxiety about the deputy and his friends. If they knew that he was U.S. Marshal Dylan Evans' son, then they might be concerned that he'd tell his father about what they'd done and face the penalty for shooting Betty and then covering up the mistake.

As he entered the railway hotel, he was certain that the man who'd shot Addie's mother had just pulled his trigger in panic. His father had told him many times that the most dangerous men he'd ever faced were the ones who were high-strung because they were so unpredictable.

"Give me a hardened, coldhearted killer anytime," he could hear his father say, "Then I can just watch for him to twitch."

He was smiling as he approached the desk and paid for one night's stay in Yankton. A team of wild horses couldn't keep him in the town for another second.

———

After he returned to the jail, the sheriff noticed that Adele was back in her previous position on her cot and wondered if Lynn had told her to do that. If he had, the sheriff's already high opinion of the young man rose a bit.

Avery hadn't even thought about bothering Addie, but had felt the overwhelming urge to find Dave Immelmann, Jimmy Ralston and Luther Bausch to let them know of the new danger that had just walked into the jail a short time ago and was now getting a room at the railway hotel.

"That was one interesting story," Sheriff Aubrey said as he hung his hat and coat on their pegs.

"How long did he take to get here? If he wasn't on that riverboat, how could he even get here so fast?"

"You have to understand that riverboats need to stop when it's dark or risk running aground or hitting an obstruction, but he didn't have to stop because he was paddling a canoe. He'd also be able to take advantage of the fast current better than a big old sternwheeler."

"So, when did he leave Fort Benton?"

Burner wasn't sure, but said, "Around a week ago. It's quite a way, but if you're not stopping much, it can be done. I'm sure the Injuns have done it more times than we'd like to know."

Avery was looking for any way to punch holes in Evans' trustworthiness, so after his questioning of Lynn's story, he asked, "Are we really sure that this kid is Dylan Evans' son? I mean anybody could walk in here and claim he was either Dylan Evans son, General Grant's kid or Bobby Lee's boy. How can we be sure he isn't some pretender who wants the girl to owe him a big favor?"

Sheriff Aubrey understood the purpose of the questioning but couldn't admit to his own reasons for confidently believing that he was Dylan Evans' son.

"Maybe you're right, Avery. We couldn't ask the girl, of course, because she'd be more than willing to back him up. I'll tell you what I'm going to do to find out. I'll take him over to see the prosecutor this afternoon and make him produce some form of identification. If he can't, then whatever he says will be worthless."

Avery was mollified to a degree after planting the seed but didn't believe his own line of reasoning. Even if the kid didn't have any papers, which most folks didn't, then Avery was absolutely sure that he'd tell his marshal daddy about how his girlfriend's mama was killed and that the local law wasn't doing anything about it.

Sheriff Aubrey watched his deputy sitting silently at his desk and could almost hear the gears in his brain whirring. He was certain that Avery was trying to think of a way to avoid prosecution for falsifying records. It was a relatively minor flaw in the litany of crimes that they dealt with on a daily basis, but when it was coupled with the belief that they'd covered up what they had to understand was a manslaughter charge

431

against Dave Immelmann that made those concerns very real. Burner knew he had a more serious problem than he'd had the day before, just when he could see the light at the end of that tunnel. This wasn't the proverbial locomotive light; this was a full-fledged explosion igniting at the end of his tunnel.

Addie had listened to their conversation and wondered if Lynn had made a mistake in confiding in the sheriff. It sounded as if he was agreeing with the deputy in doubting Lynn's identity. She may have been concerned, but there was nothing she could to but continue to be quiet. It may be an act now, but it was the best thing for her to do.

———

Lynn left his Winchester in the hotel as he stepped onto the boardwalk and turned west. He knew he was following the path taken by Addie and her mother and wanted to see the crime scene. He wasn't looking for evidence because he knew that there wouldn't be any; he just felt an obligation to visit the site where Betty had died.

As he walked, he began to think about where Addie's mother would be laid to rest. He was sure that Addie would never want to return to Yankton; just as his mother abhorred the thought of going back to Fort Benton.

When he passed the hardware store, he turned left into the alley and could see the signs of heavy traffic created by townsfolk eager to see the location of the two murders. He looked at the end of the alley expecting to see some titillated rubberneckers, but no one was there.

When he reached the spot where Addie had described, he saw some almost black blood stains on various places in the dirt, but there had been so much scuffled footprints that none of it made any sense.

Lynn turned around and walked quickly toward the main street and when he reached the boardwalk, he spotted the dark blood stains in the dry wood left by that bastard who had caused all this.

He stepped along the path trying to picture Pepper Taylor as he stumbled toward the saloon, leaving a trail of blood which had pointed to Addie and Betty. *Why had he claimed innocence with his dying breath? Why didn't he at least beg forgiveness knowing that he was about to answer to God for his sins?*

Lynn watched the trail turn into the saloon and kept walking to get his lunch. He couldn't understand why any man would be so vindictive and soulless to blame his victims for what he was going to do.

————

In Omaha, Garth was on the platform of the enormous Union Pacific station waving to the slowly rolling passenger car as the Green family and Alwen returned his farewell. It had taken him a lot of arguing to convince Benji and Al to let him stay. He'd promised to leave within a week if Lynn didn't show up, and he'd honor that promise, but he began to wonder if he could increase his chances of finding Lynn.

After the train left, Garth turned and headed for the U.S. Marshal's office to ask his new friend, Deputy Marshal Elbert Hoskins, for his advice.

When he'd seen the yard full of trains, he thought that he could take the next one north along the Missouri. He'd checked the schedule and there was one leaving that afternoon that went all the way to Yankton in the Dakota Territory. Most of that time, the train had the Missouri River in sight, so if he spotted a man in a canoe, he'd be able to get off at the next stop and head back; if not, he'd wait in Yankton.

He only had that week to wait and if he was waiting a couple of hundred miles upriver, his odds would go up considerably and he wouldn't break his promise.

It seemed like a good idea to him, but he'd ask Bert about it and maybe even see if he could come along.

————

After Lynn had gone, Deputy Sheriff George left the jail a few minutes later to find his friends and found Jimmy Ralston and Luther Bausch easily enough but couldn't find Dave Immelmann. Jimmy and Luther hadn't seen him after they'd written their statements, and Luther said he hadn't shown up at the freight yard that morning.

"Did he say anything after you left the jail?" Avery asked.

"Nope, but he seemed really quiet. I think he was feelin' bad for shootin' the woman," Luther replied.

"He seemed okay when we were writing those statements."

Jimmy said, "I think it was when you were tellin' him to be sure to write that the woman was pointin' that pistol at us like she was gonna shoot that set him off. He mighta been tellin' himself that she was really gonna do it, but once we had to cover up what really happened, he knew he'd killed an innocent woman."

Avery snapped, "Innocent? What are you talkin' about? She was a whore and had murdered Taylor! You saw the knife in his back."

434

Luther glanced at Jimmy and said, "We were all fired up, Avery. Even after Dave shot her, we didn't think things through. But when we were writing those statements, none of it sounded right. When I saw that girl cryin' over her mother lyin' dead on the ground, I couldn't see how she coulda done what Taylor said she and her mother had done."

"Did you know her innocent mother had a dagger strapped to her leg? That proves she was a whore and what that girl was doing was just an act."

Jimmy said, "It wasn't an act, Avery. Nobody is that good."

"Well, let's find Dave and make sure we all stick together. This morning, her boyfriend miraculously arrived with some tall story about canoeing down the Missouri from Fort Benton and just accidentally comes to town. He even claims to be the son of some famous U.S. Marshal, and you know what that means?"

Luther replied, "No, but maybe you can tell us."

"It means, Luther, that if he is who he says he is, then he can go back to his daddy and tell him what happened. Then his father can come up here with some deputy marshals and arrest us all. He's got jurisdiction anywhere in this country."

"Arrest us for what?" asked a startled Jimmy Ralston, "All we did was change our story a bit."

"We conspired to obstruct justice for manslaughter, Jimmy. That's what we did. Dave is guilty of manslaughter for what he did; or didn't you know that?"

"He just panicked; that's all," Jimmy quickly replied.

"He shot her when he shouldn't have, and that makes it manslaughter. When we covered up for it, then it makes us all criminals."

"So, what do we do, Avery?" Luther asked.

"We find Dave, then we wait for a day or so. Her boyfriend is trying to get her to talk, but if she doesn't, then even if he went back to Denver and told his old man, it won't matter. She didn't even talk to her lawyer, so as long as she keeps her mouth shut, we don't have anything to worry about."

Luther and Jimmy shared a look before Luther said, "Alright, Avery. Let's find Dave."

Avery nodded, then asked, "Have either of you checked his room?"

After two head shakes, Avery led them down the street to Fletcher's Boarding House.

———

When he found himself alone in the jail with Addie, Sheriff Aubrey turned the desk chair around until it faced the cell.

"Miss Price, may I call you Addie? Lynn doesn't use Adele, so if it's alright with you, I'll use Addie."

Addie listened but didn't move as she stared at the wall.

"In a little while, I'm going to the hotel to pick up Lynn and then we'll go to the prosecutor's office. There's a very good chance that when we leave, the charges against you will be dropped. Lynn believes, and I agree with him, that as long as we keep that news private, the safest place for you is right where you are. He'll show up just before the train leaves and take you with him."

Addie finally rolled over, then sat up and asked, "Why do you both believe that I'm safer here?"

Burner was pleased to hear her voice as he answered, "We both understand that my deputy covered for his friend who shot your mother. I'm sure that Avery knows what a danger you represent to him and the others if you talked. If he hears about the dropped charges, I don't know what he and the others would do. So, if the prosecutor does drop the charge, then we can't let him know about it until you're gone."

"So, I won't see Lynn until tomorrow?"

Burner smiled at the question. Here was a young woman facing the possibility of hanging, yet she was asking about seeing her boyfriend before asking the more serious questions.

"I'm going to give him my key to the jail when we leave the prosecutor's office, and I'm sure that he'll make quick use of it. You won't be a prisoner if he comes, so I'm not doing anything illegal. I'll feel better knowing that he'd be giving you protection, too."

Addie finally smiled at the sheriff and said, "Thank you, Sheriff. I've been wrong to mistrust you."

"I don't blame you a bit, Addie. And call me Burner."

"Burner?"

"My Christian name is Bernard, but I didn't like Bernie, either."

Addie laughed lightly then said, "I was never too fond of Adele myself."

The ice broken, the sheriff asked, "Lynn said that you told him what really happened, so I'm not going to ask you about that night. I'll hear it when we talk to the prosecutor. He even told me about your mother and why she had the dagger, so don't concern yourself with that, either. But what I was curious about was why he would let you and your mother get on that boat without him. He obviously cares very much for you."

Addie let out her breath and said, "He said that he had private things to do, and although he never said what they were, I'm sure that it had to do with the timing of his birth. We were born just days apart; six days, thirteen hours and twenty minutes apart by his calculations. That told me that he was worried about the man who may have been his birth father."

"It wasn't Dylan Evans?" the sheriff asked in surprise.

"Lynn's probably not sure because of the timing. You see…"

Addie explained her belief for Lynn's arrival and determination to stay in Fort Benton but didn't know if he'd found the answer before he left and asked that the sheriff not mention it to Lynn.

She had rushed through her explanation as she kept her eyes on the door, expecting Deputy George to enter at any moment.

Sheriff Aubrey didn't expect to see his deputy anytime soon because he was sure that he was hunting for his friends to let them know about Lynn, but he still had locked the door to give Addie time to return to the cot.

After she finished, she said, "I've got to get back now. I have a lot of thinking to do."

"Go ahead and I'll unlock the door. I still don't think that Avery will be returning very soon."

Addie had turned around to walk to the cot when she stopped, looked back and asked, "Why not?"

"He's probably chatting with his friends about what to do if you start talking," he replied, then added, "I wish I had a second deputy."

————

His only deputy and his friends hadn't found Dave in his room or anywhere else, and it had them worried. They began to suspect that he'd taken the morning train out of Yankton just an hour earlier and that would leave them holding the bag.

————

Since leaving the jail after writing his statement, Dave Immelmann had been sliding deeper into the pits of guilt for what he'd done. As soon as the bullet had left his Colt, he knew he'd made a horrible mistake and all he could hope for was that he'd missed. But he hadn't missed and had killed that girl's mother. Her loud cries of loss and then her angry accusation had haunted him all night and kept him from sleeping. *Why had he even cocked the hammer?* He knew that they weren't in danger from those two women, even if they had trapped and stabbed that dead man in the saloon.

After leaving the jail, he should have gone to work, but couldn't face any of the others, so he kept walking to the riverbank. He had spent almost an hour staring at the flowing water without seeing it as he relived that horrible night.

439

When he returned his mind to the real world, he pulled the offending pistol from his holster and stared at the Colt that he had treasured since he'd bought it a few weeks ago. He drew the hammer back to the first click and opened the loading gate before rotating the cylinder until the empty brass was exposed and used the rod to push the expended round free.

After closing the gate and releasing the hammer, he holstered his pistol and stared at the blackened brass cylinder in his palm, knowing where the missing bullet had gone.

He didn't pay attention to his cold, damp britches as he sat on moist mud of the riverbank and examined every minute detail of the remains of the cartridge.

Finally, he stood, hurled the brass into the river, then turned and walked downriver for two hundred yards. He stopped, then glanced to the east and began walking away from the river.

Avery had left Luther and Jimmy at the freight yard as he continued walking to the jail, unaware that his missing friend was striding just four hundred yards to his southwest on a parallel path.

Dave had reached the depths of guilt and self-loathing after leaving the river and as ashamed as he was for committing that unforgivable act, he'd compounded his shame by lying to hide his guilt.

He reached the south side of Yankton and kept walking as he stared in front of him, knowing where he had to go.

———

LYNN'S SEARCH

Lynn had finished his very early lunch and was sitting in his room in the railway hotel thinking about what he would say to the prosecutor and then to Addie when he saw her again.

Avery had returned to the jail, hung his hat and told the sheriff that he'd found nothing unusual on his rounds, but had been pleased to see the girl still laying with her back to the outside world. She must not have talked to her boyfriend after all.

Dave had made his way through the back alleys and finally arrived behind the saloon and stepped onto the same spot of earth where the woman had been standing when she had looked at them with curious, but frightened eyes. They weren't the eyes of a murderer, but he had closed them forever.

He stood facing the alley, pulled the weapon that had ended her life, then cocked the hammer and placed the cold muzzle against the right side of his head.

There were no loud saloon noises to mask the sound of the gunshot, so within seconds of the echoes reaching the street, two nervous passersby slowly entered the now infamous alley and soon found Dave Immelmann's body.

One stayed while the second rushed to tell the sheriff. Both knew Dave Immelmann and it didn't take a lawman to realize who had pulled the trigger ending his life or why he had done it.

Larry Grinnell burst into the sheriff's office, and exclaimed, "Come quick, Sheriff! Dave Immelmann's offed himself!"

Avery had to keep from retching when bile filled the back of his throat as he and the sheriff grabbed their hats and hustled out behind Larry.

Addie had heard the man's exclamation and wasn't sure what impact it would have on her situation, but that was secondary to her. She felt as if her mother had received some measure of justice for what the man had done, but at the same time, felt a sprinkling of compassion for her killer. For him to do what he'd done because of his sense of guilt meant that he wasn't the evil monster she'd tried to make of him. He was just an average man, and maybe even a good man, who'd made a terrible mistake. Now, he was dead, just like her mother; *but what good had come of his death?*

————

Larry didn't have to lead the sheriff and Avery all the way as a crowd was already forming at the mouth of the alley and several men had begun to walk toward the scene.

They pushed their way through the crowd and soon reached the end of the short alley where the found Dave Immelmann's body sprawled on the ground with the large exit wound on the left side of his head visible to the curious eyes of the onlookers.

"Break it up! Go home, all of you!" Sheriff Aubrey shouted.

The men who were hovering near the body slowly turned and left, then after he made sure that the area was empty, Burner took a knee near the body, picked up Dave's hat and laid it on his head.

After he stood, he turned to his deputy and asked, "I can guess why he committed suicide, Avery. He felt guilty for shooting Mrs. Price."

Avery wasn't about to give in that quickly as he stared at Dave's body.

"Are we really sure he killed himself, boss? I mean, we didn't have any witnesses and maybe that boyfriend wanted revenge against him for killing her mother."

Burner snapped, "That's his pistol on the ground near his hand, Avery. Her boyfriend, if you noticed, carries a Smith & Wesson. There's no doubt in my mind that he killed himself, but we can get an autopsy done to make sure. Does he have any family?"

"He's got a brother, but he lives down in Sioux City."

"Well, I'll leave it to you to let him know about it. I'll go see Ed Freeman again and you stay here to keep out the spectators."

Avery nodded as he watched the sheriff pick up Dave's gun, then give the barrel a sniff before examining the cylinders.

"This was just fired, and the empty cartridge is still in the top cylinder," Burner said before he walked back down the alley, leaving Avery with his dead friend.

———

As the sheriff walked to the mortuary, he worried about what impact Dave Immelmann's suicide would have on his deputy. Avery's almost instantaneous suggestion that Lynn had somehow murdered Dave bothered him immensely, and Burner worried for Lynn and Addie's safety. He knew, if anything, Dave's decision to take his own life would only add more support to Addie's side of the story that Lynn would

443

present to Hiram Lefkowitz this afternoon. It was what would happen afterwards that gave him concern.

————

Lynn hadn't heard the gunshot or any of the excitement that was happening just two blocks from his room as he lay on his bed reviewing what he'd be telling the prosecutor.

He had to avoid even mentioning his father because he didn't want the lawyer to believe that he was trying to exert influence. That would only be necessary if he didn't believe Addie had told him the truth, and if he didn't believe her, then there would be no reason for him to talk to the prosecutor in the first place.

If the prosecutor dropped charges, he'd ask the sheriff if he could stay with Addie for the night so they could talk. He was sure that if he asked, the sheriff would give him a wink and suspect they'd do more than just pass a few words, but he didn't mind. Besides, who would believe that they'd never even shared a quick kiss since they'd met.

He smiled at the thought as he looked at the ceiling and calculated exactly how long he'd actually spent with Addie before she left Fort Benton and came up with three hours and twenty minutes; exactly two hundred minutes or twelve thousand seconds. Yet, somehow, he believed that the last eleven thousand and fifty seconds were just time for confirming what he'd felt when he'd first met her and had that shot of lightening rip through him. But once they boarded that train, they'd spend a lot longer than three hours and twenty minutes getting to know each other.

Now he just needed to convince the prosecutor to drop the murder charge.

LYNN'S SEARCH

_____

As Lynn waited for the sheriff to pick him up to see the prosecutor, his younger brother, Garth, was sitting in the U.S. Marshal's office in Omaha talking to Deputy Marshal Elbert Hoskins.

"I can understand why you might want to take the train, but are you sure that your father would want you to go out there by yourself?"

"It's just a way to get closer to Lynn, Bert. It's not exactly dangerous or anything. I'll just get on the train in three hours and sit there."

"I could tell the boss that I heard about a problem with the sheriff up in Yankton. He won't care if I'm gone for a couple of days."

Garth grinned and said, "I've got to get my stuff from the hotel. I'll see you at the station, Bert."

Bert nodded, then as he watched Garth leave the office, rose and headed for the marshal's private office to give him his concocted story, knowing that as far as the boss was concerned, he could have said that he was investigating an invasion of the town by moon men.

_____

Three hours later, Garth and Bert Hoskins were crossing the Missouri aboard the train that would stop in Council Bluffs across the river, then turn north for Yankton, about another hundred and fifty miles away. It wasn't scheduled to arrive until early the next morning after making its many stops along the way, but Garth would still be watching the river as often as he could, hoping to spot Lynn paddling along in his canoe.

445

Bert didn't regret accompanying Garth because he wanted to talk to Lynn Evans anyway. Benji had told him that it had been Lynn who had arranged for his move to Denver to work with Dylan, and Bert was hoping to convince Lynn to do the same for him.

————

Lynn was waiting for the sheriff in the lobby when he first heard chatter about the suicide of the man who had killed the murdering whore.

He wanted to interrupt the conversation to ask for more information but knew that he'd get the accurate story from the sheriff when he arrived. He suspected that the sheriff would be delayed by the man's self-inflicted death, so he wasn't concerned after he'd been sitting in the chair for over an hour.

————

After notifying Ed Freeman of the body that had to be picked up, Sheriff Aubrey had quickly returned to the jail just in case his deputy got there first. He didn't believe that he would do anything to the girl but wasn't about to take the risk.

When he entered the empty office, he relaxed and headed for the desk.

"What happened?" Addie asked from her cot.

"Dave Immelmann put a .45 through his head in the same spot where your mother had been standing when he killed her. There's no question that he committed suicide, so it won't change anything."

"Are you still going to take Lynn to the prosecutor?"

"Yes, ma'am. That is now my top priority. We need to get you and Lynn out of Yankton so things can quiet down."

Addie was still facing the wall as she said, "He wasn't the monster that I made him out to be; was he? He felt so guilty for what he'd done that he couldn't live with himself."

"No, Dave wasn't close to a monster. I liked him, but he was too much of a follower and wanted to be important."

Addie didn't say anything else as she stared at the wall. *Why should she feel so sad about the man's death?* He'd killed her mother, even if it was accidental.

Deputy George returned to the jail a few minutes later, but didn't remove his hat as he asked, "Boss, could I take the rest of the day off? I'm kinda shook up after seeing Dave's body."

"Go ahead. I'll see you in the morning."

Avery just turned and left the office, closing the door behind him as Burner watched. Having him out of the way meant that he could take Lynn to Hiram's office now, but he was worried that he might return with his two remaining friends while he was gone.

He figured that nothing would happen that soon, so he stood, grabbed his hat and said, "I'll be back soon, Addie."

"Okay," she replied from her cell and listened as the sheriff closed and locked the door.

Once she was alone, she sat up and stared through the window at the road traffic outside. The sheriff's concerns were obvious, and she had no protection as she sat in her big cage. All she could do is sit and wait.

———

Fifteen minutes later, Lynn and the sheriff were sitting with Hiram Lefkowitz as he listened to Lynn as he presented Addie's version of what had happened.

The prosecutor was well aware of Lynn's famous father, which hadn't hurt his credibility at all. As he had been hoping for any reasonable excuse to drop the charge, he'd made his decision to do just that soon after Lynn had started. Now, he was just listening for the details; convinced that they were factual.

When Lynn finished the narrative, he ended by expressing his firm belief in the accuracy of Addie's version by adding that he'd given her and her mother more than enough money to reach Denver safely and there was no motive for them to try to rob anyone.

After Lynn stopped talking, Hiram glanced at Burner then said, "I was reasonably sure that the statements provided by the witnesses were, in the least, inaccurate, Mister Evans. The version you just presented of what had happened that night is much more believable and if I decided to take this to court knowing that you'd testify, I'd be a fool. I'm going to drop the charge and Miss Price is free to go."

Lynn smiled, then said, "Thank you, sir. Sheriff Aubrey and I have decided that we need to keep that information a secret until I escort Addie to the train in the morning."

"That's probably a good idea."

Lynn then asked, "Have they buried her mother yet?"

The sheriff replied, "They were going to do it this afternoon. Why?"

"Can we have the mortician just embalm her body so we can take it with us on the train? I don't believe that Addie would want to have her buried here."

"Of course. I'll write out a quick note in case he has any questions."

Sheriff Aubrey pulled out the same small notepad that still had the vital information for Beatrice price on the top sheet, then ripped it and Adele's page out and wrote his note on the third. He handed all three to Lynn, who slipped them into his jacket pocket.

He and Lynn then stood, and Lynn shook the prosecutor's hand as he thanked him again, before they left the office.

Once in the hallway, the sheriff reached into his pocket and handed Lynn his office key.

"I figured you might want to spend some time with Addie after it's dark. I'd sleep better knowing you were there to keep her safe, too."

"Thanks Burner," Lynn said as he dropped the key into the pocket with the notes.

After waving to the sheriff, Lynn headed to the mortuary to make the arrangements to move Betty's body to Denver. He hadn't broached the subject with Addie but couldn't imagine that she'd be happy knowing she could never bring herself to visit her mother's grave.

The sheriff reached the jail before he realized that he'd given the key to Lynn and had locked himself out of his own office.

He could have gone back to the hotel and asked to borrow the key again, but it was already mid-afternoon and he decided that he'd just make his own rounds before going home, so he left the front of the jail and started a stroll to the west.

———

Addie had spotted the sheriff in the window and when he hadn't unlocked the door, she began to worry. *What had happened at the prosecutor's office? Didn't he believe Lynn and now the sheriff was trying to avoid giving her the bad news?*

She stood and walked to the bars at the far corner of the cell to get a better view through the window but didn't see anyone or anything to help her to find answers to her new questions.

She finally returned to her cot and resumed her now customary position, knowing that whatever had happened was out of her control; just as everything else had been since that night.

———

Garth hadn't seen any signs of canoers or anyone else on the river since the train had turned north, and now, it was behind a line of bluffs and the river was no longer visible.

"Do you think he's still coming?" Bert asked.

"Lynn is a lot like my father. If he says he's going to do something, then he does it."

"It's a long way down the Missouri from Fort Benton, Garth and a lot can happen."

"I know, but I'm not worried about him as much as I am about his princess."

"His princess?"

Garth laughed then began explaining what he and Alwen had come to accept as fact about Lynn and Mrs. Price's unnamed daughter. He knew it sounded silly, but it passed the time as the train chugged along the rails.

———

Lynn had been getting more anxious as the afternoon wore on, and finally headed to the diner for an early supper. As he walked along, he kept his eyes peeled for the deputy, but didn't know what his friends looked like, so he had to pay attention to most of the passersby.

He made it to the diner and ordered a big steak; not because he was particularly hungry, but to give him a reason to just stay longer until the sun finally set. It was the middle of October, so it would be going down soon.

Lynn didn't even taste the steak much as he slowly cut the meat and placed it into his mouth. He could have been eating an alligator steak for all he knew.

———

Avery was sitting with Jimmy and Luther in the same saloon and at the same table where they'd been when Pepper Taylor had stumbled into the barroom, but they weren't playing cards.

"I can't believe that Dave's gone," Luther said quietly as he stared at his empty whiskey glass.

"And to go that way is even worse," Jimmy said.

Avery said, "He made his own choice and there's nothing we can do about it. We have to think of ourselves now."

"What do you mean, Avery?" Luther asked.

"I figure that when Dave shot himself, it would give our prosecutor enough reason to let that girl off without going to trial."

"So? What difference would that make? She leaves and we're okay."

"But what if she convinces her boyfriend that we all lied to protect him, and he tells his U.S. Marshal father about it?"

"We did lie, Avery," Jimmy replied, "and I'm not going to lie anymore."

"I won't either, Avery. We shouldn't have done it in the first place. If you'd just let Dave tell the sheriff what had happened, he might not have even gone to jail."

Avery said, "Don't you two understand that you can go to jail for lying about it? You could spend five or ten years in the territorial prison."

"I don't care," Jimmy replied, "I'm just sick of this whole mess."

Avery watched as Luther nodded, then snarled, "You two are a pair of sissies. I don't know why I wanted you for friends," then tossed down the last of his whiskey and stormed out of the saloon.

Luther watched him go and asked, "What do you think he's gonna do, Jimmy?"

"I don't know, and I don't wanna know."

Luther nodded and said, "Let's stay here for a while."

"Yeah. I think that's a good idea."

————

Deputy George had stomped less than a hundred feet along the boardwalk before he slowed and then stopped as the sun set in front of him. He'd lost all of his support now and felt vulnerable. He was too smart to do anything violent because he knew he'd either die in the process or hang afterward.

He crossed the street to head for his room to think about what he should do. He assumed that the sheriff would ask for his badge soon, and he didn't relish the idea.

By the time he entered his room and closed the door, he thought that the best thing to do would be to pack his things and take tomorrow's train out of Yankton. His father had been the Wright County Sheriff for years, but didn't hire him as a deputy after a very big argument, so he'd taken the train west out of Iowa and eventually gotten this position. He figured that if he returned with two years of lawman experience, he'd be able to convince his father to bring him on after all.

————

Lynn had stretched his supper to the limit, so he finished the last dregs of his coffee, left fifty cents on the table and left the diner.

The sun was almost gone, but the sheriff had said that he could visit Addie after dark, and it wasn't quite dark yet. But he figured it was close enough, so he bounced across the street and headed for the jail. He still kept a watch for the deputy and his friends, but he was anxious to see Addie again. He had so much to tell her but assumed that the sheriff had told her about the dropped charges.

———

Addie had finally shifted to a sitting position with her back against the wall as she waited in the dark cell and watched the door.

It had been a long, tense wait already, and her nerves were on a knife's edge as she waited for the sheriff to return. She couldn't imagine his deputy doing anything; not when she was locked inside the cell, but the fear was still there.

She was concentrating on the door when she caught a shadow crossing in front of the window out of the corner of her eye. She turned quickly to look at the window when she heard the sharp click of the door's lock followed by the slight creak from the door's hinges as it swung open.

She saw the shadow enter, and knew he wasn't the sheriff, but seemed too tall to be the deputy. Addie was about to ask who he was when she heard her answer.

"Addie?" Lynn asked as he closed and locked the door.

"Lynn!" she exclaimed as she rushed to the bars.

Lynn didn't stop to light a lamp, but hurried to the wall, removed the large key ring from its peg and approached the cell door where he began trying to get the right key into the barely visible lock.

"What are you doing? Are you breaking me out of jail?" a startled Addie asked as she walked toward the door.

Lynn finally managed to insert the key into the lock, and as he turned it, replied, "Yes, ma'am. I'm bustin' you outta here and we're gonna make our escape to my canoe and row outta Dakota Territory."

Addie didn't know how to react as she stood dumbfounded near the swinging cell door.

Lynn left the key in the lock as he stepped inside and for the first time since he'd left her on the *Alberta*, he wrapped his arms around her.

When he felt her embrace, he whispered, "I'm only kidding, Addie. Didn't the sheriff tell you what the prosecutor said?"

"No, he didn't come back, so I thought that he'd decided to continue with the trial and the sheriff was too embarrassed to tell me."

"Oh. It's probably because he gave me the key to the jail and locked himself out. Anyway, the good news is that Mister Lefkowitz, the prosecutor, dropped the charge and you are now free to leave anytime."

Addie felt a huge release of worry and tension as she squeezed Lynn and said, "Thank God! I was so worried all afternoon. The sheriff told me that if the prosecutor dropped the charge, I should remain here for my safety but that you'd be staying with me. How long will you stay?"

"Until sunrise. Then I'll go and pack my things, buy us our tickets and I'll return around 9:30 to escort you to our train. It arrives much earlier, but they have to service it and turn it around, so it won't leave until just after ten o'clock. We'll be able to get on board right away, though."

"It sounds as if you've got it all planned out."

"At least until we get on the train," he said before finally stepping back.

He took her hands and said, "Let's sit down, Addie. We have a lot to talk about and I think the twelve hours until sunrise won't be nearly enough."

"I have a lot to tell you, too, Lynn," she said as they walked across the cell and sat carefully on the small cot in case it collapsed from their weight.

Once they were seated, Lynn said, "Before we talk about anything else, Addie, I wanted to make sure that I did the right thing about your mother."

Addie quietly asked, "What do you mean? What could you do about her?"

"They hadn't buried her yet because of the autopsy, but I asked the mortician to prepare her body for transport rather than immediate burial. He said it was pretty much the same thing anyway, so I arranged for her to come with us to Denver rather than be buried here. Is that what you would have wanted, Addie?"

Addie felt tears sliding from her eyes as she nodded and whispered, "Yes. You can never imagine how much the idea that she would be here where I couldn't visit her. I owe her everything; even more than just my life. The thought that she'd be just another forgotten grave in a faraway place was crushing. Thank you for being so thoughtful, Lynn. It means so very much to me."

"She'll always be close to you, Addie. I could almost feel the love you had for each other in the brief time that I knew her."

"When we spend more time together, I'll tell you how much she really did for me, but now, we can talk about you and what happened in Fort Benton after we left. Why did you stay?"

"I had to sell the bank. Most folks in town didn't know that my father's name was still on the deed for the bank, and my parents never really cared about it, but when I told them I had to go to Fort Benton, they asked me to sell it and didn't even care about how much they were paid."

"That's not the real reason; is it? I know you probably had to do that, but I don't think it would have taken very long especially as you could have given it away. I think I know the real reason for your going to Fort Benton and why you couldn't leave. You didn't know who your real father was. Is that it?"

"No. It's close, though. I knew who my real father was before I left. I'd suspected it for a long time, but my parents never treated me any differently than my brothers or sisters, so it didn't matter to me. They're such remarkably kind people that I really didn't want to know."

"What happened to make you leave?"

Lynn explained the situation with Ryan and how he'd goaded him into finally asking his parents the question and how they had answered him honestly and without reservation; holding back nothing.

"But after Ryan died, why did you feel that you had to go to Fort Benton? What were you searching for?"

"Before we even left the Double EE that night, I was already dealing with the knowledge that I was Burke Riddell's son. Although I had never done anything to make my parents ashamed of me, I began to wonder if there wasn't a seed of Burke Riddell's evil lurking inside of me. I'd never done anything that put me into a position where I had to test myself and knew that I had to know who I really was or live with the possibility that the seed would suddenly sprout."

"But why Fort Benton and how would you know?"

"How I would know was a mystery to me, but I felt that the best place for it to happen was in Fort Benton."

"Did you find your answer?" Addie asked softly.

He reached over and took her hands as he replied, "Yes, Addie. I had that question answered and know it will never resurface. I'm Dylan Evans' son and sent him a telegram before I left to let him, and my mother know."

"Can you tell me how it happened?"

"I have to, Addie. Ironically, it was your departure that lit the fuse."

As Addie studied his face in the dark cell, Lynn began telling the story, beginning with his arrival on the docks. He didn't skip his frustrations at his own ignorance or his many mistakes, but didn't leave out the danger, either.

It took almost forty minutes of non-stop talking before he reached the climax in the house where he'd been conceived. It was only then that Lynn found the emotion begin to overtake him.

"...after I shot the sheriff on the porch, I walked back into the house and spotted Dan Billingsley entering my mother's old bedroom. I knew he was planning on luring me inside and I knew with absolute certainty it was there that I would have my answer.

"Even after putting those three holes in the wall and hearing him scream in pain, I didn't know. It was only when I saw him on the floor glaring at me with his pistol on the floor four feet away that I began to realize the test was there. I hated the man for all that he'd done and knew that I could kill him without penalty as I had my pistol pointed at his face.

"But I heard my father's voice; my only father's voice, telling me that it was always wrong to shoot an unarmed man. So, even as Billingsley taunted me and almost begged me to shoot him, I lowered my pistol. At that moment, with two dead men on the first floor and the room still filled with gunsmoke, I was at peace, Addie."

"I can hear it in your voice, Lynn."

"Even as I walked him down those stairs, Addie, I was already thinking of some way to leave Fort Benton and reach you before you arrived in Denver."

"I missed you too, Lynn."

"It was more than that, Addie. I know it sounds silly, but I was worried that once you met my brothers, you'd forget all about me and by the time I arrived in the springtime, you might be married to Alwen already."

Addie laughed then said, "That is silly, Mister Evans. I don't care if he's an Adonis, I'd never forget you for an instant."

"Charlie Red Fox knew why I felt as if I had to leave and thought I was being foolish but helped me to get here."

"Now we're together and you've told me what happened after we left. What do we talk about next?"

"Tell me about what happened to you and your mother once you boarded the *Alberta*."

Addie's tale took less time than Lynn's and ended with her surprising arrest.

By the time they were up to date, the streets were dark, and the jail was in even deeper shadows.

After all the talk about shootings and death, Addie and Lynn spent more time just talking about their lives and families, so Lynn wound up taking most of that time to provide Addie with a brief summation of each of the adult Evans, including John Wittemore and his grandmother, Meredith, who still lived in Denver.

As he talked about his Uncles Bryn and Kyle, he passed on the stories of how each of them had found his own long, difficult path that finally led to Denver.

The siblings and cousins, despite their quantity, didn't take as long.

When he finally completed his family history, Addie asked, "How will I fit in, Lynn? Where will I live?"

"It'll be your choice, Addie, but I think you'd be most comfortable in my parents' home. They have plenty of room now that the older boys, me included, live in a small house nearby. You'd really like Bethan, too. She's fourteen now but she's a match for any of us in riding and shooting."

"I can't ride a horse, Lynn, and you know I can't shoot a pistol, either."

"If you want to learn to shoot, I'd be happy to show you, but you do have to learn to ride. I'm going to have to borrow a horse until Griffin is returned in the spring, but you can pick one from the herd. We can go riding together, Addie."

"What are you going to do now that you're no longer worried?"

"I think I'll follow in my father's footsteps and become a lawman. I may not be a deputy marshal, but after the past month, I'm convinced that's what I'm meant to be."

"Can you be a lawman when you're only seventeen?"

"I don't think so, but I'll train even harder until I'm old enough."

Addie then quietly asked, "What about me? What can I do?"

Lynn looked at her shadowy face and as much as he wanted to tell her what he wanted her to do with her life, he knew that it was much too soon.

"You can decide after you're settled in, Addie. You never know, you might want to strap on a pair of shooters and put on a badge yourself. You could be Sheriff Addie Price, the terror of evil men throughout the territory."

Addie laughed but didn't say what she had hoped he would have answered to her question. She knew that he had provided the humorous response to avoid the obvious, but she could understand why he had and could live with the delay. It was going to be a long train ride before they reached Denver. The only possible bump in that road was Deputy George and his friends.

They continued their long talk, avoiding the serious topics. The only interruption was when Lynn escorted Addie to the privy and then used it after she exited before walking back into the jail.

The predawn arrived and they were still conversing, but the long night had drained each of them.

Lynn finally stood, took Addie's hands in his and lifted her to her feet.

After a night spent in the dark shadows, even the dim light of the predawn seemed bright, so as they stood faces just inches apart in the jail cell, each could clearly read the other's eyes.

Lynn didn't see any reason to hide the obvious any longer and whispered, "I love you, Addie."

Addie could almost hear his words before they crossed his lips and sighed before whispering, "I love you, Lynn."

He leaned forward across those few inches and kissed her softly.

Addie felt her knees weaken as she felt his lips on hers and wished it had been in any other place except this. But the bars surrounding them no longer mattered as she pulled him closer to extend the kiss and add her own passion.

Lynn was lost as he wrapped his arms around Addie and wished that he had done this earlier, but even then, knew if he had, he might miss the predawn entirely.

When the kiss ended, Lynn still had Addie in his arms as he said, "You'll never know how much I wish I could stay."

"I have a very good idea, Mister Evans. You forget where I slept, or tried to sleep, for much of my life. I imagine that you'll probably find it difficult to walk out of here, too."

"I haven't forgotten, Miss Price, but maybe that's why I didn't kiss you earlier, too. I'd love to continue, but I really need to get back to the hotel and start packing. You should try and get some sleep. I'll be back in about four hours to escort you to the train.

"One more kiss before you go?"

Lynn didn't answer before he kissed her again and let her know without question that it would be awkward for him to walk to the hotel.

They finally parted and Lynn made a point of limping toward the door as Addie laughed. She was still laughing as he closed, but didn't lock the cell door, then picked up his hat, left the key on the desk, and headed for the jail door. He turned, then smiled and waved at Addie in the dim light before closing the door and heading back to his room to pack.

CHAPTER 12

Garth had given up looking at the Missouri as their train approached Yankton after the long night's journey. He didn't regret his decision but wished that there weren't so many stops along the way. Then the train had spent a couple of hours in Sioux City to replace some bearing on the locomotive, too. He had done the arithmetic and with the delay, the train had averaged just fifteen miles per hour. He thought he could have ridden to Yankton in less time, but he didn't have his horse with him, so it really didn't matter.

––––––––

Lynn had quickly packed and checked out of the hotel before heading to the station to get their tickets. He bought two tickets to Denver when he spotted the smoke from the arriving train on the southern horizon.

"Wasn't it supposed to be here already?" he asked the ticket manager.

"Yep. She had to have some maintenance done down in Sioux City, but it won't change the time she rolls outta here."

"That's good to know because I don't want to be sitting on the platform very long."

The man behind the cage didn't ask why he had to leave but assumed that it had something to do with those murders and wasn't about to stick his nose into that mess.

Lynn thought about going to the diner for breakfast but decided to make sure that Betty's casket was on the loading dock. So, after slipping the tickets into his jacket pocket, he walked around to the other side of the depot and spotted the cargo awaiting shipment. He didn't see a real coffin but hadn't expected to find one as he examined the longer crates and soon found one with his name on it and a large cross carved into the wood, which probably let the workers know its contents.

Satisfied that the mortician had done his job, he turned and was heading back to the other side of the platform when he heard the locomotive's bell ringing from the approaching train.

He really needed to have his breakfast, but decided he'd wait until after the train arrived. There was no reason for his decision, but he just wanted to look it over after its unscheduled service.

He was standing on the side of the platform and the locomotive hissed and squealed as it slowed while Lynn watched the moving parts for anything that looked amiss and wished he'd listened to his father and Uncle Bryn more closely when they started talking about steam engines. He had never shared their enthusiasm for the mechanical beasts.

As Lynn studied the passing locomotive, Garth was watching the buildings as they slid past his window. Just as it reached the station, he spotted a lone man on the platform and blinked. He was tired from the boring trip and wasn't sure if it was even possible.

"Lynn?" he asked aloud as he stared.

Bert heard Garth and looked out the window. He'd only met Lynn when he'd stopped in Omaha and had the issue with

465

Jack Mitchell, but as he looked at the man, he sure looked like Lynn Evans.

"Let's go!" Garth said as he stood and snatched his travel bag.

Bert was smiling as he picked up his saddlebags and trailed the excited boy down the aisle while the train slowed.

Lynn had only checked one side of the locomotive, but it had seemed okay to his ignorant eyes, then turned to get his breakfast.

He had barely made it across the platform when he heard a shouted, "Lynn!", behind him.

He turned and was stunned to see Garth racing across the platform, his travel bag bouncing in his hand and his hat ready to blow off of his head.

"Garth?" he asked loudly as his brother slowed.

Before Garth reached him, Lynn noticed his older companion walking behind him, saw the familiar U.S. Deputy Marshal badge on his coat and soon recognized Elbert Hoskins, the youngest deputy in the Omaha office.

"What's wrong? Why are you here?" Lynn asked quickly when Garth skidded to a stop in front of him.

"Nothing's wrong, Lynn. I just figured I'd come up here to wait for you on your canoe. I didn't know you were here already. Are you waiting for the train?"

"Yes, sir," Lynn answered, then offered his hand to Bert and said, "It's good to meet you again, Deputy Hoskins. When I saw you with Garth, I thought that you'd heard about what had happened here and had come to help."

It was Bert's turn to be surprised as he asked, "What kind of trouble?"

"I don't have much time to explain out here, but let's head to the diner to get some breakfast and we can talk while we eat. You should put that badge in your pocket for now, too."

"Alright," Bert said as he took off the badge and slipped it into his pocket, wondering what had driven the suggestion.

Garth was on his brother's right and Bert was on his left as they stepped quickly along the boardwalk.

As they walked, Lynn said, "I won't go into too much detail right now, but Addie is in the jail. She had been charged with murder after she and her mother were attacked at the end of the alley just past that hardware store. The deputy and his friends who came down the alley, thought they had murdered the man who planned to assault them, and one of them panicked and shot and killed Mrs. Price. The prosecutor dropped the charge yesterday, and she's still in the jail for her protection. I was going to pick her up just before the train left, but now that you're here, maybe I'll do it earlier."

Bert wanted to ask more questions, and Garth was almost bursting, but neither said a word as they passed the alley.

As they continued past the saloon, Lynn said, "The sheriff is a good man and was concerned that his deputy had lied in his statement, so we were both worried about what he might do if Addie was free to leave. Yesterday, the man who actually shot Mrs. Price put a .45 through his head in the same spot where she died, and I'm not sure how the deputy will react."

Bert finally said, "It sounds like a real mess."

"And it's one that I'll be glad to leave behind," Lynn replied as they reached the diner.

————

Sheriff Aubrey arrived at the jail just after the train arrived and saw Addie sleeping on her bunk. He knew that Lynn had been there when he found the door unlocked and then discovered his office key on the desk.

He tried to be quiet so Addie could sleep as he settled in. Avery wouldn't be here for another hour, and Lynn should arrive an hour and a half later, so Burner didn't expect any trouble. It was what would happen after they'd gone that was his problem now.

He knew he'd have to fire Avery but would wait for a week or so. It would be a tense week.

————

Avery had packed and was in the livery saddling his black gelding to walk him to the station when he looked out the big doors and spotted Lynn walking with a boy and a man on the opposite boardwalk.

He stopped getting his horse ready and walked to the barn doors and watched them as they headed west. He assumed they were going to have breakfast and the two with Evans had just arrived on the train. He just didn't know who they were.

After he watched them enter the diner, he returned to his horse and finished getting him saddled. As he worked, he continued to think of who would have come to Yankton to see Evans. If they had both been adults, he would have been sure that at least one of them would be his father, but one was far too young. He must be Evans' brother and the other one was probably his older brother; the deputy marshal in Denver. He had no idea how they could have arrived so soon, but their presence meant that his plan to leave on the train was dashed into dust.

He had some jerky and hardtack in his saddlebags and had all of his savings in his pocket. He thought that the best thing for him to do was to make his escape on horseback and just ride south to Sioux City. He'd wait for a few days, then ride to Clarion in Wright County to see if his father would give him a job. He'd put this whole nightmare behind him but cursed that night when Pepper Taylor had stumbled into the saloon.

———

Over breakfast, Lynn explained what had happened in Yankton and then had to answer Garth's question about his last days in Fort Benton before he started his long canoe trip down the Missouri.

Bert listened in fascination as Lynn calmly described the shootout at the house. Lynn didn't feel the same emotion that had filled him when he told Addie earlier, but kept it almost clinical.

When he finished to take a big bite of ham, Garth exclaimed, "Wow, Lynn! You shot a deputy and a sheriff!"

Lynn swallowed, shook his head and replied, "No, Garth. I shot the sheriff, but I didn't shoot the deputy. The sheriff shot him in the head because he thought he was a traitor."

"I bet it was still pretty scary."

"It was, but it had to be done."

469

Garth looked at his older brother and asked, "Are you okay now, Lynn?"

Lynn paused with his fork just inches from his mouth as he looked at Garth, then smiled and replied, "I'm better than okay, Garth. It was a terrible time, but I'm glad that I went to Fort Benton."

"So, we get to meet the princess in a little while?"

Lynn had just put the forkful of scrambled eggs into his mouth, so he just raised his eyebrows as he tilted his head.

Garth laughed and said, "We didn't know Addie's name, and your first telegram confused everyone when you said the princess was lost. So, we all thought of her as a princess."

Lynn swallowed the eggs and replied, "She is a princess, Garth; the prettiest princess I've ever seen."

"Are you going to marry her?"

"That's a real stretch; isn't it, Garth?"

"I don't think so."

Lynn just smiled at his brother and polished off the last of his breakfast.

———

Before they exited the diner, Avery George had ridden out of Yankton before heading south on the road that paralleled the tracks.

As he passed the jail, Sheriff Aubrey was at the window waiting for him to show up to the office and watched his deputy ride past.

LYNN'S SEARCH

After he was certain that Avery wasn't returning, he turned back to Addie, who was sitting at the desk finishing the breakfast that his wife had prepared for her.

"I think I just lost my deputy."

Addie had a buttered biscuit in her hand as she asked, "Why would he leave?"

"He probably guessed that I was going to fire him. I'm not disappointed that he's gone, but I am concerned that he still has his badge."

"You don't think he'd try to shoot Lynn when we're going to the train station; do you?"

"No, but I'm sure that he'll be looking for him. He's probably a lot more concerned for your safety."

"I'm worried for his. He took so many chances up in Fort Benton and to get here that I feel it's just a matter of time before the odds catch up with him."

"It sounds like he's learned a lot from his father. What you told me about that gunfight in Fort Benton sounds like the actions of an experienced and skilled lawman. He thought before he acted. I can't tell you how many young men, and old ones too, do just the opposite."

"Like Dave Immelmann."

Burner didn't reply as he walked back to the desk and sat across from Addie.

"Your train leaves in a couple of hours, Addie, so Lynn should be here in another ninety minutes."

"I'm ready. Please thank your wife for the breakfast. It was much better than the ones from the diner."

"She wanted to come with me to talk to you, but I explained that there was a danger with Avery acting the way he is, so she stayed home. I was kind of surprised, to tell the truth. Usually, she always gets her way."

Addie smiled before polishing off the biscuit and lifting her cup of coffee to her lips.

Just as she took a sip, there was a loud banging on the front door, making her spill of the lukewarm coffee onto the desktop.

Sheriff Aubrey stood, then walked to the door but before he unlocked it, loudly asked, "Who is it?"

"It's Lynn, Burner."

Burner smiled at the young man's anxiety to see Addie but could understand it as he unlocked the door.

Lynn entered, handed his Winchester to Garth, then slid his saddlebags to the floor as he quickly walked toward the desk.

Addie's face had flashed into an uninhibited brilliance, even though she had expected to hear his voice on the other side of the door.

As Lynn hurriedly walked around the desk, she stood and without a smattering of hesitation, they embraced as if they'd been separated by years and hundreds of miles.

Lynn released her after ten seconds but kept his arm possessively around her waist as he turned.

"Addie, I'd like to introduce you to my brother, Garth and Deputy Marshal Bert Hoskins."

Garth was staring at Addie with wide eyes as he said, "She really *is* a princess, Lynn."

Addie smiled at him and said, "It's nice to meet you, Garth. Lynn has told me so much about you that I feel as if I know you already.

"And it's nice to meet you as well, Deputy Hoskins."

Bert wasn't wide-eyed, but he was obviously impressed as he replied, "Thank you, ma'am. Please call me Bert."

"My Christian name is Adele, but please call me Addie."

Lynn then said, "Garth wanted to get as far up the Missouri as possible to find me canoeing downriver. He dragged Bert along for company."

Burner then said, "Did you see Avery leaving town?"

Lynn turned to the sheriff and asked, "He's leaving? What about his friends?"

"I don't know about the other two, but my deputy rode out of here just a few minutes ago. I'm a bit surprised that you didn't see him. I imagine he's heading south."

"We'll keep an eye out for him, but I don't think he'll so anything; especially not with Bert and Garth here."

"When are we leaving?" Addie asked.

"Well, the train isn't going anywhere for another two hours, so I was wondering if you'd like to take some of that time to have a nice, hot bath."

Addie's eyebrows shot up as she exclaimed, "I'd love a bath! Where can I go?"

"We'll keep guard while you use the bathtub in the barber shop. I used it when I arrived, and it was worth the dime."

She turned to the sheriff and asked, "Can I leave most of my things here until I'm finished?"

"I think that can be arranged, Addie," Burner replied with a grin.

Addie quickly donned her jacket and hat, then picked up one of the bags before Lynn took the bag from her hand.

She took hold of Lynn's left arm then they followed Garth and Bert out the door and turned right for the barber shop.

As they walked along the boardwalk, Addie listened as Garth told Lynn about the Greens' departure with Alwen and how he and Martha seemed to be smitten with each other.

"Are we going to send dad a telegram before we leave?" he asked when he finished.

"I think we'll wait until we get to Omaha. We have a four-hour delay until we pick up the train to Cheyenne. Then after the twenty-hour ride west, we'll have another delay in Cheyenne to catch the southbound train to Denver. At least that's only a four-hour trip."

"Okay."

They turned into the barber shop and Lynn expected some form of protest from the barber about letting a woman use his bathtub, but the man was very pleased to be able to help the young woman who had endured so much since she'd arrived in Yankton.

After Addie disappeared behind the curtains to enjoy her bath, Lynn took a seat next to Bert while Garth had his hair trimmed.

"How is life with Marshal Claggett?" Lynn asked, already knowing the answer.

"He's not there as much as he should be, and when he is, we all wish that he wasn't."

Lynn laughed, then said, "You know, Bert, I think my father still has one more open slot after stealing Benji. Would you like me to mention your availability in my telegram?"

"I wouldn't mind at all," Bert replied as he glanced at a grinning Garth.

"I'll do that, and I'm sure that Garth really didn't bring you along for protection, either. He's pretty handy with that pistol of his."

"I noticed that you both wear Smith & Wessons instead of the Colt or Remington. Why is that?"

"Brand loyalty more than anything else. My father bought some of the Model 1s and 2s when they first came out because they used metallic cartridges. My mother and aunts used the Model 1s, and he and my Uncle Bryn used the Model 2s. Uncle Bryn took his pair to war with him. Naturally, when they came out with the Model 3, which shoots the bigger .44 cartridge, he ordered a batch of them and when we were old enough, he would give each of us one."

Bert grinned as he asked, "What does he give your sisters?"

"Bethan uses a Model 3 and is as good a shot with it as we are. She's handy with the Winchester, too."

"You're kidding!"

"I never kid about guns or Bethan. She handles her horse like any cowhand and helps with the herds, too."

"So, she's a tomboy."

"Hardly. Bethan is only fourteen, but she's very much a girl, even when she's shooting or riding. The only thing she doesn't do on the Double EE is geld the colts."

"Is she squeamish?"

"Not at all. When I was going to geld a handsome colt, she watched, and I asked her if she wanted to do it. She said that she was just watching right now so she'd be able to geld her husband when she got married."

Bert laughed as he shook his head, saying, "I don't think I'd want to be the sorry boy she chooses."

"She was just joking, but I personally think that she's going to have a hard time finding a boy or man who can meet her standards. If she does, then he'll be a very lucky man."

"She sounds like an extraordinary girl."

"She is, and so is the young lady taking a bath behind the curtain. She's been through so much in her life, yet you'd never know it by just talking to her. She's strong yet resilient. I simply can't measure just how remarkable she is."

LYNN'S SEARCH

"It sounds like you're pretty hooked, Lynn."

"I was sure that she was the right one the moment we met, and nothing has come close to changing that belief."

"Are you two going to get married?"

"I'm only sixteen, Bert, and Addie is less than a week younger. I know we can, but we both want to spend more time together."

Garth hopped out of the barber's chair and Bert said, "I may as well get a trim," then he and Garth switched chairs.

Garth was rubbing the back of his neck as he sat down and asked, "Is Addie going to stay with us on the Double EE?"

"Yes, sir. I think she'll stay in the big house with mom and dad. Bethan will be like a sister for her and she'll have Cari, Brian and Conway to keep her company, too."

"It'll be nice to have you back in the house again, Lynn. Alwen missed you, too."

"How serious is it between him and Martha?"

"I'm not sure. They were hard to pull apart for the first few days, but now it's not so much."

"I guess we'll see how they are when we get to Denver."

Garth then asked about the gunfight in Fort Benton, which seemed to fascinate him, so Lynn repeated the story, adding some of the details he'd had to skip in the shortened version he'd told in the diner.

Just as Bert stepped down from the barber's chair, Addie stepped out of the curtains. If Garth thought she looked like a princess in the jail, he didn't know how to measure her appearance now.

Lynn stood and smiled at her as she handed him her bag.

"That was perfect! Thank you, Lynn," she gushed before she kissed him.

"You look spectacular, Addie," he replied.

"I feel much better. I'll get my jacket and hat on and we can head back to the jail to pick up our things and then get on our train."

Lynn nodded, handed the barber a silver dollar, which more than covered the bath and two haircuts, then pulled on his hat and followed Garth and Bert out of the shop with the freshly scrubbed Addie on his arm.

When they entered the jail, they were greeted by Burner and his wife, Mary, who'd decided that it was worth the risk to meet Addie after all.

The pressing demand to go to the train depot kept the introductions brief, and after loading his saddlebags over his shoulders, Bert took Addie's bags and Garth held his travel bag and Lynn's Winchester in his hands as they waited for Addie and Lynn to say their farewells to Burner.

Lynn shook the sheriff's hand as he said, "You're a good lawman and good man, Burner. I feel privileged to know you."

"I'm glad to have met you too, Lynn. You did your father proud."

"I hope I never do anything to disappoint him."

LYNN'S SEARCH

"I don't believe you can."

After Lynn stepped back, Addie hugged the sheriff then kissed him on the cheek.

"Thank you for all you've done for me, Burner. You're a good man."

"Thank you, Addie. You take care of Lynn now and keep him from doing stupid things like paddling a canoe a few hundred miles."

Addie smiled as she replied, "I'm not sure that it's remotely possible, but I'll try."

She then turned, took Lynn's arm and walked out the door.

As they headed for the train depot, despite the sheriff's opinion, Lynn was on high alert, expecting the disgruntled deputy to take a shot at Addie. He'd lost everything since that night, but only had himself to blame. If he'd told the truth from the start, Lynn doubted that his friend would have even been charged for shooting Betty. But men like him never blamed themselves; it was always someone else's fault.

They reached the depot without seeing ex-Deputy George and Lynn bought a ticket to Omaha for Bert and another ticket to Denver for Garth.

He still hadn't mentioned the thick bundle of cash in his money belt; not even to Addie. He had decided almost as soon as he'd discovered it that it was his parents' money, and there was no reason to even talk about it.

———

479

By half-past ten, the train had reached its top speed of thirty miles per hour as it rumbled south.

Addie was sitting at the window on the left side of the car with Lynn next to her. Their bags and saddlebags were in the seat in front of them and his Winchester was leaning against the wall beside Addie. Garth and Bert were seated three rows back.

"I'm so relieved to be out of there," Addie said as she watched the scenery pass.

"I know the feeling. It's how I felt when I left Fort Benton. There is something a bit odd about this whole thing that I never mentioned because I haven't thought about it since I learned about your arrest."

Addie turned away from the window and asked, "What's that?"

"When I finally reached Yankton after leaving my canoe on the bank downriver, I remembered a girl named Libby Perkins that I'd met on the *Alberta*. Her family was going to Yankton."

"And you were planning on seeing her again?" Addie asked with arched eyebrows.

"No, ma'am. It's just that when I heard you'd been arrested, I thought that if it was necessary, I could talk to her father. He would be the judge to hear your case."

"You're kidding! You met the judge on the boat?"

"Only a couple of times, but Libby seemed interested, so I talked to her more often, but with her two brothers usually hovering nearby."

"That is strange, but I'm glad that it didn't come to a trial."

"So, am I. I just wish that your stay there didn't have to come at such a cost."

Addie nodded, then turned her eyes back to the window as she wiped them dry. She knew that her mother's body was in a crate in one of the boxcars and tried to separate the damaged physical remains from her perfect soul.

She stared at the landscape as she remembered her mother and found it difficult to recall a day when she was able to go to sleep happy. Her mother had a terrible life and Addie silently thanked her for enabling her to have a real future. It may have been Lynn who rescued her from the forbidding life that awaited her, but it had been her mother who had made it possible.

She was still deep in thought when the train passed a rider and she quickly nudged Lynn and asked, "Isn't that the deputy?"

Lynn had been watching her more than the scenery, but quickly glanced behind her head and spotted the lone rider.

"I'm sure you're right, Addie. At least now we know where he is. I was actually a bit concerned that he might be in the stock car with his horse."

"I hadn't thought about that, but now that he's gone, we can finally put Yankton behind us for all time."

Lynn leaned over, kissed her then said, "We'll do just that, sweetheart."

Addie smiled at Lynn, then instead of looking out the window, began asking about the Double EE and his family; soon to be her family.

————

The train arrived in Omaha at four-thirty in the afternoon, and the train for Cheyenne wasn't due to depart until 8:10, so that gave them time to get the long telegram sent to Denver and have a good supper.

Bert had to leave to report to his boss about the very real situation in Yankton, which he would blame on the deputy, who'd made a run into Iowa, but wasn't worth a pursuit.

Lynn wrote the telegram to his father and knew it wasn't nearly enough information, yet it would have to do until they reached Denver.

————

The sun was gone when they boarded their westbound Union Pacific train. They were all pleased that there weren't as many towns in Nebraska, so the train wouldn't stop as often as the one from Yankton. It was still going to be a long train ride, though, and they'd bought some reading material at the newspaper stand at the depot before boarding.

————

Dylan was locking up the office while Bryn waited when Cal Lewis came trotting down the boardwalk.

"Marshal! I got a telegram for you!"

Dylan dropped the keys into his jacket pocket and waited for the boy to reach him.

Cal handed the yellow sheet to Dylan while Bryn rummaged through his pockets for a nickel.

Dylan anxiously unfolded the message, knowing that they had probably come from either Garth or Lynn.

His eyes quickly read:

US MARSHAL DYLAN EVANS DENVER COLO

IN OMAHA WILL ARRIVE IN DENVER TOMORROW
NEED BURIAL SITE FOR BEATRICE PRICE
DAUGHTER ADDIE WITH ME AND GARTH
WILL NEED HORSE AND SADDLE FOR ME
WILL EXPLAIN ALL WHEN WE GET HOME
DEPUTY HOSKINS WANTS TO FOLLOW BENJI
THANK YOU FOR BEING MY FATHER

LYNN EVANS OMAHA NEB

Dylan let out a sharp breath and handed it to Bryn as Cal waited.

"No reply, Cal. Thanks for getting this to me before we left."

"You're welcome, sir," he replied before jogging away.

Bryn handed it back to his brother and said, "There must be quite a few stories behind all this."

"We haven't built a family cemetery on the ranch yet, Bryn. Do you think it's time?"

"I think so, and I have just the spot, too. We can just have the burial for Mrs. Price there, and then build a proper cemetery later."

"Let's head back and tell the family."

Bryn nodded then mounted Maddy and waited while Dylan stepped up on Crow. They headed west as the last shades of red left by the setting sun faded, then turned south for the Double EE.

LYNN'S SEARCH

———

Their train rocked and clicked across the iron rails as it rolled west across the Great Plains, and Addie slept with her head resting on Lynn's left shoulder.

Lynn was still awake as he thought about their future; as he was sure that his and Addie's were bound together. He wished he was older, so there wasn't that burden of not being recognized as an adult by the state. He and Addie could legally marry, of course, but after that things became more than just uncertain.

What he wanted to do and what was available for a sixteen-soon-to-be-seventeen-year-old were two different things. He wasn't worried about money after sending the twenty-four thousand dollars to his father for the sale of the bank; knowing that he would get an equal share with his brothers and sisters. It was just that gap before he turned eighteen that now bothered him.

As the night landscape slipped past the window, Lynn looked down at Addie's peaceful face and smiled. He realized that she was the most important part of his future now and the rest would follow.

Even as she slept, Lynn decided that he'd have a house built for them on the Double EE, then they'd marry, and he'd work on the ranch for another year and continue his education as a lawman. He may not be able to work with his father, but there always seemed to be a slot available in the Denver County Sheriff's office.

He took a deep breath, then kissed the side of Addie's forehead before closing his eyes and waiting for sleep to take him.

CHAPTER 13

Early the next morning, the Double EE was a busy ballet as arrangements were made for Addie's arrival.

Bryn had marked the location for the cemetery before he and Dylan left the ranch. Flat Jack would drive the carriage with Gwen, Erin and Bethan and pick up Katie before the train arrived while the rest of the family remained on the ranch to welcome Lynn home and to meet the princess.

Alwen would ride and lead a second horse for Lynn along with Garth's gelding and John and Kyle would ride as well.

Martha Green had volunteered to babysit young Colwyn and John for Katie while she was at the family gathering.

Gwen had been stunned with the news of Betty's death but was happy that Lynn was bringing her daughter to the ranch. She and everyone else speculated about just what had happened on that trip from Fort Benton that cost Betty's life.

After arriving in Denver that morning, Bryn stopped at Kyle's house before he went to the office to let him and Erin know about Lynn's return while Dylan stopped at the Wittemores to tell John and their mother.

Everything was in place well before midmorning, so Dylan and Bryn returned to the office where Dylan explained what was happening to the other deputies who weren't out in the field.

He then called Benji aside, who had just stopped by before doing some house hunting, to ask him about Bert Hoskins, who he had never met. Benji hadn't been surprised that Bert wanted to escape from the presence of Marshal Edgar Claggett and gave an honest appraisal of the young lawman.

"We need some young blood around here, Benji. We're all getting old."

Benji laughed and said, "You're still a kid, Dylan. You're what; thirty-five? I'm closin' in on forty."

"It's kind of scary how fast time just seems to disappear sometimes; doesn't it?"

"You got the right of it. You could be a grandpa pretty soon, boss."

"You don't think we'll share the same grandkids; do you?"

"My Alice seems to think that Martha's losing interest; but not for the usual reason. I think it's because she wants a husband who doesn't risk getting shot every time that he leaves the house."

"I guess it's out of our hands anyway, Benji. I wonder how Lynn and Addie get along. Gwen already thinks that there's something there and I haven't any idea where she could have come up with that notion."

"Gwen has a sixth sense about folks, Dylan. Or haven't you noticed?"

Dylan grinned and replied, "Trust me. I noticed. She steered Bryn to Erin and had a hand in Kyle's discovery of Katie. At least this time, I know that she didn't do anything."

Benji shrugged and said, "You never know, boss."

Dylan was still smiling, but when Gwen had mentioned it to him, she had seemed so sure of herself; just as she had been when she refused to even think of a boy's name before giving birth to Bethan. He'd been married to her for seventeen years now and he still was in awe of his diminutive wife.

———

The southbound train was just eighteen miles out of Denver and Addie was clutching Lynn's left arm like a vise. She had only vague memories of her father and then much too vivid memories of the men who visited their house, but the one constant had been her mother. Now she would soon be thrust into an alien world that Lynn had described as almost a fairyland where everyone actually cared for each other; a world where she wouldn't be subjected to either ridicule or aggression. *How could anyplace be that wonderful? How could she possibly fit in given her own family history?* Her only anchor now was the man who had set her free from her old world and was bringing her into his.

Lynn knew that Addie was nervous because she'd stopped talking an hour earlier. Except when they were sleeping or eating, most of the train rides had been a continuous conversation. He hadn't attempted to soothe her nerves because he knew that he'd said and done all he could before they even boarded the train. Now it was in the hands of his family; especially his mother and Bethan.

———

The crowd of Evans filled a good portion of the train platform as the locomotive pulling Lynn and Addie's passenger car passed.

LYNN'S SEARCH

Just before it lurched to a stop, Lynn stood, handed his Winchester to Garth who was already in the aisle with his travel bag, then hung his saddlebags over his shoulders and lifted Addie's bags from the seat and waited for her to stand.

Addie saw the crowd of smiling people on the platform, then took a breath and stepped into the aisle in front of Lynn and behind Garth.

Garth hopped from the passenger car and moved aside as Addie stepped onto the platform much more sedately, then turned and waited for Lynn.

Lynn was loaded down with saddlebags and Addie's bags, so Addie took his left arm as they walked to the gaggle of Evans. She tried to smile but wasn't sure she succeeded as Lynn escorted her to meet her new family.

She was sure that the couple in front was his mother and father, so she steadied her eyes on Gwen; the woman who had accompanied her mother to Fort Benton and had asked her son to bring her away from that accursed place.

Gwen wasn't surprised at all to see Addie latched onto Lynn and could easily see the anxiety in Addie's eyes. It would have been surprising if it hadn't been there. She knew that if her mother's body was accompanying her that something horrible had happened to them on the trip. Whatever it was, Gwen knew she would make Addie feel as welcome as possible to dispel that anxiety.

She stepped away from Dylan and the others and soon reached Lynn and Addie.

"Welcome home, Addie," she said with a warm smile.

Addie found a real smile as she replied, "Thank you, Mrs. Evans. Lynn has told me so much about you."

"I can tell you stories about him that will make him blush, Addie. Let's get this crowd back to the ranch."

While Gwen was meeting Addie, the entire male side of the Evans clan slid over to Lynn's other side.

Lynn looked at his father and said, "I have a lot to tell you, Dad. The only sad thing about the whole journey was losing Betty Price. She was shot and killed accidentally in Yankton before I arrived."

"J.T. Downey's taking her body to his mortuary and will put her into a proper casket. We have a place for a new family cemetery on the Double EE and we'll have the burial at ten o'clock tomorrow. I'll leave it to you to tell Addie."

"Thanks, Dad," Lynn said as Alwen, Kyle and John relieved him of his bags and saddlebags.

"Where's Griffin?" Dylan asked as they turned and walked with the women away from the track side of the platform.

"He's still up in Fort Benton, but Slim will ship him here on the first riverboat in the spring."

"Slim O'Hara is still there? If it was anyone else, I'd think that you'd seen the last of your horse, but Slim will send him back with a new set of shoes and probably in better shape than when you left him."

After leaving the bags and saddlebags in the carriage, each of the men mounted as the women climbed into the carriage and buggy.

LYNN'S SEARCH

Addie was in the center of the back seat with Erin on her right and Meredith, the family matriarch on her left. Gwen sat directly across from her with a very pregnant Katie and Bethan.

Once they were rolling, Gwen smiled and said, "As shocking as it is to see so many Evans in one place, there are even more at the ranch and Katie's two babies are still in her home, so it may be overwhelming at first. None of us expect you to remember our names right away."

"I think I know most of your names already anyway. Lynn talked about you all a great deal. I may have some difficulty with the children, but I can probably get most of the adults right."

"Just remember that I'm the shortest one in the whole crowd."

Addie laughed and said, "Lynn told me the name the Crow Indians gave you and I can tell that it was well earned already."

Gwen was pleased to see Addie's worries fade and then she had help from her older daughter.

Bethan asked, "What do you think of my oldest brother?"

Addie blushed as she replied, "I think he's wonderful."

Bethan grinned and said, "So, do I."

"You surprised me, Bethan. From the way Lynn described you I almost expected to see you on a horse wearing britches with a six-gun strapped around your waist while you smoked a cheroot. You're dressed very ladylike."

"Except for smoking, you'll probably see me in britches on a horse with my Smith & Wesson in a day or two. You can join me if you'd like, Addie. The Double EE is a big ranch with a lot of interesting places."

"I'd like to do that, Bethan, but I've never ridden before."

"I'm sure that Lynn will show you."

The rest of the drive to the ranch was filled with small talk. Each of them knew that the more serious conversations would take place at the ranch when the whole family was gathered together.

Gwen was certain that she and Dylan would be having a private talk with Addie and Lynn after most of the extended Evans clan left their house.

———

The loud talk among the male riders was more substantive but revolved around Benji Green and now Bert Hoskins more than anything that had happened in Yankton or Fort Benton. Even Garth managed to keep from repeating what Lynn had already told him. He understood that it was Lynn and Addie's story to tell.

As he rode among his family, Lynn felt at home long before he even saw the Double EE. He could see Addie smiling and talking to his mother, sister, aunts and grandmother in the carriage, which was a relief; but not at all surprising.

For the first time since leaving Fort Benton, he could feel the money belt pressing against his stomach and would be glad to be rid of the cash.

LYNN'S SEARCH

He had so much to tell his family, especially his parents, and the money was far down on that list. Most of all, he wanted to talk to them about Addie. Although he'd already decided what he wanted to do, he would still like to hear what they would say.

———

Addie spotted the first buildings on the Double EE and was stunned. Lynn had told her about the different houses and barns but seeing them was a revelation.

"Who lives where?" she asked Gwen as she stared.

Gwen didn't have to look before she replied, "This access road leads to Bryn and Erin's house and barn. The small house to the east is where Flat Jack and Alba live. When he first built his house, Bryn hoped that Dylan and I might eventually come here, so he built it on the south edge of the northeast section.

"When we did move here, he deeded the adjoining section to us, so we built our house to the south about four hundred yards. We built a second house and that's where Lynn, Alwen and Garth live now."

"Lynn said that Bryn owns sixteen sections. It's hard to imagine that much land."

Gwen smiled at Addie and said, "He did have sixteen sections, but that's another subject for later. We'll be going to our house. That's where the rest of the family is gathered."

As the carriage turned down the access road, she had her first glimpse of the large corral teeming with horses of all sizes and colors.

493

"Look at all those horses!" she exclaimed.

Bethan said, "Those are the ones that are saddle broken and can be sold or used by the family. There are two large herds out in the pastures, too."

Addie stared at the horses and then searched the western horizon for the herds but didn't see them. She guessed that they were on the other side of the hills and wished she could ride just to see them.

————

Forty minutes later, the entire Evans family, minus Kyle and Katie's two young ones, were gathered in Dylan and Gwen's immense parlor.

Garth had brought Addie's things to an empty upstairs bedroom across from Bethan's room, then returned quickly to be there when the storytelling began. He could afford to miss parts of it but wanted to hear it again.

When everyone was settled, Lynn and Addie were sitting close together on the settee holding hands.

Lynn began by saying, "When I left the Double EE more than a month and a half ago, I didn't know what I would find when I stepped on that train to Kansas City. I only knew that I had to go, or I'd never be truly confident in myself.

"The first serious thing to happen was when I stopped in Omaha and rode out to the Mitchell farm to tell them about Ryan..."

It took Lynn more than forty minutes to describe what had happened in Fort Benton and the long canoe trip down the Missouri. He didn't mention the cash he'd found in the canoe, nor did he talk about the reasons that he had to go with Sheriff Martin and Deputy Granger to the Riddell house, knowing the danger it held. He reserved those subjects for his parents.

He finally let Addie pick up the story when he reached Yankton. Lynn could feel her hand tighten on his and knew that it would be much more difficult for her to tell what had happened.

"Of course, I had no idea that Lynn was so close when we reached Yankton, and my mother and I had already decided to leave the *Alberta* there to take the train to Denver. After our boat had picked up the survivors from the *Princess of Ohio*, I noticed that one of the men was following me. By the time we reached Yankton, I was afraid that he might trap me, so I took a steak knife from the dining room and hid it in my purse for protection. Then, on the night we disembarked…"

Addie didn't gloss over her mother's deception to get to her hidden dagger, nor did she disguise her rage and hatred of the man when she plunged her knife into his back. It was only when she reached the point where she and her mother were looking at the four men with their pistols pointed at them, that her voice began to fail.

"…and then…then, my mother tried to tell them that she didn't know how to release the hammer and one of them…"

Lynn put his arm around Addie and as tears fell from her eyes he said, "One of them, a friend of the deputy sheriff, overreacted and fired. It was one of those panicked shootings that you always told me about, Dad. He wasn't malicious in any way. On the day before we left, he felt so guilty about it that he went to the same spot and used the same pistol to end his own life."

Lynn then took over the rest of the narrative, explaining how Sheriff Aubrey and the prosecutor were hoping to hear the truth so the charges could be dropped.

He ended the momentous tale with Garth's unexpected arrival in Yankton, and after he said his last word, the full room was completely silent for almost a minute.

Addie had stopped crying, but Lynn still held her close.

When no one said anything, Lynn looked at Addie, whose dark blue eyes were already on him and said, "Tomorrow morning at ten o'clock, your mother will be laid to rest here on the Double EE. There wasn't a need for a family cemetery before, so one will be built around her grave. I'll talk to you later about her grave marker. Did you want to have a minister there?"

Addie shook her head slowly as she replied, "No. They were of no help to my mother when she was alive and those that took notice of her at all were no better than the men who came to visit her."

Lynn looked at his father, who just nodded. He'd asked about a minister on the ride back and Lynn had told him that he didn't think that Addie would want one there for the reason that she'd given.

———

Once the silence ended, the questions began and as they were being answered, the family began a parade into the dining room to collect plates of finger food.

The reunion lasted until early evening, when John had to drive Meredith and Katie back to Denver in the carriage. Kyle shook Lynn's hand and kissed Addie on the cheek after Katie had embraced her.

After the lamps had been lit and only Dylan and Gwen's immediate family remained in the big house, Gwen sent Alwen and Garth to their house with Lynn's saddlebags and had Bethan take control of her younger sister and brothers.

The fire was popping and sending sparks onto the brick hearth as Lynn and Addie sat alone with his parents.

Lynn finally was able to remove the bulky money belt and when he set it on the table, it was obvious that it contained much more than a copy of the bill of sale.

"Dad, I sent you the money from the bank sale before I left Fort Benton."

"I know, and we've already created six, four-thousand-dollar bank accounts for you and your brothers and sisters. You'll need to go there with Kyle in the next couple of days to sign the account papers."

"Thank you, Dad, but there's something else. After I left in the canoe that Charlie Red Fox gave me, I found a leather pouch under a bearskin. This is what was inside."

Lynn opened the money belt and began pulling bank notes and setting them on the table.

"I haven't done an exact count, but I know that there's at least thirteen thousand dollars there. I'm pretty sure that Charlie Red Fox knew where Dan Billingsley had kept some of his embezzled money and didn't want him to be able to use it to make an escape. This belongs to you and mom."

Dylan glanced at Gwen, then said, "No, Lynn. We don't know that. Maybe Charlie Red Fox found it near the Crow village and thought that you deserved it. You can deposit it in the bank when you go there to do your paperwork."

Lynn was startled before he said, "No, Dad. That's not right. It's got to be your money because it's the only possible source for that much cash."

"I told you before you left that we didn't care if we saw a penny from that bank sale and we're very happy to be rid of it. From what you told us, I believe that you've earned it, Lynn, and I don't want you to split this up among your brothers and sisters either. Just deposit it in your account and let it sit until you need it."

Lynn stared at the pile of banknotes, sighed and said, "Alright, Dad."

"Now, what else did you want to talk to us about?" his mother asked.

Lynn glanced at Addie before replying, "I want to marry Addie, but I'm only sixteen. She'll be turning seventeen six days, thirteen hours and twenty minutes after I do, and I know that we can get married legally now, but I think it would be wiser to wait a little while."

"I was sixteen when I married your father," Gwen said.

"I know, Mom, and I'm grateful that you did. I just want Addie to get adjusted to living on the Double EE and being around the family. Then there's the other reason."

"Which is?" Dylan asked.

LYNN'S SEARCH

"Since I was barely old enough to wear long pants, I wanted to be like you, Dad. I wanted to be a lawman, but it was for the wrong reasons. When I was just a foolish boy, I thought it was all excitement and shootouts, just like most boys. As I grew older, I saw the other, more routine parts of the job. I also began to understand the dangers and the long hours spent on the trail in nasty weather. Being a lawman wasn't a glamorous job; it was a frightening and sometimes a thankless way of life.

"But even as my perceptions changed, I continued to learn the skills to be a lawman from you; the best lawman and finest man I've ever known. I wasn't sure that it was the life for me, but I still learned every day. I learned a lot more than how to track or read and handle men; I learned what it took to be a good man.

"When I went off with Ryan, it was because he'd goaded me into asking about my birth father. He said that I probably had the soul of Burke Riddell hidden deep inside me and I was just like him. That frightened me more than you can imagine. I'd heard story after story about Burke Riddell for as long as I could recall, and none of them had a single hint of anything good about the man.

"After I returned with Ryan's body, that fear still lingered and I knew that I'd never know if what he'd said was true if I stayed here. I had to go out on my own to find the answer. I didn't know how I'd get that answer or where I would find it, but the only place that made sense was Fort Benton.

"I told you everyone the facts about that night, but I didn't say why I decided to go with Sheriff Martin and Deputy Granger knowing that they'd probably try to shoot me in the back. It was because I had an overwhelming belief that I would only find my answer in that house. Logically, it made no sense at all, but I was drawn to the place like a magnet.

"After the gunfight with the sheriff, and I saw Billingsley go into the bedroom, I knew that was where I'd find my answer, and I did. When I had an unarmed, wounded Dan Billingsley under my pistol, I could have shot him without a single question being asked. He even taunted me to try to make me shoot him. But I heard your voice, Dad. I heard you telling me that there was never a reason to shoot an unarmed man; no matter what he'd done.

"I was furious with Dan Billingsley as I pointed my pistol at him, but your voice made me release the hammer and holster the gun. It was then I knew that Burke Riddell was nothing but a dead memory. I also realized that following in your footsteps would be the best possible way to show the respect, honor and love that I have for you; my one and only father."

As Gwen squeezed his hand, Dylan could only nod as he looked at his oldest son. When he'd gone to Fort Benton, he had known why he had to leave, and now, his deepest hope at been realized. Lynn had gone from the Double EE a confused boy and had returned a confident, strong young man that any man would be proud to call his son, but only Dylan could make that claim.

Gwen finally asked, "So, what are your plans now, Lynn?"

"I'd like to have a house built for me and Addie, then for the next year or so, I'll work on the ranch with the horses and learn even more from dad. When I'm eighteen, I'll get find a job as a lawman. Eventually, I'd like to join the marshal's service and work with dad and Uncle Bryn, but I'll need the experience first."

Addie then looked at Lynn and asked, "When did you ask me to marry you, sir?"

Lynn smiled and replied, "That was coming next, ma'am. Will you marry me, Adele Gwendolyn Price?"

Addie nodded and replied, "Yes, Lynn Robert Evans. Whenever you think the time is right, but don't wait too long."

"I won't."

Gwen then asked, "Your middle name is Gwendolyn?"

"You shouldn't be surprised, Mrs. Evans. I'm sure that my first name would have been Gwendolyn if my father hadn't insisted on naming me after his mother."

"Addie, I think you should start calling me mom."

Addie beamed at her future mother-in-law as she said, "Thank you for everything, Mom. I was very nervous about meeting everyone, but you made me feel so comfortable right away; you and Bethan."

Dylan then said, "About that house, Lynn. While you were gone, Bryn and I talked about our children and the Double EE. He said that he'd never use the south twelve sections for anything. The man who practically gave the land to Bryn had the sixteen sections broken down into one-acre lots to sell to prospectors as gold claims. There wasn't any gold, but the surveys are still there. So, what he decided was to break up the twelve sections into forty-eight quarter sections.

"We don't figure we'll have that many children among all three of us, so each of you can choose two quarter-sections anywhere from those forty-eight and he'll transfer the land to you. After you make your selection, you can have your house and barn built there."

"Then I don't have to leave the Double EE."

"Nope. You'll have your own piece of land and your own home. You and Addie can go exploring whenever you have the time. Right now, I imagine that you're both pretty exhausted from the trip."

"I am a bit tuckered out, and I know that Addie could use a good night's sleep. Can I leave the cash with you for the time being, Dad? I don't think my stomach will ever return to its normal shade after wearing that money belt so long."

"I'll take care of it. Your mother and I will head out to the kitchen and talk to Bethan for a few minutes, then she can show Addie to her room. We'll see you for breakfast, Lynn."

Dylan then stood, took Gwen's hand, and they smiled at Lynn and Addie before leaving the room.

Lynn then asked, "Are you all right, Addie? You went through a lot today."

"I'm fine, but I am tired. You have an extraordinary family, Lynn."

"I know, and you'll make it even more amazing, Addie. I'm sorry that I hadn't asked you about getting married, but it just kind of popped into my head when I started thinking about the house."

Addie smiled and replied, "I've been thinking about since I met you, Lynn, but I didn't think it was possible once we left Fort Benton."

"When I met you and felt that lightning bolt, I first thought it was just because you were so beautiful, but the more I talked to you and got to know you, I realized that it was because I loved you and knew that you were the right woman for me. I still feel a jolt when I see you, Addie, and even if it fades over time, I know I'll never love you any less."

Addie threw her arms around Lynn and almost rammed him into the back of the settee as she kissed him.

Lynn was overwhelmed by her passion and having her almost on top of him, but fully engaged in sharing his own passion as he pulled her even closer.

Having Addie pressed tightly against him had its expected effect but having his parents and Bethan at the other end of the hallway acted as an effective brake to anything beyond kissing.

When they finally ended the kissing session, Lynn gasped, "I wish we had that house already."

Addie's lips were just inches from his right ear when she whispered, "I'd settle for the barn."

Lynn laughed then painfully separated from Addie.

"I've got to go to the small house now, Addie. I'll see you at breakfast."

Addie nodded before accepting one last quick kiss from Lynn, who rose from the settee and walked awkwardly to the coat rack where he donned his coat and hat.

He knew better than to return to Addie's side of the room, so he just waved and exited the house.

Seconds later, Bethan popped into the parlor, smiled at Addie and said, "I'll show you your room now, Addie. That's assuming you can walk better than my brother could."

Addie laughed, then followed Bethan up the stairs.

———

After breakfast the next morning, everyone prepared for the burial at ten.

At the appointed time, the entire Evans family was gathered beside the open gravesite.

The spot picked by Bryn was on the southwest corner of the three sections that he would keep as the Double EE. It was on the top of a flat hill that wasn't big enough to call a plateau.

When anyone stood on the hill and looked west, the Rocky Mountains filled the horizon. To the east, the family houses dotted the start of the plains and Denver's growing skyline was visible to the north. The south vista was a mix of rocky and grassy areas with one almost river and several creeks crossing the land and would eventually be dotted with the houses of the next generation of Evans.

But today was about Beatrice Louise Spencer Price; Addie's mother and protector.

The hearse slowly made its way up the hill to the hole that the diggers had created earlier.

Addie was holding tightly onto Lynn's hand as she watched her mother's casket slide from the hearse and then lifted to the hole.

Tears flooded her dark blue eyes as they lowered the heavy oak casket that weighed more than her mother ever had.

LYNN'S SEARCH

No words were said before the diggers began shoveling the dirt in place, and soon they and the undertaker had driven away in the hearse.

Lynn slowly looked at each member of his family; young and old. As much as Addie grieved today for her beloved mother, he knew that each of them would help her to overcome her grief. They would fill her days with love and understanding, just as they had since he'd been born.

Soon Addie would be a full member of the family and then they could build their own legacy. Their children would never experience the pain that she had, and he would always make every effort to make them proud of their father; just as he was proud of his father – Dylan Evans.

EPILOGUE

After the burial, it was less than a week before the site was converted into a proper cemetery. The gravestone had arrived and been put in place. It was a simple stone that read:

Beatrice Louise Price
April 11, 1841 ~ Oct 16, 1873
Beloved Mother and Guardian
To Addie

It was Addie's decision not to use Adele because the only people who called her that didn't know her.

―――――

Over the weeks that followed, Addie selected a handsome, deep brown mare she named Chloe because she didn't know any women with the name. She began her riding lessons with Lynn and sometimes with Bethan as Lynn began spending more time with his father and Bryn.

They selected their two quarter sections that first week, and not surprisingly, it was the pair that was along the western edge and abutted Bryn's southwest section. It was the closest to the new cemetery, so Addie could visit her mother's gravesite whenever she wished.

―――――

As Addie was easily adjusting to her new life, in Clarion, Iowa, Avery George was having a much more difficult time trying to fit in.

When he'd returned to his hometown, he expected to be well received by his father despite their big row that had driven him away and with his two years' experience as a deputy sheriff, also assumed that his father would be pleased to swear him in as his own deputy.

But his father was anything but welcoming when Avery walked into the Wright County Sheriff's office. When he saw his son suddenly reappear after leaving in a huff two years earlier, he was just short of disgusted.

He'd received a telegram from Sheriff Aubrey in Yankton giving him a brief summation of what had happened, and that Avery might be heading his way.

Hector George hadn't expected any less from his firstborn son after he'd gone, and had only been surprised that it had taken two years.

Avery was furious at his father's second rejection and had made quite a scene when he left the jail, threatening everyone from his mother to that girl who had caused him this second round of humiliation.

When Avery George rode away from Clarion the next day, he rode with his old friend, Homer Edwards. Homer had been one of the primary reasons for Avery's fall from his father's grace, but after Homer had married, Avery saw no reason to stay.

Homer was still married but deserted his fat wife who was already pregnant with their second.

As they rode west, glad to be free of any responsibility, Homer suggested that he ditch the Avery and start calling himself something different and more menacing.

Avery had always hated his name, so it wasn't a hard sell, and thought as long as he was going to use a different name he'd go to the top and crown himself a king.

When he'd told Homer that he'd be called King George, Homer had laughed and said as long as he was going to be a king, he should be royalty as well.

So, as they left Iowa, they rode as King George and Prince Edwards.

Now they just needed to find a way to make serious money.

————

Construction would begin on Lynn and Addie's house in the first week of November, but they had to extend the access road to the site first, and weather would probably hold up construction more than a few times, but they hoped to get the exterior work completed before the real nasty weather arrived.

The more time that Addie and Bethan spent together, the closer they became. In addition to helping Addie with her riding and even showing her to shoot, it was the quiet time that they shared in their bedrooms that strengthened the bond. Bethan would share secrets about Lynn that had them both giggling and Addie would pass along lascivious information about men to Bethan that even Gwen wouldn't have told her.

The sisterhood that they shared, even more than anything that Lynn or Gwen did, made Addie feel like family and made Bethan feel even more mature than she had before.

LYNN'S SEARCH

Lynn had deposited the $13,655 into his account, but still didn't know what he would ever do with that much money. The house, barn and corral had only cost him $1630, and was only that much because he'd taken his father's advice and made it much larger than he'd planned to allow for children.

Lynn and Addie still spent a lot of time together, and she was introduced to baseball, which she enjoyed, and met Peanut and his family. The small donkey and his wife, Hazel had a big jack named Wally, a slightly smaller jenny named Acorn and a new tiny jack the young children had christened Chester. She's smiled as the small patriarch of the donkey family seemed to strut before his tiny herd proudly proclaiming his donkey-hood. He was getting even scruffier as he aged, but Peanut was still in healthy.

The winter arrived in spades, just after the house was completed, but it was still a shell inside without furniture or accessories. The cookstove and bathtubs were in place, but the heat stoves hadn't been installed yet, so the only source of warmth were the cookstove and the two fireplaces.

The lack of furniture didn't prevent the house's use as a rendezvous for Addie and Lynn, but they did have to avoid the inevitable.

They'd planned on getting married on Addie's birthday, March 11th. It wasn't quite spring and there would probably be snow on the ground, but neither expected to be able to hold out much longer.

U.S. Deputy Marshal Bert Hoskins arrived on December 8th and moved in with John and Meredith, at least temporarily.

On January 12th, in the wee hours of the morning, Katie gave birth to Meredith Anna Evans and Grandma Meredith was ecstatic with her latest granddaughter.

On January 16th, with a blizzard howling down from the Rockies, Flat Jack fell from his horse as he was trying to move the herd into the canyon. Alwen and Garth were with him and brought him back to his small house with a broken hip.

He seemed to be recovering when he contracted pneumonia and died on January 28^{tht}. Despite the frozen ground, they buried him in the family cemetery. Alba was disconsolate with his loss and moved back into the main house with Bryn and Erin for the comforting company of the children.

———

The snow had actually melted when Addie's seventeenth birthday arrived, and she and Lynn were married in the Denver County courthouse. They couldn't hold the ceremony in Judge West's chamber due to the size of the audience, and even the main courtroom was overcrowded, but none of that mattered when Lynn Robert Evans finally married Adele Gwendolyn Price and she officially became a member of the Evans family.

The celebration was held in Dylan and Gwen's home and in a fitting sendoff, the married couple, dressed in britches and heavy boots, mounted their horses, each wearing a pistol. They waved to the mass of family and friends on the porch and rode west along the extended access road into the spectacular Rocky Mountain sunset.

When they reached their fully furnished house, Lynn took the horses to the barn and while he unsaddled the animals, Addie started fires in the two fireplaces and two of the heat stoves.

By the time Lynn entered the house and took off his gloves, heavy coat, hat and gunbelt, Addie had already shed her outerwear and much of her other encumbrances. The long wait to release their pent-up lust was over and within a minute, the house was filled with sounds only unbridled passion was capable of producing.

It took three riotous sessions of lovemaking to finally reach the point where they could use their new bed for rest.

As Addie felt Lynn's warmth across her back and thighs as his arms held her close, she remembered those long nights listening to her mother working in the next room and how much it had sickened her. For years, she thought that she could never be with a man and when she'd agreed to go with Dan Billingsley because she thought there was no other solution, she'd been revolted with the idea.

Then she'd opened their door and her eyes met Lynn's. From almost that instant, Addie knew that if she ever took a man to her bed, it would be him. Now they were together, and it had been even more thrilling than she could have imagined.

She'd listened to Lynn explain to her and his parents how he'd searched for the answer to his true self but had never told him of her own concern; that she would have to become what her mother had tried so desperately to prevent. One day, maybe she'd tell him that he had answered her own fateful question and given her a life that was beyond her biggest dreams.

Author's Note

Okay, I reached my recent goal of writing sixty books in three years and I'm exhausted. I'm going to take a break before I start the fifth one in the saga and do some editing and do something quite different.

I'm planning to write a collection of goofy Western short stories before starting the next one.

I'll try to cut down the length of the fifth book. I thought this one would be shorter, but it's even longer. Just a hint about the next one in the saga; it'll be the first book in which the primary character is female. I've scattered quite a few hints in this one to give you an idea who it is, so I won't divulge the title.

Have a nice Christmas and after I get this online, I've got to get some presents wrapped for my own Christmas Elf.

LYNN'S SEARCH

1	Rock Creek	12/26/2016
2	North of Denton	01/02/2017
3	Fort Selden	01/07/2017
4	Scotts Bluff	01/14/2017
5	South of Denver	01/22/2017
6	Miles City	01/28/2017
7	Hopewell	02/04/2017
8	Nueva Luz	02/12/2017
9	The Witch of Dakota	02/19/2017
10	Baker City	03/13/2017
11	The Gun Smith	03/21/2017
12	Gus	03/24/2017
13	Wilmore	04/06/2017
14	Mister Thor	04/20/2017
15	Nora	04/26/2017
16	Max	05/09/2017
17	Hunting Pearl	05/14/2017
18	Bessie	05/25/2017
19	The Last Four	05/29/2017
20	Zack	06/12/2017
21	Finding Bucky	06/21/2017
22	The Debt	06/30/2017
23	The Scalawags	07/11/2017
24	The Stampede	07/20/2017
25	The Wake of the Bertrand	07/31/2017
26	Cole	08/09/2017
27	Luke	09/05/2017
28	The Eclipse	09/21/2017
29	A.J. Smith	10/03/2017
30	Slow John	11/05/2017
31	The Second Star	11/15/2017
32	Tate	12/03/2017
33	Virgil's Herd	12/14/2017
34	Marsh's Valley	01/01/2018
35	Alex Paine	01/18/2018
36	Ben Gray	02/05/2018

Made in the USA
Columbia, SC
28 December 2019